Xanthippe

Eileen Ebert Smith

The Janzen Press
P.O. Box 2254
Palm Springs, CA 92263
619-861-5788

To every member of my wonderful family
especially Trent W. Smith M.D.,
plastic surgeon and polo player par excellence,
and
to the memory of my father, Edgar Philip Ebert Ph.D.
whose reflections on Xanthippe inspired this story.

Foreword

It was not Xanthippe's carrot colored sheath of hair, or her lissome way of walking, like a cat, nor even her devilish gift of mimicry that caused talk. What really set people's tongues wagging were her wild and crazy escapades. For one, she was often seen racing around the country-side on a horse! Granted her father was a renowned riding master, there are certain things that nice girls just don't do!

She is still pining for her first love when her parents betroth her to Socrates, a controversial cult leader, who challenges long-held beliefs and takes orders from a 'Daemon'.

Unfamiliar surroundings and the characters she meets following her marriage bring a mixture of laughter and rage, a new approach to an old affair, and some hitherto undiscovered strengths.

Xanthippe wearies of her husband's ideologies, yet hears them until they become etched on her mind. A turning point in her life comes when she does battle with Zeus himself!

Much has been and continues to be written about Socrates. On the other hand there is little to be found about his wife beyond random comments about her sassy tongue and bad temper.

After twelve years of meticulous research and writing, author Eileen Ebert Smith presents a captivating new view of Xanthippe and her place in Greek history.

Jill, of Bang Printing, said it all in a note to the author: "Until working on your book, I was never at all interested in Greek history. Your introduction to the many characters involved makes it all come alive like never before."

M. E. Robertson
Palm Springs, CA 1994

The Cast of Characters and a Bibliography appear at the back of the book.

Chapter One

Soft breezes stirred an acrid fragrance of hay. Mount Pentellicus was aflame with purple and rose and, in the clear bright light of a soaring sun, Xanthippe and her mare made long leggy shadows on the stable wall.

"Let me have just one quick run on Iris, and I promise you I will spend an extra hour doing my chores," she implored, her face radiant with hope.

"No! Get back to the house where you belong. I tell you, young woman, if you don't quit heckling me I'm going to sell that damn filly for hound rations." Palen's voice was gruff, but there was an indulgent grin on his swarthy face. Despite himself he was captivated by this female.

Twelve years ago he had been sick with disappointment when he got her instead of the son he craved. He had even chosen a name, 'Xanthippus', in honor of Pericles' father.

Some chaps, in the same situation, solved the problem by buying a boy from an impecunious kinsmen. But all his relatives were richer than he could ever hope to be and had no need to sell a son (There were also a few whose boys he would not have taken as a gift!)

Time was when one could sire his namesake with any woman he wished. No longer since Pericles' edict that children born out of wedlock, or from liaisons with foreigners, were not eligible for Athenian citizenship. Later, when Pericles himself fathered a bastard by his mistress from Miletus, the laugh was on him because not even he, the Archon, could get his law revoked! It was lucky for him that he already had two legitimate sons by his first wife before divorcing her to take Aspasia into the palace (a deed for which he was still highly censured).

Yet who could blame him for succumbing to the blandishments of a hetaira? Those women knew how to frenzy a man out of his mind. Their mastery of the art of erotica made Athenian wives appear to be less imaginative than a flock of sheep. A reminiscent grin creased Palen's face.

"Papa? What are you smiling about?"

"I thought I told you to leave!"

Knowing that any further pleas on her part would only serve to annoy him further, Xanthippe gave her shoulders a compliant shrug. "I'll go as soon as I give my sweet little mare this carrot," she said, but still she lingered. Although the gods lived on Mount Olympus, as far as she was concerned, Papa was Zeus, and being with him in the paddock . . . Paradise.

"I think she's beautiful!" she had told him, when one of the brood mares had foaled prematurely and thrown a worthless filly.

"Beautiful?" he had snorted. "Should we name her 'Iris' for the Rainbow Goddess?"

When no one had offered to buy the sorry little creature, he had presented her to Xanthippe. The look on her face had almost made the birth of an unmarketable horse worthwhile. Then, to his amazement, in less than a year, Iris began to acquire some manners and style.

It had been winter and biting cold, the night Xanthippe was born. "Hair the color of fire and a face to match!" Phaenerete, the midwife, had chuckled, indicating a sprout of orange fuzz on the baby's head. "There's nothing wrong with the little scrapper either. Listen to her yell!"

He had to admit, if only to himself, that he was intrigued with the 'little scrapper' from the day she sat up, looked him in the eye, and said "Papa" Her first word. It just proved that, despite her unfortunate gender, she was brighter than a new gold coin.

When he had hefted her up in front of him on his mare and cantered around the ring, she had gone wild with joy.

At five she was riding alone, well balanced, hands confident on the rein. That was the year when, after many miscarriages, his wife, Nikandra finally managed to bring an infant to term, a boy, thank the gods. His name was Elefterous, for his great grandfather who was a distinguished horseman. Nevertheless, it soon became evident that Elefterous the Second did not, nor ever would, share either his grandsire's or his sister's zeal for horses.

"Here they come! Scat!" Palen flung out his arm as if to sweep Xanthippe bodily out of the barn. The time had come for him to clamp down on her habit of strolling into the paddock whenever she pleased. Now that she was twelve, some of the men who came to buy horses, or race the chariot, were beginning to regard her with more than a purely avuncular interest.

Small wonder! Her very appearance was startling. That combination of grape-green eyes, hair the color of a noon-day sun, and a blue tunic, made her look almost incandescent, standing in the light that came streaming through the open stable door.

"No doubt about it, she's the one who should have been his son," Xanthippe heard one man say as he dismounted.

"A cursed shame she wasn't," Palen agreed.

Stung by his remark, she kicked a stone loose from the dirt and sent it flying. But its impact on her toe hurt less than her father's words.

Except for her ownership of 'Iris', nothing was as good as it had been before Elefterous was born. These days, when her father was not with his clients, he was schooling her brother who, at five, was old enough to ride. But the dunce didn't know a mane from a tail. What's more he howled every time he was hoisted onto a horse!

"Sit back! Stop hunching over her neck. GRIP! Grip with your knees, for the godsakes, you're bobbling around like a cloth doll!" Palen would shout in a voice harsher than a hound's bark.

His comments fell like a rain of hail-stones on everyone, including the wealthy 'aristoi' who came to improve their racing skills. None of them took exception but Elefterous. He, poor soul, was so (literally) unseated by his father's reproofs that, quite often, he lost his balance and fell to the ground.

As if having a brother were not enough to contend with, it seemed that, whenever she did have a chance to enjoy herself in the stable or paddock, one man or another always showed up to bluster, "Run along! This is no place for a girl."

After first making sure no one was around, she would circumvent these dictates by darting into an unused stall where a split between two wall boards provided a splendid view of both paddock and racing ring. Here, hidden from view, she could see what went on in the charmed world of boys and men.

As usual her hound was at her side. "He can be your pet," Papa had said, handing her the runt of a litter. "You might name the little fellow 'Cerberus' for the three-headed beast that guards Hades' gate." And Cerberus, who was now very big, had been her loyal companion ever since.

An argument was in progress in the paddock. Men seemed always to be bickering about one thing or another. When their disputes accelerated past the power of rhetoric they were settled on the ground. There had been times, when, peering through the wall, Xanthippe had seen contestants pummel one another until blood ran. "Why," she would wonder, "can they behave in so fine a fashion, when girls are reprimanded for the least cross word?"

Pericles was today's topic of dissent. "He says he's a democrat but he's more of a tyrant than Peisistratus. The difference is that Peisistratus didn't try to dupe people. What's more, the water pipes he installed a hundred years ago still benefit us more than all that white marble on top of the Acropolis ever will! Why, I ask you, was the temple in which our ancestors worshipped Athena not good enough for the Archon?"

"How dare you impugn a man for glorifying the goddess of our Empire? You should be charged with impiety!"

Xanthippe could see her father's flaming face, hedged by its bristle of black beard and brows, and his dark eyes glowering over a nose, so deformed from falls and fights it looked as if it had been hewn by a drunken sculptor.

"The problem with Pericles is he was born rich and never had to do a day's work. That's why he's so profligate with our tax money! By Zeus, his ardor for erecting temples, and music halls will pauperize the empire!" said another.

"If you ask me, his ardor concerns an erection that has little, if anything, to do with empire building!" This time it was Lysicles, the sheep farmer, who spoke. He was a huge man whose voice was a bellow, and his laughter even louder. "I catch an occasional glimpse of the comely Aspasia when I cart lamb to the palace." He gave his comrades a wink.

"Tell us." said another. "Since you're so familiar with what goes on there, have you ever discovered whether Pericles takes off his helmet in the privacy of his own home?"

"For all I know he wears it when he lays his lady."

Xanthippe grinned. According to rumor, the reason that no one ever saw the Archon without his helmet was because, on the night before his mother gave birth to him, she dreamed she was being bedded by a lion. Which, explained his monstrous head.

"Perhaps his helmet brings him good luck. He has three sons, that is, if you include his bastard. Maybe we should all try wearing one when we mount our wives", jested another.

"Think of that, Palen! If you'd worn a helmet Xanthippe might have been a boy after all!"

"I fathered four sons but not because of what I had on my head!" shouted Lysicles amidst renewed roars of laughter.

"Thank the gods I sired two by my former wife before the worthless slut moved into the Archon's bed and whelped two for him. But she also left me with a daughter for whom I must arrange a suitable betrothal. And, while we're on the subject, Palen, if you keep on permitting your Kokeeno to ride, mark my word, she'll not only be headstrong, she'll break her virgin's veil! Then try to find a man who will agree to take her off your hands! Believe me, I'd better not catch Hipparete astride a horse!"

Xanthippe pursed a sour mouth. The mere sight of Hipponicus made her want to vomit. It was not his appearance alone that set her on edge, nor the fact that he disapproved of girls who rode horseback, nor even his habit of appraising her as if she were one of her father's horses, but something indefinably nasty about his furtive glances.

She sighed. How distressing it was to despise the father of Hipparete, her best and, in fact, her only friend.

The men were beginning to drift away from the stable and out toward the ring. Still squinting through her eye-sized window, Xanthippe was waiting for a chance to slip away unseen when a rustle from behind startled her.

There, inside the stall stood Alcibiades, a thoroughly disagreeable fellow who came out from Athens with other boys to race the chariot. He was the nephew and ward of Pericles, and so, thereby, related to her father, which meant she had to endure his hectoring at clan affairs.

Because of his beautiful face, close cropped, golden curls, and imposing stature, everyone said he looked like a god. But picking fights was his favorite sport so if he *were* a god he'd be a son of Ares who 'rejoiced in the delight of battle'.

"You know better than to sneak in here and eavesdrop," he lisped. "Get out! Don't just stand there! Do as I tell you!"

"You can't make me!"

"Oh yes I can. When I give orders I expect to be obeyed!" Alcibiades stepped toward her.

Cerberus' hackles rose. With a menacing growl, the hound fixed his eyes on the boy and inched forward.

"Stay, Cerberus!" Xanthippe put out a restraining hand.

"That dog is daft! He'd have to be to tag after you. His tail is too long. I think I'll cut it off."

"Go away! You have no right to tell me to leave. This barn belongs to my father, not to you!"

"If your father caught you here he'd be the first to run you off. Do you think you're a boy? Or don't you know the difference? Ha! I am now going to lift our tunics and educate you." His face agleam with mischief, Alcibiades grabbed her garment. This time the rumble in Cerberus' throat was more ominous.

"Let go of my tunic, you hind part of a mule! I already know the difference!" Xanthippe balled her fists. "If you put a hand on me I'll stand by and watch my hound tear you apart!"

"Bitch! What you need is a good thrashing. One of these days I'm going to give you one!"

"You wouldn't dare, you noisy mouth!" Assuming a lordly air she pursed her lips. "I am Pericleth preciouth nephew. When I give orderth I am obeyed!" she mocked. "By the gods you can't even talk! Try giving my hound an order and see what happens. He won't understand a word you say."

"No one makes fun of me! No one!" Alcibiades screamed, his face contorted with rage. Again he advanced and again he was stayed by the hound.

"Alcibiades!" someone shouted. "Where are you? Come to the ring! It's your turn at the chariot."

"Remember, I warned you. I'm going to give you a lesson you will never forget!" Alcibiades snarled, making a coarse gesture. "You've had it coming ever since you jumped out of that hollow tree, you crazy she-demon. I swear to the gods no one mimics me and gets away with it, especially a nobody's nothing like you!"

"Go piss on yourself!" Xanthippe had heard those words employed to great effect by her father, however, they might sound less well coming from her. Also what if Alcibiades were to reveal her hiding place? Unfortunately, he was correct in assuming that her own father would be the first to chase her away. With this in mind she fled, muttering, "The next time I'll let you go after him, Cerberus."

Persons with red hair were inevitably nicknamed 'Kokeeno'. But a 'Nobody's Nothing?' Unforgivable!

Papa claimed arguments were good for people. He also maintained that every important, successful person had at least one enemy. So she had hers! And, one way or another she'd find a way to make that lisping son of dogs eat dirt.

Two years had passed since their first skirmish but, like Alcibiades, she remembered every detail as if it had been yesterday.

She had been sitting at the foot of a big hollow tree that towered over the family burial ground. Ever since she was a little girl it had been, to her, whatever she wished, a theater, temple, or a palace in Athens. There were times when she had actually seen the face of Zeus there, leering at her from the recessed shadows on its gnarled old trunk.

Cerberus was off in pursuit of a woodcock, and she had been playing 'pretend' when voices, and the smell of wood burning, had drawn her attention. Hastily she had crawled into the tree's musty sanctuary to hide, alert and listening.

"Look, Critobolus, he's wiggling his legs. Maybe he'll poke his head out!"

She'd had no problem recognizing Alcibiades' shrill lisp.

Then another voice, stronger and more articulate said. "Oh come on, Alcibiades, I'm tired of watching you torture that poor thing. Anyway, we shouldn't be here. If Palen discovers we left the paddock we'll be in real trouble. I've seen him lose his temper over less."

Emboldened by curiosity, Xanthippe had emerged from the tree to see Alcibiades, less than six feet away, holding a tortoise tied to a thong, and dipping it back and forth from a bonfire into a pool of water.

"Stop! You're hurting it!" she had shouted, lunging at him, and raking his cheek with her fingernails.

Taken by surprise he had staggered back, touched his face, and discovered it was bleeding. In a rage he had dropped the half dead tortoise, snatched Xanthippe by the hair, and struck her a blow that sent her reeling.

"Alcibiades! You hit a girl!" His friend had exclaimed.

"Thith ith no girl, Critoboloth, she ith Hecate, the wicked witch. If you aren't careful she'll put a curth on you." Apparently emotion accentuated Alcibiades' lisp. Retrieving the tortoise he had flung it at her and snarled. "If you're tho fond of thith dirty old turd let him thleep in your bed. One look at you and he'll crawl away tho fatht you'll think he ith a rabbit."

She had been on the verge of tackling him again but, "Don't let him upset you," his friend, Critobolus said, putting his hand on her arm. "He doesn't mean half of what he says."

"Oh yeth I do," Alcibiades' had retorted. "You wont get away with thith!" Still glaring at her, he had flounced away, scrubbing at his cheek.

She recalled narrowing her eyes, pointing a rigid finger at him and muttering, "May Hecate, cross your path and bring curses on your yellow head."

"I can't imagine what got into Alcibiades, going after a girl half his size," Critobolus marvelled, shaking his head. After stamping out the fire, he had given her a comradely wink, and followed his companion.

Today Alcibiades had called her a 'Nobody's Nothing.' Back then it had been 'Hecate'. 'Hecate' the dreaded two-faced goddess of the night, who distilled a poisonous drink from hemlock and could turn herself into a white mare who made nests in hollow trees and lined them with horse hair, entrails, and the plumage of exotic birds.

The tortoise, meanwhile, having survived its ordeal of fire and water, was lumbering into one of the clumps of asphodel that ringed the graves. Had the creature been worth such a fight? Xanthippe asked herself now. Who knows?

But something else had happened that day, something really important! She had fallen in love and made an important decision. When she grew up she was going to marry that handsome Critobolus.

Chapter Two

Churning from side to side, Nikandra implored the god of slumber to close her eyes, but to no avail. A grandiose moon, hanging directly outside her window, was flooding the bedroom with light but that was not the sole cause of her insomnia.

Palen had ridden away again this afternoon without a word about where he was going or when he'd return. It was the sort of thing he had been doing ever since she was still bleeding and torn from giving birth to Xanthippe. Now here she was again, wide awake and plagued by uneasy imaginings long after Mother-Phyllys and the children had gone to sleep.

Thirteen years ago, on her wedding day. Palen had brought her to this place. After a two hour journey through endless stretches of gray-green terrain that dissolved into a far-off haze of thickets and foothills, they had come to this farm in the hamlet of Cholargus. As they turned down the lane, the sight that met her eyes bore no semblance whatsoever to her roseate images of what life, as the bride of an Alcmaeonid, was to be. Instead she had seen an inelegant huddle of smallish buildings, fashioned from uncut rocks, and dwarfed by a triptych of mountains looming in the background.

The house itself was U-shaped around a courtyard in the center of which stood the family altar. It was here that she had bowed before the ever-burning flame to make obeisance to Apollo Pythian, Artemis, and the rest of Palen's family gods whom, she, as his wife, was henceforth expected to worship.

Equally disheartening was the fact that, except for some of the men who came on business, she had seen little of her 'aristoi' in-laws with whom she had hoped to mingle. To date, her socializing with

Alcmaeonids was limited to clan affairs, which indicated that her husband was little more than a trivial twig on a prominent family tree.

With Phyllys, her mother-in-law, she had toured the slat-roofed kitchen court, a loom room, two first floor bedchambers, and a labyrinth of food caves. By the time a laundry laver and, two waist high amphorae, had been inspected, she was already longing to be back in Athens.

Finally, after ascending a rough outdoor staircase that clung to one side of the house, they came to three more rooms that appeared to have been fastened, as an after-thought, onto the roof. She recalled having been heartened by the sight of a blooming olive tree doing its best to soften an otherwise bleak landscape outside this very room.

"This is your bed-chamber" Mother Phyllys had said. "As you know my son sleeps on the ground floor and will, of course, expect you to visit him there."

Prior to marriage no mention had been made about the giving or receiving of pleasure in a marital bed. Therefore Nikandra's wedding night had brought about an activity more to be endured than enjoyed. To her surprise, as time went by, matters improved and she found herself experiencing a few unexpected delights when Palen lowered his bulky body onto hers.

In no time she'd become pregnant and he was overjoyed. But, "I don't give a damn what you call her," he had stormed, beside himself with frustration, when the 'son' he had been so confident of getting turned out to be a girl.

His mother was disappointed too, but kinder. 'Naturally we can't call her Xanthippus, but Xanthippe' would do nicely since 'Hippe' (horse) represents her father's vocation and his clan. And, as a grandmother, I too shall have a new name," 'Yiayia Phyllys' had said, giving the stirring stick in her hand a merry twirl.

Palen had given lackluster consent yet, oddly enough, he had taken a liking to his unwanted daughter. Nonetheless he'd been more than ever determined to beget a son. However now, when he summoned Nikandra to his bedchamber, he was as indifferent and abrupt as if they were hounds, coupling in the barnyard.

Despite his continued activity, and her prayers to Artemis, five conceptions had gone awry. Following each loss she had wept inconsolably, stifling her sobs to keep from irritating her husband because he despised shows of emotion.

As he regularly pointed out, it was her fault, not his, that he was still without a son and heir. Blind to how these catastrophes affected her, he would storm off to the paddock, little knowing or caring what it meant to carry a child in one's womb for several months, only to lose it in one uncontrollable gush.

It was around the time of her fourth mishap that he took to disappearing on his mare. Then, six years ago, praise the gods, especially Artemis, she had been delivered of a live son. All the same, Palen was still leaving home. Like today.

Convinced by now that the elusive Morpheus was not going to come with his sleeping sand, Nikandra quit her bed, went to the window. and tilted her heart-shaped face upward. The moon was so low in the sky it seemed near enough to touch. Perhaps, at this very moment, the goddess Artemis was flying across it on her big black cat!

Impulsively pulling a cloak over her nightdress she trailed down the outside staircase, around the house, and into the courtyard. "Summer or winter, I've been cold ever since I left Athens," she mumbled, tugging the wrap closer to her shoulders.

It was chillier out here than in town. Worse yet was the eerie silence, broken only by the occasional wail of a wild animal. Everything looked different at night. The mountains, Parnes, Pentellicon, and Hymettus, all three bulked like purple monsters against a moon-bright sky, and behind them the stars, like little lightning bugs, frozen in fathomless space.

The worst thing about living on a farm was having no one your own age with whom to share the choice bits of tattle that were so relished in town.

She gave a start. What was that sound? For a moment or two she held her breath, then relaxed. Probably a bat. The whir of their wings could sound loud in this unearthly quiet. An owl maybe. Owls were very vocal on moon-lit nights. They also ate mice and their nests stunk. She shuddered. Xanthippe loved all those weird creatures. One never knew what she might drag in next. Or what she'd do. As if being born female weren't bad enough, she was an odd child, prone, for example, to wander with Cerberus into areas where no girl had a right to be seen.

One could, perhaps, understand why the stable held such fascination for her . . . but not the ancestral burial ground! Equally provoking was her irreverent way of mimicking people, a habit that, for some reason, Palen seemed to find amusing.

Xanthippe adored her father. Unperturbed by his bluff ways, she pranced at his heels like a shadow, faithfully copying every move he made. Slick as a garden snake she eluded her household tasks in favor of toting feed buckets and cleaning harness for him in the barn. All in all, from the moment she had come into the world, her behavior had been a source of consternation.

Godsname! Where can he be? Unbidden images rose to taunt Nikandra. Although it was some time since she herself had enjoyed a visit to his bed, she was, nonetheless, his wife., and should not have to be wondering if, at this very moment, he was receiving his pleasure from a courtesan!

"Small wonder I can't sleep," she was thinking when the clatter of hooves interrupted her reflections and, moments later, in came Palen.

"I'm starved," he announced, after showing some surprise at finding her still awake and seated downstairs in the courtyard. "I had supper but that was hours ago. Bring me a jug of wine and something to eat."

Quickly Nikandra snatched up a lamp, lit it at the altar flame and hastened to the storage cave wondering, as she went, whose cooking he had enjoyed earlier in the evening.

Silently he consumed the cheese and olives, and sipped the brandy she brought back and placed before him.

"I went to a symposium in Athens. A fancy affair," he said at length, as she was wondering whether to stay or leave. "Hipponicus invited me. His father was the host."

"Xanthippe goes to the house of Callias when she visits Hipparete. And now you! How I would love to go there!"

"I picked up some prospective customers, fellows who have heard about my horses. They're coming tomorrow to take a look. By Zeus, I wish I could breed them faster."

"I too!" Emboldened by his apparent good humor Nikandra leaned forward. "Tell me more about the symposium.

"There were flute girls and dancers, but the main event was a debate."

"Did you see Elpinice?"

"What would Callias' wife be doing at his symposium?"

"I've heard they give parties together and ask the men to bring their wives."

"Bullsballs." Palen popped a handful of olives into his mouth and studiously aimed the pits at a water jar.

"Who were the debaters?"

"One was Protagoras, a Sophist master of logic. I couldn't understand what he was talking about half the time. Those city fellows are full of wind. I do recall him saying that there are two sides to every question because nothing is totally true."

"Who was his opponent?"

"Socrates, the son of Sophroniscus."

"And of Phaenerete! You mean to tell me that the son of Phaenerete was there?"

"Yes. Phaenerete. The old trot."

"Whatever was he doing at such a fine gathering?"

"The bugger is much in demand these days and I am forced to admit he speaks up boldly and seems unafraid to address any subject. They say he was once a disciple of Protagoras. If so, by the gods, he turned the tables on his old master tonight! Socrates swears there's only one truth and each man must find it for himself, by bits and pieces. He puts it this way, 'On earth 'Truth' appears as broken arcs, but in heaven a perfect round.' It sounds nice but I don't hold with a man who forsakes his father to gad around town asking people to define virtue and truth. 'Search for truth within yourself,' he says, "What does a wild man like him know about truth? What he knows best is how to amuse or irritate, depending on who's listening. Most of his followers are crazy as a pack of three eyed loons."

"What else did Protagoras say?"

"That man is the 'measure of all things' and truth changes according to how he sees it. He also says sensations are all that count and nothing is true unless it's felt."

"Then what?"

"Socrates repeated that it's people who change, not truth and, if you keep looking for it, without prejudice, you find it for yourself. Something like that. His device is to badger people with questions until they no longer know what they're trying to say. I fell asleep and missed most of the rest. Anyway, toward the end, he had his old master so tangled up that poor Protagoras ended up sounding like a complete idiot."

"Did that make him angry? Protagoras I mean."

"Not at all. He clapped Socrates on the back and said, loud enough for everyone to hear, 'Some day you will be one of the world's greatest sages.' Which, of course, is a chamber-crock full of . . ."

"Tell me more" Nikandra asked quickly. After twelve years she still had trouble accommodating to Palen's coarse comments.

Over the rim of his cup Palen studied his wife's face. She looked uncommonly well. Her large brown eyes sparkled and her skin gleamed beneath the moon's silvery glow. Setting his Metaxa aside, he mopped his chin and stood up.

"Come," he said.

Regretful that their conversation had ceased so abruptly Nikandra got to her feet and followed him to his quarters. How nice it had been, sitting in the courtyard alone with her husband. Especially when he was being so friendly and pleasant. This night had turned out ever so well! It had been different. And special.

Later, when he sent her back upstairs. there was a look of contentment on her face. "At least I know where he was tonight, and what he was doing," she said to herself.

Chapter Three

"It appears to be floating in the sky!"

"Mark me, people will still be coming to see it a hundred years from now!"

"That temple symbolizes everything we stand for!"

"I thought it could never be done!"

Pericles' dream of bringing Athens to a new pinnacle of glory had been realized and, on this, the first day of the Greater Panathenaea, cascades of citizens, foreigners, freed men, and slaves, were pouring down the broad Athenian Way. "Flawless!", "Ethereal!", "Sublime!" they exclaimed, vying to find superlatives equal to the grandeur of the newly completed Parthenon. But Socrates, ambling along beside his parents, was so lost in contemplation that he neither saw nor heard.

"Stop daydreaming! Look up!" his mother cried, tugging at her son's cloak. "We're four squares from the Acropolis, and I can already see the gold tip on Athena's spear!"

But it was his father who caught his attention. "That statue proves Phideas is a genius," Sophroniscus said. "But one of these days, you, my son, will surpass him."

Socrates did not replay. This was not the time or place to contradict his parent. Yet, today, tomorrow or next week, it would still be difficult to soften the blunt blow of truth.

His father and forebears had always been loyal 'sons of Daedalus' the eponymous ancestor of sculptors. Therefore it would shock him to learn that his only son had chosen not to follow further in his footsteps. Even though neither parent had ever insisted that he do anything against his will, they'd have trouble coming to grips with this.

For over a year, every marble cutter in Athens, had been laboring, even by lamp light, to complete their orders in time to see them gracing the Acropolis on this day of days. A depiction of three sisters, had fallen to Socrates' lot. After meeting the two younger ones, and scrutinizing their features, it had been relatively easy for him to carve satisfactory likenesses of both. But the eldest was dead and, despite verbal descriptions, he'd been unable to establish an image of her in the eye of his mind. Then, five weeks ago, something strange had occurred.

He could not recall just how long he had been sitting in his father's workshop when a vision came of the sisters, all three, in a row, at the foot of steps leading up to the broad natural plateau atop the Acropolis hill. Standing tall between the other two, the deceased was clearly defined by a shapely head, slender neck, and a handsome, albeit elongated nose. She had a beautifully delineated but somewhat sardonic mouth, and eyes that held a look of mystery, like those of an Egyptian. As for her body, it was more austere of line than the somewhat sensual figures favored by Athenians.

Socrates knew perfectly well how easy it was to drift from intense concentration into a light sleep. But this was no dream. Leaping to his feet, and holding the image in his mind, he had begun to carve. Trancelike he labored, chisel in a hand that moved as if controlled by some outside force, fashioning and refining that enigmatic central figure.

Nine days ago, he had stood back, appraised his work and found it good. Then, as he was putting his pumice stone aside he heard the voice.

Thirty years ago when he was a boy of six, it had come for the first time. The Phantom, Daemon, Spirit, call it what you may, was inaudible in the ordinary sense. It was not discerned in the ear but through the medium of the mind.

No one else heard it, and he could do so only in a state of perfect stillness. At such times, instead of advising him which course he should take, it told him what not to do. Convinced that it was the 'God of all gods' who talked to him through the medium of this 'Daemon', Socrates, in turn, took care to obey.

On that particular day the advice had been clear and explicit. "The profession of your father is not for you," Nine words. No more. Yet they left no doubt. 'The Three Graces', as he had named the piece, was to be his last sculptured work. Nothing, henceforth, was to impede his on-going search for the elusive Truth that lies above sham posturing, and pretense.

It meant separating myth from fact, something that could only be done by questioning people about the validity of long accepted teachings and deeply rooted beliefs. To do so he, personally, must be entirely free from prejudice and fear.

More risky yet was the task of persuading others to face their own excesses. The money, power and lust, with which man cossets himself, are not handily relinquished.

He would, of course, be censured for abandoning his father's vocation. But a seeker after wisdom and truth cannot afford to be swayed by public opinion. Still, when one comes to know himself as he truly is, the estimation of others is no longer a matter of concern.

Self discovery is the work of a lifetime, however there are compensations to be accrued along the way . . . inner peace, contentment, and joy.

As a youth he had known sensual gratifications. Many! It was later that he discovered something infinitely more satisfying, the sublime experience of being in harmony with the universe. Only twice had he experienced this transcendental state. For all he knew, perhaps no more than a few moments had passed because he'd had no sense of time. Even so they had lasted long enough to transform his life.

While Socrates and his parents approached the Hill, Palen and his family, were taking advantage of the foot baths that greeted travellers when they walked through the city gates.

Open mouthed, Xanthippe stared at little mud-brick houses, standing in rows on narrow cobbled streets, as if a giant Laestrygone had stacked them, one against the other. Pots of basil bloomed on every window ledge, and clothes flapped from terra cotta roof tops like colorful sails.

Housewives shook orange and yellow mats from blue shuttered windows while, in the street below, an impatient donkey kicked beneath his load of garlic and onions. Birds, frenzied by the day's unbroken brilliance, called to their fellows, one lording it over the rest with his shrill insistent biddings.

"Although I rarely want to come to town I always enjoy myself when I do", said Yiayia Phyllys. A black bonnet, the signature of widowhood, rode atop her white hair, and her dark eyes sparkled in a face so sun bronzed and feathered with wrinkles it resembled an aging apricot. "But each time it seems bigger than before." she added.

"Everyone in the Empire must be here!" Nikandra sighed. Ever since her marriage she had dreamed of returning to Athens in fine clothes and jewelry. "I wish I had some gold bracelets and an ornament for my hair."

"That thread of pure gold I gave you to wear around your neck when you married my son is ornament enough," Phyllys retorted, her voice faintly tinged with asperity. "Your peplos is very becoming." she added, appraising the gown on which her daughter-in-law had spent many hours.

Two lengths of creamy linen, that Nikandra had woven in the loom room, were joined at her shoulders, girdled at the waist, and draped to fall in folds to her slim young ankles. Dusky tendrils, escaping the coil of hair she had moored to the back of her head, curled in charming disarray around her face, and her eyes were bright with excitement.

"Look!" she said, as they drew near the Acropolis, "There by the stairs! Phaenerete and her husband! The man with them must be their famous son. Shall we go and speak to them?"

Xanthippe had no use for Phaenerete whom she held, at least in part, responsible, for the arrival of Elefterous. So it was with ill concealed impatience that she paused while the two families exchanged greetings.

"Is it really twelve years since I brought you into the world, Xanthippe?" Phaenerete asked. "And you must be five by now!" She wagged a pudgy finger at Elefterous.

"Make a salutation," Nikandra prompted her daughter. "To Sophroniscus, Phaenerete, and their son Socrates."

Obediently Xanthippe bent a knee to all three. But it was Socrates who captured her attention. Never had she seen such astonishing eyes! Huge and sky-blue, they bulged from his wide snub-nosed face, and stared at her with such marked intensity she felt that he was gazing directly into her head. If so, he'd know she was thinking that he looked like Silenus the goat god. Unflinchingly she returned his stare.

"My son did that." Phaenerete indicated the memorial. "Name of god, the middle one looks like Xanthippe!" Nikandra gasped. "Did your model resemble my daughter?"

"In a way," was the oblique reply. Again Socrates regarded Xanthippe. "It would appear that you are the central figure," he said. The resemblance was uncanny, as if he had somehow immortalized the woman she was, as yet to become.

"The parade!" Elefterous shouted as a sound of music coming from Athens' Dipylon Gate, heralded the marchers.

"See how the poor things hesitate and balk. They must know they're to be sacrificed," Xanthippe commiserated as the lowing of oxen, being goaded toward the temple added their mournful accompaniment to the lively sound of flutes.

A company of flag bearers, stepping smartly, came into view, then youths carrying jars of sacrificial wine, and behind them, maidens with libation bowls, and baskets of flowers. Musicians, plucking briskly at the strings of citharas which rode on their hips, marched to their music.

"I see Callias and Hipponicus!" Nikandra pointed to a company of public ministers, elders, marshals, and military commanders striding by. "The richest men in Greece! . . . And we are related to them, Xanthippe" she added unnecessarily.

"I know. I know," her daughter yawned. "You've told me so a hundred times."

Old men, chosen because they were still lithe and handsome carried olive branches from the tree of Athena. Dignitaries in the exotic costumes of their native lands, resident aliens in red capes, and Heirophantes, the most exalted order of priests, walked with solemn measured tread.

Tray bearers moved in stately array. Cavaliers, in short colorful cloaks and broad brimmed hats, reined high strung steeds to keep pace with the marchers' slower step.

With their mouths full of sweets bought from roving vendors, Xanthippe and Elefterous gaped at athletes, whose bodies gleamed with olive oil, as they wove in and out of the parade. Behind a roped off section of highway, charioteers leaped in and out of their vehicles as they raced.

Just when everyone felt that nothing could surpass what they had already seen, a massive wheeled craft, built like a ship, and bearing Athena's new gown, hove into view. Spread like a sail over the yardarm, its embroidered sheath of jewels reflected the suns' rays with prisms of light.

Thousands of frenzied spectators watched the majestic craft being manipulated down the Athenian Way. Roars of acclaim rose from their throats as it slowly advanced up the west slope of the Acropolis. An imponderable feat!

"The 'Young Arrephorai' did some of the needle work on that sail," Nikandra said, unable to resist bringing up a worn-sore subject, namely, the small select group of aristoi girls with whom she hoped Xanthippe would, one day, find herself affiliated. "I wonder why Hipparete hasn't come to visit you lately. Are you sure you were pleasant and polite the last time her father brought her to the farm?"

"Yes, Mama, I am always friendly and polite. But not because I want to be one of those witless 'Young Arrephorai!"

People were starting to follow the queue up toward the Parthenon, Conceived by Pericles, and constructed by Ictinus and Callicrates, it rose in lofty grandeur high above.

Within its 'Cella' stood yet another gold encrusted statue of Athena before which they paused to bow. All but Xanthippe. Face up, she gazed, fascinated by a necklace of snakes that encircled the goddess' head.

"Let's go!" Palen said, heading back toward the steps.

"I don't like seeing my daughter's face on a dead woman's memorial!" Nikandra worried, her eyes fixed on the 'Three Graces' near the bottom step. "Is it an omen? What do you think it means?"

"Probably that Socrates fancies skinny women with long noses", was her husband's rejoinder. "Don't fret, Nikandra. Everyone knows he's queer. That's all there is to it. He runs with a pack of wild men and poses questions that any fool could answer. 'What is virtue? What is love' he asks. Who cares? I think he has pebbles in his head. Hurry your feet or it will be dark before we reach home."

Flat sheaths of red hair whipped like flames around Xanthippe's head as she, staying a few paces behind her father, twirled in the light of a setting sun, feathering the air with her hands. In a wealth of mimicry she was the juggler, making six golden balls dance in the air.

"Name of god, everyone is staring at her!" Nikandra moaned. "Why is it that no matter where we go she attracts attention? People are always looking at her!"

"True." Phyllys nodded. "There's a kind of magic about Xanthippe, an 'eironia' one might say. I only pray that the Fates never cast a shadow on that lovely glow. Do you realize that she has been mirroring all of us, as well as everyone she sees, from the time she was two? And she does it as if she actually becomes the person whom she parodies!"

Chapter Four

Her intimate evening with Palen in the courtyard had begun to seem a bit unreal to Nikandra, like a dream. But now, three months later there was little doubt about what had occurred that night because she was pregnant again.

Having acknowledged her condition, she instituted a weekly trudge into Cholargus to visit a small shrine of Artemis.

"Please," she begged the goddess after an offering of wheat and maza cakes, "Let this one be another boy."

As, one by one, the months plodded by, like feet mired in mud, a horrible memory continued to surface . . . something she had witnessed as a child. It was her mother's face contorted by the grimace of death and, on the same blood soaked pallet, an infant lying lifeless and grotesque. What if that was what the Fates now held in store for her?

Such matters never bothered Palen. All he cared about was getting another son. "You managed to give birth to two live children so who knows? You might do it again," he'd say.

He had been jubilant when Elefterous was born but his good humor hadn't lasted. Before long he was voicing his displeasure with the child. One of her problems had been an inability to nurse the baby satisfactorily. The poor little fellow was always hungry. No matter how often she held him to her breast and tried to soothe him he wailed night and day. It had been a great relief when, at last he could digest goat milk and eat solid food. But, although he didn't cry quite as often, he stayed cranky and fretful.

Elefterous was totally unlike Xanthippe, She laughed easily, was fearless, and sat a horse better than any boy who came to Palen for instruction. Elefterous, on the other hand, had neither her courage or charisma.

But even if his sister were able to jump a mare over the moon, she'd never be allowed to chant the Mysteries that prevented one's father from having to wander, lost and discarnate, in shadowy realms when he died. That was for sons to do.

Therefore it was Elefterous, the first-born male, who would some day stand at Palen's grave and recite the sacred words.

But Palen was still very much alive, and longing for a son with whom he could ride, race, and have a good time!

* * * *

When, at long last, Nikandra's pregnancy ran its course, she delivered so quickly there was no point in summoning Phaenerete, and it was Phyllys who tied the cord.

"Another boy! A big one too!" she exclaimed, gleefully displaying living proof that Nikandra's oblations had found favor with Artemis.

"This one looks like me," Palen rejoiced.

"The gods have forgiven me," Nikandra sighed happily.

"Forgiven you for what, Mama?" Xanthippe wanted to know.

"I'm not sure. But if they were angry they aren't now because they gave me another son."

"Hmmm. . ." Xanthippe gave her brother a look that was dark with distaste. To her way of thinking, a red-faced midget who smelled, and hiccuped until his crib sounded like a basket full of crickets, was no cause for thanks.

Palen, ignoring the axiom that one should wait two weeks before announcing a birth, promptly dispatched Andokides, the stable slave, to bid clansmen and friends to a 'Day of Recognition'.

"He was just born," Nikandra protested weakly.

"Stop fussing. Anyway he looks older. And no silly superstition that a baby is a fetus until it has survived its first ten days is going to make me wait to tell the world we have another son! If people are stupid enough to believe old wives tales that's their problem, not mine!"

"Some of your fancy relatives were here for Elefterous' Day of Recognition," Nikandra recalled. "Do you suppose Elpinice and Callias might come this time? Or what about Pericles and Aspasia? I'd give anything to meet her. Anything!"

"Are you daft?" Palen clapped a hand to his brow. "He goes nowhere

22

unless it serves a political purpose. And no matter where he goes he never brings her. Everyone in Attica knows he avoids even chance encounters with Hipponicus!

"This time we'll invite Anytus."

"Why him?" Having managed to give her husband another son Nikandra felt more at liberty to speak up.

"You ask me why I invite the largest purveyor of leather goods in Athens?

"Great gods, woman, I'm just thinking ahead! Someday Anytus' son, Astron, will inherit everything he owns! Are you so besotted over producing two boys you forget we have one, as yet, unclaimed daughter? Anytus wants to make a name for himself in politics so any alliance he might have with an Alcmaeonid, even me, would be to his advantage. And he'll make one if we betroth our daughter to his son."

"That homely boy who comes here to drive the chariot?"

"The same. But the money he'll inherit will make him look more handsome."

"But Xanthippe is scarcely twelve years old! I was fourteen when your mother and my father signed our contract."

"Your father took a chance, waiting so long! Plenty girls are already married and have families by then. Besides it's never too late to lay a little groundwork!"

"Won't Anytus know that's why you asked him?"

"He'll think it's because his clan belongs to the same phratry as ours, and we observe mutual feast days."

"I see . . ." said Nikandra, wearing a puzzled frown.

*　*　*　*

Prisms of light were just beginning to brighten the sky as the women entered the kitchen court to finalize their preparations for the new baby's 'Day of Recognition'. The atmosphere was pungent with mingled fragrances of mahlepi, oregano, and garlic and everything was in readiness when the guests began to arrive

"We left two newly weaned lambs for your second son in one of the empty stalls," Lysicles announced, striding into the courtyard with his wife. Next came Phaenerete, the rotund midwife, and Sophroniscus, her tall, lean spouse. Together they resembled the juxtaposition of a circle and a line.

Nikandra was thanking General Gryllus and his wife, Clymene, for a silver mug etched with an image of Aphrodite, astride a goose, when she saw Callias and Elpinice, probably the most esteemed couple in the clan of Alcmaeonid.

"Thank you! How good of you to come! We are honored!" she gushed. Her hands were fluttering like panicked sparrows as she accepted their gift, a silver bank made to look like a rabbit, and filled with gold coins.

"We are pleased to share your happiness," Elpinice replied with a smile. In her sixties she was still very beautiful.

But when Xanthippe saw Hipponicus standing behind his mother her nostrils flared with disgust. How could a glorious woman like Great-aunt Elpinice give birth to such a creature?

His mean little eyes were curtained in flesh and his skin so pocked with lumps and pits it belonged on a hog. His lips, like earth-worms, were purplish and moist, and they twisted when he spoke as if he feared being overheard. Even the sound of his oily voice was nauseating. But, because he was one of the rich relatives, Mama admired him.

"Have an almond cake! May I give you some wine?" she would urge, skittish as a colt, when he came up to the house after buying horses from Papa. With him today was a girl who appeared to be not much older than Xanthippe.

"Allow me to present Allys, my future wife," he said pompously, She, in turn, bent her knee, then, smiling sweetly, did the unthinkable by turning her back on the women who were segregated in one end of the courtyard, and joining their husbands!

"Can one of you tell me why we keep hearing rumors of war with Sparta when we have a Peace Treaty that was supposed to be good for thirty years?" she asked, gesturing daintily with jewel bedecked fingers.

Although not a man appeared to take umbrage at her encroach ment on their all-male province of war and politics, the women shifted their feet, and Lysicles wife frowned. And when, in lieu of the reprimand she deserved for her show of boldness, Hipponicus gave her an indulgent pat on her bottom, there were audible gasps.

It was Elpinice who, in response to a sign from Callias, discreetly drew her son's bride-to-be aside.

Anytus, the leather merchant and his wife were last to arrive. Her smile was cordial but he was a dour faced man with obsidian eyes, amber teeth, and a long jutting chin.

He returned Palen's greeting with a thin lipped smile and, upon sighting Callias, Hipponicus, two of his host's more eminent relatives, he hastened to join them. Behind him strode Xanthippe parodying his walk.

"Stop doing that!" Nikandra seized her by the ear. Go talk to that person Hipponicus brought. She seems not to know how to behave at a social function."

Before Xanthippe could comply, Palen clapped for attention. "We are ready to begin," he said importantly, and nodded to his mother. She, cradling the baby in her arms, bowed before the ever burning flame and handed him to Nikandra who, in turn, paced three times around the altar, then lay him on the ground at Palen's feet.

"Clansmen and friends," he said loudly, when he retrieved the infant. "I present my second son, bred by me, and born into the world by my wife. His name is Marc, for my father who died in the service of Athens when I was three years old. I never got to know him, nonetheless I take pride in reciting the Mysteries every week at his grave.

After anointing Marc with a mix of water and wine Palen raised him aloft. Then, cradling him in his left arm he took a jug of wine in his right hand and poured a libation for the gods.

"Mighty Zeus, Mother Hera, Athena of the Empire, Artemis, Apollo Pythian, Hermes, and you the gods of our clan," he cried, "Smile on this lad and bless his days!"

Guests formed a Mystic Circle and solemnly passed the replenished vessel from one to the next until it was drained. "Yiasus!" They shouted the ancient toast three times, to Marc, his family, and his forebears.

The ceremony was over and when the baby, having been duly recognized, was returned to his crib, Phyllys, Nikandra, and several neighbor women hurried into the kitchen court, their cheerful chatter sounding a final note to religious ritual.

Beads of juice bubbled on the crusty surface of a pig, roasted golden brown over a bed of crimson coals. When its fat and bones were sacrificed, according to the law of Zeus, the meat was carved, put on a platter and placed alongside bowls of eggplant in oil, rice, pickled artichokes, horta boiled with herbs, goat cheese, and baskets of bread still hot from the oven.

"This one is to Papa Palen," Lysicles laughed, raising his drinking cup when everyone had been seated.

"Yiasus! To Papa Palen," everyone echoed, happy in the manner of all Athenians who are afforded an opportunity to drink wine, share food, and gossip.

"The first Day of Recognition my wife and I were privileged to attend, here in the house of Palen was for you, Xanthippe," Lysicles said. "That was almost thirteen years ago, around the same time that Phaenerete, here present, delivered Aspasia of a son the Archon never intended to beget. Am I correct, Phaenerete?"

Giving him a significant look, Lysicles' wife tilted her head toward Hipponicus. References to Pericles' mercurial love-life not only peeved him but made his parents and all the others uncomfortable as well.

Adroitly Elpinice returned the conversation to Xanthippe. "Tell me, she said, "what do you think of your new brother?"

"I don't like him."

"I didn't like mine either." Elpinice smiled, instead of laughing like the rest. "Also, you have two brothers to cope with, I only had one. I thought my parents preferred him to me. Perhaps they did! But that was not his fault. Later on we became friends. So will you, with Elefterous and Marc. Speaking of friends, my granddaughter told me to tell you she is looking forward to your next visit."

"Nikandra, Palen, this has been a memorable occasion," her husband said. "The sun will soon be setting so we must be on our way."

Nikandra's hand went to her heart. One more drop of happiness and her cup would overflow.

Pulling herself up Phaenerete gave her garment a tug where it had become lodged between her buttocks, and declared that she and Sophroniscus were also about to leave.

"What do you suppose got into my husband?" Lysicles wife whispered to her neighbor. "I was afraid his remark might get Phaenerete going on again about the night she delivered the palace bastard. Thank the gods Elpinice didn't give her a chance."

One by one people were beginning to go. "We wish we could stay longer. If only it didn't take so long to get back to Athens," they said and went to re-hitch their carts. "It has been a splendid day," others commented as, one after another they filed through the gate.

While bidding them 'Adio' Nikandra noted that Palen and Anytus had sequestered themselves in a corner of the courtyard and were deep in conversation.

"We shall discuss this matter further, but now we too must leave, Where is my wife?" she heard Anytus say.

* * * *

When everyone had gone Phyllys put away what was left of the feast while Nikandra banked the altar fire and dreamed of social triumphs that might accrue from having Palen's elegant relatives here today.

A noisy sigh drew her attention and she turned to find Xanthippe, slumped in a corner fingering Marc's silver rabbit. Impulsively she put the altar broom aside and sat down beside her. "You look sad. Is something troubling you?" she asked softly.

The sympathy in her mother's voice was so unexpected that a tear, quivering on the edge of Xanthippe's eye, slid down her cheek.

"Thank you for bringing firewood and doing so many helpful things. You were a good girl," Nikandra said. "I don't know how we would have managed without you. It was Marc's Day of Recognition but you deserve recognition too."

With that she left the courtyard. "I always kept this by my bed," she said, returning with a little lamp. "My mother gave it to me long ago. Now I want you to have it. Shall we light it?"

Upon receipt of a vigorous nod, Nikandra touched the wick to the altar fire and, together with her daughter, watched a small new flame come into being. "It's one of the few things I was permitted to bring with me when I left the house of my father," she said, handing the lamp to Xanthippe. "I guess I was waiting for just the right moment to pass it on to you."

A howl from the crib basket told Nikandra that Marc wished to be fed so she went to nurse him and,clutching her treasure, Xanthippe climbed the outside stairs to her room.

For awhile she sat on the side of her bed, cradling the lamp and staring fixedly at its orange-blue flame.

How sympathetic Mama had been! As for Papa, one would think he only had two children, his sons. Still, it was obvious that he was already bored with Elefterous. Before long he'd also weary of Marc who couldn't do anything better than drool, wave his arms and legs, and give people an idiotic grin. Papa would soon discover that one good daughter is worth more than two good for nothing sons.

* * * *

By noon, the next day, everything from bowls to benches and tables that Lysicles had helped Palen set up in the courtyard, were back in their proper places.

"May I give you some more water with wine," Nikandra asked Palen, still lingering over his meal. He gave his head a negative shake.

How nice it would be, she was thinking, to talk over yesterday's events with him, gloating a little over the triumph of having achieved a combination of tasty food and spirited guests. It would also be interesting to hear what he and Anytus had talked about.

"Perhaps a bit more moussaka?" she urged. "I'm glad we had some left over from the party. It tasted good, didn't it?" This too was met with silence. "Are you sure I can't get you something else?"

"For the godsakes, woman, hold your tongue!" Palen snapped. "You've been twittering at me ever since I sat down to eat. What's heckling you?"

"I'm wondering what you and Anytus talked about yesterday. Did you say anything to him about a betrothal for Xanthippe?"

"It was mentioned."

"What did he say?"

When I introduced the subject he acted off-hand. However he did try to find out what kind of a dower his son could expect our daughter to have."

"So . . . ?"

"Nothing was decided. These things take time, you know. But I have a feeling he's interested.

Chapter Five

Education was so highly revered that, before a boy entered school, his lessons were often initiated at home. Therefore, when Elefterous turned five, Palen engaged Archos, a short, stout savant with blueberry eyes, a round red face, and hair that stuck up from his head like the cockatoo on a rooster.

This so-called 'paidogogus' was expected to introduce his charges to sums, letters, and the history of the gods, and monitor their physical fitness and social deportment as well.

Surprisingly, Palen acquiesced to his mother's proposal that Xanthippe should also be tutored, for at least one hour a day. Not, as he explained, that he held with educating females, but, "After all, they are responsible for household accounts, and a little instruction in numbers can't do her any harm," he had allowed. "Just bear in mind that no man wants a woman who gets too smart for her own good, so for godsake, don't over-do it."

Archos, having recovered from his initial shock at finding a girl in his courtyard classroom, quite enjoyed the novelty of receiving undivided attention from at least one of his two disciples.

Xanthippe, on her part, was spellbound, especially when, after giving cursory attention to the subject of numbers, she found he could tell stories, even better than Yiayia Phyllys.

However, whereas Phyllys made the gods sound like nice, pleasant people, describing Uranus, for example, as 'smiling benevolently' down on his mother, the earth goddess, Archos saw him as "a totally remote being whose cold eyes are stars that gaze with utmost scorn at the violence on earth."

He also had a novel version of Zeus, whom, he said, "has a heart that swarms with fury so great it impels him to fling bolts of thunder and lightning that torch the forests, inflame the earth, and cause both sea and land to quake and heave."

He was at his best teaching Thespian art. Thanks to Pericles' dispensation of free tickets, he attended the Theater of Dionysius whenever he managed to escape his paidogogical duties. Following these excursions, having sated his passion for drama, he would return, even better equipped to fan Xanthippe's fires. Nor was she daunted by his continued insistence that she memorize lengthy passages from Homer, Euripides, and Aeschylus.

"The theater itself is like a big bowl. The 'orchestra', a round stage, is at ground level, along with sixty-seven thrones for high officials. The rest of us sit on a rise of seventy eight tiers of wooden benches." he explained. "The actors, 'hypocrites' they're called, change costumes and masks in little huts. A chorus of fifty 'tragoidoi' wearing goatskins and masks, tell the audience what's going on."

After two years of hearing him describe, and often enact, the tragic dramas, and comic satyr plays, he witnessed, Xanthippe was still begging for more. "Did the 'hypocrites' in 'Agamemnon' seem real yesterday? Tell me about Clytemnestra's costume. What was it like?"

To answer your first question, there isn't a man on that stage who fails to make his character come alive!" Archos said, his ruddy face ablaze with enthusiasm.

"It's hard for me to picture men in the roles of women."

"They do remarkably well. However I must admit that you have every bit as much talent."

Intoxicated by his compliment, Xanthippe ran to the ash grove. Quietly, within the familiar recess of her hollow tree, she waited until she clearly saw herself masked, and wearing a costume befitting her chosen role. Then she emerged from the tree to declaim her lines on a stage of moss and grass.

As always, whether speaking the words of Clytemnestra, Medea, or Antigone, behind her make-believe mask, she pictured Critobolus, the charming charioteer, as her chief protagonist.

* * * *

"I heard a disturbing story in the paddock yesterday", Palen reported at breakfast. "The prophetess Diotima is said to have had a vision in which she beheld hundreds of Athenians dying of a plague. The sight was so hideous that she has remained in seclusion ever since. They say she does nothing but pray, day and night, begging the gods not to allow what she foresaw to come true. My personal theory is that most of those old heifers who claim they can foretell future events, get their messages out of a wine jug. But not Diotima. She's considered to be completely reliable."

"That really scares me," Nikandra murmured.

"You're always afraid of something. I'd prefer being taken by a plague to dying of fright!"

"You should have heard the story Melissa told me yesterday while we were working in the vegetable patch," Phyllys said, lowering her voice. With a slight bend of her head she indicated the sixteen-year-old who was chopping onions on the other side of the kitchen court. "I wonder why slaves always seem to know what's going on sooner than we do?"

Palen had found the girl recently in a slave ring. "My father bought Andokides' parents when they became slaves after the Persian War," he had recalled. "They worked, had Andokides, and finally died here. Now he needs a woman. He's almost thirty! If he and Melissa have children we'll be able to get a little more help around this place."

"Melissa claims that several weeks before the Parthenon was finished, one of the artificers fell off the roof," Phyllys persevered. "He was so badly hurt no one thought he'd live. When Pericles learned what happened he went straight-away to the shrine of Athena and was praying for the poor fellow when the goddess herself came into view! 'Tell the priests to take turns sweeping their hands, palms down, over his body until he regains consciousness,' she said. 'Then have them feed him all the pig broth he can swallow.'

"The priests and physicians didn't believe him. They thought he'd been addled by the Furies. But he swore everything he said was true so they went ahead and did as they were told and four days later, that man was back on the job!"

"If a god or goddess talked to me I'd die the way Semele did when she looked at Zeus!" Nikandra gasped.

"Semele did not die of fright. Zeus burned her up with a lightning bolt," Xanthippe corrected her mother.

"You know more about the gods than any girl in Athens. I guess we can thank Archos for that." Phyllys commented with a smile.

"I wish I did." Nikandra sighed. "I always have trouble sorting them out. One story I'll never forget is about the Goddess Thetis, and a man who was drowning until, all of a sudden, he saw her!"

"How do you know he saw her if he was drowning?"

"Because he didn't drown after all. The moment she appeared he was tossed up on the beach."

"I think the gods manifest themselves to mortals more often than we think," Phyllys said. "Simon the Cobbler believes they disguise themselves as lapwings. He says he can hear them speaking to him through the rustle of oak leaves."

Nikandra shuddered. "Birds scare me the most. If one brushes against the house, especially a raven, it means something dreadful is going to happen. A raven flew in the window the day before my mother died in childbirth."

"You women may have nothing better to do than chatter all day but I have to work. I'm going into town to show my yearling in the Agora." Palen said pushing himself away from the table. "What's wrong with you, Xanthippe? You look as if one of your mother's ravens flew up your nose."

Xanthippe compressed her lips. No one, least of all 'Papa' must suspect that, after listening to some of these tales, she was sometimes too scared to sleep. However, now that she had his attention, this might be a good time to speak to him about something else, something that had been occupying her thoughts for some time.

Before she could speak she was interrupted by Melissa. Still red-eyed and teary from the onions, she was now engaged in cutting up an octopus. "Eh no lak dis kine fesh," she complained noisily over her task. "Et smull bad."

"Bar bar bar," Xanthippe repeated, pursing her lips and making a dour face. "Melissa always sounds as if her mouth were full of meal."

"Xanthippe! I have told you and told you to stop mimicking people," Nikandra expostulated. "Melissa talks that way because she is a barbarian. Can't you understand? That's why they call Persians BAR-BAR-ians. If you don't stop making fun of everyone you're going to get yourself into trouble!"

"Too bad she can't do that at the Theater of Dionysius. People would fall off their benches!" Palen chuckled.

"Papa!" Xanthippe exclaimed, seizing her opportunity. "Take us there! To the Theater of Dionysius! I beg you! Please!"

"Who's notion was that? Your mother's? Or Archos? Is that damned paidogogus putting ideas in your head?"

"Neither one. It was Hipparete, Kallia, and the other girls in town who get to go to the Theater of Dionysius whenever they wish. They talk about it all the time.

"Lysicles' wife says Euripides has finished a drama he has been working on. The name of it is 'Alcestis' and it's to be presented at the next feast of Dionysius. That will be three weeks from today." Nikandra interposed eagerly. "It would be such a treat to go! May we? Please? We can get some of Pericles' free seats."

"No! For the last time, NO! I can't afford to idle my time away spending an entire afternoon at the theater even if I don't have to pay an obol. I have enough on my mind without having to watch a bunch of hypocrites suffering on a stage. Besides you know how I hate crowds."

"No time," Nikandra complained under her breath grabbing a pile of soiled laundry. "No time' he says, but he always manages to find some when he wants to go on a wild boar hunt, or chase after flute girls at some fancy symposium, or guzzle kokineli at the taverna in Cholargus. The gods alone know where else he goes! But the moment I ask him to take his own family anywhere he has work to do! Come help me, Xanthippe!" Standing bare-armed at the laver she seized a wet cloth and wrung it as if it were the neck of a foe.

"If Papa really wanted to take us he would," Xanthippe echoed, for once in accord with her mother.

"Just then, to their surprise, Palen returned. "I've been thinking," he announced. "The God of Fertility gave us two sons so perhaps we owe it to him to celebrate his Feast and pray that at least one of them turns into a decent horseman."

* * * *

The magnificent Theater of Dionysius, the sounds the sights, the crowds, surpassed Xanthippe's wildest dreams! The costumes and masks were beyond belief. Archos had been right about the actors too. They really did seem to be the persons whom they wished to portray.

How shocked she had been when Admettus allowed the God of Death to take Alcestis. Would Papa do such a terrible thing? Or, for that matter, would Mama be willing to die for him? Weeks later, those sad lines were still repeating themselves, over and over in her head.

Regally she strode across the courtyard, re-enacting that scene, picturing Critobolus as the king for whom she, the beautiful queen, was about to surrender her life for the man she loved.

"It is enough that I should die for you!" she cried.

Critobolus would not be as cowardly as Admetus, or so afraid to die he'd let her to do it for him! Not he!

"Do you not see the Winged One glaring under dark brows?" Xanthippe's voice was now a throaty whisper. "It is Hades come to drag me away to his House of the Dead."

It had been impossible to keep from sobbing when Eumelus' sang his sad song of farewell. "O Mother, Mother, harken to me! I am calling to you, your little bird has fallen on your grave!" she chanted, clutching her budding young bosoms.

"Name of god," Nikandra groaned, listening to her daughter's dirge. "How long do you suppose we'll have to put up with that?"

"She is incredible!" Phyllys marvelled. "What a blessing it was for her to be given an opportunity to see a drama. Thank the gods Palen continues to condone her lessons with Archos. That daily hour with him means a lot to her."

"I'm afraid he might decide she's learning more than it's good for a woman to know," Nikandra said, nibbling her lower lip. "I worry. What will we do with her when Archos leaves? Or worse yet, when she can no longer be permitted to ride a horse? She may well be the brightest girl in Attica, as far as reciting poetry is concerned, but when it comes to learning how to do housework she behaves as if she didn't have good sense. Being able to recite poetry will do her no good in the long run."

"Look on the bright side," Phyllys said. "Marc is far from finished with his tutoring which means that Archos wont be leaving here for some time to come. As for horses, Xanthippe will readily give them up when the right man comes along."

34

Chapter Six

Archos had departed early in the morning, bound for Athens to celebrate a Feast Day for the Muses. "Memorize this quotation from Homer while I'm gone, Xanthippe," he had said. "It goes, 'The man is happy whom the Muses love. For though he has sorrow and grief in his soul, yet, when the servant of the Muses sings, at once he forgets his dark thoughts and remembers not his troubles. Such is the holy gift of the Muses to men.' "

But, instead of learning her lines she gravitated toward the paddock. Except for Andokides, who was mending a fence, no one was around, so she went on into the stable where Palen was grooming a gelding.

"Ye Gods, Xanthippe! You again?" he scolded. "How many times must I tell you not to set foot in this barn without my permission?"

"You said I wasn't to come if anyone else was here, and no one is. May I work Iris for awhile? Please?"

"No!" Palen shook his head. The time had come, once and for all, to wean this headstrong young creature from a situation that had grown out of hand. Admittedly it was his fault. He never should have told her that Iris belonged to her in the first place. But then who would have guessed that the odd looking weanling would become so notable? Even the markings on the animal's hide were settling into a shining pattern of orange on white!"

Funny how a girl and a horse can have so much in common, both slim and elegant, both 'kokeenos' with minds of their own. What's more, the care and schooling Xanthippe had given that young mare were, without doubt, responsible for Iris' superior health and performance.

She had also cajoled him into hitching Iris to a chariot and then persuaded him to show her how to drive it around the track. He'd always known she was bright but, by the gods, how she had amazed him that day! Graceful as a dancer, she had accommodated to the cart's erratic movements, balancing on firm feet, knees bent, body flexible, making just the right counter- moves as the floor rocked beneath her. Only for a moment had she grabbed his arm to steady herself, then, after a few turns, she had taken the reins!

By now even his own mother, who had also ridden as a girl, was beginning to insist that Xanthippe be made to understand that a young woman's future depended on more than knowing how to train a horse.

Alcibiades presented another problem. Until recently Pericles, his guardian, had permitted him to buy many fine animals. That, in turn, encouraged the patronage of other wealthy clients. Now, as a sixteen year old, the lad was free to use some of his dead parents' fortune, and he wanted Iris at any cost.

Of further concern was the fact that Anytus no longer seemed interested in pursuing their dialogue about betrothing Astron to Xanthippe. Was he angling for a more pretentious connection? HA! As if that donkey-grinned son of his could be considered a prize, even if he did stand to inherit his father's entire stinking leather business!

"Please, Papa?" Xanthippe's voice broke in on Palen's musings. He had almost forgotten she was still there.

"Oh, go ahead," he grudged, "But, before you work Iris, take Enyo out. She's in foal and should be stretched. Give her a short run, then slow her to a walk."

"May I ride her beyond the farm?"

Palen gave a nod. Despite his misgivings how could he deny a girl who had somehow managed to turn that pitiful weanling into a racer?

* * * *

Cantering across the pasture Xanthippe made a conscious effort to sit erect and well back on the saddle blanket like her father. But the mare's gait was smooth, and the day so deliciously limpid, that she relaxed and, abandoning discipline, allowed Enyo to wander at will, even when it came to stopping here and there for a nibble!

Wild thyme, camomile, oregano and mint crushed fragrantly beneath Enyo's hooves and, as far as the eye could see, scarlet field poppies preened in the crystal light.

Shepherds in dark blue work chitons paused in their work to wave, and tenant farmers with ozier baskets of olives on their heads smiled, surprised to see a girl riding by on a horse.

How good it was to escape Mama's maxims, like the one about aristoi woman having to sleep on fine bed linen even if they themselves had to weave and wash it.

My aunt never married, poor soul", Nikandra had said yesterday, "but she taught me how to be a good wife, and to behave myself. Everything, in fact, that a woman needs to know. And," she had hesitated a moment, "your father has a man in mind for you."

Mama had refused to divulge his name but who cared? How stunned she and Papa would be to know that whomever they might have in mind, their daughter had no intention of marrying anyone but Critobolus. They'd object if he weren't rich but, if necessary, she herself could make money. Lots of it.

For one thing, she had demonstrated her ability to train horses. Or she might persuade an influential Alcmaeonid relative that, even though she was a woman, she should be given a chance to work in the Theater of Dionysius.

Perhaps Critobolus would like to live on a farm. That would be easy. Instead of going to his house they'd come to hers. She could see them now, driving the chariot and helping Palen with the horses while Nikandra, Phyllys, and Melissa attended to the cooking and housework.

She had paid scant attention to where Enyo was taking her but suddenly her day-dreams were interrupted. There, just ahead, gracing a pair of dusty crossroads, stood the temple, taverna, and several little houses that comprised the township of Cholaragus. She recognized them from the day she'd come here with her mother to make a sacrifice to Artemis before Marc was born.

To Xanthippe's surprise, Enyo stepped up her pace and, as if knowing where she was going, clopped down the middle of the road until she came to the row of houses. Then, quite on her own, she stopped dead in front of one that had a box of flowers on the window sill.

Except for some men who were eating in front of the taverna, the town seemed deserted. But of course! The sun was riding high and people were probably indoors because it was nearing the time for dinner.

"Name of god!" Xanthippe gasped. "Mama will be furious!"

* * * *

"Where have you been?" Nikandra fumed, brandishing a quern. "I had this and everything else laid out for you to grind barley-meal! Your grandmother and Melissa have been in the vegetable patch all morning, which left me to clean up the house and prepare this dinner! Elefterous got sick after his riding lesson and vomited three times, all over the kitchen court, and your father will be here any minute wanting his noon-day meal! Everyone around here seems to think I have the strength of a Titan but I don't. I'm only a mortal!"

"What's all the noise about?" asked Palen, coming through the door.

"Xanthippe behaves like a boy and you encourage her!" The words sounded like little slaps coming from Nikandra's agitated lips. "I try to keep her indoors, then you go ahead and permit her to ride abroad in the sun. Before long her skin will look like pig's hide. And what man wants a freckled female who sits a horse more skillfully than she can bake a loaf of bread?"

"Oh for the godsakes, hold your tongue", Palen exploded. "Women should be encouraged to exercise outdoors. Take the Spartans, not that I have any use for the bastards, but their wives are more fertile than ours and it is because they are told to build their bodies and get plenty of fresh air. General Gryllus says so and I believe him."

"Fertile indeed," Nikandra snorted. With an exasperated grunt she slammed down the stone roller. "Even General Gryllus would have to agree it takes more than fresh air to make a girl fertile! I'll wager his precious little Kallia isn't allowed to run about in the sun! Small good that sort of thing does any girl when it comes to getting a husband. And you're the one who frets because she is still not formally betrothed." Tearfully she ended her tirade.

"Be patient, woman! Stop fretting. I'm as anxious as you to make a good contract. I gave Xanthippe full rein this morning because her riding days are numbered. Our sons are the ones who should be learning horsemanship. Furthermore I have neither the money or animals to supply three children with pleasure horses! But I still think she should go out in the open, at least once in awhile."

"Then let her work in the vegetable patch where she can have all the 'open' she wants!"

Knowing that a wife must inevitably submit to her husband's wishes, Nikandra did so, this time saving face by stipulating that Xanthippe always be made to finish her chores before leaving the house. "Whether it be to study with Archos or get some fresh air." And the latter "only if she is wearing a pilo on her head," she said, referring to the conical bonnet used by noble women to protect their complexions.

No longer elated over her ride, and feeling herself to be, somehow, the source of her parents' strife, Xanthippe was savagely scraping remnants of food from bowls when she heard the clatter of carriage wheels in the driveway

Nikandra cocked her head, "Who can that be?" Her face grew brighter. "Maybe it's Hipparete in her fancy carriage!"

They ran to look. Sure enough, there was Hipponicus, riding his stallion down to the paddock, and at the gate, Hipparete, being helped to alight by the slave who drove her carriage.

"It's such an honor to have you come all the way out here to visit my daughter," Nikandra exclaimed. "You haven't been here for a long time. We missed you! Name of God how time flies! Look at you! So grown up! And how is your dear Grandmother? I'll find some cakes and milk and make a party for the two of you. You're probably thirsty and hungry too after your long ride from town."

Still chattering she hastened to the food cave, grateful that, at least now and then, a pleasant event such as this came along to brighten her dreary days.

"Shall we go back to the ash grove and play make-believe or are we too old for that sort of thing?" Hipparete asked.

"I pray to die before we get that old," Xanthippe said fervently. "Let's go!"

"I'll never forget the first time we came out here," Hipparete panted as they ran. "We pretended we were charioteers and used our tunic belts for reins. You always made me be the driver because you wanted to be the horse. And your hollow tree was the stable."

"Now it's the Theater of Dionysius."

"Today let's play that the burial ground is Delphi and we are here to consult the Oracle! We can take turns being the sibyl. You first. Sit on this stump. It's the sacred tripod. Pretend we see vapors rising from the sacred Castalian springs! I'm the supplicant! Speak to me, Celestial One! Tell me what the future has in store. Whom does Apollo say I shall wed?"

"Parakolo oraios tharma deos ela doe," Xanthippe mumbled, coining words that sounded like those her father employed when he addressed the gods, and rolling her eyes until their green irises nearly disappeared. "That means you will marry a handsome rich man who owns many beautiful horses and lives on a very large farm."

"I'd rather have many beautiful sons," Hipparete giggled. "But, did I ever tell you that I used to be wild with jealousy because you had a horse and I didn't. Perhaps I still am."

"You? Jealous of me? I don't believe it!"

"I think I'd be divinely happy if I lived on a farm. I always have a glorious time when I visit you. But then, it's fun to be with you no matter where we are!"

"Efkharisto! Now you be the sibyl. What do you see for me?"

"I can't talk in tongues like you so I'll speak plain old Greek. I see you becoming the first woman hypocrite to perform at the Theater of Dionysius. I also predict that you are going to marry a remarkable man!"

"Does he have black curly hair?"

"No, he's bald," Hipparete replied with a shriek of laughter.

"You just lost your job! Anyway I have something else for us to do. Follow me and for the godsakes don't make any noise."

Walking stealthily behind rocks and bushes Xanthippe led her companion to the stall with its view of the paddock and ring.

Hipparete's eyes were shining. "I remember doing this when we were six years old," she whispered.

"Once Papa caught me and said he'd beat me with his horse whip if he ever saw me here again," Xanthippe recalled. "By now he may have forgotten. But today they're all out there racing the chariot and if we hunch down and stay quiet we can probably watch without getting caught."

"There's Alcibiades," Hipparete gasped as the golden haired youth came thundering down the track in their direction. "My brothers dote on him. So does Father."

"I hate him. He thinks he's Zeus. I remember the first time you told me you hated Alcibiades. It was after he'd made that nasty threat about cutting off your dog's tail. My father wants to betroth me to him."

"You and Alcibiades? Do you want to marry him?"

"Not really. He does such wild things I think he's a bit mad But he is amusing. Last week he and my brothers were playing 'knuckle bones' in the street when a man came along in his cart and Alcibiades lay down in front of it to keep him from interrupting their game!"

"Then what happened?"

"The driver cursed him but reined his donkey and went around."

"Thtop your cart, commoner!" With arms outspread Xanthippe lay on the stall's earthen floor. "I will rethitht your attempt to interrupt thith game of knuckle-boneth even if you run over my armth and legth".

40

"You are really naughty! Oh! Here comes Critobolus! He's gaining on Alcibiades! I could sit and look through this slit in the wall all day long! But, may the gods forbid, if my own father found me here, he'd rave like a zealot! He makes such a fuss about your horseback riding that if he thought . . ." Hipparete's voice trailed off. Apparently she had decided not to pursue the subject of her father thoughts.

"Here comes Astron, the poor bastard", Xanthippe whispered when another chariot came careening around the track just as Palen, standing behind the lad, took the reins to keep him from from tipping the cart. "Astron can't race worth an owl's hoot. If he lives to be a hundred he'll never be a charioteer. He follows Alcibiades and Critobolus like a dog but he's uglier than a dog. He looks like his father. Oh po po po! They're heading in! We must get out of here. Fast!"

Grabbing Hipparete by the hand Xanthippe led her out of the stable and once again stooping behind shrubbery and fences they avoided detection and reached the courtyard panting and giggling.

"That was exciting, watching those boys race." Hipparete said breathlessly, "Has your father ever said anything about wanting to betroth you to one of them?"

"No but Mama has hinted he has someone in mind. I tell you I'd rather drink hemlock than marry a man I didn't know or love. Tell me, how well acquainted are you with Critobolus?"

"Not very. Sometimes he comes to our house with Alcibiades to play at games with my brothers. He's handsome isn't he?"

"I want to marry him."

"You what?" Hipparete's mouth dropped open. "What does your father say about that?"

"Nothing so far. I haven't told him".

It was then that Andokides came into the courtyard to inform Hipparete that her father was looking for her.

"I wish I didn't have to go! I'm glad you're my friend. Please come to Athens soon and visit me again. I'll ask Father to send a carriage for you. He's probably in a rage now because he couldn't find me the minute he wanted to leave. Allys, the girl he expected to marry got betrothed to another man and since then my father . . ." her lip trembled slightly but again she failed to finish what she had started to say.

"I hope she comes back soon", Nikandra said, watching the carriage disappear in a cloud of dust. "Maybe one of these days she'll be able to help you join the 'Young Arrephorai'. I wish you'd spend more time in the loom room learning how to do fine stitchery."

"Mama, you've already told me, . . . and told me! I think it might be more fun to join the Hetairai."

"Don't let me hear you talk like that! A hetaira is not a good women! The whole lot of them are foreigners. Only nice young women like Hipparete and Kallia can invite someone to join the Arrephorae! And of course it has to be a person who also, like you, has aristoi blood "

If Kallia is any example of a nice young woman then I don't wish to be one!"

Chapter Seven

A bevy of neighboring wives had come to stitch coverlets with Phyllys and Nikandra, but their tongues were busier than their hands. Xanthippe, who had been put to polishing altar vessels in the courtyard, could hear every word. Cautiously she moved closer to the loom room window,

"If we had to pay for admission to the Theater of Dionysius I'd never get my husband to go. I don't care how popular a drama might be, that man falls asleep the moment the chorus starts to chant. Thank the gods women have separate seating. Even from up where I am I can hear him snore."

"Be grateful he goes at all. Mine prefers a seat at the Cholargus taverna."

"I felt very privileged to attend this year's Feast of Dionysius," said Lysicles' wife, tossing her needlework aside with the air of one who, having attained the heights, can no longer be bothered with matters mundane. She was a scrawny little woman with small darting eyes that made her look like a chicken searching for bugs.

"I wanted to cry when Alcestis' son was grieving at her grave," Nikandra reminisced. "But I didn't," she added bravely. "My husband has no use for tears."

"It's time you learned to control yourself! You'd weep if you found that a mouse had died in the flour sack." he had said, just yesterday, when he caught her crying because a batch of bread dough failed to rise.

"We may have more to cry about than you think. Now that summer is almost here, my husband predicts we'll be at war with Sparta any day," reported the pig farmer's wife.

"In spite of all the talk and rumors I still can't believe it" Phyllys exclaimed. "That silly young woman who came here with Hipponicus and challenged the men with questions may be more intelligent than she looks. Women aren't supposed to think about anything but cooking and housework but I, like that girl, think we have a right to know what's going on, I too would like to know what became of the peace treaty that Callias negotiated with Sparta. After all it's the women who become widows, and the children who are left fatherless because men can't settle their disputes without killing one another."

"To say nothing of those who come home too broken and maimed to function," said the pig farmer's wife.

"You'd think we suffer enough giving birth to their sons without the additional burden of bearing war's heartache," Nikandra added gloomily. "When I think of all the pain I had to endure . . ."

"Shall we bring out some food for our guests?" Phyllys interrupted.

With their hostesses safely out of earshot the other women leaned toward one another and lowered their voices. But not enough to prevent Xanthippe from overhearing.

"Thank the gods we were spared having to listen to Nikandra describing her birth throes again," said one.

"You would think she was the only woman who ever had a baby. Something must be troubling her today because she hasn't made a mention about how she hobnobs with Palen's aristoi relatives."

"She will, before the day is over! Just give her time."

"Such airs she puts on, as if she, not he were the Alcmaeonid. Anyway I doubt if there's not much more than a drop of their elegant blood in his body!"

"Their Xanthippe is an odd one. Can you feature permitting your daughter to straddle a horse in full view of men?"

"Of course not. It's indecent."

"Have you ever noticed that she doesn't resemble anyone else in their entire clan? Who among them has hair that can be seen two fields away? I've sometimes wondered if she even belongs to them. Maybe someone who wanted to get rid of a daughter left her in Palen's barn right after she was born."

"He'd be more inclined to keep a litter of kittens than a stray baby girl."

"But suppose it was he who got someone's daughter in trouble. Even though every one of us saw Nikandra swollen three times her size before the child was born it might have been a still-birth, like all those others. Then, by a pure chance, this red haired infant shows up!".

"Godsname! When it comes to creating a drama, Sophocles could take lessons from you!"

"I, for one, don't think we should be voicing such naughty ideas, especially not here in the house of Palen!"

Xanthippe did not recognize the woman's voice, but was, none the less, touched by her integrity.

"I, myself, always felt sorry for Nikandra, poor thing," Lysicles' wife sighed piously.

"I remember how sorry our husbands felt for Palen. All those pregnancies and nothing to show for any of them but a red haired girl. It's lucky for Nikandra she finally produced those two lads. But something tells me Palen still can't accept the fact that she gave him a girl who should have been a boy, and a boy, who should have been a girl. You can tell it's Marc who is his favorite. Palen surely did crave that second son."

"Did you ever know a man who wasn't set on having all the sons he could sire? We have three and my husband would be pleased to have me give him three more." Lysicles' wife preened. "However he admires Xanthippe. Says she doesn't miss a trick. Don't look now but she's out there this very moment, listening to every word we say." she gave her head a significant jerk toward the window.

"It's time to eat. We have a table set in the kitchen court." Phyllys said, coming through the loom room door. "Xanthippe!" she called through the unshuttered window, "Will you come and join us?"

Not trusting herself to speak Xanthippe shook her head. Just now the very thought of food made her sick. Uneasily quelling he sour spittle that slid across her tongue she fled to the ash grove. Her pace did not slacken until she tripped over a grave stone and plunged headlong into a thicket of brambles. Feeling as if her chest were about to burst, she pulled herself up, hobbled over to the tree and, leaning against its sturdy trunk, plucked barbs from her skin. Blood oozed from a gash on her leg. After erasing it with a dribble of spit she sat, hugging her knees to her chin, lost in thought.

Until this morning she had never doubted her father's love. Sometimes he'd scold, or yell, but he was like that with everyone. What mattered was that he'd given her a horse and a hound, and seemed pleased to have her around when no one else was in the barn and they sat together polishing stirrups and reins. Yet if what those women said happened to be true, Alcibiades was correct in calling her a 'Nobody's Nothing' a person whom not even Papa or Mama would have wanted from the day she was born. Who'd give an owl's hoot if she lived or died? Yiayia Phyllys? Possibly.

Critobolus? At times, when he came to race the chariot, he'd stop to talk with her and appeared to enjoy her company. Yet he, like Yiayia Phyllys, behaved that way with everyone.

What to do? She couldn't just keep on sitting beside this tree. Not here where her Grandfather and other dead relatives still existed, in some obscure fashion, down below. What if one of those 'little people, as they were called, came up from the under-world right now!

Hastily Xanthippe got to her feet, brushed herself off, and began to run, then walk, on into the woods. Cerberus, loping on ahead of her, turned back from time to time to assure himself his mistress was still there. Yet even the presence of her canine companion was not enough to lessen her sense of desolation.

The grove was dappled with shadows and only a few spears of light still threaded the sky when Xanthippe came out of the trees and into a meadow. Taking a deep breath she pressed on through an area that looked vaguely familiar until, all at once, she knew where she was! Cholargus! The little hamlet to which she had come with Enyo who walked down the main street as if she knew where she was. Everything looks different when one is on a horse instead of on foot.

Hunger was gnawing at her gut by the time Xanthippe reached the crossroads. She hesitated. Bursts of raucous laughter erupted from the taverna when, suddenly, the curtains that covered its entrance parted and a woman emerged from what was commonly considered to be the sole bastion of men. "Zeus!" she gasped, "Where did you come from? You don't belong around here do you?"

Xanthippe shook her head. "No," she faltered. Then, gathering courage, "I decided to . . . not to go back where I came from. My parents don't want me," she added lamely.

"Poor thing. You look like you'd been pulled through a rat-hole. I live over there." With her thumb the woman indicated the other side of the road. "Come, along. I'll bet a gold coin you've not had supper! By the way, my name is Femma. What is yours?"

Heartened by the prospect of something to eat Xanthippe introduced herself and followed the woman across the street to a small one room dwelling with a colorful flower box on the window sill. Now she remembered! Enyo had paused here the morning they had come, by chance, to this tiny township.

"It's getting dark. While I turn up these lamp wicks you can empty yourself." Femma pointed to a receptacle under the bed.

"You will feel still better after you wash. The water jug and bowl are on that stand. Then we'll have some of the bean stew I put on the stove this morning. And the flat bread I bake for a living. I had just delivered a batch to the Taverna when I came out and saw you."

She was pink cheeked and pretty. Black curls hung in wild disarray to her shoulders, her eyes sparkled, and her full lipped smile was as comforting as the succulent aroma that floated from her cook-stove.

"You look better already." Femma said when Xanthippe had refreshed herself. "Go ahead, Sit down. Help yourself " Carefully she placed two steaming bowls, and a loaf of warm bread, on the table.

Giddy from the fragrance of ham and garlic Xanthippe was glad to comply.

"Tell me why you ran away. What makes you think your parents don't want you?"

The meal was delicious, and Femma so sympathetic and easy to talk to, that it wasn't long before Xanthippe was pouring out the whole story.

"Don't let anything those neighbor women said bother you," her new-found friend said earnestly, as she replenished the bowls. "My guess is that they're jealous, because, compared to you, their own children probably look like moles! As for that boy, Alcibiades, he sounds like an arrogant prig. Don't let him upset you either. People like that aren't worth a second thought. Tell me more about the handsome one. You say his name is Critobolus? Perhaps he shares your warm feelings but is too shy to let you know."

* * * *

Preparations for supper were underway when Phyllys noted that she had not seen Xanthippe since early afternoon.

"Probably in the paddock," Nikandra said, "mimicking every everyone she sees and picking up obscene expressions."

When Palen came in from the barn he said he had no idea where she was. Neither did Archos, Elefterous, or Marc.

Search the ash grove and see if she's there. Then come right back! I'll return to the paddock and ask Andokides."

But the slave also denied having seen her.

"Perhaps she's asleep in her room," Phyllys suggested and toiled up the stairs to investigate.

"She's always running off like this," Nikandra fretted.

"Cerberus never lets her out of his sight. Has anyone seen him?" Palen asked. There being no replies he went outside and shouted their names.

"I've heard reports that wild boar have been seen in the area." he said grimly when he returned. "I think I'll saddle the mare and take a look around. I shall get Lysicles and some others to help." Within moments Enyo's hoofs could be heard, pounding up the lane.

"If anything had has happened to her I will forgive myself for being cross with her," Nikandra quavered, twisting her fingers.

"Ask Artemis to bring her back," Phyllys' counselled, the anxiety on her face disavowing the confidence in her voice.

It seemed forever before Palen returned. With him were Lysicles and his sons along with others who had been rounded up to assist in the search.

"Is she here?" they asked and knew from the look on his mother's face that she was not.

They were discussing what to do next when the outer gate inched open to reveal the object of their search, standing uncertainly on the threshold.

"Xanthippe!" Nikandra cried.

"For the gods' sake where were you?" Palen yelled. "You look as if you'd been in a cock fight!"

"You look terrible!" This from Elefterous.

"Are you hurt?"

"What have you been doing?"

"How did your tunic get so torn?"

"Hold your tongues and let her speak?" Palen shouted above the din.

"I ran away," Xanthippe said, with a defiant tilt of her chin. "According to the neighbors I'm not wanted here because I'm a girl. Alcibiades said the same thing. He, told me I act like a boy and he tried to lift my tunic to prove I'm not . . ." She paused to swipe at her nose. "A lady I met told me I should come home. She fetched me in her cart."

"You ran away?" Palen roared, "What a typical dumb female trick! I should take a whip to you, scaring the bowels out of everyone! Look around and see how many men have searched the countryside for you, wondering if you'd been swallowed by a boar!"

"Where is the person who brought you home?" Phyllys asked. "We should thank her. Do you know her name?"

"She was in a hurry to go back to her house. I met her across from the taverna in Cholargus. She fed me and says she knows you're a famous chariot racer, Papa. Her name is Femma"

"Oh po po ! So Femma gave you supper." Lysicles laughed. "I'm sure it was tasty! They say that anything you get at Femma's house is sure to be good!"

His comment was met with several broad grins and a few ill disguised chuckles.

"Nikandra, bring our neighbors some wine and cakes," Palen commanded, ignoring the sheep herder's comment. "These men left their supper tables because a foolish girl had a notion to run around the countryside like a head sick loon."

Still trying to hide their mirth over whatever had struck them funny the men declined his offer.

"Efkharisto (no, thank you)", they said.

"You are tired and we must go"

"We're glad you're at home again, Kokeeno".

One by one they spoke and shuffled toward the gate. No sooner had they gone than Palen turned on Xanthippe with so fierce a scowl that she burst into tears.

"Stop blubbering! What makes you think you can control a horse when you have no command over yourself?" he bawled.

"You'll never see me cry again." she vowed, meeting his eyes headlong. "Never!" she repeated through clenched teeth.

"Don't be so hard on her," Phyllys rebuked her son."Have you already forgotten how frightened you were when we couldn't find her? Just thank the gods she's home safe!"

Palen did not respond. There are times when I could take a whip to her, he thought, glumly contemplating this girl-woman whom he sometimes hated and always loved. Tonight's escapade would make him the prize butt of jokes for miles around. At this very moment people were probably already falling apart with laughter.

"Did you hear about Palen's daughter dining with Femma?" they'd be asking one another, Femma! The only whore in Cholargus!

"What was it you mentioned about Alcibiades, Xanthippe?" Nikandra inquired.

"Not now," Phyllys remonstrated. "She's been through enough for one day. I suggest we leave any further questions until tomorrow. What we need to do now is to assure her that she is wanted and loved. Come with me to my room, Xanthippe, and we can talk awhile before you go to bed."

* * * *

Instead of allowing herself to be segregated upstairs, as was the custom with wives, Phyllys had elected to share a bed chamber with her husband on the ground floor throughout their short-lived marriage. Still not bowing to tradition, she continued to retain it after his death.

Delicately fragrant of herbs and spice, like its occupant, that room was, to Xanthippe, a sanctum of delight. Here she had heard the legend of Odysseus, the romances of Pyramus and Thisbe, Orpheus and Eurydice, Endymion and Selene and, best of all, Phyllys' own story.

"It seems so 'all of a sudden' that you have grown too tall to fit into my lap." Phyllys laughed. Her face sobered. "What a scare you gave us, 'Kale Pai'."

Xanthippe patted the fleshy wattle that hung beneath the old woman's chin, and gave a sigh of content. Never had the endearment Kale-Pai, 'precious little one' fallen so sweetly on her ears.

"I'm sorry I worried you."

"I forgive you, on one condition. If you ever think of doing such a thing again you're to tell me about it first."

"I almost turned back when it began to get dark but I couldn't, not after all those dreadful things I heard about myself today."

"Such as . . .?"

"That instead of me Papa would have preferred a litter of cats.

"The giddyheads! His problem is that, like all men, he is afraid to die without leaving a son behind to say the ritual prayers at his grave. Believe me, from the day you first said 'Papa' he has adored you. You are his pride and joy."

"You're prejudiced," Xanthippe said, smiling broadly. "Oh Yiayia, I'm glad to be at home again, sitting here with you. Before we go to bed tell me a story, the way you used to. The one about Grandfather Marc looking into your eyes until you thought you were going to swoon."

"My heart melted like goat butter on a hot stove!" Phyllys chuckled. "If only you could have seen him dance a 'Dithyramb'! How he tossed his head and performed the most intricate steps with skill and grace! He could out-dance or out-hunt anyone. But he proved his manhood by showing me that, I came first in his heart. It takes a real man to give his love unreservedly.

"I shall marry for love the way you did. No match-maker for me!" Xanthippe declared stoutly. Critobolus might think of her as an amusing child, but the time would come when he too would look into her eyes, and realize that she, Xanthippe, was a woman!

"Why, I wonder, do neither gods nor mortals ever seem to know pure bliss for more than a brief time," Phyllys sighed. "My life was flawless until Athens warred with Persia. I've told you how patriotic I felt was when my dear husband sailed with a fleet commanded by Elpinice' brother, Cimon. I was proud to learn that he served in Athens' great victory over the Phoenicians at the mouth of the Eurymedon River."

Xanthippe nodded. It was an oft-told tale but she never tired of the telling.

"When word came that he had perished at sea I began to realize what we had was too perfect to last. So here I sit, some thirty years later, a widow wondering what purpose that or any war ever served. I just pray there's nothing to all this gossip about a war with Sparta. Such a thing could finish the Athenian Empire, and all of us along with it! But that is unlikely, so we wont waste time worrying about it," she said,

"Those women who came to sew said the battle will begin within a month." Xanthippe said. That had been almost as bad as the other things they talked about. Papa might go and die like his father! Or what about Critobolus! However these were thoughts Xanthippe kept to herself.

"My story is not a sad one," Phyllys said, patting her granddaughter's hand. "Believe me, I am content, knowing that what we had was very rare. I am also doubly blessed to feel free to share all my precious memories with you, Xanthippe . . . Oh my dear! It's getting late. You have had a difficult day! You should be in bed."

"May I sleep in your room tonight, Yiayia Phyllys? At times when I climb the stairs to my room I feel as if something scarifying, like a monster Hecantocheire, is coming up behind me, to grab my heel with one of his hundred hands."

"You have a great imagination. But let's suppose you happen to be right. Wouldn't Cerberus be there to protect you?"

"He would if it weren't for Mama. She says he smells like a pole-cat and is not allowed on the second floor. But he does sleep on the bottom step so if anyone tried to get by him he'd bark so fiercely he'd even scare off a monster." Remembering how the hound had protected her from Alcibiades' rude advances, Xanthippe grinned.

"I came to say goodnight," Nikandra said, appearing unexpectedly.

"Are you feeling better, Xanthippe?"

"Yes, Mama."

"You must be tired. It's very late."

"She can sleep with me tonight," Phyllys said. "I think she's still shaken by today's experiences."

"Well then . . ." Irresolutely Nikandra stood in the doorway, then, "Goodnight," she said, feeling sad and older than her years. How contented the two of them looked, she thought. Yet it was she, not her mother-in-law, who should have been comforting the truant. A stab of jealousy, vague regrets, and a desire to gain Xanthippe's affection, stirred uncomfortably in her breast. Yet how to capture the love of a daughter who so obviously preferred sitting with her grandmother, or working for her father, to enduring the company of her mother?

There had been a bond between them, or so it seemed, the night of Marc's Day of Recognition. But it was short-lived.

"Starting tomorrow I'm going to try again to get along with her," Nikandra promised herself. "I'll start a pleasant conversation and, bit by bit, we'll become friends."

* * * *

"Tell me more about the little skirmish you mentioned having with Alcibiades," Nikandra said next morning in the kitchen court where she and Xanthippe were twisting garlic bulbs into braids. She would not, she had decided, mention yesterday's escapade. At least not just now.

"It was over a year ago. He tried to chase me out of the stable."

"Well, you can't fault him for that. You shouldn't have been there in the first place. What were you doing?"

"Having a conversation with Cerberus."

"Don't be sassy. You can't converse with a hound. What was that about Alcibiades lifting your tunic?"

"I told you last night. He said he wanted to show me the difference between a boy and a girl."

"Name of God. What happened next?"

"Oh, Mama, stop asking questions! I was in the stable minding my own business and suddenly there he was." Dropping her garlic braid on the table, Xanthippe minced across the floor. "He said, "Hath no one told you that girlth are not thuppothed to be theen in thtableth?"

Nikandra's acquaintance with Alcibiades was limited to seeing him at clan gatherings, but the parody was unmistakable and she couldn't keep from laughing. "I agree. He was wrong to tease you," she said, picking at the redolent cluster in her hand, "However you must be careful around boys. It's best to stay away from them altogether. They are prone to do things like . . . like lifting your tunic and that can get a girl into trouble.

"As you know, Alcibiades is related to us. He's a direct descendant of Alcmaeon, Megacles, Cleisthenes, Hippocratus," One by one Nikandra counted them on an abacus of fingers. "The next time you see him again, don't quarrel. Be friendly, Invite him into the courtyard. I'll give you both something to drink and a bowl of the almond cakes I save for guests.

"I wouldn't care if his parents were Hera and Zeus! He's worse than Hipponicus, and Hipponicus is despicable. If you wish to give Alcibiades your precious almond cakes invite him into the courtyard yourself."

"Don't speak to me in that tone of voice, Penroula! You seem to forget I'm your mother!" Disgusted with her attempt to initiate a friendly conversation with this quarrelsome girl, Nikandra thrust a pail at her and sent her off to fetch water for the pots.

Melissa shook these down this morning," Phyllys reported, coming into the kitchen court with a basketful of olives. "We must get to work on them right away."

Stifling a yawn Nikandra hung her finished garlic braid on a peg, sat down opposite her mother-in-law, and reached into the basket. Gloomily impervious to the morning sun that streamed through the slatted room, spattering everything it touched with light, she divested the purple globes of stems and silvery leaves and dropped them into a jug of brine.

Why was it that she and Xanthippe could not exchange five sentences without having cross words and misunderstandings? It would appear that, no matter what a mother did or did not do to gain accord with her daughter, the Erinyes had already decreed that such a thing was never meant to be.

* * * *

Scowling darkly, Xanthippe strode, stiff-legged, to the well. Her mother had called her 'Penroula'. A bad girl.

It would be a pleasant relief to return to the crossroads of Cholargus and have a really intelligent conversation with Femma, who not only listened, but seemed to understand.

"You look like you're marching off to war," someone said. Xanthippe had no need to turn and see who it was. She knew.

"I saw you hiking to the well when I came up the lane," Critobolus said. "So I hitched my horse to a tree and came to say 'Kalimeera'. It's been awhile since we've had a chance to talk to each other. But I keep an eye on you. I hear you aren't riding Iris these days because you did something that upset your father. Whatever it was, you have my sympathy. I've locked horns with Palen myself. And with my own father as well. I'm seldom the one who comes away victorious.

"You may not know it," he went on, "but I often stay on here after our chariot races, just to see you handle that mare when you think that no one else is around. You are incredible! And very attractive with your hair hanging loose and blowing around your face."

"I've hidden behind trees to watch you race," Xanthippe confessed, having, to some extent, recovered her composure, and, along with it, her tongue, "You are better at it than any of the others."

"Alcibiades doesn't share your opinion. He's so sure he's going to win at the next Olympiad he's already lording it over everyone else as if he were Zeus. But right now I must head back to Athens so I'll get there in time for supper. Perhaps we can find some time to talk again later."

With that Critobulous was gone.

Chapter Eight

Palen was still fuming. Thus far not a soul had dared tease him about his daughter's supper with Femma but he knew damn well her escapade was titillating the entire country-side. Her reason for running away might seem justifiable to a female, but not to him. She must be punished!"

Silently Xanthippe heard her sentence. "You are not to go near the paddock for six weeks. And if you ask to ride, the answer is 'No!'" He held her chin in a vise-like grip between his forefinger and thumb. "I swear by the gods, one more stunt like that and you'll have real cause for regret."

"No one can take care of Iris the way I do," she mourned when he released her chin. He did not deign to reply.

She had yet another blow in store when, as she stood on a knoll that overlooked the track, she saw Alcibiades cantering Iris around the ring. "This mare will soon belong to me!" he shouted in passing.

Atticans scorned stirrups. Instead they mounted with the help of a leaping pole and depended upon formidable metal bits to control their steeds. So, pity the horse whose rider, like Alcibiades was inclined to haul on the rein.

"Papa! Iris is mine! You gave her to me!" Xanthippe cried. He's so heavy-handed he'll pull on her mouth 'til it bleeds!" Again her appeal met with stony silence and, dangerously close to tears, she fled.

Silently, in her bed-chamber, she withdrew a terra-cotta Goddess Artemis from its wooden chest and propped it on her wash-stand. The little figurine, a gift from Yiayia Phyllys, served as a repository for her inmost thoughts. She had formed a habit of talking to it soon after Elefterous was born.

"They coddle him as if he were the Archon, and hang over his crib making silly-talk," she'd lament, listing her grievances one by one. "But they treat me like a slave. 'Bring the water jug! Fetch fresh diaper-cloths! Yammer, yammer, yammer!'

"I pray you, let things be nice again," she begged now, searching the goddess' vacuous painted eyes. "Please, make Papa stop being angry and don't let him sell my mare to Alcibiades!" However Artemis, like Palen, remained mute.

If only there were real someone, a flesh and blood someone, in whom to confide. There were some things one could not tell, not even to Yiayia Phyllys or Hipparete.

Femma? Neither a relative or a neighbor but she laughed easily and was full of fun. She was also a compassionate person who gave good advice. Femma was a friend!

"For now there's little you can do, Xanthippe," she had said. "When you are older you can make your own decisions, and, if you have real courage, fight for them."

Despite Papa's dictum that she must never visit Femma again, Xanthippe knew she would. But he must never find out! So, insisting that she, like his precious Spartans, needed out-door exercise, she donned a hat and set forth.

Upon arriving at Femma's house she pulled the bell-rope and waited. There was no answer and she gave it another tug but still no one came. Then, just as she was about to leave Femma opened the door "Xanthippe!" she exclaimed. "I hope you aren't running away again?"

"No. Not that I haven't given it some thought," Xanthippe grinned. "But this time I'm here just to see you."

Did she imagine it or had Femma hesitated a moment before saying, "By all means! And today, instead of bean soup I have freshly baked baklava and some mocha beans that a friend gave me to grind and make a delicious hot beverage."

"It smells divine!"

For over an hour they talked.

"There's little you can do but keep praying Alcibiades wont buy Iris," Femma said. "But, regarding your tender feelings for Critobolus, I think I can be of help. There are several things a woman can do to induce a man to return her love. In fact I'll teach you to perform some spells that are very effective! First of all one must have wax. I keep mine here" She rummaged about in a small wooden crate. "Watch as I melt some and observe how careful I am not to spill any on the stove because it can cause a fire." She settled a pot of tallow over the heat. Next we must call

56

on the goddess of mortal love. "Repeat after me, 'Aphrodite, as this wax melts, so may my beloved melt with desire.' We shall chant those words together seven times." When they had done so she with-drew a bronze wheel from her crate.

"I shall place this here on the table. Give it a whirl and say, 'Draw my lover to me, magic wheel of Aphrodite, and as you spin, may I spin into the heart of my beloved.' Listen! Do you hear dogs barking? It means the goddess is at the cross-roads! Quickly! Clash the cymbals!" Femma handed two metal plates to Xanthippe.

"That's all we can do now." she said, setting the plates aside, when Xanthippe, frowning with concentration, had performed her role. "When you're at home and the moon is full put a bay leaf in a bowl, wrap a braid of red wool around it, like a wreath, set it under the big tree you told me about and chant 'Hail, Hecate, make this potion more pow-erful than Circe's or Medea's. Let it draw my lover to me."

"Then what?" Xanthippe asked breathlessly.

"Inscribe a wheel around your bowl and say, "Magic wheel, draw my lover to me. Then, when the top of your outdoor oven at home is hot make a wheel of bran on it and as it burns call upon your family god-dess and say, 'Artemis, you who can remove the power of death, call my lover to my house'."

Again Femma delved into the box and produced a packet of herbs. "Pour this into the bowl with the bay leaf," she said, dropping some into a clay jug with a measure of wine. "And, if you feel the need, do it over again when the moon is full."

* * * *

Wanting time to think about what had transpired Xanthippe chose an alternate route home. "Left at the cross-road and I'll be on the old Dionsiou road." she said to herself.

Perhaps Femma was a diviner! She had somehow known that Artemis was one of the family's gods. And she believed that certain stones and jewels can empower you if you hold them in your hand. "You gain energy just by holding and caressing a treasured object," she said. "For example, the goddess your grandmother gave you, or the lamp from your mother."

She was contemplating these possibilities when, up to the right, she saw an ancient sanctuary. It was, as she recalled, dedicated to Asclepius, the god of healing, whose father, Apollo, taught him to help mortals to overcome their infirmities.

On impulse she turned off the road, so lost in thought she failed to see a man sitting nearby on a bench

He, on the other hand, was very much aware of Xanthippe. Tall, slender, and verging on womanhood. her hair ablaze with sunlight, in her cream colored tunic, she reminded him of a lovely white stemmed torch.

At first, when she entered the sanctuary, Xanthippe could scarcely see. Gradually, as her eyes adjusted to the semi- darkness, she beheld a huge statue of Asclepius, glowing in the light of myriad flickering lamps. Before him stood an altar strewn with facsimiles of arms, legs and other body parts denoting the afflictions of supplicants who came here to be healed.

The thought occurred that physical ailments might prove less troublesome to deal with than the emotional anguish of love, such as her own unquenchable fire for Critobolus. Even Asclepius was unlikely to know how to deal with that kind of burning. He probably had trouble just trying to identify the thicket of limbs that proliferated directly beneath his big bronze nose.

"Kalimeera, Xanthippe," someone said when she came out of the temple, squinting in the sunlight. There, standing before her was Socrates.

"Shall we sit here?" he asked, making a small bow. It was exactly as if they had planned to meet. "From this promontory one can actually catch a glimpse of the Saronikan Gulf. Do you remember the last time we saw each other, at the Great Panathenaea? As I see you today, it would almost appear that the central figure in my 'Three Graces' had come to life!" Wordless with astonishment Xanthippe sat down.

"Did you find what you were seeking?" His astonishing eyes probed hers. "I happen to believe that everyone is in search of an elusive something. That is why I take the liberty of asking what you hoped to discover. In there," he added, inclining his head toward the sanctuary in response to the quizzical look on her face."

"Happiness . . . I guess," she faltered, surprised at finding herself responding to his impertinent question."

"And what would give you happiness, my dear?"

"I'm not sure." This conversation was less real than a game of pretend. "Love, I guess, and money. However I did not expect to find either in there," Xanthippe said, pointing toward the temple.

"Do you know anyone whose wealth makes them happy?"

A strange question. Great-Aunt Elpinice was the only rich person she knew who appeared to be genuinely happy. But she, like Yiayia-Phyllys, would be serene in any circumstance.

"Not really," she replied when, after further reflection, no one else came to mind, other than Hipparete, to whom an affirmative answer might apply. "You say that you too are searching for something?"

"Yes. Constantly. I seek 'Beauty', a beauty difficult to describe. So I go about questioning others, hoping to find someone more illumined than I to assist me."

"So, Xanthippe, if, as you suggest, happiness derives from love, how would you describe love?"

His probing was beginning to annoy. "People say you teach by asking questions to which you already know the answers" she retorted, standing up, as if to go. "What is it are you doing now? Teaching or teasing me?"

"Neither. I am enjoying the company of an emerald eyed damsel whose skin is lustrous as the inside of a shell. As to my interrogation of others, I believe that wisdom is of greater value than gold. My questions are the keys to vaults of hidden treasure, intellectual treasure."

Vaults of treasure? This conversation was beginning to confirm what Papa said. Socrates was crazy.

"No, Xanthippe, I'm not deranged, just inquisitive," he chuckled. "The treasure vaults to which I refer are peoples' minds."

That proved it! He, like Femma, was a mystic! She cast spells, he read minds! How amazing to be in the company of two in one day!

"I shall try to explain," he said. "For example, do you ever say to yourself, 'Who am I?' Because in order to find the treasure of perfect happiness you must first discover who and what you are."

Sunshine, pouring through the trees, dappled his earnest pudgy face with light. Yet, aside from that, there was a peculiar radiance about the man himself,

"It's getting late. I must go home and help my mother fix supper," Xanthippe said abruptly.

"I anticipate talking with you again, my dear," Socrates said, patting her. His touch gave her a tingling sensation, reminiscent of Femma's description about the energy one gets from feeling jewels and smooth stones.

* * * *

"I saw a well-known person on my way back from Athens," Xanthippe told Nikandra upon returning home.

"Who?"

"Someone who interests you."

"Aspasia?"

"Now, Mama, what would she be doing on the Dionsiou Road?"

"Stop asking riddles! Who was it?"

"Socrates."

"Oh . . . him. You probably didn't get any way near him through the mob that tags along wherever he goes."

"He was alone."

"What was he doing way out here by himself? And what were you doing with him?"

"When I was walking down the Dionsiou road I came to that old temple of Asclepius and decided to go inside. When I came out there was Socrates."

"Did he remember you? Did you speak to each other?"

"Yes. He called me by name and recalled meeting me at the Great Panathenaea. We talked but he didn't make much sense."

"They say that even wealthy aristoi hang on his every word. Phaenerete must be very proud of him. Did you find out what it is about him that creates such a stir?"

"Not really. He says wisdom is worth more than money . . ."

"Ha!"

"But in a way I can see why he draws such a crowd. There's something rather attractive about him."

"Him! Socrates?," Nikandra giggled. "He must have had a basket over his head. What else did he say?"

"That everyone in the world is searching for something."

* * * *

Very quietly, that same evening, before it got dark, Xanthippe went on a search of her own. For a bay-leaf, three strands of scarlet wool, and a bowl.

Chapter Nine

After months of tiresome tasks on the farm, it was pure joy for Nikandra to be back in Athens, with by Phyllys and Xanthippe, en route to a feast day for women only. "There it is!" she exclaimed, pointing toward the Temple of Artemis. "Move faster! We want to find a good place to sit so we can see everything!"

"We're lucky just to be able to move in this crowd," her mother-in-law grunted as they jostled their way across a pillared portico and into the magnificent house of worship.

Awestruck, Xanthippe gaped at a multiplicity of statues and friezes flourishing everywhere. There were even paintings on the ceiling!

According to lore, Artemis customarily made her home in wooded glens but, if one were to judge from this place, she obviously preferred to dwell in splendor when in Athens.

A din of hammers being applied to three bronze gongs heralded temple girls in saffron garments who, with bells jingling at their wrists and ankles, came through a wall of curtains and danced.

"Sshh! There's the priestess!" Nikandra whispered, pressing a finger to her lips when, following the dancers' performance, a tall slim woman came to the center of the dais.

"Goddess Artemis, we have come to worship you." she said, addressing a larger than life statue of Artemis. "You asked your father 'Zeus' for the gift of eternal virginity, now we implore you to keep our thoughts pure so that we too may be chaste."

She turned toward the audience and her thick lashed smoky eyes seemed to look directly into Xanthippe's own.

"Artemis can be tempestuous, wily, even ruthless. If she wishes her bow brings death. But remember, she is also the goddess who loves children and animals, cuddles a bear cub, and races with deer. And she cares for you! From the deepest forest she will come to your aid faster than you can cry, 'Artemis, help me.'

"You know the story of Atalanta, the girl who was abandoned by her father in the woods, but saved by Artemis from certain death. Today the goddess is ready to come to your rescue and save you from the wilderness of inner death.

"Hail holy and gracious! Hail maiden daughter of Leto and Zeus", the priestess sang, raising her arms until the folds of her cloak flew back like the wings of a golden bird. "Dweller in the spacious sky! Maid of the mighty Father! Maid of the golden glistening house! Hail Virgin Goddess, most beautiful of all the heavenly Olympian host!"

Gong-beats accentuated the monotonous cadence of her paean. As their volume increased, listeners joined in. "Hail, holy and gracious, Hail, maiden daughter of Leto and Zeus . . .

Like a reed in the river she moved, bent, and swayed. Gradually her words became unintelligible, and the sound of her voice, eerie and flute-like. All over the temple spellbound women rose up, arms flailing and bodies writhing, until, overcome with rapture, some of them, swooned.

The spectacle of her mother and grandmother dancing brought Xanthippe to her feet and she was still clapping her hands and whirling when the priestess' undulations ceased, the humming faded, and celebrants, flushed and panting, resumed their seats.

When everyone was quiet the priestess spoke again. This time her voice was a throaty whisper, yet powerful enough to penetrate the temple's furthest reach.

"The moment has come," she crooned. "Artemis is with us now, here in her temple. Close your eyes and feel her presence. Be still, and pray for the fulfillment she offers. She is eagerly waiting to quicken the sterile wilderness of your souls as rain quickens the parched earth!"

Silence still reigned when the priestess turned away and, with jewels flashing in the glow of many lamps, vanished into the draperies.

Next came a scrawny old fellow whose face resembled a dry creek bed. In a voice that filtered like a reed pipe through his beard, he detailed the rewards that Artemis stood ready to bestow upon generous souls who contributed their valuables to the temple treasury.

"You said that only women came to this Feast," Xanthippe yawned.

"Men take care of temple treasuries." Nikandra whispered.

"Why?"

"SHhhh!"

By the time a sacrifice of fat had been offered to Artemis, the stench of charred flesh, issuing from an altar laden with goats, had Xanthippe's nostrils twitching

"Look! There's Clymene. See, standing with Kallia by that pillar." Nikandra said when the meat had been sliced and was being served by neophyte priestesses. Others passed baskets of bread, and bowls of sacred wine. "Let's join them. Be nice to Kallia, Xanthippe. I want no more of your mischief."

Six years later and she still can't forget," Xanthippe groaned to herself. But the recollection of the 'mischief' to which her mother referred brought a grin.

Kallia's father was a short wiry man whose stiff martial posture made him appear taller. He was good-natured and congenial, characteristics that neither his wife or daughter could lay claim to. Not only had Kallia inherited Clymene's sour disposition, she also had the buttocks of a brood mare and the ponderous bosoms of a wet nurse.

On the day to which Nikandra referred, Xanthippe had been on her swing, pumping it higher and higher, when General Gryllus came along and deposited his daughter. "You and Kallia have a nice time while I talk to your father in the paddock," he said. As soon as he was out of sight Kallia grabbed the swing and Xanthippe gave her a shove.

"You knocked me off the swing! I could have been killed!" the silly thing screamed at the top of her lungs, all the while rolling on the ground and making a great show of dying.

"Yeow! yeow!" Xanthippe was mimicking her when Nikandra came running. It was the first time her mother had ever called her 'Penroula' (a bad girl).

"She's so fat she didn't know when she hit the ground!" Xanthippe recalled protesting. "Anyway you laughed until you cried when Papa said since ravens are bad omens one must have made a dropping on Kallia's head the day she was born!"

After silencing her with a blow on the mouth Nikandra had marched both girls into the house and offered Kallia a slice of fresh baked karidopeta. A sure way to put a smile on Kallia's big mouth was to push a piece of cake into it.

"Xanthippe is incorrigible!" Mama had raised her voice to gain Papa's attention that evening when he'd come in to supper.

"Has she no sense, shoving my client's daughter around like a stable hand?" he had spat. "It appears she's developing a mean streak!"

"Stop dawdling!" Nikandra urged, breaking in on Xanthippe's soliloquy. "Clymene! Kallia! How lovely to see you!"

While the older women chatted, the girls eyed each other warily. "I've been to Feasts of Artemis that were better than this," Kallia volunteered through a mouthful of meat.

"I liked the rites today," Xanthippe said. "Especially when the priestess cast the Presence? Did you feel it?"

"The Presence?"

"It's what makes people dance and swoon."

"I didn't feel a thing. But I saw you jumping around like a hop-toad. I wanted to throw a stone at that old priest who wouldn't stop talking when it was time to eat! They should have roasted him with the goats."

"Beware, my girl!" Xanthippe quavered, screwing up her face and plucking at a make believe beard. "And hand me your jewels or Artemis will turn you into a furze tree and sheep will eat your prickles."

"You look and sound just like him! How do you do that?"

"What are you up to now?" Nikandra asked.

"She was being impious, making fun of the priest." Kallia said virtuously.

"Name of god, Xanthippe, how could you?"

"I thought the old fool talked too much myself", Phyllys said. "In any event, another Feast Day is over and we must be on our way."

"Priestesses are powerful, Kallia," Xanthippe said in a low voice. "After seeing that woman perform the Mysteries I have decided to become one myself when I grow up."

"You're crazy." Quietly Kallia delivered her parting stab.

Chapter Ten

Six months after the Feast of Artemis an aroma of ripe grapes in the sun, and the chatter of crickets, were bringing nostalgic reminders that, once again, the time had come to celebrate the autumn festival of 'Apaturia'.

Although devotion to the Empire had gradually superseded many old religious rites, this three day ceremony of thanksgiving, dedicated to Dionysius, God of the Vineyard, was still observed,even by worldly-minded clans. Leaders of one such, the Tribe of Acamantis, to which Palen belonged, had decreed that this year's event be held three miles beyond the walls of Athens, in a grove owned by Callias, and blessed with both a well and a stream.

"Take me along," Elefterous entreated, watching his elders make preparations to leave. "Xanthippe gets to go, why can't I? I don't want to stay here with Marc and the slaves!"

"Hold your tongue! You whine like a woman! The answer is 'No'! Children can't attend an Apaturia until they're ten years old?" Palen barked. "What's keeping Nikandra?" he asked his mother who, with Xanthippe was already established in the mule cart. "I could be dressed and undressed six times before my wife ties her sandals. By the dog, if she is not out here in one more moment I shall change back into my work clothes and return to the barn!"

"I'm coming!" Still mooring a knot of hair to the back of her head, Nikandra ran out into the driveway. "I want to be at my best because all of your 'aristoi' relatives will be there."

"And, just as you suspect, they'll all be looking at you. Get in the cart!" So saying, Palen snapped his rein at the mule, and, with a lurch, they started down the lane.

"Everyone else is already here," he grumbled when they pulled into the camp site. "You women, get this cart unloaded while I tether the mule."

Despite his misgivings, they were seated and ready before the seventh blow was struck on the cymbal. Callias, titular head of the phratry, was the first one to bow before a make- shift wooden altar which held two silver carafes. One was filled with water, the other with wine. When he had poured equal measures from each into a gold pitcher he gave thanks and offered a libation to Dionysius.

Another man arose and chanted the tale of the creation of man.

"The whole earth is heavy with the fruitage of a good harvest." Callias said, when the lengthy legend came to an end. "It is at this time that man also reaps his soul's harvest from the year's activities." His aging voice was weak and so difficult to understand that Xanthippe's attention wandered.

Five times throughout the summer, when the moon was at its zenith, she had painstakingly carried out Femma's instructions, invoking the goddesses and repeating the mystic words. After which she took care to hide her bay leaf, potion, and bowl in the tree trunk.

Systematically her eyes raked the crowd for a glimpse of Critobolus. He had been coming regularly to Palen's racing ring with Alcibiades and others, to ready himself for the next Olympiad, but they had not had a conversation since the day he surprised her as she was going to the well.

People were beginning to talk and move about, an indication that opening rites were over. "May Xanthippe eat with me Aunt Nikandra?" asked Hipparete as she came running up.

"Yes! Yes indeed!" was the eager answer.

Slaves had man-handled plank benches and tables into a clearing. Jugs of wine, cornucopias filled with fat purple grapes, and a feast garnered from garden, pasture, and sea were now awaiting the celebrants.

Because an Apaturia was one of the rare times when overly chaperoned young men and women were given an opportunity to mingle, they glanced about with studied nonchalance, looking for those in whose company they preferred to sit.

"I love these affairs!" Hipparete confided. "They're the only times we get to have fun with boys. Poor things, so busy studying at the Academaeia all morning and throwing the diskos, wrestling, and pushing punching bags in the Palaistra every afternoon, they have no time to play! I don't even see my brothers. Now that Hermogenes is sixteen they both take most of their meals in the androm with the men. Let's try to stay away from Alcibiades. He acts as if he owns me."

Xanthippe nodded absently. There was only one boy she cared to see. Beyond what Critobolus had said about his father being stern, she knew nothing about his family. Yet she had seen him at previous Apaturias, so they must belong, if not to her father's clan, at least to the same phratry.

"Hipparete! Come sit next to me!" Alcibiades cried, pretending not to notice Xanthippe. And, there, across the table from him was Critobolus! "I saved a place for you, Xanthippe," he said patting the vacant place at his side.

With legs trembling so violently she could scarcely stand she managed to comply. Femma's spells had begun to work!

To hide her excitement, she feigned absorption in figures of the gods, etched in black on the circumference of a two handled wine bowl being passed from one to the next. Looking up she found Critobolus staring at her as if he had never seen her until now. Boldly she returned his gaze until her heart was beating like the wings of a bird gone crazy in its cage.

She was the first to look away.

"I hear you are both going to be initiated into manhood this year," Hipparete said to the young men. "That must mean you'll be ephebes, ready to leave Athens for army duty."

She always seemed to know what to say to boys, Xanthippe thought, eyeing her friend with a twinge of envy.

"You're right, Hipparete. We'll probably leave around two months after the Olympiad." Critobolus said. Turning back to Xanthippe, he spoke in a voice that could not be overheard. "You're certainly no longer the girl who jumped out of a tree to do battle with Alcibiades. You're even more fascinating now than you were then. You are beautiful. And I intend to become better acquainted with you."

Xanthippe caught her breath. No one but Yiayia Phyllys had ever so much as hinted that she was pretty let alone beautiful! Then she remembered. There had been another. Socrates. The day they'd talked just outside the temple of Asclepius.

"You were adorable, braving Alcibiades to rescue a turtle," Critobolus said. "I hated to leave you"

"I didn't feel adorable! I was furious. When the two of you left that day I pretended I was Hecate and muttered horrible curses."

"Do you believe she builds nests in trees?"

"If she can fly across the moon I guess she can build a nest in a tree." Xanthippe giggled.

"What would you do if, you, like Hecate, could turn yourself into a white mare?"

"I'd be wild and untamable."

"You were wild and untamable the day we met! I hope you haven't changed." Critobolus grinned. "As for me, I'd like to mount Pegasus with you and fly into the sky, or anywhere else you'd like to go. Would you come with me?"

"Yes. I'd like that. But what about you, Critobolus? If you could do the one thing you wanted to do more than anything else in the world, what would it be?"

At the moment I would like to . . . " Critobolus paused and the look he gave Xanthippe sent a quiver up her spine.

"I'll get to that later." he said, "But if you're referring to what I want to do after I finish military training, I'd like to be the most famous chariot racer in Greece. I'd certainly prefer that to going into the banking business with my father. He has a way of trying to take over my life. I guess most men are like that with their sons."

Xanthippe could hardly keep from laughing. There'd be no problem with Mama and Papa over her desire to marry a banker's son! Now all she had to do was make more wheels, continue her chants and, if Femma's spells continued to work the way they seemed to have bern doing so far, Critobolus would soon declare his love!

It was almost evening when honey cakes, almonds, and fruit made their final round. But when the feasting came to an end Xanthippe could not remember a single thing she had eaten.

A musician wiped his mouth and, with flute in hand, leaped from the bench. "We are full of wine and food. Now we are you ready to feast on music!" he cried. Others joined in with citharas, pipes, trumpets, and drums, to play the wild, noisy rhythms of a Dithyramb, befitting the god of wine.

"Did you bring your flute?" Alcibiades was asked.

"I don't play a flute anymore," he said loftily. "I athk you, why should anyone ath handthome ath I am make himthelf look athinine? Fluthts puff and blow out the cheekth tho foolishly that the Goddeth Athena threw herth away when she thaw what contortionth she made."

Laughing uproariously others urged him on.

"I must admit, he does look like Apollo," said Hipparete.

"You say nice things about everyone," Xanthippe replied. "Athinine!" she murmured to herself. But she could not keep from noticing the spell he exerted. Charmed by his flamboyance, his insane fits of laughter, even his ridiculous lisp, people converged on the fair haired youth to pay him court.

Waving a white kerchief aloft Hipparete's father plunged into a circle that was cleared for dancing. His corpulent body gyrated to the musicians' frenzied melodies. Soon Palen and the other men took their turns before merging into the constantly enlarging ring. Full of fervor from wine and worship, they were moving with ever increasing abandon when Critobolus pranced into their midst and, to cadenced clapping, began to spin. Faster and faster, he whirled, around, away, and back again like a top.

"He out-danced them all!" Xanthippe gasped, her eyes riveted on him as, glistening with sweat, he bowed to frantic applause and returned to seat himself, once again, at her side.

People were beginning to drift away, families making preparations for the night, others, like Elpinice and Callias and the parents of Critobolus were returning to their more comfortable quarters in Athens. "We will see you in the morning," they said.

Gradually the dancers dispersed and weary musicians stored their instruments. One alone continued to strum his cithara, but so quietly that the lento trill of crickets could still be heard.

"My parents will return to Athens for the night but I'm camping here with Alcibiades and the others," Critobolus said. "However, before I bid you 'Kaleenikta', Xanthippe, I want you to know that being with you made this Apaturia the best ever!"

He leaned toward her. Even with his face in repose the natural upward curve of his lips gave it a look of good humor. The hair on his chest, showing above the neckline of a white linen toga, was dark, and, like the tousled curls on his head, glossy as an umberbird's wing. Everything about him caused unexpected pulse beats to flutter throughout her entire body.

Bathed in the pale effulgence of a half-moon the entire world seemed dreamlike. Wild rosemary scented the air. The lingering taste of wine in her mouth, the feel of Critobolus' hand on hers, all were part of the enchantment of the night.

"I've never seen any boy or man dance the way you did this evening!" she said, dizzy with the scent of his flesh.

"You're the one who is wonderful! I've never known a girl who could ride like a warrior, and who studies with her brothers' paidogogus. What does this Archos teach you?"

"I'm supposed to be learning numbers which, he claims are a gift from the gods and 'an expression of a mathematical thinker thinking mathematically.' Mostly we talk about drama."

"His thoughts about numbers remind me of someone I know, a man named Socrates. Have you ever met him?"

"Yes, at the Great Panathenaea. He'd sculptured an image of a dead girl who looked like me. I've seen him once since then."

"What do you think of him?"

"That his eyes are very blue and big as gulls' eggs. They gave me the feeling that he was looking directly into my head. You admire him?"

"With all my heart. He has the finest mind in the land, which is one of the few things my father and I agree upon. Father reveres him. The two of them were boyhood friends."

"I'd like to hear what it is about him that . . ."

"Critobolus!" A peremptory shout coming from the direction of the mens' encampment interrupted her.

"I must go. We'll be in trouble if your father comes looking for you and discovers that our friends have left and we're here by ourselves." Lightly he touched her cheek and walked away.

Yiayia Phyllys' romance had begun like this, at an Apaturia, Xanthippe was thinking to herself when, after rejoining her family, she snuggled into her nest of coverlets on the ground.

* * * *

Early the following day young virgins from each clan in the phratry assembled to be told, by a very old woman. what was deemed appropriate for them to learn about the magic of fertility and the mysterious seasonal rites of ploughing, sowing, reaping, and harvesting.

The sky, their preceptress explained, was the Father God Uranus who, in the form of rain, fertilized Gaea, the Mother Earth and that was why the field must be opened by a plough and prepared to receive the seed that had to be placed within its womb.

Her disclosure met with a rolling of eyes and some knowing smirks.

"Pay attention," she scolded. But when shouts were heard issuing from the area reserved for wrestling and diskos throwing contests the poor soul lost her audience altogether.

"Oh be gone with you," she snapped, spreading her hands. "Girls these days aren't interested in learning anything worth while. All they want to do is gossip and chase after boys!"

Taking her at her word the young women raced toward the games field where they were told that Alcibiades, on the verge of being bested by Critobolus in a wrestling match, had bitten him.

"By Zeus, what do you think you're doing?" one of the men who had rushed to separate the combatants upbraided him. "For shame!

Biting is for woman, not men!"

"But I do not bite as women do," was the lofty retort, "I, Alcibiades, bite like a lion. And upon my word I shall challenge him again."

"Ha! And by the gods I shall accept," his opponent rejoined.

"Alcibiades will go one of two ways," an onlooker presaged. "Either he will become one of the greatest men in Athens or he'll get himself thrown out of the country."

"Or both." said another.

Phyllys and Nikandra arose early on the second day of Apaturia, folded their coverlets, splashed themselves in the stream that ran through the property and took care of their personal needs in the short term accommodations that had been improvised for the occasion.

Now they were readying food. What seemed like a chore at home was more of a game on feast days in the company of friends. Even Elpinice, who had slaves to do her bidding was talking and laughing while she worked with the rest. Palen, meanwhile, was arguing and making his points with the men.

Xanthippe's activities, having, so far, gone undetected by the members her family was enjoying the morning repast with Critobolus, feeling as if she and not Sappho, had authored the words that Archos had given her to memorize.

She reviewed them now, making changes here and there to suit the occasion.

'He seems equal to the gods, this man who sits beside me,
and while close to me is sweetly speaking with love,
things which cause the breast to tremble
for whenever I look at him I can scarcely speak.
My tongue freezes to silence,
light flames trickle beneath my skin,
I no longer see with my eyes, my ears hear whirring.
Cold sweats and shivering make me their captive'

"Xanthippe, you haven't eaten a thing," he said. "You look as if your thoughts are . . . Tell me, where are they?"

She was deciding what to say when the insistent din of hammers on the big bronze gong heralded the most significant rite of any Apaturia, that of initiating seventeen year old males into their clans.

"I dare not be late for this", Critobolus said."

Again their eyes interlocked and Xanthippe felt as if she were falling through space. Then, with Alcibiades and other initiates, he got up from the table and went into the woods.

"Let's leave before that old crone gets hold of us and starts to tell more of her stories about ploughing mother earth! Shall we have a game of knuckle bones?" Hipparete asked. "We can ask Myrto and Kallia and some of the others if they want to play Knuckle bones'."

"A game for children", Myrto said in the clipped concise accent native to those whose ancestors came from Thessaly. Her facility for making whatever she thought or did seem the only way to think or do quickly disposed of 'bones'.

Although diminutive, she carried herself in the regal way one would expect of a direct descendant of Aristide 'the Just'. To be appraised by her cool amber eyes of a cat could make one feel judged and found wanting. Nonetheless Xanthippe was captivated by her out-spoken manner and found herself wanting Myrto for a friend.

"I hear that you are betrothed to Socrates, Myrto," one of the girls remarked.

"Who told you that? Phaenerete I'll wager! To hear her you would think the contract was already signed. She hankers for grandchildren who bear the blood of my ancestors and, since her husband and my father happen to be friends, she thinks I should marry her son. I'd run off with a bull dancer from Crete before I got into bed with him! Besides he's like his mother. He talks too much". She gave a short laugh.

"What if your father signs a betrothal contract?"

He wouldn't. Not without asking me. He may be impractical but he's fair and open minded enough to let me say 'No'."

Socrates again, Xanthippe thought. First Critobolus talking about him, and now Myrto, sounding as if they were describing two different people.

"Speaking of betrothals, the way Anytus has been courting your Papa with gifts and favors you might end up as the bride of Astron." Kallia said to Hipparete.

"May the gods forbid. If that happens I'll throw myself into the sea." Hipparete replied cheerfully. "Just having to call him 'Astron' would be too much. That name was probably his mother's idea. She's a little peculiar. 'Heavenly body'! What a major misnomer! However I needn't worry about that because, after not speaking to each other for years, Father and Pericles have come to terms and signed a contract betrothing me to Alcibiades. Instead of the ugliest boy in Athens I'm getting the wildest. But soon they'll all be in the army which is fine with me. As far as I'm concerned, the wedding can wait indefinitely. I'm in no hurry to marry him, or anyone for that matter."

"You slay me!" Kallia hooted.

She had changed, Xanthippe observed. For one thing she'd lost weight. And her full lipped mouth had begun to look sensual rather than surly. She was also obviously paying more attention to her apparel because it was not only free of food spots but carefully draped! Several fine gold chains adorned her neck, and, her hair, instead of hanging in unkempt strands across her shoulders, was becomingly dressed and bound by filigree clasps.

"Does anyone know what a girl can do to make a man fall so madly in love with her he'd gladly go to Hades' pits just for the privilege of holding her in his arms?" Kallia asked.

"Great gods!"

"Oh come now, let's be honest. You know perfectly well we'd all like to know the answer to that."

Amid shrieks of laughter only Xanthippe stayed silent. How surprised they would be to discover that she herself already knew how to make a dream of love come true.

"One of our slaves makes a Persian love potion," a girl named Theora volunteered.

"Does it work"

"What goes into it?"

"You catch a lizard and grind it up and cover it with wine. Then, just before nightfall, you pick some flowers and knead them over your threshold with a quern and while you are doing so you repeat over and over, 'He' (whoever he happens to be) loves me.' Next you invite him to supper and put some of the lizard mixture in his wine".

"And he vomits and drops dead over the threshold that's conveniently covered with squashed flowers," Myrto said drily.

"If a person isn't betrothed do you suppose the potion could help her get a contract?"

"I'm not sure," Theora said dubiously. "Ask the slave who gave you the recipe."

"Has anyone heard the rumor that Crito has a betrothal contract in the making for Critobolus?" Kallia asked. Xanthippe felt beads of sweat breaking out all over her body. Certainly Kallia was mistaken. Were Critobolus betrothed he would not have looked at her and talked as he did last night.

"He's old enough." Myrto said.

He's being initiated today." "Do any of you know what the men do in their rites, the part that's supposed to be kept secret? I've heard some stories about what goes on!"

"Only that they get very drunk, and if a female so much as goes near where their Mysteries are being observed even if she only peeks she'll be tried by law and imprisoned,"

"What you say about women being punished by law reminds me of the time I tried to get my father to take me to an Olympiad," Xanthippe said, catching everyone's attention.

"Did he?" Myrto asked.

"No. He said women are forbidden by law to go near any of the events. If anyone disobeys she must pay the penalty.

"Which is . . .?"

"Getting tossed over a cliff. The decree went into effect after a woman sneaked into the games disguised as a man because she was her son's trainer. But when he won the foot race she got so excited she ran out onto the track and her toga flew open and it was decreed that one can only attend an Olympiad if he is naked."

"Name of a god!"

"What happened to the woman?"

"The law had not, as yet, gone into effect so she was saved" Xanthippe finished, satisfied by the rapt attention with which her story had been received

"How fascinating!"

"You told it so well I could actually see the poor thing's toga flapping!"

"What a ghastly experience!"

"I happen to know what the men do at their ceremony," Myrto said, slanting wise eyes at her companions when the comments and laughter subsided. "Men!" She gave a light laugh. "They're all like children."

Impressed by her sophistication, the others moved closer, with cries of "Quickly! Tell us! What do they do?"

"Did any of you notice the long tubular grip-sacks they were carrying when they went into the grove?" she asked.

There were several nods.

"Well, as we're told, Dionysius represents the grape bearing vine and after the harvest he, or it rather, is pruned . . . actually torn to pieces and eaten until there's nothing left of him but a stump. But like Persephone he comes back to life each spring as the ever procreating vine or penis and his children are the grapes.

"So, to celebrate his fertility the men drink wine and chant and dance wearing huge phalluses made of balsam and painted red. They fasten them to their bodies and sing crude songs with leather bladders under their arms that they squeeze to make noises like farts. And the-seventeen-year-old initiates are also given big 'wands' of their own to wave!"

Following several enthusiastic outcries Myrto still had more. "Finally the phalluses are heaped on the altar as a form of surrender to the power of Dionysius. Can you picture them, Alcibiades for example, leaping about wagging one of those things? And being serious?"

"I can!" Xanthippe cried, still aglow with the heady sensation of success. It was the first time that girls from town had appeared to regard her as, not just as a horse breeder's daughter, but one of them.

Picking a round piece of bark from a fallen birch log she thrust it between her legs and, holding it erect, flung back her head shouting, "I am Alcibiadeeth, the greatetht prick in Athenth and thith ith what maketh me a man!"

Dropping the bark she assumed a woe begone expression. "Oh thee how thad I am", she wailed. "I have lotht my thplendid penith!"

Her performance was greeted with such howls of laughter that, spurred to even greater histrionics, she retrieved the object, whirled it madly over her head and flung it into the air.

You are the funniest person I ever saw," Iodice exclaimed, wiping tears of laughter with the hem of her tunic. "But for the godsake none of us must tell a soul what we were talking about!"

"Not only she but all of us could be accused of impiety,." Kallia said grimly pointing finger at Xanthippe. "We might even be brought before a tribunal!"

"You're right! According to my father on this is a day when men dance with God!" another girl chimed in.

Now her companions were regarding Xanthippe as if she were an oddity, like Lysicles' lamb, the one born with five legs.

"I think you showed poor taste, making fun of Hipparete's betrothed." Kallia added.

"Don't be a goose!" Hipparete exclaimed. "Look at me. I'm still laughing. I think she was, she is, marvelous!"

But the jollity had ceased.

Late in the afternoon celebrants, still decked with fir branches and yellow berried ivy, emerged from the grove. Liberal portions of ivy and grape wines, both sacred to Dionysius, had apparently been drunk in his honor because some men promptly fell asleep on the ground while others grabbed their wives and returned to the woods.

Critobolus, Alcibiades, and their fellow initiates, having fortified themselves with food that had been placed on a long table, armed themselves with another jug and wandered toward the games arena while the girls, no longer voluble, picked at their own supper following which they were prodded into helping the older women.

"The moment we're finished here I am going to get some sleep", Hipparete yawned. "I'm almost too tired to stand up."

Thoughtfully Xanthippe placed two woolen covers on the earth and rolled into them. The euphoria induced by this morning's conversation with Critobolus had evaporated, leaving in its place a heavy sense of depression. What could have prompted her to parody Alcibiades in front of those girls, some of whom she scarcely knew?

Hipparete was her friend but the others? Would they tell their parents who would in turn tell hers? She had already intercepted a few disdainful looks being cast her way at supper.

"Artemis," she whispered, "Don't let me get into trouble and don't, oh do not let that rumor about Critobolus be true."

As Xanthippe had guessed, Critobolus father was a member of Palen's phratry but belonged to a different clan. And, since each clan has its separate Roll Call, she would be denied the thrill of seeing him indoctrinated into manhood.

Just as the presentation of brides, babies and newly initiated sons, was about to take place on this, the third and last day of Apaturia, Alcmaeonids were astonished to see Pericles arrive to personally present the name of Alcibiades, his nephew and charge.

Before the twitter of excitement he created could turn into a tumult, Callias asked that the cymbal be pounded for order, and the Archon was ushered to the center of a ring of chairs in the first row. Hurriedly other, lesser clansmen, and their families, arranged themselves on the rise above to watch Hipponicus bow to the man who had seduced his wife.

In truth, so much attention was focused on Alcibiades, his famous uncle, and his prospective father-in-law, that others who were being introduced seemed to fade into anonymity. When Pericles departed right after his nephew had pledged eternal fealty to the ancient Tribe of Acamantis, the buzz of voices could not be altogether stilled.

"Xanthippe, it's easier to get to my house from here than from Cholargus. Ask your mother if you may come home with me today for a visit," Hipparete suggested when Roll Call was over. "You can return to the farm in my cart."

"I'd like that!" Xanthippe said, knowing that Nikandra could be relied upon to say 'yes'.

"Good! But you seem downcast. Is something troubling you?"

"I made a fool of myself yesterday."

"Forget it. You gave all of us a laugh. Pay no attention to Kallia's mean mouth. She's always like that. Hmmm, I wonder what she's up to now." Hipparete gave her friend a nudge. "See, over there with Alcibiades. What do you suppose she said to make him look that ugly?"

Turning about, Xanthippe met Alcibiades' eyes, and saw a look of implacable hatred undeniably, directed at her.

Still as a statue she returned his stare. "If looks had the power to kill we would both be dead," she said to herself.

If only I could turn him over to Myrto," Hipparete sighed. "She belongs to a note-worthy family, but they have no money. What she needs is a rich husband. He could give here everything she wants and she might be able to make him behave. "They'd be good for each other."

* * * *

The final ceremony of thankfulness, and obeisance to Dionysius was short lived, and the time had come for 'adios'.

"Pericles spoke to me!" Nikandra exulted as she packed bedding into a cloth sack. "He was very friendly wasn't he Mother-Phyllys? And he not only remembered who you and Palen were, he called you by name! When you introduced me to him I almost fainted. How did I look? Did I seem nervous? I was, you know. Oh I do wish Aspasia had been with him. I've always wanted to see her."

"Will you stop raving, and finish what you're doing, so we can be on our way!" Palen complained.

"Mama," Xanthippe said, touching Nikandra's arm, "Hipparete invited me to her house. I'll stay there for two days, and come home in her carriage."

"What about your chores? And Archos? I've never known you to miss a minute of your time with him!" Nikandra said. But, as Xanthippe had surmised, she capitulated.

Chapter Eleven

The house of Callias sat high on a overlooking Athens. On clear day, one could even catch a glimpse of the Gulf.

"I can never quite believe people actually live here. I always feel like I'm in the Temple of Artemis," Xanthippe marvelled.

The rooms seemed limitless. Many were as big as Femma's entire house, and several were used solely for visiting! The family dining room seated eighteen persons and, of course, there was an andron for men. Perhaps the most impressive feature was a tremendous banquet hall where, years ago, the celebrated painter Polygnotus had inserted the portrait of a much younger Elpinice into a mural on one of its walls.

It would be very nice to dwell where fountains splashed in three courtyards, and slaves were always on hand to gratify your every wish, Xanthippe thought, with a faint tinge of envy.

"An army could encamp in this place and there would still be room for more." she said.

"You forget how big our family is," Hipparete said. "Me, for one, and Grandmother, Grandfather, Father, my brothers, cousin Iodice, and twenty slaves, to say nothing of guests from all over the Empire."

Flowers growing in terraced gardens scalloped the hill with a rainbow of hues. Following a brief but intense shower, raindrops glistened on spider webs and butterflies flirted in a plot of asphodels. A platoon of ants. marching across the flagstone walk, contributed to the illusion that this was truly a garden of the gods.

"The trees look like they're wearing clean green clothes!" Hipparete said gleefully. A few puddles still pocked the ground and, on a whim, she jumped into the center of one and splashed her tunic. "I hate growing up", she grumbled, giving the wet garment a shake.

"And I." Xanthippe echoed fervently.

"I get so weary of being told to do stupid things like preparing pickled fish. Look at these cuts." Hipparete thrust out her hand. "When I am betrothed to a boy who owns thirty slaves why should I be taught to work as if I were going to be one myself?"

"It seems to go with being a woman. Be glad you only need to know how to do these things so you can tell if all those slaves are doing what they're supposed to. Why is your father so set on having you marry Alcibiades?"

"He wants to strengthen family alliances. Alcibiades was three when his parents died and Pericles became his guardian. I was born four years later, about the time you were. If Pericles hadn't lusted for my mother, my betrothal contract would have been signed before I was six."

"Do you ever miss her, your mother?"

"Not really. I was an only baby when she ran to Pericles. I don't even know where she is. But that's ancient history, and apparently Father wants to let bygones be bygones. After all, Pericles is the man who rules the Empire. Besides which his precious nephew says he's in love with me. Not that I believe it! The only person Alcibiades is in love with is Alcibiades. But for some strange reason everyone, including my family, seems to adore him."

"I don't."

"Nor I. I wish I did. But if, as they say, we're going to war with Sparta, the boys will stay in the army and Athens will have a huge crop of spinsters. So I should be thankful just to be betrothed. Has your father said any more about having someone in mind for you? I could tell, by the way you and Critobolus looked at each other the other night that you care for each other. "Do you think the little rumor Kallia let drop about him being betrothed might have something to do with what your father said?"

Xanthippe gasped.

"It could, you know."

"Kallia and Myrto are looking for you." Hipparete's cousin, Iodice called through the garden gate.

"Oh, Xanthippe. You're here too," Kallia said coldly, when they returned to the house. "Hipparete we missed you at the Young Arrephorai meeting this morning."

The conversation turned to activities and people unfamiliar to Xanthippe, but she was content to let her thoughts drift. What if Hipparete were right! Palen had taught Critobolus how to race the chariot, and both fathers belonged to the same phratry, so they had to be acquainted!

"Will you young ladies join me for supper?" Elpinice asked.

When they were seated and a libation of wine poured for the gods Elpinice raised her eyes toward Mt.Olympus. "Render us rich and flourishing and give us wisdom, Queen Demeter," she prayed.

While slaves served Lobster in lemon sauce, there was lots of chatter about the Apaturia. Uncomfortably conscious of Kallia's disdain over that ill-begotten parody of Alcibiades, Xanthippe was fearful it might be alluded to in front of Aunt Elpinice. It was almost a relief when the topic turned to war.

"I married an Alcmaonid which doesn't mean I must approve of Pericles," Elpinice said flatly. "He exiled my brother and stole my son's wife, so by now I'd be content if I never set eyes on him again. He could get us into a war that would spell the end of Athens as we know it. Yet I would welcome Aspasia. She is real woman. Callias has always been good about inviting husbands to bring their wives to dine here, not just on the occasion of a birth, a wedding, or a funeral, but for the pleasure of their company. Can you feature Aspasia being permitted to do such a thing in the palace of Pericles? My guess is that she sometimes longs for the days when, as a hetaira, she could do as she pleased."

Myrto wore a look of pure delight. It mirrored Xanthippe's own reaction to a glorious woman who dared to speak in so noble a fashion.

This was a most exciting evening!

"It distresses me to realize that you young women have never known anything other than a male dominated society." Elpinice continued. "Your grand mother and I were far less restricted, Xanthippe. I wish you could have seen her tackling that farm before your father came of age. I, for one, approve of the way he permits you to ride."

"I seldom hear that said, Aunt Elpinice. But I'm not at all sure how much longer the word 'permits' will apply. I'm afraid it will soon be the past tense 'permitted'. When did this 'male dominated society', of which you speak begin?" she asked.

"A good question! I've talked too much. Who has an answer?"

"I can try", Myrto said, elevating herself slightly on her couch. "It probably got its start on the island of Lesbos where Sappho, a poetess and teacher of music and dance, became so influential that some of the Lesbian men feared she'd take away their power. So they got her exiled. But to give them their fair due, or at least the few who had good sense, she was ultimately brought back and honored by having her image stamped on a gold coin before she died.

"I've read some of Sappho's poetry," Xanthippe said.

Elpinice' violet eyes widened. "You two are well informed! Xanthippe, where on earth did you find Sappho's poetry? I was not even aware you could read!."

"I got the script from my brothers' paidogogus.

Elefterous is in public school now but Archos still teaches Marc and me."

"A script! Such things are hard to come by. This man Archos must think the world of you. Just be sure your father never finds out about it unless you want to see your paidogogus tossed bodily over the fence! I fear Palen is not one to appreciate Sappho." Elpinice chuckled.

Xanthippe grinned. The thought had already occurred to her that not even the liberal academician, Archos, would dream of putting forth ideas as daring as those she had heard discussed tonight. Nor would her father tolerate them if he did.

* * * *

It was late and the house dark and quiet. Xanthippe, too stimulated to sleep, stood in front of the open bed chamber window and stared at a star-jewelled sky. Critobolus lived in Athens. Perhaps at this same moment he too was gazing into the heavens and thinking about her!

How luxurious it was to nibble figs, brought by a slave and placed beside a pitcher filled with flowers. Apparently the only thing Hipparete had never been able to lay claim to was the ownership of a riding horse!

Beds in the house of Callias were soft as the fur on a cat, she thought drowsily curling up beneath a cover of softest wool. Ah yes! It would be glorious to live here, or in any house, providing she shared it with Critobolus.

He was still on her mind when she was awakened the next morning by the companionable chirping of birds outside her window. Otherwise all was still. However the sweet pungency of a Persian spice, Mahlepi, told her that someone, probably a slave, was also up and baking bread.

Quietly so as not to disturb anyone she dressed and, smiling imperiously, smoothed her tunic as if it were silk, adjusted a would-be cluster of jewels at her throat and, walking regally as a queen, descended the marble staircase.

On the bottom step she was assailed by an uneasy sensation of being observed. Cautiously she looked around and saw Hipponicus. He was scantily clad and his hair and beard were wet, indicating that he had come from one of the bathing rooms she had seen on her first tour of the house.

Something about the look in his eyes, and the way he ran his tongue across his slimy lips made her want to turn and flee. Instead she held her ground and bobbed a salutation.

"I see that you too are an early riser," he said, coming toward her.

Apprehensively gripping the stair rail she stood very still.

"Xanthippe?" Hipparete called over the balcony. "Ah! There you are! And you, Father?" A sober look crossed her face.

"I'll be down right away and join both of you for breakfast!" she said hurriedly.

* * * *

Xanthippe was pleased to find that the slave who conveyed her back to Cholargus, was not talkative. His silence allowed her time to think about her visit, and sort out some of her emotions.

When she and Hipparete were nine years old, they had pledged eternal friendship by making tiny incisions in their right thumbs and pressing them together. "By mingling our blood we become two bodies with one soul inspired," they had repeated solemnly. "From henceforth we are friends forever!"

With all her heart Xanthippe had meant what she said. But the vow had not included amity for Hipponicus. Furthermore, after her most recent encounter with him she had come to a sure decision. He was to be avoided at all costs. But how grievous it was to know that both the father, and the future husband of her friend, were unmitigated scoundrels.

Chapter Twelve

"I sold two yearlings today," Palen said. "And one of these days we may have something else to celebrate. Get a jug of Metaxa and bring it to the courtyard. It's a nice evening."

Nikandra could tell he was in a rare good humor by the broad smile on his face. Also because, when he had poured brandy for himself, he offered some to her.

"What was the other thing you were going to tell me?" she asked. "You said we might have something else to celebrate."

"Maybe . . . maybe not. What I mean to say is, there's nothing definite so far, but Anytus brought up the subject of a betrothal for Astron and Xanthippe again. Perhaps he's begun to realize that anyone who gets our daughter can consider himself fortunate. Not just because she's an Alcmaeonid, or that we've put aside a decent marriage portion for her, or even that she knows how to run a household. At least I hope she does! Considering all the tutoring she's had she ought to know everything there is to know about doing sums."

Some of Nikandra's chronic fatigue seemed to fall away as she digested her husband's tidings about the impending disposition of their daughter. What a comfort it would be to have the matter settled. It would be a dream come true to see her married into a wealthy family.

"Shall we tell her?" she asked.

"No, we'll keep it to ourselves awhile. For one thing, Astron has to serve his term as an ephebe, so it will be at least three years before he's free to get married."

"You're sure this is the right thing to do? Betroth her to Astron I mean. He's most unattractive, with those boils on his neck and . . ."

"And a chin like a grain scoop. Yes, I agree he's no Adonis. But how many times have I heard you say you want Xanthippe to have a rich husband? Well, believe me, if this works out she'll get one. So stop worrying because, if nothing goes wrong, Xanthippe will get one" He reached out and patted her hand. "I'll pour some more Metaxa," he said, "and let's have a few of those almond cakes you insist on hoarding for company."

When he chose, Palen could be companionable, and almost tender, Nikandra thought as she went to get the cakes. How nice life would be if he were always like this.

On the other hand it might be easier were he consistently unpleasant. That way his fits of temper would not have the power to catch her unaware.

"This business of getting her betrothed has burdened my mind almost from the moment she was born." he said. "She may be nothing but a girl but, by Zeus, she's bright. I only wish our boys had some of her horse sense. But she's fourteen years old, and if we don't soon get this business settled, she'll end up without a man at all. Sadly he shook his head. "Name of a god what a wonderful son that girl would have made."

* * * *

"I seem always to be either too hot or too cold." Nikandra complained, using a fore-arm to wipe her flushed face. "Xanthippe! I don't think you have heard a word I said all afternoon."

She was right. Her daughter's mind was far removed from the kitchen court where they were grinding wheat. In truth Xanthippe had been trying to remember how exactly, that rumor about a betrothal for Critobolus had been worded. But to Nikandra she said, "I've been wondering if I'll still have to do this sort of thing after I get married."

Instead of answering, Nikandra clapped the flour dust from her hands, mounded the wheat, and shoved it into a bowl. This, she was thinking, might be the time for the two of them to talk about matter of women and men. Despite Palen's advice to the contrary, a few well-chosen words might also be dropped about a contract of betrothal for being under consideration. "I'm tired of working." she said. "Let's quit and have some cakes and wine. Stay here and wait for me."

Having rummaged through the sour smelling wine cellar she

returned to the kitchen court with a jug of kokineli, stacked a platter with almond kourabiedes, poured the wine and seated herself somewhat formally across from her daughter.

I'd like to discuss a few things with you that I hope you will find interesting," she said with an apologetic little cough. Taking a sip she eyed Xanthippe warily over the rim of her cup.

"You are approaching the, uh, peak of womanhood. That is, you are . . ." she faltered. "What I mean to say is girls your age are vulnerable. That's the word I was looking for. Vulnerable. A young woman's behavior must always remain above reproach. She should try to stay away from men and boys, that is until she marries one of them. That applies even when she is betrothed. So you must stop talking to them in the stable yard or at clan meetings unless you're with a grown-up."

"Stop fussing, Mama. I promise you I shall remain as chaste as a fish until I get married." Xanthippe replied, thinking that the time she had spent in the company of Critobolus had apparently not gone unnoticed. But Nikandra's face unfailingly betrayed her every emotion and was, at the moment, altogether free of guile.

"Don't be flippant. Just take care that you mean what you say. Horrible punishments await the female who gets herself in trouble. Never forget. No matter where you are or what you do, someone sees. I refer, not only to the gods, but the neighbors.

"You've said all that before. Please Mama, quit rambling and get to the point." Xanthippe said uneasily. What if, the gods forbid, some of the adults had heard about her mimicry of the mens' Mysteries.

"These things bear repeating. A girl needs always to be on guard against gossip and mischief. She must never do anything that might encourage . . . fits of ecstasy." Delivered of her message Nikandra shifted her bench and leaned against the wall. "Why are you staring it me?"

"I was thinking about Pyramus and Thisbe, the lovers who killed themselves because their parents forbade them to marry, I was also wondering if you had ever been in love."

"Love! I fear that your grandmother has filled your head with romantic nonsense. Had her husband not died so early in their marriage she would long since have quit talking about what a perfect man he was. Instead she'd have found out that life is too difficult to support romance for very long. Amorous adventures are for gods, not mortals. Even so, goddesses have their share of trouble too. Look at Hera! And she's the wife of Zeus! Daydreams and sentimental stories are for young girls. Yet I must say, it would be nice to be one again, a girl I mean. I'm getting so old. Next year I'll be thirty. I hope you'll marry a thoughtful, um . . . lover. When your father asks me to visit his bed-chamber he's always in such a hurry." Nikandra's face reddened. "But I guess it really doesn't matter since most of the time I'm too tired to care one way or another."

Retreating uneasily from her mother's confidences Xanthippe moved to safer ground and surprised herself by saying, "I appreciate all the things you do for us, Mama. You work very hard."

"That's because I like things to be nice." Moved to tears by the unexpected accolade Nikandra mopped at her eyes. "I'm afraid the wine is affecting me," she said apologetically. "While we're on the subject of marriage, I think I may safely say that your father recently spoke of contracting a betrothal for you".

"To Critobolus?"

"Critobolus? The son of Crito? Good heavens no."

"Then tell Papa he's wasting his time. I intend to make my own choice and not get tied to some pig's ass like Hipponicus or anyone else he picks up in the paddock which could include someone I'd never even seen!"

"If you continue to say such nasty things you won't get anyone to marry you at all! Not even a pig's ass, to use one of your obscene expressions. In fact you ought to be grateful to have a father who is doing his best to give you a chance to get married at all. It's a terrible thing for a woman to remain single and have to be supported by her father forever! Or her brothers! The daughters of Athenian citizens are expected to make proper marriages. My own betrothal to your father was settled properly by his mother, my father, and a matchmaker.

"If you say 'proper' one more time I shall scream."

"Proper is a good word to keep in mind, young woman. Even though we did not belong to the same clan or worship the same hearth gods, your father and I have a good marriage."

"You forget. I live here too where I can see what happens to a 'properly arranged' marriage. Papa orders you around as if you were his slave. 'Nikandra! Bring me food and wine,' he says or, 'This bread tastes as if you made it yesterday. Bake a new batch.' 'There's dog dirt on the floor!' 'I need clean clothes.' He doesn't need a wife, he needs a keeper! You may be able to put up with all that but it's not for me."

"How, please, do you intend to find your great love?"

"You think I am so unattractive that no man will look at me unless Papa bribes him with my dowry?"

"Oh, Xanthippe," Nikandra despaired, "Why can't we get along and enjoy being together? Other mothers and daughters don't have scenes like this!"

"They probably do and keep it to themselves for fear of what 'some one might think' which is all you ever worry about."

Nikandra's face was that of a child who has been unjustly slapped and Xanthippe's anger dissolved.

"It's not your fault, Mama. But I'll die before I marry someone I don't love just so Papa can get me off his hands.

"Most girls would thank the gods to find a husband of means, And this one will inherit a fortune. How can you fault that?"

"I don't. But money isn't everything. No matter who, or what he is, I don't want him."

"Well . . . a contract hasn't actually been signed yet because he'll soon become an ephebe and will have to do his service."

"So go ahead and tell me who he is."

"Astron, the son of Anytus. He comes here for chariot racing instruction."

"Astron!" Speechless with horror Xanthippe pressed both palms to her cheeks.

"You're getting flour in your hair," Nikandra observed.

"Speaking of pigs' asses, Astron is king of the swineherd! How could you and Papa think of doing such a thing to me? Name of God! What does Yiayia Phyllys say about this? Surely she can't approve! Believe me. Mama, I, like Thisbe, will plunge a sword through my heart before I marry the son of Anytus!"

"Aren't you being a bit overly dramatic? After all, this isn't the Theater of Dionysius. As I said, the contract hasn't even been signed, but take my advice and pray it will be. If all these rumors about a war with Sparta come true you'll be lucky just to find someone who can grow a beard!"

* * * *

A week later Xanthippe still could not credit what her mother had said. Astron was the ugliest boy she had aver seen. His laugh was the bray of a donkey and he had a tiresome habit of trying to attract attention by telling stupid jokes. Worse yet, he kept her from spending even a few moments alone with Critobolus because he was always tagging after him when the boys came for chariot racing. The very idea of being his wife made her sick.

Only when she was listening to Archos could she be free, for awhile at least, of these nagging anxieties. But this was his day to go to Athens.

"I have some weaving to finish in the loom room," Nikandra said. "Keep an eye on the boys and see to it that they finish the assignments Archos gave them before he left."

However she was hardly out of the courtyard before Elefterous gave a disgruntled sigh. "I'm tired of this." he said, slapping down his tablet. "Please, I beg you, tell us one of your stories!"

Irritating as they might be, Elefterous and Marc could always be depended upon to provide Xanthippe with an audience of two. Whether she clawed the air like a hundred-handed Hecantocheire, or turned into a giant Laestrygonian and lunged at them with hideous growls, they would scream with horrified delight. The more noise she made in the telling, the more they loved the tale. Today's choice was the saga of Hephaestus being thrown from heaven by his father.

"Thrown by angry Jove sheer o'er the crystal battlements from morn to noon he fell, from noon to dewey eve, a summer's day, and with the setting sun he dropped from the zenith like a falling star . . ." She was well into her tale when frantic barking coming from somewhere in or around the stable yard alerted her to the fact that Cerberus was not nearby. "Don't move until I return. Finish your lessons!" she called back over her shoulder as she ran.

No one was in the paddock so she hurried around to the back of the stable It was there that she found Alcibiades, trying to hold Cerberus at bay with a whip, while the hound, hair bristling and one paw extended, appeared ready to spring.

"Call this crazy animal off!" he yelled.

"Come." Xanthippe said quietly and beckoned to the hound who, after one final growl padded to her side. Unable to resist temptation she fixed her adversary with a contemptuous smile.

"I now have one more reathon to even the thcore with you! Jutht wait and thee," he snarled, his eyes narrowing with hate.

"I too have one more reathon to even the thcore with you! Jutht wait and thee! Pfffft! You think because I'm a girl you can scare me but you're more afraid of my hound than I am of you," Xanthippe snapped as, with her head held high she stalked away followed by a now docile pet.

Partly concealed by a scruff of bushes she paused on the crest of a hillock, and was not surprised to see how many chariots were in the racing ring. Palen was so highly respected a master of chariot racing that, with the Olympiad in view, more boys and men were arriving every day.

From where she stood she could see Critobolus, prone on a sheet beside Alcibiades, while slaves massaged them with olive oil to keep their backs and shoulders from getting stiff.

The sight of his unclothed body made her think of figures she had seen of the gods. Unlike those marble statues, his forehead was probably glistening with sweat beneath his tousle of curls. And because both boys were uncovered she'd be in more than ordinary trouble if anyone caught her watching them.

Wrapped in sheets they entered the stable. When they came out again they wore identical white racing chitons, girded at the waist with hammered metal belts. Both boys were tall and handsome. Beyond that all semblance ceased. Alcibiades behaved like a madman, his wildness accentuated by a shrill lisp, On the other hand Critobolus was calm, smiled easily, and his voice was articulate and mellow. She ran up the lane. Perhaps he'd ride and stop to talk for awhile! But soon, to her dismay, he and Alcibiades trotted by without a glance to right or left.

* * * *

It was day-break in the month of Anthesterion. Trees, no longer dormant, were awakening to spring's caress and the Sun God's golden arrows were making restless shadows shift and prance all over Mount Hymettus.

"We'll use winter wheat." Phyllys said in the kitchen court where she and Xanthippe were making phyllo. "This won't take long so you'll have time for your hour with Archos. The trick is not to tear it," she went on as they stretched their creation to gossamer fragility. "Handle it with the same light touch your father taught you to use on a rein."

"I don't know why he bothered." Xanthippe grumbled. "He claims I was born to sit a horse, then makes me work in the kitchen while he teaches Elefterous and Marc.

"You mustn't criticize your father," Phyllys said, scattering nuts and currants over the phyllo. Now, roll it, put it in the oven, and join Archos."

Instead of going to the tutor, Xanthippe surveyed the paddock and racing ring. No one was around so, cautiously she tiptoed into the stable and found her father sitting by himself. "May I help you, Papa?" she asked, pointing to the bridle he was cleaning. Giving a nod he handed her some head-gear to polish and, for awhile, they worked in silence, sitting on a wooden bench beside the stable wall.

"I could be of great help to you at the Olympiad," she said, holding up a gleaming helmet. "See how this shines. Others may not approve of my being there at first, but once they see me handling your racers, they'll realize that you breed horses who are not only fast but well dispos…tioned. You really should arrange for me to go!"

"Can't you get it into your head that females aren't given entry? To make sure they can't sneak in, no one who goes to the Olympiad wears clothes. It's the law, and to break a law of Athens is equivalent to disobeying Zeus!

"Will you take Elefterous and Marc someday?"

"Yes." Palen hung the bridle on a wooden peg. "But I wish things were otherwise because I'd like to take you. It's something to see . . . every road across the Peloponnessus clogged with wagons, carts, horses, mules, hucksters, contestants and spectators, all hurrying to arrive on opening day."

"What happens when they get there? You say it lasts five days. What do they do all that time?"

"Hold on! If you talk any faster you'll swallow your tongue! On the first day we go to the Sanctuary of Zeus at the foot of the 'Hill of Cronos' for sacrifices, prayers, and qualifying oaths. The next day is for javelin throwing, wrestling, sprinting, running and jumping with weights, in a stadium that seats thousands. The wrestling is very popular and fierce. Another main event is the two hundred yard sprint. The third day is mostly for religious ceremonies and a big sacrifice to Zeus. On the fourth, wrestling, boxing and some 800 meter runs are featured.

"What about the horse events?"

"They're held all week, in the Hippodrome. That's where I am with my charioteers. The bareback races and shows of skill in horsemanship get pretty wild!

"After more religious rites on the final day, the lucky ones attend a 'victor's banquet'. "I wish you could go with me, Xanthippe, I must admit, you do have remarkable skills when it comes to horses. Especially Iris. I think I'll let you go ahead and work her in the ring. No oftener than once or twice a week, mind you! And then only at sun-up or late in the day. If anyone sees you driving a chariot they'll think I'm as crazy as . . ." Palen scratched his head, ". . . as crazy as Socrates," he said. "Run! Here come the men! "

Chapter Thirteen

"I want to give a dinner-symposium for the fathers of my young charioteers," Palen announced. "I've decided not to hire a 'mageiros'. Why pay someone to cook when I have a mother and a wife who can put together some of the tastiest food in Attica? I'm counting on you women to make the affair a success. Xanthippe can help with the serving."

Nikandra's insistence that no Athenian virgin should ever be seen in a man's dining quarters, went unheeded. Xanthippe, contrary to her mother's forebodings, viewed the prospect with optimism. For one thing it presented her with an opportunity to find out what went on behind the door's of a man's andron. Also it would be like playing the role of serving girl in a drama.

A maelstrom of activity, the like of which had not been equalled since Marc's Day of Recognition, followed Palen's directive. Frantic as a bird in a wind storm Nikandra goaded Xanthippe into laundering coverlets for the twelve couches that rayed from the table in Palen's small dining room. "Thank the gods for Archos," she said fervently. "He's no help in the kitchen but he keeps the boys from being underfoot.

Using a mixture of ground rotten-stone and olive oil, Melissa polished bronze bowls and serving pieces until they gleamed. She, poor thing, was seven months pregnant, and bouts of nausea had her forever running out of doors with her hand clapped to her mouth.

Phyllys' job was to prepare the edibles that could be safely stored in a food cave. "Did Palen tell you Callias sent word he can't come?" she asked. "HMmmm, he must be getting too old to come out here and then return to Athens in one night."

Nikandra hid a smile. Her mother-in-law was every bit as old as Callias but it was hard to imagine anything slowing her down.

Everything was in a gleaming state of readiness when the invited guests appeared. At the outset, when Xanthippe entered the andron with her platter of sea-urchin, smoked fish, capers, and bulbs in sour-sauce, she had a few moments to pause, unobserved, and watch the undulations of a hired flute girl. The men, were in high spirits and looked strangely unfamiliar, bedecked in ivy and ribbon crowns that had been fashioned for the occasion.

Lysicles, whose two younger sons were among those training for the Olympiad, was the first to see her. "Look who comes bearing gifts! None other than young Xanthippe!" he shouted. "The young lady who rides a horse almost as well as her father! I watched her trot old Enyo back when you were not yet six hands high! And now, by Zeus, you're almost as tall as I, but a lot better looking, by the dog. You're going on fifteen by now, aren't you?"

General Gryllus, the next to help himself to a wine-sop, surveyed her with bright penetrating eyes. Even his formidable mustache and beard could not conceal his jovial grin. It was hard to believe that, as people claimed, this short cheerful person could be a fearsome foe in battle. As a long-time steady client he had been invited tonight although his son was not, as yet, a charioteer. "What a pity my boy 'Xenophon' is only six months old," he said with a mock sigh. "Otherwise I would be trying to persuade your Papa to discuss a marriage contract."

With a blush Xanthippe smiled back at Gryllus and, turning to the man with whom he had been speaking, found herself face to face with an older image of Critobolus. The resemblance was so startling there was no doubt in her mind as to his identity.

"Have you two met?" Gryllus asked. "No? Well then, permit me to present Crito, the father of one of your Papa's finest young charioteers. Crito, this is Palen's daughter."

"My pleasure." said Crito. To Xanthippe's disappointment, he accepted a tidbit and returned to the conversation he'd been having with Gryllus before she appeared with her tray.

At her side was Andokides, serving crayfish, a task for which he obviously had little zest. "You wanting some more diss fesch?" she asked someone else, involuntarily parodying the slave's woe-begone expression and uneasy gait. It was Lysicles' roar of laughter that told her it was not only one man who had witnessed her performance but everyone in the room, including her father. And her father was not amused!

Then she saw Anytus, staring at her as if he were evaluating a brood mare, and a chill ran up and down her spine. Gritting her teeth she offered him the tray.

Beside him stood Hipponicus, also staring from beneath his hooded lids. "You play the role of a slave girl very well," he said.

"Hipparete often talks about what great fun it is to be in your company. You must know some very interesting games." The words came in a whisper from one side of his mouth. "They tell me that girls with red hair conceal sensuous secrets beneath their gowns". Slyly, he patted her firm young buttocks with a pudgy hand.

With that Xanthippe's pleasure in her task evaporated. Gripping the tray she ran from the room, green eyes flashing with rage. "What am I supposed to do when they talk to me?" she asked, back, once again, in the kitchen court.

"Nothing!" Nikandra declared emphatically. "Don't speak to anyone! If I had my way you wouldn't be there in the first place! Your father has made a bad mistake. What will those men think, seeing his own daughter serving food in his andron? It's indecent." Flushed from the heat she snatched a casserole of lamb in paste out of the bake-oven and set it down.

"I'm inclined to agree." Phyllys said. "So, while Andokides pours more wine and clears away the first dishes, you pass the meat without saying a single word."

Gritting her teeth Xanthippe returned to the andron. But, after setting plates before everyone else, she could no longer avoid Hipponicus.

Because the room was small, his couch was positioned in such a small space that she had to turn sideways to approach him.

A sphere of corpulent belly protruded from his richly draped chiton, and there was a look of evil in his flesh encased eyes.

She was cautiously placing his plate on the table when, feigning interest in his food, he slipped a stealthy hand beneath her tunic and inserted a rudely exploring finger. The others, talking, laughing, and eating, were scarcely aware when, flame-faced and furious, Xanthippe pulled away from him and raced from the room.

"I wont go back in here! You can't make me!" she exploded in the kitchen court. "Pregnant or no, Melissa will have to serve because I quit!"

"Melissa fainted which leaves only you and Andokides. Go clear the table and give them these towels and the bowls of scented water. Andokides can pass the honeyed fruits while you help your father pour more wine. Then you may leave and not return. So just go! There's nothing else we can do."

"Palen, if those women of yours were men they could run the most popular mageiros establishment in Athens," someone was saying when Xanthippe returned to the andron.

"You speak truly, sir," Hipponicus rumbled. "The wife and mother of my esteemed relative are both superlative cooks. His daughter also appears to be developing in ways that make her look much more attractive than she does astride a horse.

"I admire women for their talents, fine needlework, weaving, wine making, and cooking, to name but a few. Yet, after much pondering I have reached the conclusion that underneath, they are all the same." He slanted his eyes at Xanthippe who was handing finger bowls to the other guests.

"Fellow seekers of wisdom, I ask your leave to begin the speech-making by quoting from Semonides, a poet who maintains that mans' greatest danger lies in being beguiled by womanly wiles." Taking a long haul on his wine cup Hipponicus hauled himself up to a sitting position and began.

"From the beginning the god made the mind of women
A thing apart. One he made from the long haired sow;
While she wallows in the mud and rolls about on the ground
Everything at home lies in a mess.
And she does not take baths but sits about
In the shit in dirty clothes, getting fatter and fatter."

Here he paused to enjoy the laughter that greeted his prose before plunging on.

"The god made another from the evil fox,
A woman crafty in all matters.
She doesn't miss a thing, bad or good.
The things she says are sometimes good
And just as often bad.
Her mood is constantly shifting.
The next one was made from a dog, nimble,
A bitch like her mother.
She wants to be in on all that is said and done
Scampering about and nosing into everything.
She yaps it out even if there is no one to listen.
Her husband cannot stop her with threats
Not if he flies into a rage and
Knocks her teeth out with a rock!"

Faster and faster Xanthippe sped about the room, ignoring the disapproving glowers that Palen was sending her way, snatching dishes with a clatter to avoid hearing any more of the odious discourse. Hipponicus was no longer smiling and, as he continued to speak, a hint of anger crept into his voice . . ..

"And when her husband is still in shock
From finding out about her
The neighbors are having a good laugh
Because he made a mistake in his choice,
For each man likes to regale others with
Stories of praise about his own wife
While at the same time finding fault with
Any other man's wife.
We do not realize that we all share the same fate.
For Zeus created women as the greatest of all evils
And bound us to them with unbreakable fetters.
Therefore, King Hades welcomes into his realms
All men who fight with each other because of a woman."

To the sound of hands banging on the table Hipponicus acknowledged the applause with a nod and, once again, reclined on his divan.

After filling her carafe of wine, Xanthippe, on a pretense of wishing to replenish his goblet, returned to his side.

* * * *

Weeks later people were still chuckling over Palen's flame haired daughter emptying a pitcher of wine on Hipponicus."

"Mark me that was no accident! By the gods, they say lightning bolts were coming out of her eyes."

"I'll wager it was not simply Hipponicus coarse piece that riled the maiden. The old fart was probably after her curly red brush. I tell you no one's daughter is safe around that man, not even his own. He fancies himself to be a master of the art of love."

"His former wife must not have agreed with that else why did she leave his bed?"

"Name any woman who wouldn't have left him for a chance to go to bed in the palace."

"Palen should have hired another helper. Whoever heard of a man so stingy he'd ask his own daughter to serve his guests?"

The tale, told over cups of Aeolian 'kafe-vari-glyko' in the tavernas, gained color with each repetition.

It was Alcibiades who, several days after the party, came to Palen and said, "You must be ready to slit the throat of whoever spread the story about your daughter's encounter with my future father-in-law. It's all over Athens. But I'm not here to spread tales. I have more important matters on my mind.

Palen noticed that when Alcibiades was dead in earnest he no longer lisped.

"On my sixteenth birthday, I received the first portion of my inheritance. There'll be more when I marry and the rest when I have a son, so I am in a position to buy Iris for any price you ask. I want to take her to the Olympiad where, as your devoted disciple, I shall honor you by winning. I know I can. Now is the time for you to sell her, not only to prove the character of your particular strain, but because she's still sound and not, as yet, damaged by the rigors of the race. You once promised that when I was ready for the Olympiad you'd sell me any horse in your stable at a good price. I'm ready! And Iris is my choice. I don't ask for a bargain. I want to pay whatever you ask."

In his foment of rage at Xanthippe for having, once again, made him a laughing stock, to say nothing of the insult she had dealt a fellow clansman, Palen acquiesced.

"Very well. Give me time to decide on a price," he said. "You have my word. The mare is yours with one stipulation. She's mine until the last chariot race we shall run here at the farm, before going to Olympia."

Palen was not the only one to be fuming over his daughter's erratic behavior.

"How could she have done such a thing? And to Hipponicus of all people!" Tiny furrows criss-crossed Nikandra's brow. "She'll never be invited to join the Arrephorai because, after what she did he won't permit Hipparete to be her friend anymore. And Anytus! He's such an admirer of Hipponicus he may decide not to sign the marriage contract. After the show she put on who would want her for a daughter-in-law?"

"Xanthippe is at a difficult age. She is still a child but one who in the process of becoming a woman." Phyllys countered. "The changeover is never easy.

Furthermore, although she won't say what happened, I feel sure he did something nasty or she would never have spilled that wine on him. I detest men whose minds are lodged between their legs!"

So saying she marched out to the paddock and, placing work worn hands squarely on her hips, faced her son.

"Stop brooding." she scolded. "You've haven't spoken to Xanthippe for three weeks. Your churlish manner is making all of us uncomfortable. Don't you realize that it is unhealthy to hang onto ill will? Besides which, you know as well as I, that if you hadn't been so insistent on having Xanthippe serve in your andron, that episode with the wine would never have occurred. Be that as it may, you still have no cause to be upset. Your symposium was a success. They had a fine time. We could hear them laughing and enjoying themselves all evening long, and they ate as if they were starved. They stayed on and on. As I recall it was quite late when they left."

Palen did not reply, but the look he gave his mother was charged with resentment. Nonetheless she persevered.

"Hipponicus has been here several times since your affair so apparently he bears no grudge. I'll wager he was probably as amused as anyone. So what harm was done? You know perfectly well that as long as you continue to breed a fine strain of horses, he and all the rest will keep coming here to buy. So why continue to punish Xanthippe? I dislike seeing a man as intelligent you being so hard on his daughter. I swear, there are times I think you feel a need to chasten her for being a girl."

Instead of answering Palen continued to scowl and Phyllys, having said what she came to say, returned to the house.

She might be partially right, he mused uncomfortably. Still it was too late now to change his mind, at least in so far as his promise to Alcibiades was concerned. Be that as it may, until he could figure out how to tell her that he had sold Iris he would permit Xanthippe to return to the paddock and train her. Furthermore he would try to be more cordial at supper.

* * * *

Under Archos' supervision the boys had been committing their family prayers to memory and it was Marc's turn to perform. When the libation had been poured for Hestia, Goddess of the Hearth, and following a bit of prompting from the paidogogus, he ducked his head and recited,

"Hestia, in all dwellings of men and immortals,
To you the sweet wine is offered, first and last

At the feast. Never without you
Can gods or mortals banquet."

"You gabble your words like a duck," his father said, frowning. "Can't you get him to do any better than that?" he demanded of the paidogogus.

"I shall try harder," Archos apologized, his round face pink with embarrassment.

For awhile no one spoke. But when Palen poured himself another goblet of wine Marc darted a mischievous glance at Xanthippe.

"I heard a man in the paddock say a funny poem. Want to hear it?" he inquired. When he grinned his two large new front teeth gave him the expression of a bright faced squirrel. Without waiting for an answer he sing songed the words.

"Xanthippe poured a jug of wine
On an uncle come to dine
Soon his toga was as red
As the hair upon her head."

"Enough!" Palen' voice was knife sharp. "How is it that you can recite a stanza of swill like that but say prayers as if you had rocks in your mouth?

And I have had enough of your giggling. Any more and I'll give you a treatment you won't find so funny. Sometimes I wish I could take the lot of you to the Agora and sell you in the slave ring!"

So much for cordiality, he thought. Pushing himself away from the table Palen wiped the oil from his face with a corner of his toga and quit the kitchen court. Not long afterwards Enyo's hoofs were heard clattering down the lane.

* * * *

In bed that night, as she had ever since her father's symposium, Xanthippe shut her eyes tightly, and tried to block out the memory of Hipponicus' groping hand. But the thought persisted, ugly and obsessive.

It had been awhile since Mama's halting explanation of men's' ways with a woman. Not that the information had come as a surprise but, viewed in the light of Hipponicus' furtive pawings, the idea of so intimate a transaction was revolting.

Perhaps she would not marry at all! Instead, she'd remain beautifully pure and inviolate, like the virgin goddesses, Hestia, Athena, and Artemis. She could do so if chose to become an actor, for who would ever guess that behind one of the masks was a real woman and not someone who only pretended to be.

Chapter Fourteen

At times, when her brothers were memorizing their lessons or doing sums, Xanthippe had the tutor all to herself. But this was not one of those days.

"Look at Xanthippe's nose, Elefterous." said Marc. "It has a sharper point than my stylus." He held up the pen with which he had been scratching numbers onto a wax tablet.

"Look at me trying to act smart with a mind the size of a toad's testicle!" Xanthippe mimicked his childish treble. "Marc, if you don't stop vexing me I'll give your noisy mouth a blow that will close it for a month!"

"Your hour is over, Xanthippe." the paidogogus said briskly. "Boys! Get busy at once or I'll double your memory work!"

Without a moment's hesitation Xanthippe headed for the ash grove. She had not visited it for awhile, partly because Palen had taken to appearing unexpectedly with the boys to teach them the ancient rituals for the dead. With preparations for the Olympiad on his mind he had probably already been here early in the morning for his prayers.

"Come!" she encouraged Cerberus. Her loyal companion was aging, and, instead of chasing woodcocks and butterflies, he now preferred to poke along at her side and, when they reached their destination, to lie in the sun and snore.

Giving him a pat she knelt and, reaching into the hollow tree, brought out the bowl, she had pilfered from the altar vessels. It was still entwined with three strands of red wool, but Femma's potion had dried out, leaving a dusty residue of wine and withered herbs. "Hail Hecate, draw my lover to me," Xanthippe whispered, stirring it with a finger before restoring the bowl to its hiding place.

Leaning against the tree's huge trunk she was content for awhile, simply to look upward and watch the sunlight shimmering on the leaves. Gradually her irritations and anxieties began to dissipate. No further reference had been made to Astron, which seemed to indicate that the betrothal contract Nikandra had mentioned was not going to materialize. Anything was possible. Astron might even die in the army.

"Artemis, forgive me!" Xanthippe whispered, mortified to have harbored such an ugly thought, especially on hallowed ground.

In her tunic pocket was a scrap of papyrus on which she had written four lines that the chorus chants in the scene where queen 'Alcestis' returns to life. Hastily she fished it out and studied the words. Then, rising to her feet and clutching her nubile young bosom she sang.

"Spirits have many shapes

Many strange things are performed by the gods,

The expected does not always happen,

And God makes a way for the unexpected!"

A sound of hoofbeats pattering on the leaf strewn terrain caused her to jump and look up just as Critobolus rode through the trees, ducking his head to avoid being slapped across the face by a branch.

"Well done, Xanthippe!" he applauded, halting his horse. "Forgive me for startling you. But wasn't I lucky to arrive in time to hear your lovely song!

"What's more, the words fit the moment, don't you think?"

While he dismounted and tethered his horse, she sat down again and tried desperately to gain control of tremors that were rocking her body.

"I've tried to join you any number of times but that buffoon Astron is always on my heels." Critobolus said, turning toward her. "Today I managed to elude him. I was hoping I'd find you here. Just being with you might bring me luck in next month's race, the last your father has scheduled before we go to the Olympiad."

"I wish I had a talisman to give you."

"What about that?" He sat down beside her and fingered the scarf she wore on her head. Momentarily she was seized by a wild impulse to touch his hair. Instead she removed her scarf. "I pray it helps you win." she said, handing it to him and pushing back the damp hair that clung like twisted strands of copper to her forehead.

"Papa says that shortly after the Olympiad you and several others will become ephebes. Are you looking forward to being in the army?" she asked, calmer now. "Do you think you'll enjoy travelling and living in encampments?"

Their eyes caught and held. Xanthippe was accustomed to looking directly at anyone with whom she spoke but with Critobolus it was different. And more exciting. Mama had spoken about 'fits of ecstacy' but she certainly had not described anything like this!

Palen had schooled her well in the art of controlling a runaway horse , even so it was not easy to subdue her rampaging emotions, even though her heart was racing, her face remained impassive. But when she looked at him unbidden recollections of his naked body, oiled and gleaming in the sun, came to mind.

"It's very pleasant out here," Critobolus said, lying prone on turf worn smooth from many dramas enacted beneath the tree. "Comfortable too." He patted the earth. "Lie here beside me and look up into the trees."

Timorously she complied and rolled down beside him.

"Don't be so tense, Xanthippe. Relax." Gently Critobolus traced her features, eyelids . . . forehead . . . cheeks . . . mouth . . .

"What's the matter?" he asked when she recoiled.

"It's that . . . You touched my nose. My brothers keep teasing me about it because it's too long."

"Your brothers are crazy. It's distinctive. So is this." Critobolus lifted a sheath of hair from her shoulders and allowed it to drift through his fingers. "I have never seen its equal. Is it copper . . . gold? . . . Or fire?"

At that moment it was as if her throbbing body had taken on a will of its own. What's wrong with me, she wondered, battling frantically for self-dominion even though all she really wanted was to have him put his arms around her and hold her close.

"Someone at the Apaturia remarked that you were . . . " She was going to say 'betrothed' but . . .

"You excite me," Critobolus whispered and touched her forehead with lips as delicate as the wings of a butterfly. Then he pressed them to her mouth. No one had ever kissed her before. It was a lovely sensation, warm and sweet, like drowning in a sea of bliss, and she responded eagerly. Another kiss and Kallia's rumor was forgotten altogether.

"No." she sighed as his caresses became more intimate. But instead of resisting further she allowed herself to be swept along in the grip of this strange force. Nikandra's contention that Athenian women who lost their virtue were hauled into court and dealt with by contemptuous officials seemed a small price to pay. No wonder Pyramus and Thisbe preferred death to separation!

"Come to me, Xanthippe." Again his mouth sought hers.

"We mustn't."

"We must!" It was a command. Almost roughly he pulled her closer and, moved beyond reason, she surrendered to the clamor of her body. Blissful anguish, unimaginable pleasure, and, for a moment, searing pain. Then pure delight.

It was late afternoon when Xanthippe sat up and began to re-arrange her disheveled hair.

"Oh my god", her lover said in a low voice. "I've dreamed of this ever since you sat down beside me on the first day of Apaturia . . . even before then. And, if possible, making love to you was even more wonderful than I had imagined. But I never meant to . . . I would never want to hurt you."

"I love you."

"We can't allow anyone to find us here." This time he evaded her eyes as he spoke. "But we must meet again."

Something about the look on his face brought swift sobriety. Nudged by the cold finger of fear Xanthippe now wanted only to get away as quickly as she could. "I must get into something clean before someone sees me," she thought, conscious of the scarlet mark of an irretrievable loss now staining her tunic.

And before Critobolus realized what was happening she had jumped up, straightened her tunic and, saying, "I should have been home hours ago," she turned and was gone.

"I'll find a way . . ." he began, but she was already beyond reach of hearing whatever it was he had started to say.

An explanation would have to be made about what she'd been doing all afternoon. Oh no! She stopped in mid flight. What if her menses stopped!

Panting from emotion as well as exertion she considered calling upon Artemis for help. But that unpredictable virgin Goddess might choose to visit vengeance on a girl who so mindlessly surrendered her maidenhead so she addressed her prayer to Aphrodite instead. And Hecate. After all it was the witch of the yew tree and the goddess of physical love who had brought Critobolus into her arms in the first place!

General Gryllus saved Xanthippe from inquisition. Hearing his and other voices coming from the courtyard she knew she'd be able to slip up to her room and don fresh clothing without being seen."The Spartans pretend to want arbitration but I distrust them. And our colonies aren't much help," she heard him comment as she passed by the courtyard gate.

They were still talking when, after hurried ablutions and a change of clothing, she returned. "By Zeus most of this country's problems derive from allowing foreigners to flock here like flies," Palen opined, shaking his fist. "Athens is full of pro-Spartans and every last one of them is bent on stirring up sedition! What's more I hear that rabble-rouser Socrates agrees with them"

"Not necessarily. He's in Potidaea with Pericles' troops right now." Gryllus replied. "I'm sure you can't help but wonder how these skirmishes will affect the Olympiad."

"I just thank the gods that it's dependably inviolate from war and politics."

"Well! Here's Xanthippe! Kalimeera, young lady! I have some news of interest for you women. Aspasia was accused of impiety and brought to trial by that notoriety seeking comedian Hermippus. The 'uncrowned queen of Athens', is generally held in low esteem so it came as no surprise to anyone when she was found guilty. But, by Zeus, she's been condemned to death and even her severest critics are scandalized!"

After this awesome news had been worked over Gryllus headed back to Athens and with so many other things to pre-empt the conversation, Xanthippe's silence and her long absence went unnoticed.

There was more talk and commotion the following day, when men who came to the race told how, yesterday, Pericles had made the most impassioned speech of his career, denouncing Aspasia's trumped up trial so convincingly that the verdict was revoked and her life spared.

Aspasia and Pericles, must have experienced the same intimacy that she herself had discovered with Critobolus, Xanthippe thought to herself. Their romance had been illicit too and it was only recently that they had been given priestly dispensation to marry.

Which was only right because how could anything as wonderful as being in love be wrong?

Chapter Fifteen

Every morning, just at first when Xanthippe awoke, she was aware only of a new dawn. Then, on the heels of consciousness came a sick sensation that something was very wrong. Quickly she would close her eyes and burrow under her coverlet, longing for sleep to come again.

Today it was the clatter of pots and Nikandra's voice calling her name that forestalled further escape from reality. Now, fully alert, she remembered. Palen had sold Iris to Alcibiades and, as if this were not already more than she could endure, Critobolus was avoiding her.

It was close to a month since they had made love under the hollow tree and, in all that time, she had scarcely seen him. Also, when they did encounter one another, he appeared ill at ease, evading eye contact, and treating her like a stranger. Could it be that he scorned her for capitulating to him?

At least one good thing had happened . . . the return of her menses! Which meant that her indiscretion in the ash grove was not going to be publicized by the advent of a baby.

"Mother-Phyllys is in the loom room and Melissa is sick again so I'll tend the chickens and leave you to clean up this mess in the kitchen court." Nikandra said when her daughter appeared.

Content to be left to herself, Xanthippe attacked the cooking utensils and scrubbed the hard earthen floor. There were times when this sort of activity helped to keep painful thoughts at bay.

A ratatoo of hoofbeats pounding up the lane gave evidence that a crowd of spectators, as well as participants, was beginning to arrive on this the day of Palen's big racing event. And, Xanthippe was thinking her father would have to throw her out bodily if he wanted to keep her from standing where she could watch.

How could he have done anything so cruel as to let her train and care for Iris knowing all along he was going to sell the mare to Alcibiades? Certainly nothing she had ever done or could do merited such punishment.

"Kalimeera, Xanthippe." Critobolus said, riding up on his horse and intercepting her as she was heading for a knoll near the racing ring. For a moment she thought he was going to ride on but, without looking directly at her, or dismounting, he said, "There's something I must tell you. It concerns an argument I had with my father during which we disagreed violently over a matter that is very important to me but which he wont even discuss. He is a very opinionated man, yet, as my parent he . . ."

"Move on!" Alcibiades yelled, riding up before Critobolus could finish what he had started to say. "Why are you wasting your time with her when you should be down there getting ready for the race?"

"Go get ready yourself," Critobolus snapped. "I'm sorry," he said to Xanthippe. "Perhaps we can finish this conversation later. So saying, he followed Alcibiades, and they trotted toward the paddock.

"We're ready to start!" Palen shouted. "Since the track can take no more than three chariots at a time, the winner of each race gets to go again! Enter the ring!" he directed Lysicles' eldest son. "Alcibiades! You're next. Move on in. You, Hermogenes!" He pointed to one of Hipparete's brothers. "CHARGE!" he shouted when they were lined up on the track.

In unison they plunged forward but, to everyone's open mouthed amazement, it was not long before Alcibiades fell behind. The more he used his whip and yelled at Iris the more she refused to respond.

"For the godsake, what's wrong with you?" Palen yelled. "They'll throw you out of the cavalry if you can't do better than that."

As Xanthippe had feared, Alcibiades was driving Iris and tugging at her mouth with one of the monstrous metal bits he insisted on using. It was all she could do to keep from screaming as she watched the mare's obvious misery. No longer able to keep away, she ran from the hillock to the fence and stationed herself at the gate.

A wheel, coming loose on Hermogenes' cart, saved Alcibiades from total disgrace. While it was being tightened he flung his rein aside and, jumping out of his chariot, cried, "I demand a re-run! Bring my second horse." he commanded his slave. "This one isn't worth a damn!" Then he saw Xanthippe. "You're the one who ruined her." he snarled.

When the changes had been made the race began anew. This time Alcibiades came in first.

Progressively, by the process of elimination, the field narrowed down. Some chariots crashed. A few capsized. Several racers were thrown, others cut and bloodied. Only two men remained. One was Alcibiades. His grim determination to vindicate himself was obvious.

Palen meanwhile, was too intent on the races to notice his daughter's presence by the fence. That is, until she ran to where Iris, still hitched to the chariot, stood by the track. He, like everyone, was stunned to see her spring into the cart, take up the reins, and go charging down the course.

Faster and faster she raced until an abundance of orange hair whipped loose from the band around her head to stream symmetrically with the mare's flying tail. Gradually she closed in on the two who'd had a head start. It was like a dream in which time seemed to stand still while she herself was soaring through space.

Alcibiades, trying desperately to drive her off the track, moved closer to her chariot. But he barely grazed it before she edged past him to take a definite lead. When she crossed over the finish line and slowed to a stop there was a mighty roar and pandemonium.

"It looks like the lady made an ass of you, Alcibiades!" someone shouted amidst tumultuous cheers. Then she saw her father. "Get out of that chariot and into the house before I beat the hell out of you here in front of everyone! You have disgraced me," he rasped. Rigid with rage, he stalked from the track, leaving Xanthippe alone in a multitude of men. No longer cheering, most of them were regarding her with disfavor.

Chapter Sixteen

"Oh po po po what now?" Palen muttered to himself.

It had been a miserable morning from the moment he came into the stable this morning and stepped on a hoe. When things start out like that you can bet your last oboloi that nothing will go right for the rest of the day. To prove it, here came Anytus, riding into the paddock, with a look on his face that augured no good.

There was something evasive about the look in his eyes when the two men exchanged salutations. Despite his wealth, power, an eligible son, and what appeared to be a betrothal contract rolled up in his hand, he was a repulsive son of a bitch.

Silently Palen poured two measures of wine from the jug he kept in the barn and gave one to his visitor. Anytus, after a preliminary gulp, peered dismally into his goblet as if hoping to find therein what it was he had come to say.

"Young people no longer respect their elders, often because their parents don't discipline them," he said, giving Palen an oblique look. "That chap Socrates is much to blame. He should be run out of Athens. For some unknown reason he seems to bewitch young people. They tag after him and he puts wild ideas into their heads. 'Discover who you really are,' he tells them, trotting about in his bare feet. I ask you, who in Hades' pits would you be if you weren't who you were? He also encourages my son and others to ignore the sacred teachings of their fathers. What's more, I understand that even girls are somehow being influenced by his impious philosophy, notably your own daughter."

Grimly he finished his drink, and cleared his throat.

Sensing the direction in which Anytus was going Palen replenished his wine cup and handed it back without a word.

"Sooner or later what I'm here to say needs to be said. I shall try to be brief. I must do everything in my power to protect my son because I fear he is too easily influenced. Above all else he needs a trustworthy, steadfast woman to be his wife. Your daughter, sir, does not fit that description, and I am not about to condone Astron marrying someone who does one outrageous thing after another. As a matter of fact I had already begun to wonder about Xanthippe even before she ran away from home, and ended up having supper with Femma."

"Leave Femma out of this," Palen growled.

"As you wish. But let me tell you, I have no intention of signing this betrothal contract." Briskly Anytus got to his feet, and thrust the piece of parchment at Palen.

Palen, in turn, let it drop on the ground. "You and I have had an unwritten agreement for ten years!" he shouted. "Am I to understand that your word is worthless?"

"By the gods there is nothing wrong with my word! The problem is that when you first mentioned a betrothal contract I had no idea your daughter was going to become the butt of gossip all over Athens. Even Astron says he doesn't want to marry her. I don't usually let him tell me what to do. But this is one time I agree with him. He's my only son and heir and I want him to marry well. May the gods be willing he will live to do so. You realize that he will soon be going into the army, maybe even to war!"

"Godammit, man, your treachery leaves me saddled with an unbetrothed sixteen year old at a time when every young man in the Empire may be going to war. But let me assure you, that darling only son of yours is no prize. You can tell him for me not to come around this farm again! And he can forget the Olympiad too because he certainly won't be going with me! Nor will he be missed! Half the time he doesn't even know what he's doing."

By this time Anytus was ready to come to blows with him but, knowing that he'd be the one who would take a beating, he dashed out of the stable, lurched aboard his horse, and galloped away.

"What is it, Palen!" Phyllys exclaimed, noting his ashen face when he tramped into the house.

"This!" He held out the ripped papyrus. "Xanthippe's betrothal contract!" Anytus refuses to put his name on it. He rode out here this morning to inform me that his son can't marry my daughter because she has gained herself the reputation of being the craziest woman in all Hellas!"

114

* * * *

Discord hung over the kitchen court like a cloud and, in the laden atmosphere, a rumble of distant thunder was akin to the sound of marching troops. For the first time in memory Palen failed to instigate prayers and a libation to the gods before supper, Elefterous picked at his food, and even the dependably merry Marc was quiet and solemn.

Ever since the races his rage had been steadily fomenting. The family had scarcely risen from the table before it exploded. "I have never taken a whip to a female and I don't intend to now even though the gods know you deserve it!" he lashed out. "You will never mount a horse or drive the chariot again! I swear to Zeus I've reached my limit."

"Don't worry. I won't. The gods forbid that I end up like you and ride rough-shod over everyone," she retorted.

"Hold your tongue!" Palen shouted, raising his arm. Instinctively Xanthippe extended her hands to ward off a blow. But instead of hitting her his flailing fist collided with an open pot of boiling chicken stock that was sitting too close to the edge of the stove top. It went toppling and, as it fell, Xanthippe was deluged with a scalding sheet of liquid and she screamed.

"Nikandra, quickly! Bring a handful of comfrey root and some shoots of aloe vera!" Phyllys cried. "You, Palen, ride into town and purchase an infusion of Cynoglossum Officianale from Eryximachos the physician to ease the pain and keep the child from being scarred."

"Scarred!" Nikandra wailed, watching helplessly as the poultice of herbs she had brought was applied to welts that were already forming on Xanthippe's arms.

That was when Lysicles' wife chose to make an appearance. "I was on my way home from the Agora and decided to stop by and return this wool-carding rake you loaned me," she said by way of explanation. "Since no one answered the gate bell I came on in." As she spoke her busy eyes glanced from one to the other.

"A pot of soup was accidentally spilled on Xanthippe", Nikandra said hastily.

"Papa threw it at her." Marc volunteered and received a silencing cuff.

The guest, having deposited the tool she'd brought, was already on her way to add even more excitement to the story of Xanthippe's chariot race.

* * * *

Meanwhile, Palen, upon leaving the physician, hurried on to the Altar of the Twelve Gods and, after offering a sacrifice of wheat, he purchased the votive figurine of a maiden and lay on the altar of Asclepius.

"This represents my daughter Xanthippe," he said. "She is headstrong and stubborn and I know you agree with me that no female on earth should be so untamable. But you, the God of Healing, already know it was my mistake to allow her privileges that fathers should reserve only for sons. For that I apologize to you, Asclepius, and I promise to use better judgment in the future. What happened was not intentional and that is why I ask you to heal my daughter."

Then, somewhat subdued by what had transpired he went home.

* * * *

Marc, like Elefterous, was now old enough to attend school. But it was decided that for awhile, at least until he, like his brother, had been duly enrolled and established in the little Academeia of Cholargus, Archos would stay on.

Knowing that, especially after her impetuous actions at the chariot race, her own future was more than ever precarious, Xanthippe continued to take advantage of her daily hour in the classroom. It would come as no surprise were Palen to cancel it even before the paidogogus left for good. Therefore, even when she felt too miserable to move she went.

"Xanthippe! Where on earth were you?" Archos asked, looking curiously at the disheveled young woman when she came dragging into the courtyard. "Marc and I have been here all morning and lessons are almost over," he said. "But come, sit down. You can finish the day with that quotation I gave you to memorize from 'Works And Days'"

A verse that would sound gloomy even when prattled by Marc, she thought, drawing a deep breath.

"Badness you can get easily, in quantity.

The road is smooth and it lies close by.

But in front of excellence the immortal gods have put sweat,

And long and steep is the way to it, and rough at first.

But when you come to the top it is easy,

Even though it is hard." she stammered, thinking that Hesiod could have written those words expressly for her benefit.

"What ails you?" Archos blustered. "Six weeks ago you declaimed an entire passage from 'Hippolytus' and spoke with such eloquence you could have put any actor in the Theater of Dionysius to shame!" The words were hardly out of his mouth when his eyes fell on her bandaged arms and his face grew even more ruddy with contrition. No wonder she had trouble concentrating after what she'd been through!

"I'm sorry", she whispered.

Six weeks ago she had been living in a dream world, confident that Critobolus planned to confirm his love for her by asking his father to speak to hers about a marriage contract. But she hadn't seen Critobolus since the race!

How glibly she had quoted Phaedra's tragic stanza. Now it returned to taunt her.

"Oh, I am miserable! What is this I have done?
Where have I strayed from the highway of good sense?
I was mad.
'Twas a madness sent from some God that caused my fall.
I am unhappy, so unhappy! The tears are flowing
And my face is turned to shame'"

It was a relief to hear Archos say her classroom time for the day had come to an end. Not wanting to face whatever tasks awaited her in the house she drifted aimlessly across the yard to where her old swing still dangled from its branch.

Solemnly Xanthippe regarded her disfigurement. New tissue was forming over the burns and, although her skin was still an angry pink, there were no major blemishes, save for one. Nikandra had been the first to notice. Until then no one had mentioned the nasty accident, almost as if they were pretending it hadn't happened.

"There's only one scar left on Xanthippe's arm and it looks exactly like the snake that winds around the staff of Asclepius!" her mother had exclaimed. And, as if she were telling one of the dark tales that were as much a part of the loom room as the act of weaving cloth, "It could be either a blessing or a curse!"

Palen had given a start, and said something about the wisdom of putting one's faith in the God of Healing. Then he, Phyllys, Marc, and Elefterous had peered at the weird tattoo, coiled and rising from Xanthippe's wrist to her upper arm, where it was topped by a strangely serpentine head. And, the boys, for once, refrained from making any jibes.

"Why don't you go back to the Sanctuary of Asclepius on the Dionsiou Aeropagitou Road?" Nikandra suggested. "On the other hand, I've been told that it isn't used much anymore. Not since a huge temple was built for him in Epidaurus. Lysicles' wife says there are masses of serpents squirming in a pit down beneath it so it would be a good place to go if you want him to remove his sign from your arm."

But Epidaurus was over forty miles from home and available only by boat.

It would take two entire days and a lot of money, more than they could afford, to get there.

So here she was, sixteen years old and marked by a sign that, as far as her mother was concerned, indicated that she was doomed to spinster-hood. Was it, Xanthippe wondered, a retribution for all the bad things she had done? Like making fun of the Mysteries? Or making love with Critobolus?

Perhaps it was Alcibiades who had put a curse on her to get even. Yet one thing was certain. She would rather go through life with a scar on her arm than with Astron in her bed!

Chapter Seventeen

"Do you realize how many people are questioning whether you did the fair thing when you chased Xanthippe from the ring as if she didn't exist, and announced that Alcibiades had come in first?" Phyllys asked her son.

"Do you realize he's the first sixteen year old in history to win the chariot championship at Olympia? And that he brought fame to the farm of my fathers, and acclaim to me as his teacher?" Palen blustered.

"Everyone in Athens is gossiping about our daughter," Nikandra said gloomily hitting her forehead with the palm of her hand. "It's humiliating. Someone has even started a rumor that she did something offensive at the Apaturia. If only someone would come right out and tell what it was! And now this! Lysicles' wife . . ."

She stopped herself. Palen needed no reminder of his neighbor's wife proclivity for gossip. He was already upset enough. Yet now that she thought about it, he'd been acting strangely, as if something were bothering him, well before Xanthippe's most recent caprice.

"Rest assured, your daughter is no longer the topic of conversation." Palen assured her. "It's war now. A war that is going to turn the 'Thirty Year Peace Treaty' into a farce."

"Old men start wars. They should fight them. Then young men could stay home and get married." Phyllys philosophized.

"How can anyone have a decent conversation with a woman? No one." Palen mumbled to himself.

"Archos said that next week I'll be going to the Academaeia. I don't want to go to school in Cholargus! I'd rather stay home!" Marc declared, coming into the kitchen court, followed by his sister and the paidogogus.

"You stay here and I'll go to school in your place," Xanthippe snorted. "You can card wool with Mama while I learn how to be an actor."

"How many times must I tell you that girls can't go to school? And never in history has there been a woman actor." Nikandra retorted. "You never listen. A woman's duty is simply to become a wife and provide her husband with a good home and a family!"

"That is unfair! You agree, don't you Archos? You know what a good actor I'd be."

"It's true." Vigorously the tutor bobbed his head, "She has an incredibly retentive memory and great histrionic talent. I wish the day would come when girls could attend academaeias of their own. In fact Socrates said the same thing recently in debate. However, Xanthippe, if you wish, I will return from time to time and continue your lessons. At no cost!"

"Oh no he wont" Palen silently vowed.

* * * *

It may have been the sadness in Xanthippe's eyes, or simply because, after so many scandals, it seemed foolish to fret about Xanthippe's appearance since she was unlikely to get a husband in any case. Therefore Nikandra had become more lenient about allowing her daughter to wander at will.

Taking advantage of what could prove to be a brief hiatus, Xanthippe was trudging westward through territory made familiar from past excursions on Iris, when she came to a fork in the road. She paused. One path, the one to the right, led to Femma's house. After a few moments of indecision she turned left.

Much as she wanted to see her friend again, she dared risk no further trouble. Trouble was all she'd had since that halcyon afternoon when Critobolus, like the fabled lover who woke his beloved with a kiss, had aroused her from the sleep of innocence and awakened an unquenchable fire. Yes, it was Femma's spell that had brought him to the ash grove. But the sad truth was that not until a girl's wedding day was she was supposed to invoke the aid of Aphrodite, the goddess of physical love.

It was beyond a rise in the terrain, when clumps of evergreens that clung to a field of rocky crags, suddenly gave way to an endless expanse of water, that she realized she had come all the way to the Bay of

Phaleron!

Breathlessly she stepped onto the beach, removed her sandals, and savored the feel of warm firm sand beneath her feet while, overhead, a trio of hoopoe birds sounded their staccato caws. Shading her eyes with one hand she stared out to sea, sniffing its delicate fishy tang, relishing its moist salty kiss on her lips. A crab scuttled by, picking his crooked path to the water's edge. Next it was a huge shell that caught her eye and she stooped to retrieve it.

Inspired by a heady sense of freedom she twirled and danced across the cove toward some boulders that saucered out to the water's edge and blocked a view of the beach beyond. Threading her way through frills of foam that feathered the edge of lazy little waves and curled across her toes, she rounded the big rocks. There, less than ten feet from where she stood, were two naked people, laboring together in a weirdly grotesque embrace.

When the full implications of the scene upon which she had inadvertently stumbled burst upon her, she was about to turn and run. But as if her feet had turned to stone, she remained rooted to the spot while they spent their passion on a bed of pink sand.

Then he saw her.

"You bitch!" Alcibiades panted. "You turn up everywhere. Like lice! If I had a father who betrothed me to you I'd kill him!"

Astron, looking drunk and foolish raised himself and, after a glance in her direction, averted his face.

Marble returned to flesh and blood. "You can both go to Hades' pits where you belong!" Xanthippe shrieked, her voice, high and strident, born on the wind. Galvanized into action she spun about and raced back through the trees as fast as her shaking legs would permit.

* * * *

For weeks after that jarring scene on the beach Xanthippe suffered from recurrent gnawing pains in her gut. Often they awoke her at night. Again this morning it was as though her insides were being tied in knots.

The problem was not altogether new. In fact it stemmed from as far back as she could remember. But it was getting worse. An added aggravation was the way it had of grabbing her when she was beset with other problems. Nikandra's diagnosed 'Oxrhegmia' as a malady brought on by overeating. Xanthippe, on he other hand, was beginning to wonder if an attack of vomiting might, instead, coincide with anger.

Having abandoned Aphrodite, Xanthippe was also finding it hard to pray at all, even to her familiar Artemis. "Please, cause Critobolus to love me again," she muttered, soberly addressing the clay image, Conceivably the virgin Artemis was not prone to forgive maidens who fell by the wayside. At least she had answered one prayer by halting the hideous prospect of being married to the son of Anytus. 'Yccch!" Xanthippe's mouth puckered with distaste as once again, the image of Astron grappling with Alcibiades returned.

Beyond a casual greeting Critobolus had been off hand and remote, ever since he had come back from Olympia. Could it be that he and all men were, like Hipponicus, conceited fools, braying about women being either 'courtesans for pleasure, concubines for a man's body, or wives for lawful issue.' Or was it that he scorned her for allowing him to do what he did?

"Is your room ready for Mother-Phyllys' things?" Nikandra called from the bottom step,

Hastily Xanthippe put away the goddess, shoved a few more of her belongings under her bed, and smoothed the coverlet with swift strokes. She had quite forgotten that, since both brothers were now in school, Palen had decided that, except for the courtyard and work areas the first floor was hence-forth male territory.

If Phyllys minded she gave no sign, but her granddaughter emotions were mixed. Were a specter to appear in the night Yiayia's presence would be very comforting but it seemed unfair to make her leave the room in which she and Grandfather Marc had shared their few precious years together.

After failing to cram her accumulation of goods into half the space needed, most of it was consigned to a storage room which had been added to one end of the U-shaped house years before. Andokides brought up her pallet, garments, and a few other items and, before long, the room was permeated with the same delicate fragrance that had filled the air in her previous quarters.

"For your sake, Yiayia Phyllys, I wish you could have kept your bed-chamber," Xanthippe said. "As for me, just knowing you'll be near, especially in the night, makes me happy. It will be almost as nice as when I was a little girl and you'd invite me to visit you downstairs. Remember the way we'd talk and laugh? And you told me such wonderful stories! I was a lot happier then than I am now."

At the moment those care-free days seemed as illusory to Xanthippe as the games of pretend she and Hipparete used to play in the ash grove. Equally remote were the days when she had galloped Iris across a meadow, dreaming of adventure, love and romance.

Silently Phyllys took Xanthippe's hand. "Dear one, I too have had to face heartache and times when it looked as if nothing would ever go right again. It happens to everyone. But, if we want to live life at its fullest, we must cheerfully accept dark days because they make the sunny ones all the brighter. For example, in the loom room, when we embroider a pattern onto what we have woven we must use dark threads as well as light or we'd have nothing to show for our effort. The same rule applies in our lives. You alone are responsible for your feelings so watch your thoughts! Keep them cheerful. Refuse to let yourself be discouraged!"

Until now Xanthippe could not recall ever being irritated by anything Yiayia said. But her advice was senseless! How can one control thoughts that someone else causes? It is others who have the power to make you glad, sad, or discouraged!

Chapter Eighteen

Disconsolately Xanthippe peeled potatoes and dropped them into the cook-pot. It was five days since Archos had gone to another tutoring job in Athens, leaving an empty space in her life. Those hours with him had been precious, more, actually, than she had realized until they were taken away.

Reciting verse or daydreaming under the hollow tree with her hound asleep nearby, was less appealing. These days, if she went there at all, she was too beset with memories to enjoy herself. Now that she thought about it, she hadn't seen Cerberus since early in the day. Perhaps he was getting adventurous in his old age and chasing one of the deer that could sometimes be seen bounding through the woods adjacent to the burial ground.

Clapping a lid on the stew, she headed in that direction, calling his name. Nearing the hollow tree she was arrested by an unearthly sound. Quietly she stood and listened. It came again . . . an eerie whine. Then she saw him.

He was lying in a pool of blood, his dry tongue hanging from his mouth.

"Cerberus!" she screamed, and fell to her knees at his side.

His tail had been severed and blood, which at first must have pumped from the wound, was slowly oozing away. A hemp lasso ringed his neck. "What happened?" she groaned,

With an awful knowing, she recalled all the things she herself had done to precipitate this horrible deed. The first was when she had mimicked Alcibiades in the stall.

Before then, almost ten years ago, he had vowed to get even with her for mocking him under this tree. Deaf to his threats, she made him furious by doing it again at the Apaturia, and finally, by humiliating him in front of an audience at the chariot race.

Cerberus' body lay motionless and his eyes, already dilating in death looked up in mute appeal.

"Artemis!" she shrieked, "Artemis help me! Help me! Help me!" But the swift footed goddess of the hunt failed to appear and, after a final sigh of protest, her pet closed his eyes.

With a loud cry Xanthippe flung her arms around his lifeless body and lay beside him on the ground. Then she began to vomit and could not stop.

It was there that Palen, hearing her screams, found her and, after a stiff intake of breath at the sight that met his eyes, finally managed to coax her away.

"Come." he said, his voice more gentle than she had ever heard it. "I'll bring Andokides and we will . . .. we'll do what needs to be done".

"We will bury him by this tree." he said in answer to the question in her anguished eyes.

"Cry, Xanthippe", Phyllys begged that night in their bed chamber. "The look on your face breaks my heart. Don't hold it in, please Kale-Pai, cry!" Her pleas were to no avail. Tears, long blocked, refused to come.

It's time to quit pining, Xanthippe. After all he was only a hound." Palen's voice held a hint of irritation.

"Only a hound!", she screamed. "How can you say 'only a hound' about Cerberus? He was my friend. He loved me and was more human . . . than most humans!"

Actually her spirited protest came as a welcome relief. Ever since Cerberus' death she had hardly spoken, and her face had been dark and closed.

She had also continued to retch in spite of a poultice of castor bean oil that Phyllys placed on her stomach. And although the vomiting finally stopped she remained listless and still.

"What I want to know is what kind of a depraved buggering cock-sucker would do such a thing! If I find out I'll chop off his nuts!" Palen raged. "Who ever heard of a fiend wild enough to lasso a hound, sever its tail, and leave it bleeding to death in the woods?"

Little did he guess that she herself did know who that fiend was, Xanthippe thought. And that the crime had been born of a hatred even stronger than grief. And with an inward groan she chastised herself again. Had it not been for her own actions Cerberus would be alive instead of dead and buried near the hollow tree. All of this was something she would never be able to share with a soul. Not a one, not Yiayia Phyllys, Hipparete, or even Femma would understand and, less than anyone, her own father. In his opinion, or for that matter, in the eyes of the world, she and not Alcibiades would be found guilty.

As for the perpetrator himself, his precocious brilliance, coupled with an extraordinary talent for plotting military maneuvers, (to say nothing of his relationship to Pericles), had influenced his superiors to let him by-pass the indoctrination that was ordinarily an essential part of everyone's training. Instead he had already gone, as the youngest cavalry officer ever to serve the Empire, to join seasoned troops in Potidaea. To Xanthippe's way of thinking, Potidaea was so far away he might as well go to the moon because, by the time he returned, who would be able, or even want to accuse him of killing her dog?

"One of my bitch hounds is due to whelp and you can have your choice of the litter, Xanthippe," Palen volunteered with some of the tenderness she had evoked in him when she was only a child. In the past few weeks his anger at her had been considerably subdued by the tragic expression on her face.

How he loathed being an emotional weather-vane. The dichotomy of being sometimes belligerent and then, again, benign, of loving her one day, and wanting to thrash her the next, tried him sorely. Selling her mare to Alcibiades for example. It had seemed right at the time but now he was sorry he had. What really got him was that there were females in this world who held the power to influence him. And one was his, as yet a spinster, daughter.

"There will never be another Cerberus." Xanthippe declared.

"You're right", Phyllys agreed. "In a sense hounds are like humans, no one exactly like another. But although a new puppy wont take Cerberus' place, it will give you its own unique devotion"

That was the night Melissa' baby arrived, a month later than expected, and was, to Palen's disgust, a girl. Everything, in fact, seemed to be happening at once.

General Gryllus was coming to the farm more often than usual to inspect any horses that might be available for purchase by cavalrymen who, like himself, were convinced that the current negotiations with Sparta would fail and make war inevitable.

The departure of recently conscripted ephebes had been delayed by uncertainty so that, with the exception of Alcibiades, most of them were still around waiting to see where they would be sent.

And Elefterous had to be taken into Athens to have Eryximachos fasten a board onto the arm he had broken in his most recent fall from a horse. Upon returning home he had seemed positively cheery over having sustained an injury that would keep him temporarily, from his lessons in equitation.

Chapter Nineteen

"See who's at the gate. I can't. I have chicken grease all over my hands," Nikandra said, looking up from the pot into which she was cutting chunks of meat.

"It's a slave from the house of Callias. He says Hipparete has something to tell me in person," Xanthippe announced upon her return. "He brought her carriage because she wants me to return to the city with him today. May I?"

"Certainly! I'll help you get ready!" Nikandra's answer came quickly. Many fine people visited the house of Callias. What if her daughter were to make an encounter there that would lead to a betrothal! At least the visit might put her in a better mood.

Within the hour Xanthippe was on her way into Athens, She settled herself against a cushion and sighed, this time a sigh of pure pleasure. Maybe Yiayia Phyllys was right in saying that just when the whole world looked bleak something pleasant was apt to transpire. Hipparete's news might have something to do with Critobolus. He and her brothers were friends. Perhaps, through them, she knew where he was and what he was doing.

Despite his enigmatic behavior her ardor for Critobolus was, if anything, even more intense. Sometimes she wished she could forget him for awhile. But he was in her thoughts all day. And again, at night, when she closed her eyes he was still there, his bronze skin, taut and firm, hugging his fine high cheek-bones. Lying in the dark, she'd remember his mouth close to hers, his nostrils flaring and flattening like the nostrils of a spirited horse. Even when she slept, he invaded her dreams.

"No sweet barley water for us today!" Hipparete exclaimed when the carriage drew up to the front entrance and another slave came to take Xanthippe's modest baggage. "I have a jug of wine, a platter of sweet buns, and a piece of news. Yiayia Elpinice and Grandfather Callias and my cousin Iodice are at home, otherwise you and I have the whole place to ourselves."

"What about your father?"

"He's gone most of the time these days, often with Pericles now that they're reconciled."

"Is that your news?"

"No!" Hipparete giggled. "But first the wine. Although I'm not exactly celebrating what I have to say a libation is in order." She raised her cup. "Yiasu! I'm getting married!"

"What!" Xanthippe gasped. "When?" Her lip trembled and she caught it between her teeth so Hipparete wouldn't notice.

"Alcibiades was determined we'd have the wedding before he went to Potidaea. But I need some time to get ready so I insisted on waiting until he returns which, from what the messengers say, may be as early as next month. Sooner or later I have to marry him. What else can I do? The contract was officially signed two years ago. I agreed to it on one condition." She grinned and drank her wine.

"And that is . . .?"

"That I may ask my best friend to be my bridal attendant, and of course that, dear one, is you."

Alcibiades agreed to that?"

"He did. I told him it's a woman's prerogative to choose anyone she wants, and he agreed. I know that you dislike one another, but I don't want any one else to stand beside me when I make my vows. Guess what Grandmother told him! She said, 'If you object to Hipparete's request, I shall cancel the wedding' I, personally, am very fond of Xanthippe." She's a very strong minded woman".

"Great-aunt Elpinice actually said that?" Xanthippe asked with a sparkle in her eyes, the first since Cerberus death.

"It's comical to see how careful Alcibiades was not to offend any of us before he left. He'd been like that ever since the night he came here, drunk as a goat, and, just on the strength of a stupid bet he made, he'd made he hit my father and knocked him down! Surely you heard about it? The story was all over Athens. People still wonder why Father didn't tear up the contract. So do I. In fact I wish he had.

"Amazing!" Xanthippe said, shaking her head. But child's play compared to what he had done to her when he mutilated and killed her pet. What a dilemma! To be invited by her one dear friend to take part in the wedding of a despicable enemy .

"To tell the truth," Hipparete said, morosely, "I'm not looking forward to my marriage. But the wedding will be fun!"

"I wish I could laugh at life the way you do. Doesn't anything or anyone ever make you angry . . . or sad?"

"Of course. Only an idiot is happy all the time."

"You and Yiayia Phyllys are so much alike. She has her troubles but, no matter. Like you, she acts happy. When I'm with one of you I feel happy too." Xanthippe swallowed, and her throat moved with such emotion she could hardly speak. "I can't tell you how honored I am to be the one you chose."

"I love you, Agape mou. My heart hurt when I learned how much you've had to endure since I last saw you. It's as if the gods were testing you. I couldn't stop crying when I heard about Cerberus. Everyone agrees whoever did it should be in chains. On top of which you suffered . . . this." Gently Hipparete touched the scar on Xanthippe's arm. "At least I'll wager you weren't sorry about whatever it was that ended your betrothal to Astron."

"You know I wasn't. I was never more relieved! Remember, I said I'd rather die than marry him. How did you know that the contract was annulled?"

"Father and Alcibiades were talking about Anytus. They're beginning to find his attentions tiresome. Now he's trying to get Father to persuade Grandmother and Grandfather to consider betrothing cousin Iodice to Astron but they won't even think of it. One of these days you'll get a much better offer too!"

"I'm not sure. Mama and Papa are convinced I'm destined to be a spinster because my gift for scandalizing people would scare away the bravest of men. Remember when I told you I was in love with Critobolus?"

Hipparete nodded.

"I still am. And .. " Thoughtfully Xanthippe compressed her lips. No, she dared not tell her secret, not to anyone, not even Femma. "I haven't seen him for awhile. Have you, or your brothers?" she asked.

"They may have, but not I. I know you care for him, and I still hope the two of you will end up together.

"Did you ever find out why Kallia said he was betrothed?"

"Not a word. Zeus! What plots and counter-plots over who marries whom. The whole silly business should be simplified! Take Myrto. Phaenerete is determined to have her for a daughter-in-law but Myrto can't stand Socrates. She'd love to marry Alcibiades and I'd be glad to hand him over to her. If only I could! So it goes," Hipparete brooded.

"One of many things I admire about you, Xanthippe, and Myrto, is that you both dare to be different. Of course I'd rather be with you than with her. Now! Come with me. I have something to show you. It's the dress you're to wear at my wedding."

Meela, a slave gifted in the art of needlework had created a peplos even more beautiful than the one Xanthippe had day-dreamed of wearing in the company of Critobolus.

"They call it silk." Hipparete explained, watching the look of wonderment on her friend's face as she fingered the soft shining fabric. "It was brought here by boat from somewhere at the other end of the world."

"Who will be Alcibiades' groom's man?" Xanthippe asked. Critobolus was his friend. Unfortunately so was Astron.

"Socrates. I was surprised at first but Alcibiades adores the man and follows him about like an eager puppy. He's always repeating things that Socrates says, such as 'True happiness can only be had when a person gains mastery over thoughtless impulses, and learns to discriminate in his choice of food, drink and relationships.' I can usually tell when they've been together because afterwards, for awhile at least, Alcibiades doesn't get drunk and wild, and he's more considerate of me."

The gate creaked and Alcibiades came strolling in. After greeting his bride-to-be, he favored Xanthippe with a display of cordiality that, until now, was the only time she remembered seeing a look of anything but hatred on his face.

Yet why shouldn't he be pleasant? He had her horse, he'd murdered her pet, and he might even have it in his power to come between her and Hipparete. His revenge was complete! It could even be that he had influenced Anytus to cancel her betrothal. If so that would be the one thing he had ever done for which she could not fault him. For now however she would be carefully noncommittal. Her revenge would have to wait.

There was a shout of laughter and again the gate swung wide to admit Hipparete's brothers, Hermogenes, young Callias, and with them, Critobolus!

He seemed taller and more slender than she remembered, and he'd grown a beard that was trim and close cut and made his teeth look even whiter. For a moment that seemed an eternity (or was it the other way around?) her eyes locked with his, just as they had on other occasions.

It appeared that the men had chosen to join the ladies in the large family dining room. Callias sat the head of the table with Hipponicus on his right. Opposite him, at the far end of the table, sat Elpinice, regal in a purple peplos and gold chains.

Everyone was talking at once, particularly the young men, elaborating on their forthcoming adventures in far away places.

As for Xanthippe, even the presence of Alcibiades failed to disturb her. Conscious only of Critobolus, seated on the divan next to hers, she was dizzy with delight. He was still looking as if he could not take his eyes away from her face. But he did not smile, and she sensed he was trying to tell her something with his eyes.

* * * *

It was not her fabulous face alone that attracted people to Elpinice. There was a quality about her that radiated like the glow of a candle. She also had a facility for drawing people into conversations that challenged and amused, therefore, after supper, everyone spontaneously followed her into a colonnaded courtyard overlooking terraced gardens.

Critobolus, instead of avoiding Xanthippe, as he'd done 'until this evening, deftly made his way to her side, pausing to chat here and there to make it less obvious that he wished to be alone with her.

For awhile they simply stood and looked at one another. Then, "I have something I must tell you," he said in a voice that was barely audible. "In recent weeks I've come to your father's farm, not to ride or race, but just to see you. Yet, when I get there, I turn away because I have no right to seek you out until I resolve the conflict I mentioned to you, the one I'm still having with my father. But, Xanthippe, I haven't stopped thinking about you, not since our afternoon together.. I think I'm in love with you, and even though I was very wrong to let what we did happen I wanted . . ."

It was then that Alcibiades appeared. "Sorry to butt in, Critobolus," he said, "but don't you think we should leave before we're asked to? Most everyone else has left, the hour grows late, and I've already bid 'adio' to our hosts".

"They are probably the two most gorgeous young men I've ever seen and I've seen quite a few." Elpinice said when they departed. Then, reaching up, she patted Callias on the cheek. "You and only you were ever more handsome, Agape Mou".

"That's what marriage should be like," Xanthippe thought, alone in her room that night, and feeling as if she were floating on air. Meticulously she rinsed her face at a pink marble wash basin, balanced on three sculptured sea nymphs. Catching a glimpse of herself in the burnished bronze wall mirror above it, she sighed, and wondered how it would feel to see the reflection of the face Elpinice must have had when she was seventeen.

After selecting some sugared dates from a tray of sweet-meats she glanced at the bed with its carved head- board that reached to the ceiling, but, too stimulated to sleep, perched on the edge of a divan and thought about Critobolus instead.

What had he been trying to say? He had not seemed to notice her scar, possibly because she'd formed a habit of hiding it with her left hand. Nor did he mentioned Cerberus. Could it be that he had approached his father about a betrothal and been told, 'Xanthippe is a scandalous woman! You can't marry her'

Regardless of what his problem was, it could be resolved. He loved her. He had said so tonight and that was all that mattered. Of late the gods had laid some heavy burdens on her, Surely, by this time, she had paid for her mistakes and things would get better. Hopefully, before or soon after Hipparete's wedding, Critobolus and Crito would come to terms and settle their mysterious dispute. Meanwhile she would do what city girls did to make themselves desirable, crush flower petals in the bath-water, rub warm olive oil into her skin, and anoint her hair with a mix of boiled parsnip oil and yogurt.

Chapter Twenty

Potidaea was a colony of Corinth, but it was as a member of the Athenian Empire that she became vexed by taxes and rebelled. Pericles sent troops to quell the riot and it seemed no time before they returned victorious. Among them was Alcibiades, home again and ready to claim his bride.

"When are we going to draw lots?" cried Kallia, who, with Hipparete's closest friends, had gathered in the bride's bed-chamber to celebrate the pre-nuptial rites.

"Your appearance has changed so much I hardly recognized you, Kallia," Iodice commented. "What have you been doing?"

"Avoiding Feast Days," replied the girl who until now had merited her behind-the-back pseudonym, 'Belly-slave'. Nor was it only Kallia's appearance but her disposition as well that seemed to have undergone a change. Old hostilities evidently forgotten she had smiled and greeted Xanthippe with surprising cordiality which was more than could be said of some others whose jealousy over Hipparete's choice of bridal attendant was ill-concealed.

According to tradition, names had been inscribed on broken bits of pottery and placed in a basket. With a giggle, Hipparete shut her eyes and withdrew one that would reveal who had the honor of bathing the bride. And, because the winner was also foretold to be married, cheers and jests greeted Kallia when hers was the chosen name.

"You probably put your shard on the top," they teased.

There was holy water from the Springs of Kallirhoe for the bath, and a flagon of scented oil to anoint Hipparete's body for its dedication to the Goddess of Love. As she watched, Xanthippe's thoughts drifted back to the day when she herself had been indoctrinated into the Mysteries of

Aphrodite . . . but without benefit of a ritual bath.

"Kallia you're splashing everyone!" Myrto scolded. When she spoke her teeth protruded just enough to give her a judicial look. A peplos, softer than baby's skin, swirled about her hips when she walked, and a cluster of three huge sapphires clung to her small bosom. Having managed to captivate a very rich, very old nobleman, she herself had become a married woman.

"Are you still doing mimicry?" she asked Xanthippe.

"I'll wager she can't mimic me," Kallia said rolling her eyes as she sponged Hipparete's back.

"By the gods, Kallia, there's something more than the way you look that has changed, yet I can't for the life of me decide what it is!" marvelled Mara, the wife of Hipparete's brother Hermogenes. "You behave as if you have a secret. Do you?"

"I have many secrets," Kallia said archly. "But I hide them under the bed!" She reached for a bath sheet. "Wrap up in this Hipparete. Will someone please hand me the oil? Also, since we're preparing you for your wedding night we really should be discussing love. I'm told that Socrates lectures about it and since Alcibiades is a disciple of his you probably already know what he has to say. Do you?"

Reflectively Hipparete drew the sheet around her moist young body. "Just that Socrates describes love as a sort of rapture that makes the unreal real."

Myrto's laugh was brittle as the snap of dry firewood. "No wonder everyone claims that Socrates froze his head instead of his feet in Potidaea! And, can you believe, if his mother had had her way I'd be married to him! Would you marry him, Xanthippe?"

"How should I know? I've only met him twice in my life, But today, if I have the opportunity, I shall ask him how one goes about making the unreal real. It might be a handy thing to know." Xanthippe replied, careful to keep her face impassive. Myrto had a facility of making remarks that hurt.

"If you show enough interest he may invite you to be the first woman to join his group. Then you'd really cause a stir . . . which wouldn't be anything new. By the way have you heard that Anytus thinks Socrates teaches sons to defy their fathers and will disinherit Astron unless he stops following him? Was your betrothal. . ." To Xanthippe's relief Myrto's question was interrupted by the music of citharas, flutes, and songs, heralding the groom's procession as it wound its way up the hill to the house of Callias.

Now it was Xanthippe's turn to assist Hipparete, first with the wedding garment, once worn by Elpinice, then the final touch, a coronet of flowers and ribbon placed on the bride's wheat-colored hair.

With laughter and little cries of "Be blessed by the gods," the others ran down the marble stairs to take their places in a courtyard banked with flowers and filled with the most prestigious group of guests ever to assemble for an Athenian wedding. Following them was Xanthippe wearing her new silk peplos and heavy gold loop earrings, a gift from the bride, then Hipparete, walking slowly toward the family altar.

Alcibiades stood waiting, flanked by Socrates and the Archon. Looking like an incarnation of the Sun God he wore a richly draped yellow robe heavily encrusted with gold and embroidered with red chimera. On his head lay a crown of laurel leaves intertwined with scarlet ribbon. But Hipparete with her flaxen aureole of curls was a match for him. Already friends had started referring to the couple as 'the golden ones'.

Hipponicus, appearing uncommonly subdued, stepped up and stood beside his daughter while Callias, in the role of priest, inaugurated the Mysteries of marriage for his grandchild.

"Hear me, golden throned Hera, queen of immortals, chief among them in beauty. Grace Hipparete and Alcibiades with your presence, glorious lady, and let their habitation abound with peace and joy."

Next Pericles, whose abdication of responsibility for his charge was complete, made a bow, stepped aside, and seated himself with the other guests. Hipponicus surrendered his daughter to Alcibiades and she, in turn, renounced her home, family, and childhood toys. At that very moment Alcibiades looked directly at Xanthippe. Then, quite pointedly, he turned his head, as if to tell her that she, like the rest of his bride's playthings, was also now relegated to the past.

A piece of sacrificial frankincense perfumed the air. Sacrifices of lamb and wheat were offered on the altar and Athena, Zeus, Hera, Hestia of the hearth, and all the gods were once again called upon to cast their blessings on the union. Hipparete offered a prayer to Hymen, deity of the wedding night and crushed a pomegranate in her hands. "Hymen, hymenai o, hymenai o." the people chanted. Was it a hundred years or only yesterday since I heard those words at my own wedding, Nikandra wondered, as the newlyweds were showered with grain.

Together Hipparete and Alcibiades led their guests to the great dining hall through a corridor hung with russet, turquoise, and yellow tapestries brought by ship from Crete. The entrance was guarded by bronze griffins. Directly inside stood a ten-hands-tall Minoan amphora decorated with paintings of monkeys, birds and fish, and filled with sprays of golden field grass. It was said to be a prize gained by Hipponicus in his youth for throwing the javelin. Xanthippe was finding it hard to believe that the father of the bride had ever been virile enough to discharge anything weightier than a fart, when someone touched her lightly on the arm.

"May I join you?" Socrates asked."I have looked forward to seeing you here today. Ah! Kalimeera!" He paused to greet two other guests.

"Xanthippe, allow me to present my lifelong friend, Crito, and Trina, his wife. This", he told them, "is Xanthippe".

"I have already met Palen's daughter, Kalimeera, Xanthippe" Crito said, scrutinizing her with disquieting intensity.

"Kalimeera." Critobolus' mother, a sickly looking woman, echoed.

Behind them, their son had the same inscrutable expression Xanthippe had seen before. At least before the last time they had been together here in the house of Callias. That night he had smiled and said he was in love with her.

"You'll be leaving soon, Critobolus?" Socrates asked.

Critobolus nodded.

"This situation with Sparta has become untenable," Crito said glumly. "We aren't at war but we are. Who can guess what will happen? I always accepted the fact that when Critobolus was seventeen he would fulfill his obligation to Athens just as we did at his age. We gave a year of our time to the Empire. But now, after looking forward for seventeen years to having him join me at my banker's table, I am facing the prospect of waiting, the gods only know, how much longer."

"Let's hope Pericles' strategy will do the trick." Socrates replied. "You well know, dear Crito, I cherish Athens and when she calls I go. None the less I am convinced it's not only useless but immoral to oppose violence with violence. I know you agree.

"Honor me with your presence at my side", Socrates said as he and Xanthippe approached tables laden with gold platters of sheep kid, lobster, crayfish, woodcocks and exotic fruits.

Critobolus, Hermogenes, and Mara, his betrothed had already been seated. Completing the bridal table was Agathon, a budding playwright, Iodice, Callias the Second, Kallia. and Myrto, accompanied by her 'new old' spouse,

From where she sat Xanthippe could see Nikandra watching with evident delight. What a pity, she thought to herself, that someone like her mother, who adored Athens and parties and 'liked to have everything nice,' had been assigned by the Fates to spend her days in the country working like a mule.

Briefly Nikandra's face clouded. That was when the Archon, after stopping at the bride's table just long enough to offer a toast, excused himself and made his departure.

Aspasia, it appeared, had been disinclined to attend. "Women like that have a way of knowing where they aren't wanted," other guests remarked.

"Before we stopped to chat with Crito and his family I was about to say that although you were very young when first we met I already saw in you a certain 'quiddity', or, in other words, essence," Socrates said.

Xanthippe, conscious only of Critobolus had practically forgotten him. "Quiddity? Essence?" she repeated, making a pretense of sipping wine. (Not again, especially not tonight, would she allow herself drink too much and behave like a fool.)

"The word, as I use it, refers to the genuine person who can be glimpsed now and then beneath the costumes we don for public view."

"As they do in the Theater of Dionysius?"

"Not precisely. I refer to something less obvious . . . the cloaks of pretense we wear to create an illusion of being other than we really are. But always, beneath that chimera dwells the eternal 'Self' or 'essence'. Yours is extraordinary".

Again Xanthippe's attention strayed. Critobolus was hardly saying a word, while Kallia, seated at his left, chattered with great animation.

Honey wedding cakes baked in the shape of animals, birds and flowers had been stuck with small beeswax lights. When they had been exclaimed over and consumed Socrates dipped fresh linen into a golden bowl of scented water, wiped his mouth, and clapped for attention. Conversation ceased and guests waited expectantly, intrigued by this curious man whose philosophical debates had earned him a reputation for cleverness.

"I speak not only in the capacity of bridegroom's attendant and devoted friend but as an admirer of his sagacity in taking Hipparete to be his wife," he declared.

"Forgive me if I borrow from the words of Homer, who is infinitely more eloquent in expressing fine thoughts than I."

"No one is better at words than you, dear Socrates," Alcibiades shouted.

"Don't be modest. We all know that the Oracle has pronounced you the wisest man in Greece."

One of the slaves handed Socrates a brimming two handled toasting bowl and, raising it, he declaimed,

"We have now together trod upon ground where Gods have dwelled, and shared their fare, on this Mount Olympus. "Fellow Philhellenes, here we also feast and discourse like the Gods! Hipparete, Alcibiades, may those gods grant you all that is good, and give you a home vibrant with gracious concord. For there is nothing greater and better than this. When husband and wife keep their household in one-ness of mind they are a joy to their friends, a woe to their enemies, and winners of high renown."

After drinking from the golden bowl he passed it along and the musicians struck up a lively tune.

With a cheer Alcibiades ran out onto a cleared space in the center of the dining hall. Following several leaps and oscillations he waved a square of white linen and beckoned to Socrates who bounded into the ring, accepted it and proceeded to execute some jubilant maneuvers of his own. Obviously Terpsichore, Muse of the Dance had not overlooked him for, despite his shapeless body and bandy legs he was as graceful as a willow tree in the wind.

One after another the men in the party rose to accept the flag and prance a turn before handing it on to the next. Proudly lifting their heads they hopped back and forth, side to side, forming a circle with arms intertwined stamping in unison old steps inherited from their forebears. Last to enter the ring was the aged Callias slowly revolving to shouts of encouragement from every side.

Now it was the women's' turn, Hipparete first, dancing alone with lithesome grace, then the rest, taking their places, even Elpinice and Phyllys, tracing the ageless choreography.

And finally Alcibiades, returning to dance alone with his bride before taking her to his home while guests, some in carriages, others on foot formed a procession and followed.

Women and girls trailed behind the men. Up ahead Xanthippe saw Critobolus with Hipparete's brothers and her father with General Gryllus and Crito who were walking arm in arm.

At twilight well wishers conducted Alcibiades, and Hipparete, still wearing her virginal veil and crown, to their bedchamber. As the door closed, the ceremonies came to an end with everyone singing the Epithelium, a hymn sacred to marriage.

"So now you can tell everyone," Kallia said addressing her father in a very loud voice.

Heads turned toward General Gryllus. "I was unaware that we would be sharing our news tonight," he said. "For one thing my wife and I deemed it inappropriate to make an announcement until a few days after the wedding of Hipparete and Alcibiades. Yet now I may as well announce that recently my dear friend, Crito, and I formally document- ed and signed a contract to which we verbally agreed when our children were still quite young. It seals the betrothal of his son Critobolus to my daughter Kallia. We only regret that, due to the imminence of a critical war with Sparta, we will not have time to prepare for a fine wedding. Our children will be married in a small family ceremony. But believe me, as soon as we Athenians have sent the Spartans packing, and Critobolus returns from duty, we shall ask all of you to join us in a cele- bration."

* * * *

It was the day after Hipparete's marriage to Alcibiades. Phyllys and Nikandra were busy with their weaving. Melissa, with her little daugh- ter at her side, was feeding the chickens, Palen was in the barn, and the boys had gone to school.

No one was around to see Xanthippe walk, with the slow measured tread of one following a funeral procession out of the kitchen court, through the courtyard and up the outside stairs into the bedroom she shared with Phyllys.

Trancelike she opened the wooden chest that held her terra cotta Artemis. Carefully she withdrew the little figurine and, letting it lie flat on the palm of her hand, studied the goddess' expressionless eyes.

With weighed deliberation she hurled the object hard against the wall and gazed impassively as it fell in fragments to the floor. Picking up the pieces, meticulously, one shard at a time, she placed them in a pouch and carried them downstairs. Taking a spade from behind the house, she carried them out to the ash grove, to where Cerberus lay buried. Unhesitating she dug another grave. Plucking the fragments out of the pouch, Xanthippe dropped them, one by one. into the cavity. This accomplished, she covered them with dirt and stood for while staring at the mound she had made. Then, with a defiant tilt of her chin, she marched back to to the house.

Chapter Twenty-one

"All Gryllus talks about is war," Palen complained. At least it beats having to hear him brag about his precious Xenophon. You'd think he was the only man who ever had a son

"Poor soul. Like you, he was afraid he never would. With all of his war worries it's good he has the little lad to gladden him. I heard him say even though the fight in Potidaea ended so quickly, we cannot claim a real victory even though everyone thought we could," Phyllys said.

"To change the subject, Mother, what do you think made him and Crito keep their children's betrothal a secret so many years? Some say it was because their wives could never get along. Others that it was because Crito had trouble making a final decision. No wonder. It wasn't until Kallia was almost dead that anyone could put up with her, not even her father." Palen mumbled through a mouthful of bread as he hurried away.

"Have you noticed how many men have been riding into the paddock?" Nikandra asked Phyllys later in the day. "Something unusual must be going on down there. Here, Xanthippe, take this to the barn and try to find out what it's all about." She followed this unprecedented request by handing her daughter a jug of kokineli. "Put it in the tack room and, if anyone sees you, just tell him your mother thought your father might have use for another bottle of wine."

Stealthily Xanthippe slipped into the stable, and entered the room where Palen kept refreshments for his clients and looked around. Not since her impromptu performance on Iris in the racing ring she had not come near this area. Recognizing Alcibiades' voice she shivered.

"We were cut off without food or supplies in weather so cold the soldiers had to swathe themselves in wool to keep from freezing, all but

143

Socrates," he said. "His fortitude was amazing! He walked barefoot over ice as if it were a warm rug."

"The word is not 'amazing' it's 'crazy'. Everyone knows Socrates is daft", someone else said and everyone laughed.

"How are these skirmishes going to end?"

"Had you been involved you would not refer to what went on in Potidaea as a skirmish!" Alcibiades retorted hotly. "It was a short but bloody encounter and we paid a hideous price for that quick win. I myself was so badly wounded that, were it not for Socrates, I would be dead. He rescued me. He literally carried me from the field. I owe my life to him."

"A major conflict between Athens and Sparta is inevitable now," General Gryllus predicted..

"I'm against it!" said another. "We would be Greeks killing Greeks and there are those of us right here in this stable whose loyalties are divided. I myself entertain a certain respect for the Spartans."

"Well, Palen, at least you have cause to be pleased because wars always smile on horse dealers. Fighting men need good mounts. That's what brings us here. If you wish you can sell out this week."

Fearful of being discovered, Xanthippe deposited the kokineli and was about to leave when Hipponicus walked in, closing the tack room door behind him. In three strides he was beside her, standing so close that his body brushed hers, and she felt his hot breath on her face.

"Any female who hangs around a stable is asking for it," he said in a low voice. Before she could scream he put one of his hands on her mouth and grabbed her with the other.

"You don't fool me little cousin," he whispered. "There's one like you in every family so I may as well be the one to give you what you want. I've had it in mind for some time."

Feeling him rise and harden against her she recoiled and tried to jerk her head free of his hand.

"I'll take my hand off your mouth, Kokeeno, but remember, if you scream everyone in Athens will know you for what you are." Hipponicus' thick lips opened over hers, his great slobbering tongue thrusting and exploring. Frantically she flailed at him with her fists and kicked at him but his legs pinioned her like a trap.

"So you want to make a contest!" he panted. "You're quite a fighter. I like that when I 'laikazein' a woman." He laughed and pushed her against the wall.

One outcry, she thought desperately, and every man in the barn would run to witness her disgrace. And, not one of them would want to believe that the high-born Hipponicus had dared to tamper with the daughter of another Alcmaeonid without her consent, especially not if he'd seen her in that chariot race.

Hipponicus groaned and his body convulsed against hers. Then he released her. "Oh stop looking so glum! You needn't worry. I spilled my seed on the ground," he said, wiping his sweaty face with an embroidered scarf. He seemed almost ill at ease, even offered her a drink from the wine bottle she had brought.

"Just remember, no word about this to anyone or you'll be in trouble." He patted the folds of his riding tunic and re-opened the door he'd been careful to shut behind him earlier.

When he had gone Xanthippe buried her face in her hands and waited until the waves of nausea that had overtaken her had time to subside. Something had kept Hipponicus from violating her in the final sense, but she felt as soiled as if he had.

Mama and Yiayia would worry if she did not soon return to the house. One look at her face and they would know that something ugly had occurred. For a certainty she'd only have cause for regret if she told them the truth. That was a fact of life. But what could she say? A loud snort coming from the corridor where the stallion was tied gave her the answer!

Phyllys and Nikandra were shading their eyes and looking over the courtyard wall when Xanthippe returned from the barn. "What happened?" they chorused.

"Did you find out why the cavalrymen are here?"

"Godsname! What's wrong with you?"

"I tried to sneak around behind the stallion so no one would see me, and he crowded me against the wall. He's so wild I thought I'd never get away from him," Xanthippe storied. "It was dreadful. I feared he was going to kick me!"

"You look as if he did. Thank the gods you weren't hurt! What's going on in the barn?"

"They're here to buy horses. They say they'll take anything Papa will sell because Sparta this summer Sparta is going to to invade Athens," Xanthippe reported in a voice so tremulous that Phyllys offered her a cup of wine and water. "Drink this," she said. "It will soothe your nerves."

"Do you think there really will be a war, Mother-Phyllys?" Nikandra asked, clasping and unclasping her hands.

"Only the gods know the answer to that," Phyllys sighed heavily. "As

I've said all too often, there's something about a war that men can't seem to resist. It has happened before, over and over. Years ago when the Persians got all the way to Marathon everyone thought it was the end. I was only four when that war ended. Then, after less than ten years of peace, it started all over. Unfortunately, one never knows from one day to the next what might happen."

Yiayia was right, but, wise as she was she d never guess what had actually taken place today. Despite her low opinion of Hipponicus she'd be stunned to learn what he had done right down there in her son's stable.

"But if I told her she'd be the only person in the world who would believe me," Xanthippe mused as she went to bed that night. But what good would it have done? "You have endured many trials," Phyllys said gently, and bent to stroke her granddaughter's tangled hair. "It makes my heart ache to see you hurt, especially when you lost Cerberus. I often wonder why such tragedies occur in the lives of people as dear as you. But for whatever comfort it is, let me tell you, Xanthippe, that just when you think you'll never be able to smile again something is likely to happen that renews happiness. While we're talking things over, there is a matter I vaguely remember . . . ."

She hesitated . . . It was a nebulous recollection of the day Xanthippe ran away, something she had said about Alcibiades grabbing at her tunic . . . Cerberus name had come up. What was it?

Not being able to remember was one of the trials that went with getting old. Then again it could have been a dream, or simply a figment of her imagination.

Yes?"

"Sometimes I find myself wondering if you might have even a faint idea about who was responsible for what happened to Cerberus."

"If I did I'd want to kill him," Xanthippe hedged.

The truth but not the whole truth. Again she could not speak out. Alcibiades still had all the advantages. The gods alone knew what else he might be able to do to her, especially now that he was married to Hipparete.

"Well, dearest one, right now I know you find this hard to believe but eventually broken hearts heal and anger diminishes. Unfortunately it often takes quite awhile before that happens."

"What would I do without you, Yiayia Phyllys?" Xanthippe cried, grasping the old woman in a fiercely urgent hug. "When I have trouble you always try to make things easier for me. I am so glad that we can be together, here in this room. It comforts me just to know you are near. If it weren't for you I think I would want to die."

"Don't worry darling, I shall always stay close to you," Phyllys promised.

It was with those beautiful words in her ears, as well as from exhaustion, that Xanthippe fell asleep.

* * * *

The threat of a Peloponnesian war remained. That was why the Archon had called for a citizens' meeting here on the Hill of the Pnyx. Having been told to assemble on the 'Hill', citizens were talking and gossiping as they looked for places to sit.

Many were somber, fearing the worst. Some tried to lighten their spirits by making jokes.

"So we see here, Jupiter Long Pate Pericles doth appear. He ostracized Thucydides and laid aside his head, and wears the new Odeon in its stead." quipped Cratinus, an aging dramatist.

"Here's a really good one," Lysicles rejoined. " 'Fainting beneath the load of his own huge head, and now abroad from his big gallery of a pate, Pericles gives trouble to the State.' "

"Take note. I am not laughing. It's because I find that too true to be amusing." was Palen's dour response.

There was a stir. Pericles himself had arrived and at sight of him people stopped talking and settled themselves to hear his strategy. Small wonder he was referred to the 'Olympian'. Statuesque, and handsome of countenance, he made an imposing figure. Behind him, rising ten feet high, was an altar of rock, giving inflexible evidence that ultimately it was not mortal men, or their rulers but Zeus who presided in this place.

"We knew that Sparta supported the conflict in Potidaea." His resonant voice carried to the farthermost edge of the rocky slopes. "Yet, even as we were, nonetheless, making every effort to negotiate peace with honor she attacked our allies, Megara and Corcyrya. Today it becomes my sad duty to inform you that Thebes has laid siege to Plataea, another of our allies, and we again have proof that Sparta instigated the action."

There was a concerted groan as he paused to allow the enormity of what he had just said sink in. Plataea and Thebes were less than one hundred stades away. This might be called 'war in the north pasture'! A kind of pandemonium ensued until he raised a quieting hand.

"If you, the rural citizens of Attica follow the plan I have outlined, lives will not be lost, trade routes will be maintained and, most important, the Empire will still be safe for democracy!

"Our spies say the Spartans are ready to invade the Attican country-side in the spring. They have power to destroy us on land, but if our rural residents take asylum within the Great Walls before the battle begins, the enemy will find no one to fight. So they have little to gain and no blood will be shed.

"When they run out of food their only alternative will be to give up and get out. Meanwhile our navy will ravish Sparta's coastline because Athens is and always will be 'Mistress of the Seas'. Furthermore arrangements have already been completed to bring supplies to the harbor at Piraeus and from there into Athens through the Walls".

This time the outcry was not so easily quelled.

"We prefer war!"

"Death to the Spartans!"

"War! War! War! chanted a group of newly inducted epheboi.

"Are we to sit and do nothing while our fields are pillaged and our homes burned?" someone yelled.

"This scheme gives the Spartans free rein to destroy everything we've worked for all our lives!" another cried bitterly.

Repeatedly Pericles called for order. When the clamor began to abate, he spoke again. "Remember, trees though they be cut and loped grow up again quickly. But when men are destroyed they cannot be replaced."

"Pay attention to the Archon! He's right! We've had enough blood-shed and killing!" This time it was a young woman, making herself heard above the rest.

People raised their heads to see who had committed the breach. Females might be seen, but never heard, at civic gatherings.

"Can you believe your ears?" Palen rasped to Lysicles, also in attendance with his entire family. "The world is going mad!"

"In conclusion, let us try to remember that our constitution is called a democracy because it is in the hands, not of the few, but of the many. Never forget this, our laws secure equal justice for all, and our public opinion honors talent in every branch of achievement on the grounds of excellence alone. And as we give free play to all in our public life, so we carry the same spirit into our daily relations with one another. We have no black looks or angry words for our neighbor if he enjoys himself in his own way, and we abstain from little acts of churlishness which, though they leave no mark, yet cause annoyance to those who so notes them. In our public acts we keep strictly within the control of law. We acknowledge the restraint of reverence; we are obedient to whomsoever is in authority and to the laws. May the gods be with us in these trying times."

"Hogwash!" the man behind Xanthippe muttered as Pericles signalled that the meeting was over.

"I don't approve of abandoning our farms," blustered Lysicles when citizens gathered in clumps to talk and argue.

"Ship our livestock to Euboea for the summer? What does he know about sheep? Nothing. How can we be sure they'll even survive?"

Wives and mothers sided with the Archon. Generations of bellicose Greeks had dashed into battle, only to disappear forever into the shady vales of Thanatos, leaving their families penniless and bereft. Pericles ploy of fortifying people within the Walls might work.

Back again in Cholargus Palen pounded his fist on the table top until the dishes danced. "He asks us to leave the graves of our forebears for the Spartans to destroy! Men who fought for their right to abide in peace and be buried on this land would beat their breasts with shame to know that an Alcmaeonid asks us to sneak away and hide!"

"If we follow his orders there will be fewer persons who will need to be buried," Nikandra demurred.

"Oh, hold your tongue! What do women know of war?"

"More than you think," his mother sniffed.

* * * *

When Palen entered the kitchen court late the next afternoon with General Gryllus their voices had risen to a shout.

"Pericles needed Themistocles to keep him on the track. He's like a racing horse who must have a harness to keep him from running away with the cart! Now that he's rid of his only rival he has too much power."

"Listen to reason, man! His plan is good, and will probably be carried out. We'd take too great a risk remaining here."

"Women, children, and old men can retreat from a battle but not I!"

"Be good enough to remember I did not become a general by backing off from any fight, make no mistake. The likelihood is that, although I missed Potidaea, I'll soon be involved. I don't fear combat nor do you, but you owe it to your forebears to protect their lineage by taking your sons into town."

This was logic for which Palen had no immediate answer, and Gryllus was quick to press his point. "Whatever I may have to do, Kallia will stay with her mother. She'll need comfort with her bridegroom already away. So will my wife. A town house came to me recently through the death of an uncle. It's empty and it's yours for the summer. You and I are friends and I don't want my problems compounded, worrying about you being butchered on your own land. What is your answer?"

"That I am fortunate to have a friend like you," Palen said.

"We wanted to get together and talk things over," Lysicles said, arriving with his wife. As the day was chill, Nikandra invited them to sit in the kitchen court stove.near the oven. "Do you realize we're expected to make this move in less than seven weeks?" he blustered. "Seven weeks to figure out what to do so that we might have something left to come home to after our lives have been turned upside down!"

"The Fates smile on you," Lysicles chicken-faced wife said bitterly. "My husband tells me you will be in a fine house whereas we shall be forced to share a small place with my kinfolk. How we shall manage I cannot imagine."

"Did you know that Socrates saved Alcibiades' life in Potidaea?" Lysicles asked, shying away from the subject of his wife's relatives.

"From what Pericles says, foot soldiers as well as cavalrymen will be patrolling our shores while the navy does the fighting," Palen said. "For all we know, you and I may be receiving an invitation to join them any day now!"

"Which would suit me fine. I'd rather go to war with the Spartans than stay in a nasty little house in Athens fighting with my 'in-laws," Lysicles replied.

Chapter Twenty-two

Thick beds of salt always lay beneath an oven's tile floor to retain heat. But after awhile it lost its savor and had to be replaced, a task Xanthippe despised. "Hades pits," she muttered, clawing at the tiles to dislodge them. "Why this when we're leaving anyway?" Savagely scooping up the impotent salt she flung it on a pathway already white and trodden flat by the footfalls of other years.

Four broken fingernails made her think of the time Hipparete had complained about being domesticated. But never would Hipparete have to do anything like this! Nor Kallia! No wonder she had looked so smug at Hipparete's wedding! And afterwards when the announcement of her betrothal shattered Xanthippe's belief that Critobolus would never surrender to parental dictates. But was there anyone, other than Yiayia Phyllys who, sooner or later, did not? Thoughts, thoughts, crowding her mind like bats. Unconsciously her hand moved as if to brush them away.

"I'm going to take a walk," she said when her chore was finished. And there would be no indecision about which path to take. She was going to visit Femma once more before moving into Athens.

"Let her go," Phyllys said when Nikandra seemed about to object.

When Xanthippe reached her destination it was not Femma but a stranger who came to the door and said, "She doesn't live here anymore. She sold the house to my husband and moved away."

"Do you know where she went?"

"Probably To Athens," the woman replied with a shrug.

Xanthippe had trouble staying awake at the supper table that evening when a comment made by her father roused her.

"It seems Alcibiades no longer cares for the company of Anytus," he said, his first mention of the leather merchant since the latter's arbitrary termination of her betrothal.

"I wondered why he and his family weren't at Hipparete's wedding," Phyllys remarked, "But I was content not to see them. Why do you say Alcibiades is no longer his friend?"

Because shortly before his wedding he refused a dinner invitation from Anytus. After the party ended, and everyone had gone, he slipped back into Anytus' house and helped himself to twelve gold goblets!"

"I don't believe it."

"That's what they say."

"What did Anytus do?"

"He called it an honor to have his goblets admired by a man of taste, and said Alcibiades was welcome to them. That bugger would grovel in horse manure if meant pushing his way into politics."

"With that chin he could push his way through a mountain of shit," Xanthippe said." For once Nikandra was too intent on the story to remonstrate over her daughter's choice of words.

"Now that Alcibiades has come into his fortune he tosses money about as if it were water." Palen added.

"Everyone we know has more money than we do," Elefterous grumbled. "I'm tired of being a poor relation. The most interesting thing we ever buy around here is a new milk goat."

"Enough of that!" Palen said sharply. "I have too much on my mind already, without having to listen to that sort of drivel! We're being forced to move into Athens which means that the few horses I didn't sell have to be shipped to Euboea and the stallion will probably kick the sides out of the goddamn boat. We might end up being happy just to have a new milk goat! So no more of your squawking"

Succumbing to the inevitable he had sold every horse he owned with the exception of Enyo, one of her weanlings, and his best stallion so, at least for the time being, there would be available money. Yet, although he and other rural residents grumbled, theirs was a law abiding society. When everything they could garner from early spring gardens had been pickled or dried, and most of the chickens killed, plucked and salted, their women began to pack. And when his own two wagon carts had been loaded, Palen made a final leaden-footed round of the farm which, but for a few hardy sheep, already looked deserted.

In a gradual exodus farm-folk moved, hauling portable goods, even woodwork stripped from walls! Some carried tents to assure a 'roof' overhead because in Athens there was no longer such a thing as space. Some faring better than others, were bivouacked into the few empty dwellings and rooms still to be found "We can lay this at the feet of Pericles," others stormed, easily forgetting that he had been idolized by most of them for upwards of twenty eight years.

A constant hum of conversation ran contrapuntal to the buzz of flies, cheese bags, pendulous as a she goat's udder, swung from terra cotta roof tops and heavy fumes of fish, garlic, and animal offal mingled with the resinous winey breath of tavernas to make hot days seem even more so! "Athens may be the most intellectual city in the world, but it's also the smelliest," Phyllys said, pinching her nose.

To Xanthippe the reeking streets exuded a bracing whiff of welcome change if not hope. Alcibiades and Hipponicus were both far from here on matters pertaining to a Spartan attack that was apt to occur any moment, so perhaps she would have an opportunity to spend some time with Hipparete. They might even see a drama together!

Life went on in Athens almost as if nothing were amiss. There was something for everyone, bawdy delights in tavernas and houses of prostitution, debates and mental calisthenics in the Stoas, and music at the Odeon. Tiers of seats in the Theater of Dionysius were filled to capacity and, following each performance, viewers arguing for hours over which was more meaningful, Euripides' portrayal of the common man or Sophocles' depiction of the supernatural. Not even the imminence of war could curtail the gregarious Greeks!

As for boys not yet old enough to be ephebes, contests and games were provided at the Palaistra. There were also new city friends, whom Elefterous and Marc embraced with enthusiasm.

Palen, restless and refusing to be consoled by urbane entertainment, paced his borrowed house like a caged beast. "I hate this place! I'd rather be die in a battle than suffocate in these crowds," he carped for perhaps the twentieth time. "The heat and stench make me retch. I'm going to walk the 'Walls' to Piraeus for a breath of sea air, if I can push my way through the mob. Damn! I wish we had stayed in Cholargus!"

Not so Nikandra! To her Gryllus' house in the 'better' part of Athens was on a par with Mount Olympus. "This is where I belong! Look! See this! Look at this!" she would exclaim over each fresh marvel.

"Clook clook!" Palen mocked. "The way you cackle anyone in hearing distance would know you came here fresh from a hen- yard".

Unabashed she went on pointing out tinted plaster walls, mosaic floors, and most dazzling of all, right there in the house, latrines flushed by water that poured through from outdoor roof drains!

There was the Agora to be seen. "Do you remember when I told you we'd come here together some day?" she asked Xanthippe as they strolled beneath plane trees, stared at pipers piping, painters at work on their pictures, and schoolmasters holding classes in the street! One leaning against the other, booths, tents, and bazaars that boasted stunning varieties of food, clothing, jewels and wine, even silk sent by ship from afar were spread over twenty six acres of land.

"I lived on that hill when I was a girl!" She pointed at a cluster of little houses balanced on slopes that descended into the vast market place. "I wonder who's living there now."

They wandered through long colonnaded stoas where civic and legal matters were settled, ballots cast for ostracisms, and speeches made. On the periphery of the Agora they watched slaves circle naked for a buyers' inspection, and rings in which Palen and other horse dealers exhibited their stock. Then, threading their way through crowds of shoppers, soldiers, public officials, and priests, they flew from one shop to another like honey bees in a garden. The tantalizing smells of hot breads and sausage lured them away from a sweet stand and Nikandra rummaged in her money pouch. "After we make our household purchases I'll still have enough to buy each one of us a bread and hot sausage!" Her laughter sounded like Marc's did whenever he was especially happy.

"We're having a good time, Mama and I. And I have hardly thought about Critobolus, at least not more than four times!" Xanthippe marvelled.

Tripes of slaughtered sheep floated in the gutters and festoons of garlic adorned grocers' stalls where one could make selections from amphoras of brine macerated sardines, olives and goat-milk cheese. Decapitated geese, chickens, and ducks hung neck down from a line, strung like beads on hooks, luring customers to buy. There were baskets of seafood and shrimp piled high on the fishmonger's table and at the meat shop a freshly butchered suckling pig eyed them glassily from its bed of pink horta.

"What's going on over there?" Nikandra pointed to a crowd. "Why it's Socrates, making a speech!" she answered her own question. "See how they listen! Do we dare move in closer to hear?" she asked, propelling Xanthippe forward without waiting for an answer.

"No one is willingly wicked!" they heard him say. "If a man behaves wickedly it is only because in his ignorance of the truth he can't discern his own virtue. But isn't it possible to replace ignorance with knowledge?"

Some shrugged, others shouted "No." or "Yes."

"Do we further agree that knowledge leads to increased wisdom?"

Briefly the audience spoke among themselves before signifying their 'Ayes'.. "So then. once one is encouraged to search for wisdom and truth he finds it within himself?" one young man asked loudly.

"Yes, Glaucon, I am convinced that with continuing study and self-examination a man gains not only knowledge but also, wisdom and with that comes the understanding of virtue, as well as two other priceless acquisitions . . .. Peace and Contentment!

"An unexamined life is not worth living. The proof of what I say can be discovered only if one has the courage to ask himself some person-ally disturbing, but entirely honest questions. Bit by bit, we must come to grips with who, and what, we are. Incredible as it may sound, each one of us is a separate part of a single, harmonious Spirit."

"Look," Nikandra said. "Astron. See? There on the edge of the crowd. I thought he'd have gone to the army by now."

How passionately he must want to hear Socrates, Xanthippe thought, watching him disappear into the throng. If what she'd overheard at Hipparete's wedding were true, he was risking his entire inheritance by being here. Much as she disliked him, she could not help but feel sorry for anyone so unfortunate as to have been sired by Anytus. Anytus, who had told her own father she'd make a laughing stock of his son. Ha! Poor Astron was more than capable of doing that on his own.

* * * *

Summer was beating her heaviest heat onto city streets the day Palen heard that the Spartans had entered rural Attica.

Security measures were increased, and another fleet was sent to pummel the Peloponnesian coast while, from beyond the Great Walls, pillars of smoke could be seen rising against a brazen sky.

"The fiends! They are burning our homes!" men shouted. Women beat their breasts and wept. Some people even tried to storm the city gates and return to their farms. However, when visible signs of destruc-tion abated, people settled down and Xanthippe set forth to visit Hipparete.

To her relief the directions she had been given were more easy to fol-low than they sounded. "Down the Sacred Way and on through the

Kerameikos Gate. Turn right on the Road Visakiou, directly beyond the burial ground. Keep on past the Stoa of Zeus, and the Temple of Ares. When you get to Lycabettus Hill take the first road up, Pass five houses, and you'll come to mine, at the top of the hill, it's the one with myrtle vines on the outer wall."

From the courtyard one could enjoy an unobstructed view of the Parthenon. The grandeur of the house was overwhelming.

"You found it!" Hipparete cried, flinging the gate open. "I could hardly wait until you came!" She gave Xanthippe a hug. "Look at me!" she laughed. "Pregnant and fat. I'm always eating and we're about to sit down to our mid-day meal so here I go again. This afternoon, since I have no hollow tree in which the two of us can perform, would you like to come with me to the Theater of Dionysius instead?"

"Yes," Xanthippe answered a bit stiffly. This elegantly gowned, be-jewelled young matron seemed more a stranger than an erstwhile co-conspirator of make-believe.

Equally intimidating was the courtyard in which they stood. Rainbows of water splashed into a fountain from the mouth of a bronze lion with a frog on its head, Boar-hunting scenes of coursing hounds and men on horseback were painted on the wall. A marble chair, big as a throne, was carved with a scene of Theseus killing the Queen of the Amazons. By the gate, stood a magnificent life-size bronze horse, ears up, nostrils flaring, and one fore-foot extended.

"All of it belongs to my enemy, even a stable of horses, one of which is rightfully mine," Xanthippe thought bitterly.

Happily unaware of any strain on the part of her guest, Hipparete chattered on. "I'm glad you finally accepted my invitation to come and stay over-night!" she exclaimed. "Alcibiades has left again, not as a warrior this time but because of government matters. So here we are, just the two of us, free to do what we wish! I can't believe this is the first time we've been together since my wedding, can you?"

As they walked toward the theater Xanthippe found her-self relaxing. It was good to be with her friend again, and it appeared that Alcibiades had, at least for the time being, refrained from doing anything to curb his wife's cheerful disposition.

It was late afternoon, when the two young women left the Theater. However it was not the main drama 'Oedipus the King', that they talked about, but the comic relief that, as always, follows a tragedy. It had been shockingly irreverent, terribly funny, and composed by a young unknown named Aristophanes.

"I laughed so hard I cried," Hipparete declared. "I wish Aristophanes had written the drama. Sophocles is too dismal! After all that anguish I won't be able to sleep a wink. Let's sit up all night and drink wine and talk! How you and your family like living in Athens. Do you miss the farm? "

"Yes and no. Mama has never been happier! As long as Papa and the boys don't go, and no one gets killed she'd be content to have the war go on all year instead of just in the summer."

"She might get her wish. They fought at Potidaea in the winter."

"What about your brothers . . . and their friends? Where are they?"

"Patrolling the countryside, poor things. They're both hoplites and must go on foot. Critobolus is fortunate to be in the cavalry. Kallia says his post is not far from Athens. No one but the two families attended their wedding. Crito was Critobolus' groomsman and Clymene attended her daughter. Just think! A wedding with no one but parents, and Kallia's brother Xenophon! I hope you don't mind my asking but . . . I have often wondered dear one, if Critobolus still matters to you.

"Not really," Xanthippe replied, making an effort to keep her face from showing how much he still did.

"Life in the house of Gryllus is a lot easier than living on a farm. We're twice as comfortable, and have half the work. But I told Mama I'd be home by noon so I must go," Xanthippe said next morning as they sat, warmed by a gentle summer sun, and breakfasting on farina and fruit.

"This has been like old times", Hipparete said, hugging her friend.

"Marriage makes you happy?" Xanthippe asked wistfully.

"I guess so," Hipparete said dubiously. "I'm glad about this." She patted her abdomen. "The little fellow will probably be here in five months. Meanwhile as long as you are in Athens, we must get together whenever we can!"

Chapter Twenty-three

"I loved living here in town when I was a girl," Nikandra exclaimed.

It was Skirophorian, the last month in the Greek year, and time for the festival that paid tribute to the Goddess Demeter and her daughter Persephone.

Attendance on the first day was enforced by Temple and State therefore Palen, in a clean tunic, clapped a garland of leaves on his head and, striding ahead of his mother, wife, and daughter, mounted the Acropolis Hill.

The Polemarch, highest of priests, was clothed in jewelled vestments, and seated upon a throne in the Temple of Demeter. Flames danced in fiery worship on an altar while seven long-haired vestal virgins, purged and purified by spring water mixed with brine, undulated nearby.

Twelve leaping priests, sweating profusely, were engaged in an orgiastic performance around another blazing fire. One fainted and was pulled aside to regain his senses. Others waved willow wands from the 'Tree of Enchantment" and prayed for fertility and good weather.

"Someday I shall sit there," Xanthippe promised herself, noting the first row seats for those who contributed lavishly to the temple coffers. Love and romance were for fables. It was money and power that counted here in Athens.

Ten stately priestesses paced through the temple chanting mystical words considered to be pleasing to the ears of gods. On their heads they balanced 'kistai' boxes in which secret sacred talismans reposed .

"Giver of earth's good gifts, give us grace, oh Demeter, give us the life that comes only from your giving," people chanted as drinking bowls filled with sweet barley water, favored by the 'Goddess of Grain', passed through the crowd. Lifting one to her lips, Xanthippe halfway wished she were still a believer hoping to gain benefits from the libation.

The final rites, observed the following day, excluded men. Early in the morning thirty three 'sciros' (pigs sacred to Demeter and sacrificed as surrogates for women) were hauled in mule carts to the village of Sciron. These were washed and slaughtered by Mystics, in full view of all, and dispatched, one by one, into a cave.

Bawdy jokes and wild laughter, prevalent at such affairs, were unrestrained. One woman, reputedly of aristoi background, had bought an astonishing collection of dildoes and was making lewd gestures with them for the amusement of her friends. It reminded Xanthippe of her own misbegotten antics at the clan Apaturia, a blunder she would probably regret for the rest of her life!.

"This is no place for a virgin," Phyllys murmured.

The trace of a smile hovered on Xanthippe's lips. How could Yiayia, or anyone for that matter, know who had or had not managed to retain her chastity? What would she think were she to learn what lay behind the expressionless face of her own granddaughter? On the other hand maybe even Yiayia-Phyllys had a few unrevealed secrets of her own!

During a lull in the ceremonies Hipparete appeared. "I've been looking everywhere for you!" she exclaimed. "I'd like to have seen your face when they tossed those dead pigs into that cave! How could anything so gross please a goddess? If I were Demeter I'd puke. In fact I nearly did." Her face contorted.

"The earth is the womb of the world and those pigs were returned to it to encourage uh. . . more births." Nikandra rationalized. "It's a celebration of life and death.

"It also encourages Demeter to make our fields and animals and women more fertile. Demeter doesn't just give grain. She is the grain. And what she gives she can take away if she wants to, as she did when Hades stole her daughter. That was what made her so sad she let everything freeze. But when he agreed to send Persephone back every spring she promised never to completely abandon us again. So that is the reason why we celebrate the Scirophoria. This is when we remind her . . .."

"It makes a good story, Mama. even if we have already heard it a thousand times. But I'm sick of knuckling under to gods who can't decide whether they want to do me a favor or hit me on the head!"

"Xanthippe! Stop saying those things! Nikandra cast a frantic glance around to make sure no one was within earshot. "Someone could lodge an accusation of impiety against you!"

"All I hear is 'Do this! Don't do that! . Hold your tongue'! When Elefterous or Marc ask questions it's called a debate, yet I'm not permitted to think out loud!" Xanthippe clenched her fists, as if daring anyone to contradict her.

"We are not to ask questions. We simply to do as we are told. So. next month, we shall come back to this cave for the Thesmaphoria, and observe the final rites!" Nikandra stated with unyielding conviction.

"More dead pigs?" Hipparete wailed. "The stench will set my unborn baby's teeth on edge! Ah! Here are Grandmother Elpinice and Allys. Let's get their opinion."

"I beg you! Change the subject! Stop discussing the gods!" Nikandra despaired. "I have told you and told you, Xanthippe, even when you think you're alone, someone is always listening!"

* * * *

Toward the end of summer farmers joined townsfolk in paying tribute to the relatively few soldiers who, after guarding the borders, or pummeling the Peloponnesian coast, made their final return to the state cemetery in Athens.

Monuments, green with lichen and moss, were embanked as far as the eye could reach in this lovely park at the end of Cerameicus Road where those who had fallen in battle, were laid to rest amid the passionate displays of lamentation that befit such an occasion.

Articles, for use in the afterlife, were placed on each grave, and one tomb dedicated to the unknown and unrecovered.

"The bravest are those with the clearest vision of what is before them, glory and danger alike, and who, not withstanding, go out to meet it," Pericles declared.

"These men whose lives we celebrate, loved Athens, the city for whom, lest they lose her, they died a soldier's death.

"We survivors pray to be spared their bitter triumph but disdain to meet the foe with a spirit less triumphant. Just remember that Athens owes her greatness to those who have a fighter's daring, a wise man's understanding of duty, and a good man's self-discipline in performance.

"The earth is a sepulchre of famous men and their story is not only graven on stone, but remains, invisibly woven in the stuff of other men's lives."

"Pericles could move a marble statue to tears," Phyllys whispered, wiping her eyes.

"When it comes to speech-making he is the master," Lysicles asserted when, five months later he and Palen were still reviewing the fine points of Pericles' oration.

"True, but he over-blew his pipes when he said that by giving Athenians public games, free theater tickets and all that sort of thing, he enhances the entire Empire. An Administration that favors the many instead of the few, is in danger of running amok. It takes more than a pack of hounds to run a boar hunt!"

School masters should make their disciples memorize what he said about the secret of happiness being freedom, and the secret of freedom in having a brave heart!" was Lysicles resolute reply.

"Right now my main concern is how to get out of here and go home. If it weren't for that damned Thesmaphoria, and the womens' resolve to finish their prayers, we'd be there now."

They may be right. If the Spartans came upon our farms, you and I are going to need all the divine help we can get!"

* * * *

Prior to the Mysteries of Thesmaphoria, women were expected to purify themselves by resorting to an age old custom of spending three nights on a mattress of prickly twigs and avoiding known aphrodisiacs, such as pomegranates. Originally intended to encourage sexual abstinence the custom had, over the years, gradually become a ritual for everyone, even widows and virgins!

"My back still tingles from that itchy withy," Hipparete groaned when, in advance of sunrise, she and Xanthippe returned with their elders to the cave at Skiro in which rested what remained of the thirty three pigs.

"I would have slept on the hateful stuff all night but I feared it might bother my unborn child. So after awhile I got up and went back to my own comfortable bed," she confessed with a puckish grin.

When leaves from Agnus Castus plants had been strewn, and rattles brandished to repel snakes that had been lured by the smell of rotting swine flesh, a band of stalwarts chosen and blessed for their task, entered the cave and recovered the remains. When their trove had been blended with grain seed all the women received a portion to scatter over the earth.

The ritual, anything but solemn, was accompanied by bursts of mirth, so that not even Nikandra felt apprehensive when Hipparete's reaction to the mess in her hands sent Xanthippe into uncontrollable fits of laughter.

Sing you maidens and mothers," the women shouted when a statue of Demeter's reunion with Persephone was displayed.

"Demeter, greatly hail! Grant us peace so that he who sows may also reap. Return to us in the springtime and bless those who breed and those who plant, that we may feed our kine."

* * * *

By the time the service ended, Nikandra had drunk so much sacred wine she had trouble keeping her balance. Xanthippe, recalling the time she herself had imbibed too freely, put a protective arm around her waist. Nikandra, in turn was so gratified by the gesture that, wearing a look of childlike pleasure on her face, she was able to continue without further assistance.

Chapter Twenty-four

"They didn't get us!" Flinging up his arms Palen let out an exultant whoop.

Yesterday, forgetting his invectives against shows of emotion he had been visibly moved when the few spotted horses he had managed to keep, came clopping down a gang-plank at the harbor in Piraeus. And today here he was, home at last, with everything intact including, miracle of the gods, some sheep who had been left behind to exist on pasture grass. Not only had they survived, they had added some new lambs!

"Everyone! Get to work!" he ordered after the altar flame had been rekindled and the gods duly thanked for preserving family and farm. "Marc, go with Andokides to clean stalls. Elefterous, come help me re-open the well. I did a good job of hiding it. The only way the Spartans could have found it would have been if one of them had fallen in!"

Melissa was sent to tend the goats, Nikandra sorted bed- covers, and a provocative scent of oregano and garlic that infiltrated the autumn air gave promise of a tasty chick-pea stew that Phyllys was concocting in the kitchen-court.

"Look at us, barely arrived but already comfortable," she said to Xanthippe who was polishing the sacrificial vessels. "The way we mortals are given strength to handle whatever the Furies have in store never fails to amaze me."

When everything from grain to festival clothing was back in its proper place Nikandra, who in no way shared Palen's elation over quitting Athens, rose laboriously from scouring the loom room floor and massaged the back of her neck.

"Do you have to do so much so fast?" Xanthippe asked. "I guess I never stop doing what I do long enough to ask why I do it," was

Nikandra's dubious reply.

Absently she plucked at a wad of yarn, working and re- working the threads through her fingers. "Gryllus' house was so perfect and now that we're here I wish we could keep ours looking nice too," she said. "When a place is tidy, and all the copper polished, it makes me feel happy."

"You must despise housework by now, don't you?"

"No. . .Well, yes. It's when I've just finished cleaning and Papa's hounds track through and despoil everything that I hate it."

"Why don't you tell him to keep them out?"

"I could never do that!" Nikandra was aghast. "If I did dare mention it he'd just say, 'If it offends you clean it.'

From where they stood they could hear Palen's voice raised in anger. "By the gods, Elefterous, you'd better begin taking a little interest in what goes on around this place if you hope to inherit it someday," he bellowed.

"I wish Papa would stop all that shouting" Xanthippe said crossly. "He seemed so glad to be home. What put him in such a foul mood? None of us can please him no matter how we try. I'm also tired of hearing him repeat that the more he sees people the more he prefers horses and hounds."

Nikandra studied the yarn she was twisting in her hands. "Your father worries about the farm. Yet I have to agree . . . He is hard to please," she said.

Palen was leading Enyo to her stall when a series of screams issued from the house. Tossing the bridle to Andokides he sprinted up the path to find his wife, wild-eyed in the courtyard, her shrieks bouncing off the walls. Phyllys and Xanthippe were trying to calm her.

"What in Hades' name is going on her?" he roared.

Nikandra pointed. "A b . . b . . bu . . Look!" Her teeth were chattering too violently to permit coherence

A raven! Doom's harbinger had flown into the house and was careening around the loom room, wings beating wildly, its droppings spattering floor, walls, and wool.

"Don't cry, Mama. I'll get it." Marc ran to meet the challenge followed by his brother. Within moments, they were lunging at the bird with hockey sticks. It was the sight of her work room being reduced to a shambles re-oriented their mother.

"Get that thing out of here!" she sobbed.

When the raven saw a window and sailed from view she fell onto a bench and moaned, "A bad thing is going to happen."

"You're insane!" Palen shouted. "All this uproar about a bird. Is it 'female complaint'?" he asked his mother.

"Let me assure you it is not!" she replied smartly. One can hardly blame her for being fearful. War has put us all on edge. Every one of has been living in a state of constant anxiety. What we need is to get some rest and take time to collect ourselves."

"We'll call upon Apollo, Artemis, and all the household gods to deliver us from harm," she added resolutely. "We must also refuse to let this episode upset us further. Stop crying, Nikandra. A bird flew in, a bird flew out. Forget it."

"Some good the gods will do," Xanthippe mumbled under her breath. "They're the ones who probably chased that raven in here in the first place just to amuse themselves."

Despite this attempt at bravado she was disturbed. An uneasy sensation of inner turmoil was becoming more and more pronounced, especially since her return to the farm. It was as if she were different entities, with each one of her two selves drifting in opposite directions, leaving no one at all behind. And in her dreams that night she still kept hearing the sinister whisper of wings.

Chapter Twenty-five

"Poseidon is the only month in the year that's invariably gloomy. The one good thing it ever brought was you, Xanthippe, and that was eighteen years ago," Phyllys said, trying to sound more cheerful than she felt.

For awhile they had enjoyed a respite from war and a time of peace. Neither seemed destined to last. New battles were erupting near Cholargus, and rumors spread like a sour smell.

Undaunted by her unsuccessful foray into the countryside, Sparta was planning another invasion and there was little doubt that Pericles would again order farmfolk back within the Walls.

"Whether he does or does not, we stay here," Palen said emphatically. He had acquired a young stallion and re-purchased a mare he'd previously owned, one no longer useful in battle but still breedable. Except that it took time and he burned with impatience.

Nikandra's anxieties nibbled at her too. "I pray the gods you will allow us to return to the city," she sighed, fingering the edges of her shawl. "How could we defend ourselves if the Spartans did come here and find us? They might kill our sons, or all of us! Lysicles is taking his family back to Athens."

"I don't give a damn what Lysicles intends to do. Stop bellyaching. You always want money for one thing and another but how do you expect me to make any if each new rumor has me running to Athens? Right now I'm a lot more concerned with that wild colt I paid too much for. I'm going out there and break him if it's the last thing I do!"

Turning a deaf ear to his wife's litany of laments Palen tramped out, leaving a trail of mud and manure in his wake.

"I don't think he feels well," she chafed, "He acts more upset all the time. Maybe he frets about getting old. Perhaps he is ill. Do you think we should consult Eryximachos?"

Her fears were contagious. "What would we do if he died?" Xanthippe wondered aloud.

"Don't ever say things like that! It invites the Furies!" Nikandra made a sign to ward off whatever malign spirits might be lurking in the vicinity.

"Oh, Mama stop it! You'll have all of us jumping out of our skins!" With that Xanthippe picked up a meal bowl and hurled it across the room enjoying the sound of its crash.

"Displays of anger are offensive to the gods."

"Then Papa must be in trouble with them all the time!"

"Look at him," Nikandra appealed to Phyllys, "out there trying to get Elefterous to help break that crazy colt."

"Leave him be," Phyllys counseled. "He knows as well as we so that the law of Athens must be obeyed and, for now at least, Pericles is the law of Athens. When the time comes we'll move. What else can we do?"

*   *   *   *

Morosely Palen surveyed his small empire and scowled. This place was his life's blood and, by the gods, he would never take another chance of leaving it to the whims of a gang of no- good, greedy Spartans! It would be like tempting the Erinyes. No! He was not going to knuckle under to Pericles again.

The Archon's maneuver had interrupted a going business. It would be a long time before any money started coming in again. A whole week had passed with no one coming to race the chariot. Nor had anyone inquired if he had a foal. If they had his answer would have had to be "No."

What he desperately needed was another brood mare, but the army had them now. He might have to depend on Gryllus again, this time to try buying back some of his own stock. Which would make him doubly beholden to his friend.

A worse thought struck. What if Nikandra were right and the Spartans came and killed his sons! It would spell the end of an honorable family line and a heritage entrusted to him.

No one, not even his mother, had any notion of the weight it cast on a person to be the sole support of a family, to say nothing of other obligations he might have incurred along the way. Things had also gotten to the place where a man could not depend on people, Anytus and his broken promise for example. Nothing turned out the way it should these days, including the task of teaching three mule-headed children how to behave.

"Get a better hold on that line or he'll run away with you!" Palen bawled watching the young stallion buck, rear and pull as Elefterous strained at the lunge line.

"Whoa! Steady, you damned fool, or down you go!" he yelled at the colt. "What are you doing here?" he asked, seeing Xanthippe standing at the fence. "Look at that crazy colt! I tell you, there's one thing that anyone who goes into this business has to learn. Never let yourself fall in love with a horse. If you have one you can't control, sell it."

"That also applies to daughters, doesn't it?" she asked.

"The same thing applies. Hold your tongue and go back into the house!"

"I was told to inform you that the noon day meal is on the table."

"Go!"

"Wouldn't you like to come back up to the kitchen court and throw more hot soup on me?" she asked, anger replacing fear.

He could see the snake, coiled and leering on her arm. Hers was the first articulated reference to it but the episode itself had never ceased to simmer beneath their spoken words.

The set of her head had an artless elegance and its long orange cataract of hair swirled across her shoulders. At the sight of her nubile breasts beneath a light tunic, Palen felt an unwelcome surge of desire. "Zeus!" He brushed the ugly fancy from his mind before it could lodge there.

Shutting her eyes tightly she turned and walked briskly up the path, muttering to herself. "I won't cry, I will not cry."

"The way Papa yells at Elefterous he can probably be heard all the way to the house of Lysicles", Xanthippe said grimly.

"Oh, the gods forbid!" Nikandra shuddered.

"When he carries on like that I almost hate him"

"Don't say such things! Your father is upset because business has been bad ever since we got home"

"Must you always make excuses for him? He's been around horses so much he thinks he is one. He doesn't need a wife. He needs a stableman to give him his fodder, clean his stall, put fresh hay in it, and scrub him when he gets filthy. Oh and yes, to let him have his way with a mare when she's in heat! You and Elefterous should stand up to him. Anger is the only language he understands. He thinks he's a god and you treat him as if he were!"

Xanthippe was beginning to feel a kinship with the forlorn lad whose eyes no longer sparkled with mischief. After all, he hadn't asked to be Palen's firstborn son anymore than she had elected to be a girl. She had often seen her brother's lips tighten into an anxious grimace to keep them from quivering when their father upbraided him, a mannerism which only served to rile Palen all the more because it looked like a grin. "Wipe that smirk off your face!" he would snarl. "Or do you think what I have to say is funny?"

They were at it again. "When your sister was four she rode better than you do at twelve. And she was nothing but a girl. By the gods she could out ride, out think and out smart you and Marc combined!"

"Then why not teach her how to run the farm instead of me?"

"That's the last smart talk I'm going to tolerate from you."

A dull thwack was heard to accompany Palen's threat. Clearly a blow had been struck, and the wrath in his voice accelerated as the audible conflict worsened.

"His anger just grows until he loses control," Phyllys murmured, coming to the back of the house from the loom room, where she too had been overhearing the altercation.

There was an outcry from Elefterous as the sounds of a beating continued.

"No crying! Take your punishment like a man do you hear?" Palen's voice was tight and strained.

Phyllys made a move toward the paddock but Xanthippe was already ahead of her. Propelled by outrage she dashed to where her brother lay motionless on the ground, his face and eyes bruised, his toga torn and, everywhere on his person, visible marks of the pummeling he'd just undergone.

Seizing a whip used for breaking colts Xanthippe thrashed it snake-like, cutting the air with a hiss, and landing it with a snap at her father's feet.

Slowly the glazed look of wildness left his eyes as he stared at her accusing face. Breathing hard he walked away.

It was Nikandra who summoned Andokides to help her carry Elefterous into the house and insisted on bathing and dressing his lacerations herself. This accomplished she brought broth as he lay listless and apathetic on his pallet and persuaded him to taste it.

When Palen came back to the house his face was ashen and his eyes had a haunted look. Without a word he vanished into his room and did not emerge until the next morning. Then, after a brief conference with Andokides in the barn, he saddled his horse, and rode off across the field, and failed to return for supper that night.

The tension was becoming unendurable when, after ten days he returned. Obviously, somewhere, he had trimmed his beard. Also, his face looked less haggard, as if, wherever he had been, and whatever he'd done, he had come to grips with his wrath. Without explaining his absence he silently accepted the food and wine Nikandra offered him.

Palen looked up when Elefterous, still lacerated and bruised, shuffled into the kitchen court. Then, without a word, he pushed his meal aside and strode off to the barn.

Although verbally the ugly episode was a closed matter, it continued to hang in the atmosphere like a malevolent fog, Then, ever so gradually, life resumed a more normal tenor and, after a time, it almost seemed that nothing was amiss.

Chapter Twenty-six

It was in the month of Elahebolian that the Spartans marched back to Attica. Again refugee farmers poured through the Great Walls, this time to find the housing situation worse than before. Temporarily subdued by his fracas with Elefterous, Palen had allowed himself to be persuaded by Phyllys and Nikandra that, if for no other reason than the safety of his sons, he too should return, with his family to Athens.

Gryllus had been away marshalling troops to defend Piraeus when his wife turned their second town house over to relatives from Erchia which left Palen to seek lodgings elsewhere.

"Could we ask one of your relatives to help us?" Nikandra asked hopefully.

"We are not that intimate with any of them," was the succinct reply.

The sorry little dwelling he finally did manage to turn up had a courtyard that also served as kitchen. Juxtaposed were two small smelly bedrooms. Nikandra and Palen took the larger. Xanthippe and Phyllys shared the other. Elefterous, Marc and the slaves were relegated to a patch of yard behind the house. Their shelter consisted of two makeshift tents, one for Melissa, Andokides and their daughter, Pausimache. The other was for the boys. Fortunately it seldom rained in summertime but, it was decided, if it did they could all come indoors and sleep wherever they found space on the floor.

"I never dreamed that someday I'd live in such a hovel," Nikandra groaned. "It's even smaller than the place in which I grew up. I hope no one we know sees us here."

"It was your idea to move back to Athens. Are you expecting guests, or planning a symposium?" Palen asked sarcastically.

Mortified by the modesty of their new abode, Xanthippe made no attempt to get in touch with her wealthy friend. It was Hipparete who learned they were back in town and made it her business to find them. When she did she invited the women to come for a noonday meal, and their outlook brightened.

* * * *

"How good of you to come!" Elpinice greeted them a few days later when they arrived. "Callias hopes to join us later, she said as they gathered around the table. "With Hipponicus and Alcibiades off to war again he enjoys being the lone rooster in a house full of hens. Iodice looked forward to seeing you but she was sick all night and is still so miserable I insisted that she stay in bed.

How are you faring now that Pericles has brought you back into the security of the Great Walls?" she asked.

"We're having a lovely time!" Nikandra gushed. "I'm always happy here in town . . . although this year supplies are slower coming in from Piraeus than they were, and we are . . . less comfortable," she appended, catching sight of a quizzical look on her mother-in-law's face.

"How do you feel about it, Phyllys?"

"Lives were saved last summer so I can't fault the Arcon's edict," Phyllys replied. "But like most farm woman I'm happier when I have a patch of herbs to fuss over."

"It's time for me to nurse my little one," Hipparete said when she and the others finished eating. "I'll have him brought to me here"

"This has been a happy occasion and I wish we could stay," Phyllys said,when the baby had been duly praised. "But it might be wiser for us to go now and escape the Sun God's rays before they get any hotter. Tell Iodice we missed seeing her and hope she will recover quickly."

"Thank you very much for inviting us," Nikandra said, rising reluctantly. After this it would be hard to go back and face that nasty little bake oven of a house.

They had less than a mile to walk but the intense heat made the distance endless. Others seemed to be affected too. Instead of exchanging salutations in passing, they trudged the narrow streets in silence, looking downcast and wan.

* * * *

Day by day the stifling heat continued, without so much as a breeze from the sea coming through the massive Walls. Reports were spread about people being stricken with onslaughts of sneezing and vomiting. The woman next door stopped in to borrow some meal and said her husband had become so weakened with loose bowel discharge that he could no longer stand up. She looked sick too, and her breath was so fetid that the smell of it lingered after she left. Two days later her husband was dead, and within the week so was she.

Others succumbed and rumors spread that the Spartans had poisoned Athens' underground water ducts!

The next news to circulate was more terrifying yet! PLAGUE!

The prophetess Diotima's prediction had come true. Apparently her years of prayer, instead of cancelling the inevitable, had only served to postpone it.

Palen went to the Agora to buy supplies and garner news. "The place is half empty, and there's a scarcity of food." he said upon his return. "Everyone is alarmed. One fellow told me people are dying faster than they can be buried. Eryximachos is running his head off but neither a physician nor anyone else seem able to do anything. I heard, but don't altogether believe that Socrates has some sort of 'healing power'. When he puts a hand on the sick, some of them recover. They also say he can ease the others who die. He must think he's Hermes!"

On trips to the well neighbors whispered stories about people who had gone blind, lost fingers, toes, even memory. Some of the afflicted were consumed by raging fevers so fierce that even a light linen coverlet was intolerable, and death came as a relief. Agonized by unquenchable thirst several had thrown themselves headlong into cisterns.

"Lysicles would have been better off staying in Cholargus, and so would we," Palen muttered when the report came that the sheepherder's wife had died. Every day the situation worsened and although their tiny house was like an inferno, even the stalwart Phyllys was afraid to go abroad on the streets.

"I can't stand it in here another minute," Xanthippe gasped pushing back a sweaty mop of hair. "Please, Mama, let me take a few coins to the Agora and buy some grapes, if I can find any."

"No. It's too dangerous. By now we know that anyone can get the plague just by being near persons who already have it."

Nonetheless, when Elefterous and Marc were playing a desultory game of five stones in the back yard, and the others, succumbing to fatigue, were asleep Xanthippe slipped out.

What she saw, walking through the streets of Athens, was more hideous than any nightmare she had ever known. Even so she could not avert her eyes. Persons with pustules and ulcers on their flesh shuffled by until, horror of horrors, she came upon a scene so gruesome she gagged. A pile of reeking swollen corpses, too numerous for consecrated interment, had been consigned to an unholy conflagration in the street, their lifeless limbs dancing in the flames. When she could move again she hastened back to the little house which, after what she had just witnessed, looked like a haven.

Pericles' sister Ariphon expired. Xanthippus, his eldest son was next. He handled his sorrow with customary dignity, but when his second son succumbed, and he was placing a wreath on the boy's grave, Pericles broke down and wept bitterly in front of everyone!

"Unthinkable," Palen said, "for Pericles to lose control!"

"There is no plague in Sparta," people said. "What has Athens done to offend the gods? Have we been too proud? Too powerful?"

Many who had enjoyed Pericles' largesse and praised him for 'caressing' the masses were the first to denounce him. It was he who made Athens great, yet it may well be that it was also he who had provoked the gods' wrath," they opined.

"Stop riling yourselves with dissensions and complaints! Save your energy for fighting the enemy," Pericles pleaded. "We dare not lose to Sparta".

His advice went unheeded. Unable to calm the volatile populace he was brought to trial, even accused of stealing from the Treasury!

"Ridiculous!" Palen spat contemptuously. "Power may have addled his wits but no one can convince me he ever stole so much as a sugar cake in his entire life!"

In the general madness he was found guilty. Three months later when Athenians returned to their senses and repented their folly, they restored everything and made him Ruler again.

With each passing day the city became more unnerved.

"We're getting out of here." Palen said tersely when it was learned that Spartan invaders, more terrified of plague than warfare, were taking flight."

There were no objections.

"What is it?" Phyllys asked

Melissa, in the midst of frantic packing was sitting on a mound of bedcovers looking dazed.

"I hurt," the slave whimpered, peering up from her task with red irritated eyes. "Thenk des gods wu'll soon been home." Her face contorted and she fled. When the others heard her retching they paled.

"That's how it starts!" Nikandra gasped, grabbing Phyllys by the arm.

Three days later Melissa was gone. "We must tekk her wiff us," Andokides said firmly when he had salted and embalmed his wife's body and wrapped it in a coverlet. No one had the heart to deny him so he placed it in the cart which held their baggage and possessions.

"If a guard tries to stop us from passing through the gates I'll run him down! I told you women that we were crazy to leave Cholargus!" However there were no guards around to stay them when he stormed through the gates.

"Mama," Pausimache whimpered all the way home. "Mama . . . Mama"

It seemed forever until at last, they reached their destination, only to discover that this time the Spartans had found the farm. The fields were burned, the barn half gone. But the old stone house stood intact and even an Olympian tower could never have looked better to its resident gods.

"If we had stayed here we'd all be dead", Nikandra said tearfully.

"We stayed in Athens and one of us already is" Palen retorted. "My god, what a mess. I don't know where to begin."

His decision was made for him by the rigid figure that had accompanied them back to the farm and still lay, bound and embalmed on top of the second cart. "I guess we had better start with that," he said.

While they were standing at Melissa's grave in the ash-grove, Xanthippe looked at her surroundings. The plague, and the Spartans' violation of this place, made her feel as if the girl who had walked in the woods with Cerberus, and made love beneath yon hollow tree had been erased.

* * * *

By autumn one third of the population had perished. The city was overwhelmed with corpses and the stench of them was intolerable. The general consensus was that the disease had been brought into Piraeus by

Egyptian monkeys and carried directly through the Great Walls into Athens.

As if there had not been suffering enough, farms were still being overrun by a few Spartan land troops that had chosen not to leave.

It was too late for the Archon to do anything further. Broken, more than anything, by the malediction against his honesty, he too became a victim of the plague.

* * * *

Phyllys had been bending over her garden for so long her back ached. With a sigh she stood up, stretched, and watched Palen coming toward her on the white salt path. Once again the few horses that he had been able to ship to Euboea were still alive but less healthy than they had been when they went. With winter coming, he'd been working like a man possessed to get new stalls built in what was left of the barn.

"Have something to eat and rest awhile," she called, noting how weary he looked. "Your face is flushed." When he came abreast of her she reached up to touch his face and her eyes dilated with fear. "Palen! You have fever!"

"Mother!" He started to answer but collapsed instead at her feet.

"Andokides! Help me! Help! Come quickly!" she cried.

The plague had accompanied them to Cholargus. This time it was Phyllys who remained at her son's side except to go for more fresh cool cloths and bring healing herbs and broths.

"I'm the one who should be with him," Nikandra insisted when Andokides came out of room carrying pails of the vile matter that Palen discharged.

Phyllys shook her head. "You must stay healthy for the sake of your children and for Palen when he's well again. I'm old. I can afford the risk. You can't. Keep Xanthippe and the boys away from here. Elefterous and Marc can look after Pausimache. Oh how I do miss Melissa!"

"Mother Phyllys, is he going to die? Everyone who gets the plague dies."

"Not if I can help it, may the gods be favorable! Go fix the altar." Phyllys pointed to the flame on its square stone brazier. "Make it bright and inviting for the gods then prepare a barley offering and call on them."

Obediently Nikandra fussed with sacrificial pitchers and bowls. How could she pray? It was Palen who always spoke to the gods about things that really mattered. Nibbling at the inside of her mouth, she trembled and clutched the altar to steady herself. When Xanthippe came up behind her she jumped. "You scared me!" she cried. "Oh I'm so frightened."

"Many people did recover, Mama," Xanthippe reassured her, trying not to give her own fear. "Papa will too."

Wishing she could believe that herself she walked down to the half-old, half-new stable. Papa's work tunic hanging on a peg had come to assume the personality of its owner and actually bore noticeable semblance to his sturdy frame. Even a battered old cone-shaped sun hat carried the defiant tilt of his head. Ever so gently she touched it.

Why could Papa not care for her? Or, if perhaps he did, to show it with a bit of kindness now and then? For no matter how angry he made her she loved him very much. Thoughtfully scratching the snake on her arm she wished there were at least one dependable god to whom a person could turn at times like these.

Again the hideous vision of bodies piled up in the street came to haunt her. It was as if death had become a snake on her mind, coiled, evil, and ready to strike.

Where had all those people gone? She started to shiver and could not stop.

Feeling terribly alone Xanthippe leaned against one of the charred wooden beams that still sustained part of the sagging roof. The weather, matching her mood, was chilly and gray. Sounds of a horse cribbing in its stall grated on her ears while outside the trees soughed and swayed from side to side, sadly, as if shaking their heads.

"Godsname I'm thirsty," she mumbled, conscious of fierce pain in her stomach, and intolerable heat. "Terribly thirsty."

A hound's hoarse voice shredded the gloom and she started back. It was dark outside. She must have been in the stable for a very long time!

The house seemed endlessly remote as, overwhelmed by thirst, she groped her way toward it while strange colors whirled in her head. Upon gaining the courtyard she grabbed a jar from the altar and drained it of wine meant for a god.

"Xanthippe!" The voice seemed to come from afar. Distraught she tried to focus her eyes on her mother's wavering face. Finding it impossible gave up and let darkness engulf her.

An enormous red snake stared from baleful eyes. He lashed about until he caught his tail in his mouth and bit it off. Now there were two snakes who also divided, making four. These continued to multiply until snakes were everywhere, writhing on the wall, hanging from the ceiling, and slithering across the floor. One attacked her and she screamed. Then Artemis appeared followed by Demeter, Persephone and Hades, dread God of the Underworld. After chasing the snakes away the gods dissolved one by one into a single searing light.

* * * *

She awoke wondering how she came to be lying on a pallet in the loom room. Pushing weakly at a coverlet she tried to call out to someone about her thirst, then retched and felt her bowels give way.

Yiayia was there, bending over, changing bedclothes, wiping her face with cool wet cloths and offering her water.

"Everything will be alright," she soothed and administered another cold cloth that grew quickly hot on her granddaughter's feverish forehead.

"Don't go away! Please stay here, Yiayia. I feel so much better when you're with me," Xanthippe reached out to detain her benefactress.

"I'll return soon, I promise," Phyllys patted her tenderly. "Rest, 'kalepai', I'll be back as quickly as possible."

Gratefully Xanthippe looked up, wanting to thank her and say how very beautiful she was. Too tired to form the words, she closed her eyes instead, dozed, awoke, then slept again.

When she opened her eyes Papa was sitting beside her on a chair. He looked different somehow, thinner for one thing, and he was watching her from eyes that were sunk deep into their sockets. On his face was an unfamiliar expression of concern.

"You survived." he said.

"And you! We both had the plague?"

He nodded.

"I remember being in the barn, thinking that I didn't want you to die." she said with a shaky little smile. "I can't recall much of anything after that but Yiayia Phyllys coming with cool cloths for my head, and Mama with broth. Where are they? Where are the boys?"

"Mama and the boys are napping. You have been ill for more than three weeks. You're a stout-hearted girl, 'kokeeno-micro'"

"What about Yiayia Phyllys, is she sleeping too?"

"Yes, she's sleeping too. What I'm trying to say is . . .. Oh god!" Palen swallowed hard and ran his tongue over dry lips. "She's dead," he blurted.

"I don't understand, Papa. I didn't hear what you said." Then it hit her and she doubled up on her pallet.

"Oh no! Don't say such a thing!" she whimpered, "Yiayia Phyllys promised me she'd be back soon. She said, 'I shall return as quickly as possible." Where is she? I don't believe you. She wouldn't leave me! Tell me you lied! Please, Papa . . . PLEASE!" The horror in Xanthippe's eyes gave them a strange cast, like leaves in the sun.

Chapter Twenty-seven

It took a year for the rampaging plague to run its course. Speaking in awed tones of "man's inevitable encounter with King Hades," survivors went on with the business of living.

Xanthippe, still weak from her illness, was having trouble dealing with Phyllys' death. Worse by far than the loss of Cerberus, or the apostasy of Critobolus, was having to go on living without her grandmother's reassuring presence.

Assuredly Yiayia had been sent directly to the Elysian Fields, a celestial realm reserved for the blessed.

Yet even grief can be compounded by anger. Critobolus had made love to her, then married someone else, Papa had sold Iris. But Yiayia was guilty of the ultimate betrayal.

"Rest, Kale-pai, I will return soon," she had promised. Instead she had vanished into the dwelling place of the dead. Perhaps because she wanted to join her beloved husband. However that was small comfort to one who wanted her here.

Phyllys, Elpinice, Callias, all of them up in years yet too young in spirit to be abducted by the God of Death! Nor would Archos ever return as promised, to dramatize glorious tales of life and love.

Melissa? Guiltily Xanthippe retreated from memories of mimicking the slave's accent. Was she serving a new master in the Underworld, or had death released her from slavery?

And Pericles, 'The Olympian'. The intense patriotic devotion he demanded had lasted thirty years but now, in Athens' hour of greatest need, she was without a leader.

"He had the attributes of a god. What will we do without him?" wondered the very same citizens who had so recently reviled him.

So many people, irrevocably gone, along with all those nameless souls whose torched bodies Xanthippe had seen writhing on Athenian streets.

Death! Just thinking about it made her feel as if she were suffocating beneath the earth.

She too had come close to being ferried across the River of Lamentation. Where, in his vague domain would Hades have chosen to put her, a female who had dared to hurl the goddess Artemis against a wall? It would not have been paradise!

General Gryllus, now a widower, came to felicitate Palen on out-smarting Death.

"Clymene lived long enough to see Kallia married, and leave Xenophon old enough to get along without her," he conceded philo-sophically.

"Critobolus has returned, thank the gods. He's going to join his father in the banking business, that is if Sparta can just leave us in peace." he added, thereby answering Xanthippe's unspoken question. Her former lover had survived!

"I persuaded Crito to let the two young ones live in my second house, the one you stayed in. They're settled and comfortable there, at least for now. But I am troubled about Kallia. She looks unwell. Perhaps my wife's death makes me overly sensitive." He sighed heavily.

"Don't think!" Xanthippe told herself fiercely. Critobolus is Kallia's husband. This longing for him must cease.

"I'm going into town to sympathize with Hipparete over the deaths of Elpinice and Callias," she said later, having gathered from Gryllus that Alcibiades was not in Athens.

"You have no business walking so far! You might get sick again!" Nikandra demurred and spread her hands helplessly when, despite her remonstrances, Xanthippe set out.

Though an evil smell still clung to city streets, a stench that not even strong winds from the sea could dispel, stout hearted citizens were making a comeback from catastrophe.

"There goes Palen's old maid daughter. Nice tits but a temper like her father's," someone remarked loud enough for her to hear as she passed by a taverna.

"Stupid fool," she muttered, quickening her steps. In the prosperous section of Athens she slowed her pace to cool wrath still boiling at the man's impudence. 'Palen's old maid daughter'. The truth of it was what hurt the most.

Upon reaching her destination she stopped to catch her breath before pulling the bell.

"What a happy surprise!" Hipparete cried. "I've been terrified ever since I heard you were struck by the plague. But look at you! Not even a mark on your dear face. Come, sit down. You must be exhausted."

Gladly Xanthippe complied and accepted a cup of wine. Her walk into Athens had seemed more arduous than on previous occasions.

"Isn't it remarkable how good friends, who haven't seen each other in months, just take up where they left off? It's as if we'd never been apart!" Hipparete marvelled when, after sharing their sorrow over the death of loved ones, they talked about the horrors of war and plague.

"Plague is worse than war," Xanthippe said.

"I agree. A plague is so close at hand that you're constantly reminded of death. Wars, on the other hand, are usually fought elsewhere so one is less aware of what's happening."

"War killed Grandfather Elefterous but it was plague, not Sparta, that did away with Yiayia Phyllys, your grandparents, and Allys . . . and almost got Papa and me."

"I still can't bear to think of it!" Hipparete's face clouded. "Alcibiades came back alive from Sparta yesterday and has already gone to look for Socrates. I pray he finds him. War, political maneuvering, all of it, has a bad effect on him. Life is never easy is it!"

"What's hard about having everything one could possible want?"

"You sound as if you were scolding me."

"I'm sorry it seemed so," Xanthippe said hastily.

After years without the exchange of a single cross word, they were at odds and she was to blame.

Pretending that nothing had happened, they chatted aimlessly about one thing and another, but the silent sound of Xanthippe's anger hung over them like a shroud.

"Stay," Hipparete urged softly when Xanthippe arose and made as if to leave. "What with your illness, and Great-aunt Phyllys' passing, you've been through a lot. Don't go until we, you, and I are happy just to be together again. Life is too short for anger. You're right. This is a beautiful place. I was wrong to complain."

Mollified, as well as embarrassed, by her uncalled for outburst, Xanthippe sat down again and they talked a bit longer before she returned to Cholargus.

* * * *

"Athenians are becoming degenerate, like athletes who win championships too easily and grow slack," Socrates told a crowd in the marble colonnaded Stoa of Attalos. Many in his audience were young men recently returned from patrol duty.

Palen and Lysicles moved closer to hear what else he had to say and were joined by Crito the banker.

"Is discipline a thing of the past in Athens? And if so is it irretrievable?" asked Hermogenes, the son of Hipponicus

"Have you observed how diligently Athenians still obey umpires in contests and take orders from choir trainers? Or seen the excellent discipline they continue to maintain in their fleets? It seems to indicate that discipline has not been abandoned altogether. Would the laxity you mention perhaps be only a temporary lapse, due to incompetent leaders?"

"Yes," Hermogenes said emphatically.

"Ah! You agree then that although the discipline of Athens has lessened it is not past recovery, providing, we become more thoughtful in choosing those who rule."

"This fellow Socrates doesn't seem to worry about making enemies in high places," Lysicles observed. "He has the courage to speak his mind." He lowered his voice, "It could get him into trouble with Cleon."

In the scramble to succeed Pericles, Cleon, a harsh violent man, became Archon.

To detractors the stink of his tanneries on Pandrossos Street was an extension of his personality. There was little doubt in anyone's mind that he was one of the 'incompetents' to whom Socrates referred.

"Cleon sees eye to eye with Anytus, and Anytus hates Socrates guts. If those two team up he'll be in danger."

"To the underworld with Anytus," Palen said, scowling.

"With those popped out eyes and round belly Socrates could be the goat god. All he needs to complete the likeness is the tail of a horse," Lysicles chuckled.

"Maybe he has one hidden under that dirty old cloak he wears," Palen suggested. "Well look who's here! The old warrior himself! Kalimeera, General!" he saluted Gryllus.

"Permit me to buy a jug of wine," Gryllus said when the crowd began to disperse. "It's good to be with you. I still can't accustom myself to going home and not finding my wife."

Chapter Twenty-eight

Gryllus was there to see the stallion Xanthippe had broken on her wild (and last) ride, an animal that now gave promise of becoming a valuable chariot horse. But before long he and Palen were arguing about the Peloponnesian war.

"We have to credit the Spartans," Gryllus said. "Their officers maintain discipline and by Zeus, their orders are obeyed. You don't see them humoring enlisted men and upstart ephebes who want a say in how to deal with the ranks."

"You're no patriot of Athens! You're beginning to sound as if you secretly favored Sparta all along." Palen shook his fist. With that they began to quarrel so vehemently they almost came to blows.

"When two old friends like you and I come to the edge of violence it isn't hard to understand why anger multiplies until one city pits itself against another. Let's not add to the insanity." Gryllus said.

The dogged snarling of interminable civil war was fraying tempers everywhere. By now battles had broken out as far west as Corcyrya. Aristocrats openly supported Sparta. Democratic merchants and shippers backed Athens. Pro-Athenians massacred noblemen who, in turn, killed commoners. Some army officers, among them Alcibiades, were not sure which side they favored.

"There is death in every form," wrote Thucydides the historian, "fathers slaying sons, men dragged from their homes and murdered, some walled up in the Temple of Dionysius to perish. Something nightmarish is happening in Greece."

Armies rampaged up and down the land with first Sparta, then Athens charging to victory. People feared for their lives. Cities were being destroyed and whole populations swallowed. When a disastrous earthquake rocked Sparta, Athenians viewed the calamity as a sign that the gods were evening the score for the plague. Rampant ugliness and hatreds were themselves like a disease, filtering down to individuals, poisoning their relationships.

"He'll never change," Nikandra thought wearily later that morning when Palen threw his bowl of farina at the wall.

At noon, Xanthippe, weary of strife, packed a meal of cheese and bread when she finished working with Andokides' new wife Leah in the vegetable patch. Hopeful of recapturing some of the peace she had felt in the garden outside the old sanctuary of Aesclepius she wandered irresolutely down the Dionsiou Road.

"I don't believe it!", she gasped, rounding the bend that brought the ancient temple into view.

There he stood, almost as if he'd never left since the day she'd talked with him right on this very spot. How long ago it seemed now!

We meet again!" Socrates called out. "Have you an extra bit of cheese in your basket?" Again Xanthippe had the eerie feeling he had known she'd be there.

"Yes, plenty!" she laughed.

"Do you come here often?"

"You must come here often!"

They both spoke at once, and Xanthippe liked the vibrant sound of his laughter. "Not since the day I came out of that sanctuary and saw you." she said.

"What brought you today?" he inquired.

"I'm not sure. Perhaps I came to see the Sun God dance on the water." she pointed to the distant glitter of the Gulf, shifting from prisms of lapis to emerald and turquoise, and tossing flecks of gold back into the sky. "And you?"

"To be honest, I prefer exploring peoples' minds to digging about in nature's phenomena." With a sweeping gesture Socrates encompassed the panorama of blood red anemones, wild hyacinths and creamy almond blossoms vying for attention all around them "Seas, trees, and country places have less to tell me than men. Yet I must admit to finding this a peaceful spot in which to search my psyche. By that I mean the inner self to which I referred when we dined at the wedding of our friends. You remind me of Clytie," he said when a careless breeze loosened her chignon to free a sweep of orange hair.

"Why?"

"Like you, she loved the Sun God so much she'd sit outdoors, and follow him with her eyes as he rode across the sky until, one day, she turned into a beautiful sunflower."

Putting his finger under Xanthippe's chin he tilted her face upward. "And ever since then, Clytie has faced the sun!"

Only a touch, but with it an odd feeling of warmth and, unlike the tumult Critobolus had evoked, a sense of peace.

"Kalimeera!" An aged black frocked widow greeted them as she stumped by leading a matching black goat.

"Kalimeera!" they called, waving in return.

"I'm hungry," Xanthippe said. Reaching into her basket she withdrew the bread and cheese and divided it with Socrates.

"Efkharisto!" he thanked her. "How pleasant it is to be with you here on Mount Olympus eating food fit for the gods!

"The last time we were together you spoke of love and money as being keys to happiness," he said later, after wiping remnants of their repast from his beard with the back of his hand. "Does that still hold true? With you I mean."

"How can I say? I have no money and although I've been told that love is a god I doubt if there is ..," Xanthippe shrugged and bit her lip. "I'm no longer certain there is such a thing as love."

"Diotima Mantinice, with whom I once studied, believes that love is not a god but a spirit inhabiting the void between man and the gods, thus making the universe a continuum'. On a day such as this I am inclined to agree."

"I never thought of Diotima as one who would say anything like that. All I ever knew about her was that she predicted the plague ten years before it happened," Xanthippe said, regarding her companion with quickening interest. Perhaps Astron was not as abominable as he seemed, or as weak. After all he'd been man enough to defy his father! And for no better reason than to follow a teacher of sophistry!

"My mother and I listened to you in the Agora some time ago. Do you ever tire of talking to crowds? Some people wonder why," She hesitated.

"Go ahead. Some people wonder why . . . ?

"Why you do not follow your father's profession?"

"I don't because for some time now I've known myself to have a peculiar facility for touching the lives of others, Sometimes beneficially, and again only in brief soon to be forgotten encounters. I was also influenced by a friend, Chaerophon, an impetuous young fellow who went to Delphi to consult the Oracle of Apollo and bluntly asked if there were anyone in Athens wiser than Socrates. To my astonishment he tells me that the Sibyl's reply was, 'No, nor in all of Greece."

"You must have been quite pleased."

"Not at all. I was disturbed. 'Why?', I asked myself and, 'How to interpret such a riddle?' For I have no wisdom either great or small. Those, and other matters, instigated my search for meaning in what the Oracle said. What constitutes wisdom? What is true? What is false? At times I want to give it up altogether but my 'daemon' says 'No'. Therefore I continue to delve into the minds of others, all of which precludes working in the shop of my Father. Do I answer your question?"

"I think so . . . Can you tell me who . . . or what . . . is the 'daemon' you mention?"

"I can best describe it as a kind of 'divine inspiration', an inner voice, or spirit, that first manifested when I was a child. When it speaks I become entranced as if, in a way, I were transported to another realm. It does not speak often, and never tells me what I should do, only what I should not. To stay in touch with it I must from time to time be solitary."

"And today I interrupted."

"Oh no! I consider myself a most fortunate fellow to be blessed with the company of a damsel who not only bakes tasty bread but has a fine mind! Meetings, such as this, are the weavings of destiny!" Socrates said, fixing Xanthippe with his great blue eyes, almost as if he were casting a spell. "Once in a very long while comes a moment in time that transcends the ordinary, You have provided me with such a one today. Believe me, Xanthippe, nothing could have been more to my liking than these few hours I've spent with you."

A spectacular sunset was slicing the sky with daggers of flame when, once again, Socrates touched her, ever so lightly, on the shoulder.

"We shall meet again," he said.

* * * *

The following day, Xanthippe was in the loom room, mulling over her unique encounter with Socrates.

What a strange person, not especially likeable, yet . . . Repeatedly she drummed the loom with her foot. Thump, thump, thump . . . thump . . . thump thump . . .

"Stop kicking that thing before you knock it over," Nikandra said irritably. "You're making so much noise I can hardly hear myself think."

"Well, if I have to sit at this loom one more minute I'll probably kick it over on purpose! Please, Mama, don't we need something, anything, from the Agora?"

"I need all sorts of things," Nikandra replied, with a quirky little smile, "Two gold combs, some silk, a lobster. . .,"

"Oh Mama!"

"Unfortunately your father claims we can barely pay the taxes that keep us in this stinking war. May I give you some wine?" Nikandra reached for the jug by her side and poured a dollop for herself.

"No, thank you," Xanthippe shook her head. Apparently Mama's brief burst of levity had been induced by the goblet she held in her hand. "You said something yesterday about needing rice. Surely we still have enough money to buy an orange so we can have a treat. Rizogalo!"

With an acquiescent shrug Nikandra brought out her money pouch. "Are you planning to visit Hipparete?" she asked, doling out a few coins.

The answer was no. With all those rich aristoi friends to occupy her time who'd care to bother herself with a nobody spinster from Cholargus? Games in trees were for little girls. Nor did she wish to take a chance on seeing Kallia, who, like the others, was married and living in a fine home, the one that Gryllus had loaned to Papa a year before the plague.

Once within the city gates, and about to dip her hands in the holy wash basin. she heard someone say, "Xanthippe?"

The voice was Astron's, although she barely recognized him, lurching toward her with an unsteady gait. As he drew nigh, dark pouches, swelling beneath bloodshot eyes, and the sour smell of a taverna, gave evidence that dissipation had made him even uglier than she recalled.

"Kalimeera, Xanthippe. It'sh been a long time," he said.

"Kalimeera, Astron," she replied hesitantly.

"Too bad thingsh did not work out for you and me. It wash my shorrow that led me to the wine jugsh." His speech was slurred and difficult to understand.

"No," he amended, "It wash really my father who drove me to drink. And Alshibiadesh. Alshibiadesh told my father you would be a bad wife. Tha'sh what he did. Told him he knew thingsh about you he could not repeat. What wash it old Alshibiadesh did not tell my father, Shanthippe? Did he get you to play gamesh with him too?" So saying he cupped a hand over her breast and was met by swift retaliation.

"You drunken pig!" she shrieked, striking him a flat blow on the face.

"You haven't losht your shpunk!" He grinned and rubbed his cheek. "I remember you were angry the lasht time I shaw you." A puzzled expression crossed his face. "On the beach! I wash wish Alshibiadesh. Now he wont even shpeak to me."

"By the dog," said one of several passersby who had paused to watch the novel sight of a tall young woman with orange hair hitting a man. "Isn't that Palen's spinster daughter pummeling the son of Anytus?"

"No mistaking her! Weren't they betrothed at one time?"

"So I've heard."

"Oh, po po po! With her for a wife he might not have turned into Athen's town drunk."

"Good thinking! She could have knocked him off a wine barrel with her bare fists."

"Well. . ., " Astron expelled a wine sogged sigh. "It wash nishe to she you again, Zhanthippe." Giving her a bleary wink he turned away and shambled off into the crowd, vanishing as he had that day when she caught a glimpse of him listening to Socrates in the Agora. Apparently both Socrates and Anytus had lost him to Dionysius.

In a daze Xanthippe made her purchases and passed back through the city gates wondering what made people behave as they did. Why, after having had the pluck to defy his father about Socrates, was Astron too weak to stop being a drunken wine bibber? Or, for that matter, what would cause someone like Critobolus to knuckle under to his father?

Stranger still was a woman who kept on loving a man who was as gone from her as if he had died of the plague!

Stop thinking! Walk, don't feel! Step. . . step . . . step . . . That afternoon under the big tree was only a dream.

He is gone . . . he is gone . . . he is gone . . . Like the beat of a pulse her feet marched to the words. To break their gloomy cadence she broke into a run.

"We were just talking about you!" Nikandra exclaimed when Xanthippe entered the courtyard and found Socrates sitting there.

"You're wondering why I am here," he said, rising. "It is because I want to marry you. I came in person to ask for your father's consent because he and I are nearer the same age than he and my father."

"We were discussing money when you came in," said Palen. "I was telling him that, although we are of modest means, your mother and I managed to put aside a decent dowry for you. And I was about to ask him if he can support you and any children you may beget. So, Socrates, will you be working with your father?"

"No. Stonemasonry is not for me. I am a teacher of men."

"I'm told you refuse to accept payment for your lectures."

"My parents are comfortably fixed. Rest assured, Xanthippe and I will have enough to get along, both now and following their departure from this life." Socrates replied equably.

"Allow me to pour you a bit more wine," Nikandra babbled, fearful that her outspoken spouse might extinguish their daughter's last hope for matrimony.

"I'm sure she'd be happy to have an opportunity to live in town near her friends, wouldn't you, Xanthippe?" She cast an arch glance over her shoulder at the stupefied young woman. Wordless with disbelief, Xanthippe failed to respond.

Palen, having come to a decision, gave a short nod, reached for a stylus, and dipped it in blackwash. When the two men had affixed their names to the contract Socrates had brought, they clapped one another's right shoulder. Just that quickly the matter was accomplished.

Socrates re-rolled the document and turned to Xanthippe. "I have felt, for a long time, that we were destined to come together," So saying, he bade them 'Adio' and left.

"What do you suppose he meant by that?" Palen asked when they heard the gate shut. "No wonder they say he's peculiar."

"Phaenerete thought he'd marry Myrto." Nikandra said.

"We may wish he had. I'm not sure which is worse, an unwed daughter or a son-in-law whom people call 'energumen'.

"First you betroth me to him, then you suggest he's insane," Xanthippe fumed. Unless I fling myself into the sea I shall be forced to marry him. What else is there to do? I'm not wanted here. Believe me, I'm as eager to be gone as you are to see me go. At least Socrates, is courteous and kind."

"In that case no one can accuse you of marrying your father," Palen rejoined.

"I have to agree, he is an odd young man. But he has nice friends," Nikandra said, pouring herself a fresh libation. "His mother wanted him to marry Myrto, because of her aristoi grandfather, but I'll wager her dowry doesn't amount to much! Xanthippe is as much an Alcmaonid as Myrto, so Phaenerete has no cause to complain."

"Everyone in Athens is related to either the Alcmaonids, the Philaid clan or both," Palen snorted. "I breed horses with more discretion. And, for the godsake, Nikandra, stop referring to Socrates as a young man. He's at least six years older than you are. I wonder why he hasn't married before. Do you think he prefers men? Or it could be that he has no balls."

"Yegods, Palen!"

"Goodnight" Xanthippe exclaimed, heading for the outdoor stairs.

Yiayia Phyllys had been gone for a long time but her bed still bore a familiar indenture of her body.

In this room she had counseled her granddaughter to pray to Artemis, and to marry for love. What would she say if she were here now?

Reflectively Xanthippe rubbed her forehead. She had not seen Critobolus in three years. Yet despite his marriage to Kallia, she had never been able to conceive being married to anyone else because her body still sang with the memory of his.

She certainly was not in love with Socrates. But they were, at least, acquainted. In a way it might be a relief just to be a wife. He and she would, of course, live with his parents in what was probably a fine home. His father, Sophroniscus, was a popular artisan, and Phaenerete, a tiresome woman to be sure, was, nonetheless, the most sought after midwife in Athens.

Xanthippe herself would emulate Great Aunt Elpinice by inviting men and women to visit in what would be her new courtyard. Dear Archos had gifted her with enough education to hold her own with all the people who came. She could see them now, angling for invitations. Aspasia had been a nobody from Miletus, yet nobles, with their wives attended her 'afternoons'. Probably because she scorned discussions about boar hunts, babies and bed chambers!

With Xanthippe at his side Socrates would not only be the most sought after teacher in Athens, but the richest. To Hades' pits with Critobolus and romance. Wealth and power were what counted. Look at Alcibiades. He was despicable, but he had so much money that all Athens bowed to him. He was one of the many who should be paying huge sums for Socrates' tutelage.

Her husband would teach. She'd handle the rest! Xanthippe smiled to herself. When the money began to roll in she would buy a stallion and a mare from Papa. He, in turn, would be more than impressed when she paid his asking price instead of quibbling over the cost.

"Thanks, Archos, wherever you are for teaching me how to do sums," she whispered into the air.

Chapter Twenty-nine

Whether or not Phaenerete would have preferred Myrto as a daughter-in-law, she was prompt in asking Xanthippe to pay the visit customarily made by young women to the homes of their betrothed's parents.

"I first met Socrates' mother when you were born but I've never been in her house. Perhaps I should go with you," Nikandra volunteered.

"She's twenty one years old. By now she should know how to take care of herself," Palen reminded his wife drily.

Hoping to make a good impression, Xanthippe had chosen a 'peplos' instead of her utilitarian tunic, and the long garment was flapping uncomfortably between her legs as she marched briskly toward town.

"Forget the past with its heartaches and disappointments. Make this marriage work," she told herself, pausing to shake off sprays of dust that swirled up from the road. "If you can survive a plague you can do anything! By the gods," she vowed, "nothing can defeat me! I may be older than most brides, but not too old to make Alcibiades, Papa, and all the rest of them sit up and take note of who I really am!"

Her journey took her to the poor end of Cerameicus Road, Street of the Marble Cutters, in the part of town known as Alopeke. By this time her armpits were soaked. After dabbing at them with the hem of her dress, she gave the gate bell a yank, and waited.

Beyond the nearby marble quarries one could see the Cerameicus Cemetery and And Mount Pentellicus, visible, but looking smaller than it did at home.

She was listening to the 'plink' of chipping chisels that resounded throughout the neighborhood when the gate flung open.

"Ah, here you are!" Phaenerete greeted her. "Come in. Excuse the mess. I'm always too occupied with my profession to keep things from getting tossed around a bit."

One look and Xanthippe knew that her mother was going to be horrified. Although larger than the house in which they had been forced to lIve during that summer of the plague, it was almost as inelegant. Floor, furniture, everything was coated with the grit and dust that sifted in from Sophroniscus' work shop which was attached to the house.

Nor did the dismal courtyard, in any way, fit Xanthippe's plans for profitable afternoons with cultured people. Slabs of limestone and marble leaned against the walls, all of them covered over with an appalling accumulation of filth.

"Too many babies keep me on the go, and when Cleina, the lazy good-for-nothing, doesn't come with me to help at the birthings, she either takes a nap or gossips down by the well. At least she fetches water. Her mother was a good slave, but she's dead and I'm left with her shiftless daughter. We have one other slave, Festus, who works with my husband in the shop.

"I know you're a good cook," she rambled on. "Your grand- mother made the best bread I ever ate, and almond cakes! Ah!" Phaenerete smacked her heavy lips.

* * * *

Energized by fear that something might again forestall the consummation of a wedding, Nikandra had no time to be wondering about Phaenerete's house. Elated by the prospect of marrying off a daughter whose hand no one else had come forth to claim, she was in fervent accord with Socrates' suggestion that the ceremony not be delayed.

"My betrothed and I are both old enough to preclude any need for waiting," he'd said. Godsname, the man didn't cut words! Unfortunately he was right. By the time most women were twenty-one they had children in school!

In constant motion, she transformed the loom room into dressing quarters for the bride, gave orders to Leah, the new wife Palen had found for Andokides, and sallied forth to confront the 'mageiros', a butcher-cook, who prepared and served nuptial feasts.

To most of this Xanthippe was in silent accord. Death itself was preferable to a life dependent on her father's charity! Nor did she give a fig that the affair was scheduled for midsummer in lieu of the the traditional winter month of Gamelion because, at any moment, Socrates might be called upon to serve his country again.

Athens, on the winning side of a war well into its sixth year, showed little interest in Sparta's offer to resume peace negotiations. Like a bad habit, sporadic battles continued, and citizens, emboldened by Cleon's command to "Destroy the enemy," pointed to Athena, thrusting her bronze spear heavenward, and assured themselves that the Empire was indeed, invincible.

*   *   *   *

It was the time of harvest wheat. A blood red sun dawned over Mount Hymettus to cast its Cyclopean eye on Xanthippe's wedding day and, in the Agora, old men tugged their beards and vowed that never in history had a day been so hot.

"Aelous, God of the Winds, must be asleep" they told one another.

Nikandra, impervious to the temperature, wore her shawl and ran, in spasms of excitement, from kitchen to the loom room where her daughter stood naked beside a bath urn, her moist body fragrant with rose oil and ready for dedication.

Facing Mount Olympus, Xanthippe dipped her fingers into holy water from the Springs of Kallirhoe, and scattered the drops in a circle. Then, slowly raising her hands she mumbled ritual prayers to Aphrodite. Her performance was less than half-hearted. How sad to be viewing one's wedding night with dread instead of anticipation, just because of a long ago afternoon in another man's arms. He would be here today with Kallia and Crito, Socrates' choice for groom's man. One of the trouble makers in her life, Hipponicus, was still away at war. However Acibiades, who was steadily climbing to ever higher pinnacles of power, would be on hand to sour the ceremony.

"We're ready for the headress," Hipparete said, through a mouthful of tortoise pins. In view of her on-going advancement in society Xanthippe had hesitated to ask her to serve as the bride's attendant. In a way it had been a surprise when, with evident pleasure, she agreed.

Not deigning to answer, Nikandra reached for the 'peplos' Phyllys had worn on her wedding day, and carefully removed it from two wooden wall pegs. "We're ready to clasp the waist girdle," she said when it had been clasped at the shoulders, and draped.

199

The gown bore a nostalgic fragrance of herbs. Closing her eyes, Xanthippe could almost believe that Yiayia was here in the loom room. "You will wear it yourself someday, Kale-pai" she had said, taking it from a chest and holding it up to show. "No!" Xanthippe reprimanded herself, suddenly engulfed in old but diligently suppressed sorrow. Feelings so unbearable were to be hastily put aside.

"I picked this verbena before sun-up," said Hipparete, placing a dainty green coronet on the bride's vivid tresses.

"Now, Leah, you may bring the veil from that chest,"

"Menelaus of Troy and other well-known Alcmaeonids from the north had hair that color," Nikandra mused.

"Mother! You have said that a thousand times," Xanthippe snapped. Things were bad enough without Mama's chatter!

"They're coming!" Nikandra cried, rushing into the court- yard when the sound of flutes came floating through the window.

"You think I have no ears, woman? Po po po, I'd be happy to call this whole business off," Palen said loudly. "I'm not sure I'm going to enjoy having Socrates for a son-in-law. He's a bigger bag of wind than his mother".

"Hush!" Putting a finger astride her lips Nikandra rolled her eyes meaningfully toward the mageiros who had paused to listen, while running a skewer through the meat. "Do you want to have that spread all over Athens? First you can't wait until Xanthippe gets married, now you complain. And you didn't even have to pay a matchmaker!"

"Skasa!" he spat. "Hold your tongue!"

Clutching her ears against further obscenities Nikandra ran back to the bride's dressing room. "Hurry!" she panted. "You're not ready and they're almost here!"

"Name of God, Mama, you'll have me too upset to know what I'm doing!" Xanthippe gave her veil a jerk. and, at the sound of the gate bell, was seized by an impulse to flee.

"There's nothing to fear, Xanthippe," Hipparete said softly, patting her friend's hand. "I'll start out and all you have to do is walk along behind me."

Calmer now, Xanthippe followed her friend sedately into the court- yard. Amid the conglomerate of poets, dramatists, sophists, statesmen, farmers and wealthy merchants, she caught a glimpse of Myrto in the crowd with her husband, father, and brother, and, in front of her, Kallia and Critobolus!

People had waved from doorways as the groom's wedding procession moved and expanded on the road to Cholargus.

"I thought sure Xanthippe was going to be an old maid," crones said, hiding grins behind their work gnarled hands.

"Her father must have been desperate. Have you seen what she's marrying?" one of them commented.

Wearing a wedding crown of hawthorne leaves, Socrates took Xanthippe by the hand and led her to the family altar. Palen, his face devoid of expression, stood ready to perform the rites. As she stood there facing him, the entire scene seemed like blurry semi-recalled segments of a dream.

Socrates placed a ring, (wrought of solid gold to honor Apollo) on the third finger on the left hand, it being the digit that connects directly to the heart with a fountain of enduring love.

Next Hipparete handed Xanthippe an open pomegranate, the symbol of fertility. But when she crushed its sticky red fruit, and pressed it to her lips, the apocryphal smile of a blind man trembled on her lips. With that the ceremony ended and the newlyweds were showered with grain.

"The gods willing may it soon cool off," Lysicles said noisily, mopping his forehead.

"Do you suppose . . .?" Covert glances went to the bride's flat abdomen as others complained beneath their breath about the unseemliness of a summer wedding.

"No, not that."

"Her mother shivers a lot. Perhaps she chose the date."

The disposition of a daughter called for celebration and Palen had not stinted in providing one. Slaves hired for the occasion hurried about offering wine and there were three musicians to play for the ceremonial dance.

Hot coals glowed beneath a coating of ash on the altar where three sheep kids were roasted, and waiting to be taken from a spit and divested of their sacrificial fat. When the meat, tender and rosy, had been carved, the mageiros announced with a flourish that the wedding repast was ready.

It was Crito who offered the first toast and Xanthippe noticed that his nostrils flared and flattened like his son's. "To you, my beloved Socrates," he said, "and to your bride. May the Immortals allow your married life to be as if you lived in a paradise neither shaken by winds or chilled by snows, with only clear weather spreading cloudless about it and a white radiance stretching above it."

Once again Xanthippe's gaze happened on Critobolus and she

observed that when his father and the rest raised their wine cups aloft his remained still.

"Quiet!" Alcibiades cried. "It is my turn to speak." By slanting his eyes toward Socrates he managed to avoid looking at Xanthippe.

"Forgive me, dear Master, for taking liberties with the prose of your favorite bard," he lisped, " when I say, . . .

'Henceforth never be tender, ev'n to thy wife,
Nor reveal to her the import of aught that thou knowest.
But partly declare it and partly let it be hid.
Yet fear not, Socrates, death at the hands of thy wife
For exceedingly prudent she is and knows what is right'.

"You try to imitate Socrates by speaking in enigmas, do you not, dear Alcibiades," Myrto jested in the uneasy stir that followed.

Even on my wedding day, Xanthippe thought, gritting her teeth. "Fear not death at the hands of thy wife." Socrates had nothing to fear from her but it would be a pleasure to run a sword through his friend's belly!

The Sun God was descending and, as a return trip to Athens was yet to be made, the wedding dances were short lived. Tapping their stomachs appreciatively, guests congratulated Palen on giving his daughter a noble send-off.

"I shall miss you," Nikandra said. She looked worn, now that the long anticipated event was drawing to a close, and, to Xanthippe's surprise, her eyes were brimming with tears

"I will miss you, Mama," she replied.

All that Palen found to say was "Good wishes." Yet he did not appear to be entirely happy even though a spinster daughter had been taken off his hands. Something about the look on his face reminded her of the time she had awakened from plague to find him sitting by her pallet. An unbidden lump invaded her throat. Not trusting herself to speak, she sought her brothers.

Marc, who loved a party, was all smiles. Elefterous, thin and solemn faced since returning recently from his first army duty said, "I'll visit you in Athens, 'Tippy'". Then, to their mutual astonishment, she embraced him. "Please do, Elefterous. We might finally get to know each other!" she said.

Socrates assisted his bride into an ancient mule-drawn cart and they set off with a jolt. Alcibiades galloped at full speed ahead in a racing chariot, while Hipparete followed at a more leisurely pace with he others in a caravan of carriages and carts.

Looking back Xanthippe could see her family, as well as Andokides, Leah and Pausimache, framed in the courtyard gate, waving and waving.

For awhile she remained thus, her face turned back to Cholargus and her body facing Athens, half hoping this was a dream from which she would soon awaken.

Tall cadaverous Chaerophon, the one who'd been told by the Oracle that Socrates was the wisest man in Greece, strummed a few chords on his cithara and began to sing. "A little while we tarry on the earth. Then we are yours forever and forever this dark kingdom." He crooned the song of Orpheus who risked all for love by descending into the Underworld and beguiling Hades, with music, into allowing the lovely Eurydice to leave.

"I seek one who died too soon. The bud was plucked ere the flower bloomed. Love is too strong a god."

Like Alcibiades' toast, Chaerophon's selection seemed oddly inappropriate for a person's wedding night. It appeared that some of Socrates' friends were as strange as he himself was reputed to be.

"See, I ask a little thing, only that you will lend, not give her to me. She can be yours when her life's span is full."

Before long all of them were chanting the refrain. "Love is too strong a god, . . . love is too strong a god . . ."

Cholargus had long since receded from view but Xanthippe could not resist the temptation to turn around once more. And there, coming along directly behind them were Critobolus and Kallia. Catching her breath she quickly faced forward again.

"Magnificent, Chaerephon! Thank you! Socrates called to his friend. "You, like Orpheus, could 'draw iron tears down Pluto's cheek and make Hell grant what love doth seek!'"

Heat still shimmered and bounced from city walls as the wedding party moved through the gates while overhead a rising moon cast its effulgence on the Parthenon, bathing it in light.

Having arrived at the house on Cerameicus Road, friends cheered as Socrates helped Xanthippe from the cart, overturned it, and with a single blow broke its axle to symbolize her separation from girlhood.

Phaenerete tumbled out of the vehicle in which she had returned with Sophroniscus. After bidding the others to enter she sent Cleina to fetch the wine and honey cakes that lay ready for this, the conclusion, of her son's marriage rites.

"I've had enough of Dionysius' bounty for one night," she grunted, and, with a cavernous yawn. "I'm ready for Morpheus".

Xanthippe, momentarily alone, looked across the small courtyard to see the man she had just married surrounded by friends who were besieging him with questions.

"If we adhere strictly to truth, as you suggest, how can we help but incur the ill opinion of others," she heard Critobolus say and pricked up her ears.

"But when we care only about what others think are we any better off than blind men? So which is better, our adherence to wisdom and truth or to public opinion, even that of our own parents and families?"

"Even a blind man can keep his inner eye on truth!" Myrto's brother Aristides declared. "Truly, Socrates, when I stand nearby you I always feel wise and strong. But when we are apart, one from the other, I become myself again, that is to say, weak and dull witted," he added with a self-deprecating little cough.

"It would be a fine thing," Socrates chuckled, "if by touching each other we could make wisdom flow from the emptier to the fuller by a sort of capillary attraction."

"How marvelous it is to watch you cast your spell!" Alcibiades exclaimed. "Marsyas the Satyr contended with Apollo in flute playing but you need no flute, Socrates! You charm by your words! Look at me! I listen to you and my heart beats faster than if I were in a religious frenzy and tears run down my face."

Sophroniscus and Myrto's father Lysimachus were deep in conversation. Phaenerete, overcome with wine and weariness, dozed on a bench. A noisy snore escaped her and she awakened with a start. Guests, puzzled by the unorthodox turn of events glanced about uncertainly, wondering whether to stay or leave.

It's late but he can't seem to break away," Hipparete whispered. "I signalled Alcibiades but he ignores me."

"Socrates appears to forget he's at his own wedding! Have you ever seen a man less concerned with the consummation of a marriage?" asked Myrto. "Look at my brother, standing there as if he had turned to stone. Chaerophon! Sing the Epithalamium. Socrates might get the hint and take you to bed, Xanthippe."

"Yes, Papa-Crito, do that. I want to go home. I don't feel well." Kallia said peevishly.

"Be patient my dear. I'll see what I can do," Crito replied "My friends," he said, breaking into the animated circle, "This is hardly the time for you to be engaging Socrates in debate!"

"Socrates! Forgive us for detaining you from claiming your due!" Hermogenes cried, clapping a hand to his head.

"Put the newlyweds where they belong!" Chaerephon shouted. With a lusty rendition of the wedding hymn, he and the rest led the nuptial pair to their cubicle of a room and shut the door.

"I have a gift for you," Socrates said as the laughter of friends faded in the distance. "Wait. I'll return in a moment."

For awhile Xanthippe was grateful simply to be alone. But after what seemed an interminable time she opened the door and peered out. There stood Socrates, arms folded over his chest, and head cocked as though he were listening to a companion. No one else was there.

At dawn he was still in the courtyard, immobile as one of the statues in his father's shop. Exhausted from her long vigil, the untouched bride sank down on the empty marriage bed and slept without bothering to remove her veil.

Discomfiting dreams assailed her. She was a child again, troubled and confused, standing alone outside of her family home. Through the gate she saw her father on the other side holding it shut. "Go away!" he growled, "We don't want you. You do not belong here. You never have."

"But, Papa, I love you!" she sobbed . . .

* * * *

The sun was high when Xanthippe awoke to find Socrates sitting on the bed still wearing his Hawthorne crown. When he saw she was awake he removed it then lifted her wedding veil and laid it aside.

"We won't be needing these any longer," he said. Then. without further preamble, he took her in his arms. The moment she dreaded had been postponed. Now the reality of her marriage must be faced. Shutting her eyes she tried to blot out the memory of Critobolus.

For a long time Socrates held her close. Then he kissed her. Colder than Athena's statue, she remained in his arms, willing the act to be over quickly.

"Relax, Agape Mou," he whispered, tracing the outline of her face. "We're in no hurry. Allow my caresses to be a foretaste of bliss."

No longer passively waiting for him to be done, Xanthippe felt herself beginning to respond. This would not do. There must be no more such enslavement to any man. Furious at her lack of control she determined all the more not to give in to this unknown force with its power to drive her to madness! It was as if Socrates were transmitting a force so powerful that her involvement with it could no longer be escaped and her body, like a separate entity, came alive again.

Swept along by his overwhelming sensuality she seemed to be drowning in a sea of bliss, only grateful when, at last, he discharged his vitality into her and, spontaneously, she cried out with the impact of her own release.

"You wonder why I stood all night in the courtyard," he said, as she lay, still locked in his arms.

Xanthippe nodded even though, at the moment, she was actually wondering if he had noticed she was not a virgin. If so he made no sign, and she had a feeling that, either way, it would make little difference to this unconventional man.

"My daemon spoke to me last night and as I said, when he does I must listen"

"How can you stand still all night, listening something that isn't there? What did he or it say?"

"Everyone has an 'inner voice', Xanthippe, yet so often, in the company of others, we don't pay attention to it. It is difficult to get beyond a tumult of desires and into a state of quiet where it can be heard. I am still learning how to recognize that still small voice. The message I received last night was a warning not to stray from my chosen destiny."

Xanthippe frowned, and was about to question him further but he drew her close and she soon forgot his weird tale of having been detained by a daemon.

* * * *

The following day was a traditional time for friends to come bearing gifts.

Alcibiades regrets he can't be here too," Hipparete said.

"Those gold wine cups she brought might be the ones he stole from Anytus," Kallia whispered aside to Myrto. "He's just the type to find it amusing that, although Xanthippe didn't get Anytus' son, she has his goblets!"

She and Critobolus had come with a kylix, and Xanthippe's face crimsoned when she saw that it bore an etching of Aphrodite rising from foamy waves. "It is lovely," she said, wondering who chose it and how long she would be able to endure seeing Critobolus at gatherings and speak platitudes.

"His friends are devoted to Socrates," Xanthippe noted as, one after the other, they came, visited, and took their leave.

"I have never allowed myself to be wooed with either money or gifts," Socrates said when everyone left. "These things are all yours, Agape Mou, and rightly so. Now for my gift to the bride," he said, handing her an enormous 'conch' shell.

"Its surface is rough, and its pearly pink inner wall is smooth, but they are both parts of the same shell. When disturbances arise and you find that life with me is 'rough' I hope that this gift from the sea will remind you of our afternoon at the old sanctuary of Asclepius when we were in harmony with each other and the world," he said.

"Where are we going to put all of it?" Phaenerete asked, examining the goblets. "What would anyone want with these?"

Xanthippe smiled to herself. They would be put to use later, filled with wine for Socrates' paying disciples when they came to him here. But first she would have to revamp the courtyard and, godsname, what a job that was going to be!

Chapter Thirty

"No one else can take a place in your heart that already belongs to a particular person or pet. There is always room for another to give you his, or its, unique kind of love." Yiayia Phyllys had said when Cerberus died. In a way those words applied to this marriage.

There had been a time when the mere scent of athlete's massage oil made her weak with passion for Critobolus. She had been positive she would never feel like that with anyone else. Which made Socrates' power to arouse her all he more amazing.

He was also a superb conversationalist!

"What kind of games did you play when you were a boy? Tell me about yourself" she prompted him.

"I was bashful and as homely then as I am now, The girls never looked my way twice. Evidently once was enough!" He grinned. "I didn't mind because I was preoccupied with other matters, like wanting to know the how and why of things.

"I was in love with the world of ideas, so much so that people thought me odd. They still do. I irritated my teachers by asking too many questions and, in my eagerness to learn, I borrowed every book I could lay hands on. One of my Masters, Anaxagoras, also taught Pericles and Archelaus. His big idea was that, beyond our many gods, there is one infinite being, the 'Nous', Maker and Creator of all that exists. Self-ruled, itself by itself, purest, all knowing, omnipresent, having no beginning and no end, he, or 'it' forever creates, evolves, and sets all things, past, present, and future, in order."

"I thought that Chaos and Titan created the world."

"A pleasant little story, useful for the teaching of children. However if one is open-minded and willing to learn he finds Truth concealed like a palimpsest beneath the myth. The one thing I know for sure is how little I really know!"

"Is it our blood, or the air, or something in our heads that causes us to think?"

"Your mind works like a man's even though you are very much a woman." Socrates said, taking Xanthippe in his arms.

"Papa and his friends used to say it was too bad I was born in a female's body because I should have been a boy," she told him, withdrawing from his embrace. "Do you wish I were a boy?"

"Do I behave as one who prefers the body of a man?"

So, for awhile the heady combination of physical love and verbal communication helped to lessen the repugnance she felt for his house. It was when she found she was pregnant that the permanence of marriage became disturbingly real.

Socrates departed early every morning, only to return late at night. His fascination with the abstract seemed to disconnect him from the exigencies of life. To make matters worse his loquacious mother was at home all day long and only stopped talking long enough to pop food into her mouth. It was a welcome relief when her duties as a mid-wife called her away.

* * * *

Like fire from smoldering embers war flamed again when Athens, puffed by victories gained in sporadic fighting, invaded Delium, one hundred stades north of Boetia.

It was when Socrates said, "I must go," that the reality of her own dismal situation struck Xanthippe with even greater force.

"You can't!" she stormed. "Must my entire life be shaped by matters beyond my control?"

"I'm an enlisted man, Agape-Mou."

"I don't care what you are. We have matters that need your attention here at home! Look at our wedding gifts, crammed under a coverlet in the corner of this tiny room! I married you, not your parents! I am also expecting your child!"

"It grieves me to go at such a time," he said soothingly.

"War is a senseless way for supposedly civilized persons to settle their differences. Hopefully the time will come when better methods are devised. I still shudder every time I think of being a young hoplite in Samos and seeing Athenians who had been taken prisoners and branded on the forehead with the sign of Athena, an owl! Yet as one who loves Athens there's nothing for me to do but, to the best of my ability, obey her laws 'til I can help to change them for the better."

She could not dissuade him. The Goddess Lachesis, Disposer of lots and assigner of destinies was clearly not ready to include wealth in hers! Obviously Socrates could not get rich fighting a war miles away from his students.

"How can you support so much metal in summer?" Her voice was distantly polite when he appeared, looking strangely unfamiliar, sheathed from head to foot in bronze armor. His helmet boasted curlicued cheek plates and a guard concealed his bridgeless nose. It would be difficult to bid this face- less apparition 'adio' with either intimacy or compassion.

He remained silent, as if his mind had already moved into battle, leaving his armored body behind for family prayers.

While Sophroniscus made a sacrifice to Athena and in ancient ritual language petitioned the gods to return his son safely, Xanthippe was observing that even Phaenerete's altar had a slapdash look. Fat from previous sacrifices stained its stones and the terra cotta libation bowls were cracked.

The rites ended. Socrates bade his parents farewell, kissed his wife, and clutching his sword and shield departed.

"Morning sickness is all in the mind," Phaenerete stated when Xanthippe threw up. "How would you like to be me, sixty three years old and my only child drawn into another war? So far the gods have delivered him home safely. How long can it go on?" She groaned. "For all we know he may not live to see his son! While you were away word came that Hipponicus died doing battle in Delium."

The memory of his lecherous creeping hands still had the power to consume Xanthippe with rage. Therefore, feeling somewhat insincere she called on Hipparete and offered a few lame words of condolence.

"Father and I did not get along. I never felt . . . close to him," Hipparete said, hesitantly choosing her words. "Perhaps I grieve more just because of that. I think that after the Pericles affair he hated all women . . . even me. It must have been a great blow to his pride, as if my mother had publicly repudiated his manhood. Sometimes I felt sorry for him. At others . . ." Her voice trailed off. "His remains are to be returned so that my brother Callias can perform the rites."

Xanthippe, unable to sympathize with Hipponicus, dead or alive, remained silent.

"Life is sad," Hipparete sighed. "If only we could laugh, the way we did when we were girls. Remember the time we couldn't stop giggling at the Thesmaphoria and had to hide our faces in our hands?"

Nipped by irritation, Xanthippe looked at her friend. How could anyone who lived in luxury, was pampered by slaves and fawned over by friends, call life sad? Hipparete didn't have a clue what it was to live in the wrong end of Athens next to a cemetery. Today however, she carefully 'held her tongue'.

The nursery slave brought little Alcibiades and his baby sister to be admired. After they left another slave came with cakes and wine.

"I'm glad our husbands are near one another," Hipparete said. "Socrates has such a good influence on Alcibiades that I'm grateful for every moment they're together. But I pray he will return to you before your baby comes. Couples should be together on such occasions. Alcibiades was away from me both times." She shrugged. "Nonetheless he was delighted that our first-born was a boy and gave me a rope of gold for my waist because his father's last testament stipulated that he'd get the largest part of his legacy when and if he had a son."

"Well, that's unlikely to happen in my case," Xanthippe said, her voice strained with envy.

* * * *

"You aren't getting enough nourishment," said Phaenerete at supper that evening. "Remember you are eating for two!"

"You could be eating for six,' Xanthippe thought. She had baked enough bread yesterday to last half a week, only to discover, this morning, that her mother-in-law had already crammed the last morsel into her mouth, a mouth that, full or no, poured forth endless sluices of advice. "Drink wine mixed with parsley seed. Massage your abdomen with olive oil. Use more garlic, it is the greatest medicine known to mankind!"

The thought of one more day in this tiny, airless kitchen court was unendurable. The whole house was a cage, over-flowing with soiled cook-pots, piles of dirty laundry, even wedding gifts, unused and shrouded with limestone dust, still sitting where they had been put more than a year ago.

"I'm going to walk to Cholargus and visit my family," Xanthippe said making a swift decision. "I shall stay the night so I am going to leave a pot of lentils on the stove for you and Father-Sophroniscus to eat for supper."

"You have no business walking all that distance, big as you are with child," Phaenerete chided.

Discounting her counsel Xanthippe grabbed a cloak.

"Hurry back, daughter," Sophroniscus said with his kindly smile. "May all the gods bless you".

Socrates' father was a rare human being, always cordial and kind, truly a gentle man.

Glad to shake the dust of Cerameicus Road from her feet, Xanthippe could feel her vexations begin to dissolve in the clear limpid, country air.

"I was just wishing you would come!" Nikandra exclaimed.

Age was not being kind to her. Her large eyes were heavy lidded, the skin on her face seemed to be coming loose from its frame, and the flesh on her arms hung slack.

Palen too seemed glad to see his daughter. "Look who's come calling! Xanthippe!" he said heartily. "That bulge in your belly tells me my first grandson will also arrive any moment! What brings you? How is that crazy man you married?"

"I'm here because you never come to visit me, And my crazy husband is with the troops in Delium." Xanthippe said.

"Good. He'll talk the enemy to death and end the war. You're getting as mouthy as his mother," he said with a grin.

"Here!" Nikandra filled a cup with wine and water and gave it to her daughter. This will taste nice after that long walk from town. It will be good for the baby too. If I had known you were coming I'd have killed a hen.

Xanthippe had almost forgotten how sunny and pleasant the kitchen was with Mama there pouring wine and stirring some- thing on the stove that smelled like food for the gods. "Marc is still at the Academaia. He'll be sorry he missed you," Palen said. "Did you know Elefterous will soon be an ephebe? You wont believe this! He's begun to put his mind on what he's doing when he races the chariot! I'll make a man of that boy if it kills me! Marc has more skill, of course, but, like I always said, when it comes to horsemanship neither one will ever match you."

"Nice to see you, 'Tippy. It's been awhile," Elefterous said, coming in and greeting his sister. Tall for a sixteen year old he had his mother's slim frame, large brown eyes and the tentatively hopeful smile of a blind man.

"I hear you'll soon be leaving", Xanthippe said.

"Yes, the army's getting a piece of luck," Elefterous answered wryly. I shall hate every moment of it!"

When all four of them sat down together for the noon-day meal, Xanthippe could not recall having been so content in a very long time. Mama's food tasted better than ever, perhaps in part, because she herself had not been the one to prepare it. How quickly one's viewpoint can change!

"Time to get back to work, Elefterous," Palen said when they finished eating. "Come down to the paddock and see the weanlings before you go, Xanthippe. We have two."

Leah, Andokides and Pausimache came in to ladle up their own bowls of stew and, after Xanthippe had exclaimed over how their little Pausimache had grown, she and Nikandra settled themselves in the courtyard.

"I think about you every time I light the little lamp you gave me on Marc's Day of Recognition, the one that was yours as a girl," she said, folding her hands over the growing protuberance beneath her heart. How nice it would be to have a baby girl. There were things she'd do differently than Mama had. For one thing she and her daughter would be friends from the start. This one should be a son for Socrates. Then the next time she would have a daughter for herself."

"Do you see Hipparete often, or Kallia and Myrto and the other town girls?" Nikandra asked.

"The house of my husband does not lend itself to guests. None of them would be caught dead in that courtyard even if it is full of tomb-stones". Xanthippe made a wry face. "They visit in their fancy houses. Someday I shall have money too."

"Did you hear about Lysicles and Aspasia?" Nikandra's tired eyes brightened. "A year after his wife, and then Pericles, died of plague he started seeing her. Now that the laws governing foreign women have changed they might even get married! I might even get to meet her! Isn't that exciting! Do you think she'll miss living in the palace? Mother-Phyllys and Phaenerete and I talked about Aspasia the night you were born, just two days after she had her son by the Archon."

"Wait 'til I tell that to my mother-in-law! She always wants to be the first to know what's going on! I'd like to meet Aspasia too, and ask her how she got where she did. What do you think made her take up with a sheep farmer?"

"Maybe she has a good time with him," Nikandra suggested. "You know how jolly and nice Lysicles is."

Xanthippe smiled. How good it was just to sit, quietly basking in this singular sense of well being, knowing that, as time went by, she and her mother had learned how to push aside their shutters of misunderstanding and share precious moments like these.

How much more beautiful the mountains looked, unobscured by marble dust. Why, why do I have to leave?" she lamented to herself. "Why can't this still be my home too?"

It was altogether unfair that a woman must be banished to the house of her husband!

In her heart she knew. Papa was happy to see her. Yet at no time in memory had he ever made a secret of his reluctance to house her permanently. Even so, were a miracle to occur and he did invite them to live on the farm, Socrates, with his avowed distaste for the country, would flatly refuse.

"I worry about Elefterous," Nikandra said. "He tries so desperately to overcome his fear of horses. Papa gets so impatient. He can't believe that not everyone shares his passion for them. He and I seldom see eye to eye. We're very different too." She sighed. "I think the happiest time I ever had was the year before the plague when we lived in Gryllus' town house. Remember?"

"Of course. I'll never forget. Do you remember the time you bought me a sausage at the Agora!"

"Weren't they delicious. They just don't make sausages like that anymore. Tell me, my dear, do you enjoy marriage?"

"I can't actually say. I have a husband who is so much in demand either by his disciples or the Athenian army I see very little of him! I wish you'd come visit me when Papa brings a colt to the Agora show ring. The problem is that if Phaenerete is at home we wont be able to say a word because she never stops talking. With Socrates away so much of the time I've begun to feel more like her servant than his wife."

"Perhaps all women are slaves, " Nikandra said, and looked around, startled by words she had said aloud.

"I'll wager Great-Aunt Elpinice never was! Mama, you look tired. You should have Leah do more of the work. Pausimache looks as if she's old enough to help with the chores too. I wish I had someone like her to give me a hand. Phaenerete's slave is worthless."

"Xanthippe, stay all night", Nikandra said eagerly. "You shouldn't walk so such a distances in your condition."

"That's what Phaenerete said."

"After all the babies she's delivered, she should know.

* * * *

The moon was a misty crescent that night when Xanthippe made her way up the old outside stairway, feeling a little like the lonely child of past years. The difference was that now she was married with a child of her own on the way.

Will I ever fully recover from the pain of losing her?" she wondered, looking over at Phyllys' bed.

She had lowered her increasingly cumbersome body onto her own old pallet and was seeking a comfortable position when a beam of moonlight slanted across the room to cast its light on something small and lustrous in the corner.

Curiosity won over weariness and she hauled herself up again and went to see what it was.

Almost timidly she touched the little object's shiny surface, then took it in her hand. It was the blue eye of Artemis! Somehow that single fragment had escaped her vigorous brooming to remain there on the floor until now.

Her first impulse was to throw it out the window but, as she held the eye indecisively in her palm it began to feel warm and she thrust it in her sack.

She dozed fitfully then wakened. When sleep came it brought an odd dream. She was an actor in the Theater of Dionysius. The drama was about to begin. Members of the chorus, fifty or more, wearing goatskins and masks, emerged from hidden passage-ways to take their places

Naked, she walked to the center of the stage while theater goers waited expectantly on benches that rose, tier upon tier, into infinity. To her horror she could not recall her lines! Worse yet she had no idea what the play was about!

* * * *

It would have been so nice just to stay on in Cholargus until the baby came. But when and if, married daughters visit their parents they are not supposed to stay long.

With that in mind Xanthippe bade Nikandra, Palen, and the boys 'Adio' and departed.

The house in which she lived on Cerameicus Road was as remote from the place where she had grown up as the moon from the earth. So was Hipparete's dwelling place, Xanthippe reflected as she walked back into Athens feeling like a captive who had been sold as a slave in a foreign land.

Chapter Thirty-one

The potter's wife's cousin sent word that he would soon be home. Others in the neighborhood were also comforted by messages sent from loved ones in the battle zone in Delium. As for Socrates, he might as well have gone to the moon. Not a thing had been heard from him since his departure. At least, as long as his name did not appear on the list of casualties posted daily in the Agora, no news could be considered good,

Because so many potential fathers were away at war fewer babies were being born, Phaenerete, finding herself with less to do, was often at home. Feet firmly planted on the floor, knees akimbo, her belly resting between her legs, she abandoned professional tidiness in favor of comfort. Wearing garments that spread like torn horse blankets across her shapeless bulk, she sat, day in, day out, talking tirelessly and repeating herself often.

"If you'd just do as I say and drink a pharmacopsis of fenugreek every day, and take a bit of hiera (sacrificial offering) in castor oil your health would improve." You're too thin! Eat garlic. It's the best tonic known to man!" "Drink wine mixed with parsley seed. Massage your abdomen with olive oil!"

Sophroniscus alleviated his unease by endless chipping and chiseling in the shop. To Xanthippe, hearing the rhythmic clink clink clink of his sculptor's tools, it seemed that, instead of a slab of limestone it was her head being engraved.

Unable to concentrate on the tiny himation she was knitting for her baby Xanthippe put it aside, got up and trod restlessly back and forth across the courtyard. Like an extension of her own discord a loud wail arose from the street and she ran outside to see what was amiss.

"I heard in the Agora, Athens has been disastrously defeated at

Delium!" the potter came running. There were many casualties! I pray your husband was not one of them." he added with a compassionate glance at her swollen belly,"

Grabbed by a massive cramp Xanthippe ran into the house. "Athens has been badly beaten," she told her parents-in-law.

"Just as I said! My son might never live to see his own child!" Phaenerete wailed and wrung her hands.

Another contraction clutched and held Xanthippe in its grip. "I think my labor is starting," she panted.

Phaenerete was instantly alert, her foreboding replaced by the instinctive habits of vocation. "Cleina!" she called, "Warm a distillation of hyssop! Lie down, Xanthippe, I want to see how far you have progressed."

Zealously she set about on stumpy legs to arrange the requisite jugs and potions. These maneuvers were interspersed by the mumbling of ritual prayers and an unremitting stream of chatter. When everything was in readiness she plumped herself onto a chair and continued to talk.

"I often wonder what ever possessed me to get into this business," she sighed. "After Socrates was born, I remained barren so I decided to help other women bring babies into the world. Also, as you know, I hate housework. I prefer the 'confinement' of birthing to being confined in my kitchen-court."

A moan interrupted her narrative and she probed Xanthippe's heaving abdomen. Labor was progressing rapidly "Take long deep breaths. Breathe in . . . hold it . . . Exhale. . . That's right!" she said. "There! The breathing helps, doesn't it! Now, again, in and out with each contraction. "

In the midst of her struggle, Xanthippe felt a dawning respect for her mother-in-law. No longer voluble, Phaenerete was totally engrossed in steering this baby safely through the nativity canal.

The pangs were coming oftener. As if she were one with her torment, Xanthippe was a rock being split asunder. At times she seemed to be floating above her body's power to hurt. Then the torment would return, leaving her drenched with sweat.

"Now!" Phaenerete said, "I think you're far enough along to take a little of this essence of datura stramonium to ease your delivery. 'Ah! You've crowned! Here it comes! . . . Name of god! It looks exactly like you did the night you were born!"

"A girl?" Xanthippe gasped.

"No a boy! Cleina, tell my husband to come see his grandson!"

Deftly Phaenerete severed the cord, swaddled the infant, and placed him in his mother's arms.

He looks like a little old man, Xanthippe thought, gazing at her son's wee wrinkled face and wet wisps of hair, like hers, the color of carrots. Others spoke of the ecstacy one experiences upon the birth of a child. Why then did she not feel more elated?

"What a funny little fellow! His nose is longer than his private part!" Phaenerete laughed. Retrieving the infant she clutched him to her bosom. "Sophroniscus!" she cried as her husband stepped hesitantly over the threshold. "Look! A man-child to carry on the family line, and to pray for us when we go! We'll name him 'Megalious'," she declared while tending to Xanthippe's needs after the baby had been cleaned and placed in his crib basket.

"I'll think about it," said Xanthippe, Actually she had no intention of naming her child 'Megalious' because it happened to have been the name of Sophroniscus' late father.

Xanthippe fancied 'Lamprocles'. That was what Mama had wanted to call Marc when he was born, but she'd been over-ruled. Determined not to be coerced in the same fashion, she brought out a rolled chart. The document, a gift from Hipparete, was much in vogue with young Athenian matrons. Although no one believed for a moment that the Father of Numbers' had ever know of its existence it was called 'the Pythagorean Theory of Names'. Every letter, from Alpha to Omega, was accompanied by a number from one to nine. By connecting each letter in a chosen name with its corresponding numbers, one arrived at a sum detailing the ways in which it would influence the bearer.

"Lamda-three, alpha-seven, mu-four," Xanthippe muttered. The sum of the letters in Lamprocles came to forty-six. Four and six makes ten. "Ten," she read, "is a beneficial number with honors acquired and faith in oneself. Anyone whose name corresponds to ten strives to benefit himself and others."

'Lamprocles' it would be. With such a name her son would be unlikely to spend a lifetime on Cerameicus Road. Definitely not if she had anything to do with it!

Bright owl eyes peered solemnly at her from beneath sprouts of orange fuzz, and, suddenly overwhelmed by love, Xanthippe knew what other mothers meant by 'the miracle of child-birth'.

"Kalimeera, Lamprocles," she whispered to her baby.

Although Phaenerete sulked, Xanthippe stood by her decision, as Papa always did when challenged. But, like mothers and grandmothers everywhere, there was one thing upon which she and her mother-in-law could agree. There ought to be a law against keeping a man in some far away place to fight, perhaps to die, on the day his son is born.

When Lamprocles' maternal grandparents came to see him and Nikandra's shocked disbelief showed plainly on her face. "I did not picture your house looking quite like this," she stammered.

"Oh po po po! He looks like you, Kokeeno," Palen chuckled. Seizing his grandson he hoisted him in the air.

Unlike Nikandra he paid scant attention to his surroundings.

They returned to Cholargus and Hipparete arrived the next day.

"Alcibiades just returned to Athens and I couldn't wait to tell you to stop worrying about Socrates because he too is on his way home." she said. "Now! Where is that baby?"

After assuring Xanthippe, Phaenerete, and Sophroniscus that Lamprocles was, indeed, the most adorable infant in Athens, she had further news about Socrates.

"General Laches had just ordered his men to retreat when Alcibiades, on horseback, caught sight of Socrates strutting along beside Laches. He had his head in the air and was casting those sidelong glances of his at friend and foe alike, just as he does in Athens. The General says Socrates is so valiant in battle that anyone who attacks him is to be pitied, and also that if everyone in the army behaved in like fashion Athen's honor would have been upheld and our dismal defeat would never have occurred. In any event, Alcibiades did not leave Socrates' side until he'd managed to escort him, as well as the General, past enemy lines. He believes it was the gods who gave him that opportunity to, at least in part, repay the debt he owes him for saving his life in Potidaea.

* * * *

Aspen leaves were flying, silver and white against the wind, when Socrates came home. Save for an oblique reference to some meaningful debates he'd enjoyed along the way, he said nothing about why it had taken him so long to return.

Smiling hugely he held Lamprocles in his arms. "You are fortunate. You look like your mother," he said. "Just think! You might have inherited my face!"

At supper he told how the Athenians, with seven thousand hoplites and a thousand cavalrymen handily captured Delium, then lost it again in a surprise attack by Sparta. And almost all of them had fled before General Laches sounded an order for retreat!

"Our defeat was the result of carelessness, poor discipline, and over confidence. But perhaps we can still rejoice because a one year truce is to be signed, one that will give both sides an opportunity to restore themselves.

"Athenians have lost their sense of values," Socrates mused when he and Xanthippe were in their bedchamber preparing to retire. "And I plan to work harder than I ever have to help them rediscover it."

Then, as if he were really seeing her for the first time since his return he said, "Xanthippe, a man should be at his wife's side when she bears him a son. That is where my heart was. With you."

Upon delivering himself of this sentiment he fell asleep.

Now that Socrates had come home again, the first matter to be attended to was a proper 'Day of Recognition' for his son.

"Remember, this house and courtyard will accommodate no more than twenty people at the most, and then only if they stand shoulder to shoulder," Phaenerete warned when the list of guests was being compiled.

"I agree! Let's keep it small," Xanthippe said hastily. People who had never been here before (including her own parents!) would glance down their noses at the house of Sophroniscus. It was to be hoped that in a few more years she would no longer be ashamed of the place in which she lived.

After coercing Cleina into cleaning the courtyard, Xanthippe repaired to the hot little kitchen to stuff grape leaves with pine nuts, and knead dough for the traditional bread. That and whatever else she could think of doing to provide at least the semblance of a feast. She could not help but recall how fortunate Mama had been to be blessed with willing helpers like Phyllys and Melissa when similar celebrations marked the advent of Elefterous and Marc.

But, since that was not the case here, it was up to her to make what preparations she could and leave the rest to the gods. Except that, as far as she was concerned, there were no gods. Or if they did exist somewhere high on Mt. Olympus, their list of concerns did not include doing nice things for mortals.

* * * *

Xanthippe had begun to despair. It was Lamprocles Day of Recognition. Family members and friends were crammed into the courtyard. Only one person was missing . . . Socrates!

Fortunately it was not too much longer before he appeared and the ceremony proceeded without further impediment.

"I have, here in my arms, a baby boy," Socrates said, when the traditional rites of presentation to the gods had been completed. "An infant to be sure, but it is to him, my first- born son, and to your sons, and to all the members of their generation, that we will one day entrust the destiny of Athens.

"Having recently returned from our disaster in Delium, I am filled with foreboding. Athens is the finest and brightest city-state in the world. However I am deeply concerned about her future. In years to come she may not be as lovely as she was when you and I were blessed to be given our citizenship just for being born in a place where dreams can be realized. A place where even a slave can earn money to buy his freedom.

"Our late Archon, Pericles, was blamed for problems that began long before he was born. Could it be that, many years ago, too many Athenians had already become so swollen with pride and mad for money and power that they threw discretion to the winds until now we are finally forced to face economic failure, loss of nerve, even of belief in our country's foundations?

We might say that a democracy has a thirst for liberty but gets worthless butlers to preside over its wine. When it has drunk too much of liberty's heady draught, and these so called butlers, or rulers, are not obliging, and refuse to provide more and more liberty, the people call them blackguards and chastise them.

"Soon the rulers begin to behave like subjects, and the subjects like rulers. It's so insidious a thing that the pattern even creeps into private homes. The father gets into a habit of behaving like the son and fears his children. The son behaves like the father and fails to honor his parents. 'Must have more liberty,' the boy says. The teacher fears his pupil and plays toady. Pupils scorn teachers. Old men give way to the young and are all complaisance, wriggling and behaving like young men themselves so as not to be thought disagreeable or dictatorial. By then no one knows who's in charge and a tyranny results.

I can not contain my passion for wanting to do all that is humanly possible to insure Lamprocles and his peers the wonder of living in Athens as we have been privileged to know it.

I hope to begin right here at home by encouraging my son to love books because they provide images of the world in which everything has a secret that is unlike what it seems, and in which man himself is an image of the gods.

My dear friends and relatives, I've given you a rather lengthy harangue. I have said enough, perhaps more than enough for now. Let us spill some wine into our cups and shout a loud 'Yiasus,' not just as a toast to our newly recognized son but to his entire generation and to our beloved Athens!"

Chapter Thirty-two

"Should I be flattered or fearful?" Socrates asked cheerfully.

"Who knows? I don't trust him," Xanthippe muttered. "He made a fool of Euripides in 'The Acharnians'. Soon he'll have every- one howling at your expense."

"If he makes sport of me, as he did with Euripides' mother for being a vegetable peddler, I'll make him sorry," Phaenerete exclaimed, rearing her head. "Such a snob that man is!"

Aristophanes is my friend," Socrates countered. "He won't hurt me, nor can he, regardless of what he writes since I am altogether indifferent to public opinion."

Xanthippe's first encounter with the work of Aristophanes was the summer she and Hipparete had enjoyed the comical short piece he'd written to follow a major drama at the Theater of Dionysius. Today he was the recipient of two first prizes for plays that poked fun at the great and one of Athens' most promising playwrights,

Now word was out that his new vehicle, 'The Clouds' would parody Socrates, whose familiar bare-foot figure made an ideal target for a satirist to whom nothing was sacrosanct.

Leaving Lamprocles in Cleina's dubious care, he and his family walked from Cerameicus Road to the southeast slope of the Acropolis where Pericles had envisioned, and then materialized his glorious theater. From the throngs pouring into it one might think that everyone in Athens had come for the Spring Drama.

Xanthippe, with Phaenerete puffing along behind, climbed to the women's section, seated herself, and, fingered her gold loop earrings, uneasily wondering what the afternoon held in store.

An impressive array of dignitaries and priests occupied glittering thrones arranged around the nadir of seventy-eight rows that rose from a round stage in the center of the vast bowl. But, huge as it was, a mere whisper was audible even from the top tier.

Socrates, with his father, ten rows down in the men's section had chosen to wear the threadbare himation that, in spite of frequent launderings, still managed to look tatty and soiled. This on a night when as the butt of Aristophanes' wicked wit he would be the cynosure of all eyes! Already other theater goers were glancing his way and snickering behind cupped hands.

Silently Xanthippe vowed to weave a new garment for him even if it took her six months. What hope would any man who dressed in such a fashion have of garnering large sums for teaching others?

A rustle of anticipation stirred through the crowd as members of the chorus filed in costumed as clouds and took their places on a stage set to resemble an Athenian Street.

An actor masked as an elderly farmer and another as his son lay snoring on cots in front of a little town house in which, the chorus explained, war had compelled them to take residence.

"Look at him," the farmer cried, pointing at the youth. "That precious playboy son of mine sleeping like a log and farting under five fat blankets! All right, if that's the way you want it, I shall snuggle down and fart you back a burst or two! DAMN! I'm so bitten up by blasted bedbuggering debts,bills,and stable fees from his overspending on horses I can not catch a wink!"

"YOU!" he berated his 'son', "Yes you and your damned horses! Gigs, rigs, nags, ponytails. Hell, horses everywhere! Horses in your dreams! But me, I am bankrupt!"

So far this was fun, Xanthippe thought, laughing harder than she had in a long time.

"That is an academaia," said the old man, pointing to an open classroom next door in front of which stood a sign identifying it as 'THE THINKERY'. "That place is owned and run by a fellow named Socrates. He's a teacher who claims to know a sure way to twist words and win lawsuits guaranteed to keep anyone out of debtor's prison. By the dog I'm going to send you there!"

"I won't go. You can't make me!" replied the son.

"I may be down but not for long. I'll say a small prayer to the gods and, since you won't enroll I will. Instead of dawdling here any longer, I shall go to the Thinkery myself and bang on the door," the old man retorted.

"Go bang yourself!" came a shout from the 'Thinkery' where an actor, obviously cast as Chaerophon, was teaching his 'students' how to measure the jump of a flea.

Above him, in a big basket, suspended from the ceiling, sat a man masked as Socrates. As the basket was being lowered to the stage he shouted to the farmer, "I give my promise to transform you into the perfect flower of orators."

Along with everyone from peers to peasants, Phaenerete, forgetting that he was impersonating her son, roared with laughter.

"Rise and soar while far below earth and shining harvest lie" sang the chorus.

"It is the Clouds, not Zeus who make rain," exclaimed the pseudo-Socrates stepping out of his basket. "First think of the tiny fart your intestines make, then consider the heavens, their infinite farting is thunder, for thunder and farting are, in principle, one and the same."

Now the farmer's son decided that he too would enroll in 'The Thinkery'. "You must learn to think for yourself," his teacher said, whereupon the youth went home and thrashed his father.

"Socrates tells me there's a pecking order between fathers and sons as well as rooster," he lisped.

Slowly it was dawning on the audience, a realization that it was not only Socrates whom Aristophanes wished to satirize. The farmer's profligate son, this spender and lover of horses, the man of untamed habits who spoke with a lisp, was Alcibiades!

"If you wish to imitate roosters why don't you go eat, sleep, and shit on a perch?" the enraged farmer cried as he set fire to the Thinkery. Its teachers ran from the flames, the 'headmaster' fell into fits of coughing, and the felons were caught, beaten, and served with a summons, Meanwhile, in a noteworthy display of pyrotechnics, the 'Thinkery's' walls collapsed in blazing ruins.

When the farce ended, Socrates, with cool equanimity, got to his feet and made a comical grimace, as if to prove he was as ugly as the actor's mask, Good naturedly he returned the jibes and jests that came his way (including some that were markedly caustic) and took a bow. Then, with his wife, glowering at his side, and his parents walking rigidly behind, he departed.

Hotly conscious of the contemptuous glances and patronizing looks, being cast their way, Xanthippe was fuming about the malice in Aristophanes' so-called 'wit'. Hilarious as 'The Clouds' may have been. it was too maliciously distorted to be disclaimed as mere 'caricature'.

That sly parody of Socrates had been enough to persuade anyone that he was a lying deviate who took money to pervert the young. Nor could the inference that he was impious, and a dangerous lying meddler be dismissed.

She pulled a coverlet over Lamprocles and crawled into bed. Following their marriage Socrates had told her that he did not hold with separate quarters for husbands and wives. She, in turn, had tactfully refrained from saying that in a household with only two bedrooms there seemed little else to do. But by now it seemed like a farce that he came to bed with her at all. However, tonight, when he kissed her cheek, bade her 'kaleenikta', and was about to turn over and go to sleep she grabbed him by the shoulder and, taut with rage, cried, "Aren't you just a bit upset by Aristophanes bright witty little piece?"

"I detect a note of sarcasm in your voice, Agape Mou."

"You said he was your friend! With friends like that. . . "

"Who needs enemies?' I whole heartedly agree. I have always distrusted drama and poetry because they have the power to sway one's emotions and twist the truth. What disturbs me about tonight's fantasy is its inference that Socrates is brainy in skylore, and a highbrow, always investigating what is under the earth, subverting truth, and making the weaker argument the stronger."

He yawned, and was once again about to stretch out on their shared pallet when another thought brought him back upright. "By claiming that I tread on air, talk nonsense, and take money to educate people, Aristophanes weakens my credibility. Those who know me recognize that to accuse me of accepting fees is ridiculous enough to be funny. But what about the rest, those who, in not knowing, could be misled?"

"But you don't give a fig about the opinion of others, at least that's what you say!"

"Correct! Except where discoloration of my character lessens the effectiveness of what I teach."

"I could kill Aristophanes! The 'Thinkery' Ha! You don't even have a classroom, let alone a school! And I have as yet to see a single oboloi coming from any of your disciples, more's the pity!"

"Don't be upset!" Socrates patted his wife's arm. "I was twitted in the theater as I would be at a drinking party."

Although within moments he was asleep Xanthippe's eyes were wide. In repose he looked vulnerable. There was a quality of innocence about his pudgy face that made her feel like putting a protective arm around him.

Godsname he was as rare as a three-legged goose. Who else, after being the butt of Aristophanes' wicked wit, and a punching bag for fellow Athenians, could come home, lie down, and drift into slumber with a smile on his face?

Next morning Xanthippe was still consumed with rage. Nor was it of any lasting comfort to her when, a few days later, she learned that Aristophanes' offensive travesty had failed to earn him the first prize to which he had probably, by now become somewhat accustomed.

This time it was his longtime enemy, Cratinus, who had also taken to comedy, who received the coveted laurel-wreath and purse for having written 'The Wineflask'. At least until next year's Great Dionysian and Lenean festivities, it was his name that would be acclaimed in Athens.

*   *   *   *

At dawn a batch of golden honey puffs already lay cooling on the table. Lamprocles tied to his chair to keep him out of mischief was watching his mother fold yeast and flour into eggs and oil when, at the sound of feet clumping through the corridor, Xanthippe scowled.

A burgeoning population of babies, the result of a brief cessation of war with Sparta had midwives on the go again. However Phaenerete, increasingly gimpy of gait, had turned over what remained of her own maternity work to the younger ones. Having little else to occupy her attention, she had taken to stationing herself wherever Xanthippe happened to be.

Torrents of unrequested advice poured like pellets from her lips. This time it was the care and nurture of Lamprocles that caught her attention. "You should not pick him up whenever he cries. Both you and he could use some of my tonic, the one I make with dillweed and myrrhis odorata for a sour stomach. And, pointing to a diminutive terra cotta pot, "Isn't it time he earned to empty himself like a big boy?"

"May I give you some bread with oil sop?" Xanthippe asked.

"I'm not hungry." So saying Phaenerete helped herself to a honey puff and handed one to her grandson.

"Mother-Phaenerete, have you forgotten? Sweets don't agree with him." The words were scarcely out of Xanthippe's mouth when, as if to prove her point, the little fellow vomited.

"If you gave him infusions of matricaria chaomilla in goat's milk as I've already suggested that sort of thing would not happen."

"If you didn't feed him honey puffs he wouldn't get sick."

"Sweets never hurt anyone. If he can't stand a bit of honey something must be wrong with him."

"I'll put him down for a nap."

Abandoning the bread she'd been making Xanthippe extricated the fretful two year old from his chair and carried him to her room. Crooning one of Yiayia's old chants she lowered him onto his pallet. Returning to the kitchen, she found Phaenerete kneading the dough like a mason mixing mortar.

When the leaden mass had been shaped into loaves no longer likely to rise, Xanthippe took a pail and headed for the yard. Carefully she shied away from the he-goat with his disagreeable smell, wicked pink eyes and a leer reminiscent of the late unlamented Hipponicus. Next she milked the she-goat and fed the few chickens who were plucking fruitlessly at the hard clay earth. While she was flinging laundry over a clothes rope Lamprocles' petulant cry told her he had awakened.

Activity did keep one's mind and hands occupied during the day. More trying than her endless tasks were the evenings when, at dusk, the voices of the potter and his wife floated from next door. Their conversations were as enticing as those to which she had once listened through a wall in Palen's barn.

How she envied them, laughing at the same jokes, sharing their thoughts, sometimes engaged in noisy fights. Even these had an element of harmony. The potter's wife was plain, dowdy, and her stomach was pendulous from childbirth. But the wrinkles fanning from her eyes must have come from smiling because her husband treated her as if she were the Goddess of Love.

Today's chores had been particularly trying but, exhausted though she was, Xanthippe lay awake.

Since returning from Delium, Socrates seemed to require less sleep, and when he did come to bed his presence there was less personal than Yiayia's had been in their shared room at the farm. She had at least provided the intimacy of a close and caring conversation whereas Socrates was, by now, so totally immersed in his philosophies that he no longer talked to her as he had in their first months of marriage.

Voices and sounds of laughter continued to drift across the wall and her tense body moved restlessly as uninvited visions of her neighbors making love came to mind, and her thoughts turned to Critobolus.

It was very late when Socrates came in and eased himself down beside her.

"No need to be so quiet. I'm not asleep," Xanthippe said irritably. "One of these nights you'll have to turn up the lampwick and take a good look so you will know me in case we run into each other in the Agora."

* * * *

The next morning Palen surprised her by arriving with a brace of wild hares. Staying only long enough to toss his grandchild into the air a few times he hurried on to the Agora. By late afternoon his gift was simmering aromatically on top of the stove.

While Lamprocles gnawed contentedly on a marrow bone his mother dropped dough balls one by one into the broth and wished she had some way of knowing when or if Socrates were coming home for supper. Time, for him, seemed not to exist.

"We can live only in the now, never yesterday, never tomorrow, only this moment," was his way of putting it. Of course he could always blame that damnable daemon if he were late. But this evening to everyone's surprise he came home early.

"Demeter, Queen of fragrant fields, I offer this prayer in behalf of my family. Giver of earth's good gifts, give us your grace," Sophroniscus prayed after pouring the libation. How tired and gray of face he looked. It would make his life much easier if Socrates helped him in the shop instead of running around town day and night.

His invocation was barely concluded before Phaenerete's heavy lips were smacking over a mouthful of rabbit stew. Socrates, attacking his own supper, bore marked resemblance to his dam, both of them eating with the happy abandon of pigs at a trough.

"Cleon wont be satisfied until Sparta is completely destroyed," he said, still chewing. "And battles continue to break out like pox all over Greece."

"You won't have to go again?" Xanthippe demanded, aghast.

"I am still in the army."

"You are a father!"

"I am also a son of Athens. Children do not rebel against their parents even when it seems warranted. I deplore war and I intend to pub-

233

licly disavow it when the time is ripe."

"How you can fight if you don't believe in war."

"Because obedience to your country takes precedence over personal opinion. Dissensions need to be voiced and changes made in an orderly and law abiding manner."

"Shit! What you say makes as much sense as a man jumping off Parnassus because he thinks he can fly!" Had she not been so furious when she said it Xanthippe would have, for the first time in her memory seen Phaenerete speechless. Instead she lapsed into flaming silence.

* * * *

"You married me and promptly impregnated me with Lamprocles, yet neither he nor I have seen much of you since! I did not marry your parents you know!" Xanthippe cried, when, in their bed chamber and beyond hearing of her in-laws, she finally felt free to vent her fury.

"You don't see your old friend Crito chasing all over Greece to do battle," she added savagely. "And Critobolus! He's still young but even he has served Athens long enough by now to choose to go into business with his father. Kallia is a whining bore but you don't see him deserting her at the first drumbeat to clap on a helmet and join all the assholes who, as they say, love a good fight!"

Now that Lamprocles is starting to talk I fear you may have to forego some of the epithets you picked up in your father's barn," Socrates laughed.

"But I'll be the first to admit they add color and dimension to your already excellent vocabulary. And believe me, 'Agape Mou', I would far rather stay at home and be with you but then I would be derelict to duty. As Hesiod said, 'Badness you can get easily, in quantity, the road is smooth and it lies close by . . .'"

"I know, I know, I know!" she cut in angrily, "'but in front of excellence the immortal gods have put sweat, and long and steep is the way to it, and rough at first. But when you come to the top it is easy, even though it is hard.' Well, my husband, I have had enough of sweat!"

"Archos again?"

"Yes, and a fat lot of good all those lessons do me now! I'm trying my best to forget every thing he ever taught me."

"What a pity." Socrates said, reaching out to her.

On the rare occasions when he did succumb to passion he abandoned himself as unreservedly as he did to any activity in which he chose to participate. Xanthippe, not wanting to let go of her anger, pulled back.

Her hunger for love was too intense, and his ability to transport her into a sort of mindlessness, frightening. Again and again she climaxed until at last she lay supine in his arms, her pulses still pounding.

Chapter Thirty-three

Socrates was back in uniform, this time to travel under Cleon's leadership, with twelve hundred fellow hoplites (Infantry) three hundred cavalry-men, and thirty ships. The plan was to rout the Spartans in Amphipolis, a city that to Xanthippe was as far north as the evening star.

"You can't do this! Not again!" she cried. In answer Socrates gave her an absent-minded pat and marched away, leaving her to feel abandoned and irate.

But, although Cleon aspired to rule the world, the gods evidently had other plans because the battle had hardly begun before he was killed in a surprise attack. Sparta's brilliant General Brasidias was struck down in the same fray, and the Athenians came home on the run.

"Don't go to war again, Socrates," Xanthippe entreated

"I won't" he assured her. "I've seen action at Amphipolis. Samos, Delium and Potidaea, That's enough. Henceforth I plan to devote my time to the pursuit of Truth."

"Well, at least that's better than dying in a battle," she sighed. Perhaps the day had come when he'd give her a bit more attention and admit he owed it to his family to accept money in return for the time he so freely gave to his disciples.

"I want to help you, Socrates. Don't shut me out. Let me be your partner. Tell me what you tell all those people who hang on your every word."

"Very well. I've been invited to debate with General Laches, and Nicias, our new ruler, tomorrow at the Stoa of Eumenes. We'll try to sort out this tragic business of Hellenes fighting Hellenes, as opposed to Hellenes fighting their natural enemies, the barbarians. The topic is sure to draw a crowd so come hear what we have to say. . ."

"I most certainly shall. And I have something new for you to wear when you stand before all those important people, It's a cloak I wove for you and, as luck would have it, I finished it just in time for tomorrow," Xanthippe said jubilantly.

A crowd had already collected, the following day, when she walked into the cool, shadowy Stoa of Eumenes. Apparently the crowd had been collecting there since dawn to get close enough to hear every word her husband said.

And there he stood, on a dais, barefoot, bare-legged, and clad in the same shoddy old garment he wore all the time. He hadn't given a second thought to the one she had woven for him with such care. Was this his way of saying that obedience to the State was vital but compliance to a wife irrelevant.

He looks like beggar," she heard the person in back of her remark. "Socrates can't be that poor!"

"They say his wife spends more time yelling at him than she does at her loom." said another.

Flame-faced, Xanthippe was about to turn around and accost the gossips when Socrates began to speak.

"Let us begin, Nicias, by asking ourselves in what manner should our soldiers relate to our enemies," he said.

"I am not sure I understand what you mean," Nicias replied. "Take enslavement. Do you think it just for Hellenes to subjugate people of Hellenic cities? And should they let another city do so if they can prevent it? Should it not be the custom to spare the Hellenic race, foreseeing the danger of racial enslavement under the barbarians?"

"But if Hellenes bring arms dedicated to fighting fellow Hellenes should we not fear pollution because we are asking a god to help us destroy our own people? What about ravaging and burning one anothers land? How should soldiers deal with their enemies in that matter?" Socrates countered.

"They should do no more than take that year's crops." Said Nicias.

"Pray tell me why."

"Just as there are two names, war and faction, there are two eponyms for disagreement, one domestic, the other alien. Hellenes and barbarians are enemies by nature so we 'war' with them. But Hellenes are basically friends. We might say that faction is the name for domestic hostility, war to alien."

So that's it, Xanthippe reflected. "I thought Socrates and I were at war but, according to Nicias, it's a faction,"

"In that case Hellas is sick with factions. And wherever a country is divided against itself with both parties laying waste each other's property and burning their houses, their factions are an abomination and both parties are unpatriotic!" Socrates declared. "What but greed could make them think they can profit now and be re-united later?"

"You speak easily about keeping peace, my dear Socrates, but what do we do when we are attacked by fellow Hellenes?"

"We need to revise our laws to compel the guilty ones to make amends for the harm they do to suffering innocents."

"But in an earlier talk you thrust aside the question that asked if a new constitution comes into being with people calling each other 'brother','father','son' and so on how can all these fine things be actually put into effect?" Nicias asked.

"What a sudden assault you have made on my proposals! You have no pity on a poor wretch in a tight corner!"

"Indeed, Socrates, after those words we won't let you go. So tell us, how can all that you say come into being?"

"We must discover, General, what brings about badly conducted cities that fester under the blight of poor management. Then we choose ways to make a difference although they may be small to begin with. For example we insist that those in power learn to seek wisdom. Thus politics and intellectual understanding are joined and those who pursue first one thing and then another are excluded. To accomplish this takes courage as well as wisdom."

"Explain what you mean when you speak of courage."

"Gladly. But first may I ask you to define the word for me?" Socrates asked, giving his adversary a courteous nod.

"Courage means strength."

"Would you say that a lion shows courage when he mauls smaller animals?"

"Certainly not. That is the uninhibited aggression of a beast."

"And the robber whose strength overwhelms a victim?"

"No indeed. The robber is worse than a lion. He should know better." Nicias affirmed.

"I would say that courage is an act of daring," Laches, silent until now, interjected.

"As when a man filled with red wine dares to jump from his roof top? Or a boy puts his hand in the fire?"

"Ah, Socrates, you have a disconcerting way of making what at first seems true to be false! Kindly tell us now how you define the word."

"I see it as bravery of the soul and, just as one man's body is naturally stronger than another's for labor, so one man's soul may be braver than another's in danger. For I notice that men brought up under similar laws and customs differ widely in grit," Socrates said. "Sometimes it takes greater courage to do a kindness, or stand up for a belief than to face a sword," he went on, "Perhaps the greatest courage for all of us, as individuals, lies in facing ourselves."

"And by that you mean . . .?"

"I refer to a search for self-understanding. Does it not take courage to examine our minds and motives? We speak glibly of truth yet we allow our behavior and attitudes to be swayed by public opinion. And although we talk about keeping the peace we fail in the courage it takes to address our own warlike attitudes as individuals."

"Peace depends on courageous warriors such as yourself, Socrates, and a willingness to fight! The greater our military strength the less inclined will any enemy be to threaten our peace," declared General Laches whose statement was greeted with a mixture of cheers and jeers.

"But is it conceivable that even there hidden danger may lurk?" Socrates asked, sounding as gutless as a schoolboy.

"You jest!" Laches laughed. According to Homer the single best augury is to fight for one's country!"

"And there is strength in union, even of sorry men," Nicias hastened to add.

"But suppose that in a state where military strength is paramount there are a few self-seeking warriors who prevail over lovers of wisdom by imposing policies dictated by ambition and love of glory?" Socrates countered. "Might that not result in a valiant but contentious country where good men are thrown into a court of law, ruined by false informers, put to death, banished, and supplanted by evil-doers?"

At times his ability to sway others still amazed his wife. Quite obviously there were many for whom his bear-like body and gait and even his careless dress held a distinct appeal. But the true source of his charm would be hard to define. Part of it could be his smile, the kind of smile that drew people to him in spite of themselves.

"Your husband has a way of jolting Athenians out of their cherished prejudices, doesn't he" asked Myrto, emerging suddenly from the crowd as the debate came to an end. "I'm thinking of inviting him to be the honored guest at a symposium in my home. My plan is to include wives so you may come too," she added. "I'll send a messenger to confirm it with Socrates."

It would seem that Myrto's opinion of Socrates had risen. Also, her party could well prove to be a gift from the gods. She was a real enigma, friendly on occasion and, at other times, a detestable snob bent on making a 'girl from the farm' feel like a nobody, worthless, and unwanted.

But, with a rich indulgent husband who would not only pay for a banquet-symposium but condone mixed company at the affair as well, she could handily become the doorway to financial gain on Socrates' part.

If, just because of his presence, Myrto's party happened to be a singular success he would be, more than ever, in demand, and by people who could well afford to pay him whatever he might ask.

It would be nice too if Myrto were to decide to become a real friend . . .

"Kalimeera! You stand out even in a mob like this".

Xanthippe did not need to turn her head to see who had spoken. And could it be just imagination or was he looking at her the way he had once before.

"I watched you listening to every word Socrates uttered. He was superb." Critobolus said. "Tell me, Xanthippe, does all go well with you?"

"Pretty much so, except that although I once thought that to live in Athens would be akin to dwelling in the Elysian Fields, I now sometimes find myself wishing I could go back and live on Papa's horse farm again."

"I'm not surprised. It was a great place to be. I am also inclined to think that many of us sometimes long to 'go back' as you say. Socrates claims peace can only be found by those who are content in whatever place or situation they find themselves but I think that is easier said than done."

And before she knew it they were talking as if it were only yesterday since they had been together. Happy just to be in his company once again, Xanthippe's eyes were aglow.

They spoke of horses, drama, people and places and whether women should be allowed to make their own decisions. Critobolus told how, as a banker, he helped people acquire property from the State. But there was one matter to which, as if by unspoken agreement, they did not allude. Yet that was what remained uppermost in Xanthippe's mind. The past.

A cymbal striking the hour brought a sharp reminder that time had passed all too swiftly and she bid Critobolus a somewhat guilty 'adio'.

* * * *

"By the god's beard, what does a man who keeps his head 'in the clouds' know about putting together a pact to end this damnable war?" people asked when, not long after the debate, Socrates received credit for inspiring Nicias' Peace Treaty.

"He can't even make a decent living!"

"There are beggars right here in Athens who would be unable to survive in such a sorry state," they exclaimed.

"If a slave were made to live so he would run away," said one of Socrates' friends, a man named Antiphon.

Chapter Thirty-four

A messenger brought Myrto's invitation. With it came the delight of having something to anticipate for a change. Best of all Hipparete would be there, probably with Alcibiades because he, like others who were lucky enough to still be alive, was back in Athens.

No doubt many rich and powerful people would attend. Meanwhile Xanthippe had worn her peplos from Hipparete's wedding to a rag. So, rather than postpone the purchase of new fabric 'til Socrates came to his senses and accepted a decent recompense for his services she must find some money. Stirred by her recent encounter with Critobolus she decided to go to the bankers' tables, hoping against hope to see him, as well as his father. But only Crito was on hand to greet her.

"Socrates and I are going to a symposium," she told him, "It's important for me to look my best so I'd like to withdraw some money from the dower my father placed in your keeping. It's to buy fabric for a new peplos. I've always woven my own but this is a very special occasion."

"A woman's dowry is supposed to be her security against all odds, not a source for new gowns." Crito's smile softened his words. "But there are times when a young woman deserves to be clothed in silk. So since we have recently made a small but beneficial investment for you, the answer is 'Yes'."

He was rewarded with a radiant smile. As she walked away from his booth following their transaction he noted the grace with which she made her way through the crowd and shook his head. A woman with her spirit needed more attention than she was probably getting at home. Pensively resting his elbows on the banking table, his chin propped on his fist, he considered his son. Thank the gods Critobolus had returned from the war intact. Yet, thanks to me, his father, he came home to a vex-

243

atious wife, Crito mused. Sometimes a man is better equipped to be a merchant or a banker than a kind, considerate parent.

* * * *

"I went with Glaucon to Piraeus to celebrate the festival of a new goddess, Bendis by name," Socrates said without a sign of contrition when, after an absence of two days he wandered into the house. "We were invited to dine at the home of Cephalos and stay the night.

"Cephalos the rich merchant?"

"Yes, but his real wealth is of the spirit. We had such a splendid conversation we couldn't quit and go to bed."

"What could anyone find to talk about all night?"

"We spoke of how bodily desires and distractions prevent the soul from grasping Truth, When one tries to turn away from illness, fear, the need of food, and craving for sexual satisfaction, to search for something nobler, the clamor of our incessant urges pulls us back. Perhaps wars, factions and battles all result from unmet needs! Man even fights death because he is a body lover rather than a lover of wisdom."

"Can you stop talking long enough to eat?" his mother asked.

As they were preparing for bed that night Xanthippe pointed to Lamprocles, asleep in his crib, and put a finger over her mouth Even in the privacy of their small room she must whisper when, at times, she wanted to shout.

"It's neither a holy day nor a festival. Why should we go there to eat?" Socrates asked when she was done telling him about Myrto's invitation.

"Elpinice and Callias used to ask men to bring their wives for no other reason than to be sociable. Myrto wants to do the same thing with you there to preside over the symposium.

"If you wish I shall go," was his welcome reply.

Happily she'd had just enough precious silk (the color of clotted cream), to create a most beautiful gown and when the day of the party arrived Xanthippe was ready to go.

"I promised to meet with Adeimantos and Glaucon. As soon as I leave them I shall join you at Myrto's," Socrates said.

"Anyone else would be getting rich on what you give away."

"But I am not 'anyone else'. You are becoming a scold."

"Small wonder. But I beg you not to arrive in your bare feet and for the godsakes wear your new cloak. Ah, if only you would always dress like this," she sighed, careful to appraise her husband's attire before he left the house.

"No one would recognize me." He said with a departing grin

"Tell the one about the wood chest in the sea," Lamprocles demanded when he'd been put to bed. So while she dressed her hair and lovingly draped her new garment, she narrated the watery adventures of Prometheus' son and Pandora's daughter as they navigated their great oblong craft through a flood, sent by Zeus, to drown the world

"Where's Socrates?" Myrto asked by way of greeting when Xanthippe arrived and was led through a deeply recessed door into a room so vast that the ceiling rose higher than the candelabrum's limit of light.

Critobolus was there and the look on his face told her that the creamy silk peplos was indeed effective. For the rest of the evening, not a moment would pass during which she would not be conscious of his presence.

"You look lovely, Xanthippe," Hipparete touched her arm. Alcibiades, after a curt nod pointedly turned his back.

"I hope Socrates wont disappoint us," said Kallia. "My husband can't get enough of listening to him talk." Evidently she had already imbibed a quantity of wine because her hands were trembling so badly she could hardly hold onto her cup.

"Ah! Pretty! Pretty!" Alcibiades touched a butterfly made of rubies that sparkled on Myrto's shoulder and allowed his fingers to drift down over her small pointed breasts.

"This is not one of the symposiums for which you are famous," she reminded him. "There are wives at this one, not hetairai." With a light laugh she removed his hand.

"As for hetairai,have you all heard about the marriage of my late uncle Pericles' widow to Lysicles the sheep herder?" he asked. "Perhaps she was getting more than lamb when he made all those deliveries at the palace. From royal abode to sheep farm is a long drop for a dedicated climber" (In recent years, after gaining riches, power, and prestige he seemed to have lost his irritating lisp)

"Don't be such a prig, Alcibiades! They make an attractive pair. We saw them together at Aristophanes new comedy 'The Peace,'" Young Callias remarked. "What did you think of it?"

"It's the most outrageous thing Aristophanes ever did," Critobolus broke in vehemently, "Except for his despicable "Clouds'. To this day people still retain a wrong impression of Socrates because of that piece of obscenity."

"When is Socrates going to arrive?" Myrto asked again.

"What do you suppose is keeping him?" wondered another.

"He has no sense of time," Xanthippe said, feeling some- how condemned because it was her husband who had failed to appear. Desperately she cast another glance at the door.

"Do you realize that the Erectheum has become the final structure in Pericles' master plan for the Acropolis. How sad that it was built too late for him to see it," Myrto's wealthy old husband was saying when the guest of honor was ushered into the great hall.

His mercurial face registered geniality, wisdom, and wit in turn as he went about greeting everyone. Stimulated by his presence they clustered around him, all chattering at once, like a party of statues come to life.

Not only your wife but you yourself are singularly well turned out," Hermogenes said. "Weren't you afraid none of us would know you?"

"Yes! I told her that might happen!" Socrates laughed.

As if she had never met him, Xanthippe saw her spouse maneuver the conversation, being both prompter and listener, as he stimulated others to express themselves.

"I refuse to withdraw my recommendation that the female sex must be on the same footing as the male," he said, continuing a conversation started before the sixteen guests were asked to seated in the dining hall. "In our talks about an ideal republic we're working out such a program."

"We could adopt the Spartan system," someone suggested. "Their girls take part in gymnastics and also receive a compulsory education in the arts."

"But when they grow up they're still women and, although they may wish to dispense with wool weaving, they'll have to 'weave' themselves a hard working life if they want to be equal to men."

"Sarmatian women around the Black Sea ride horses and use bows and other weapons! Have any of you ever met an Athenian woman that hardy?"

"What about the Thracians?" Alcibiades demanded. "Their women work on the land and mind sheep and cattle until they turn into skivvies indistinguishable from slaves!"

"They say that you are pro-Spartan, Alcibiades," Myrto's husband said with a slight cough. He was a tidy looking man, not much taller than his wife. Even his teeth were small and precise. "Is it true you were raised by a Spartan nurse and named for your father's best friend who belonged to the family of Endios?"

"I'm Athenian to the core!" was the quick reply. "However I admire Spartan leaders. They control their government while our democracy continues to fall into the hands of laborers, peasants, and nobodies. Going back to the equality of women, I advocate that the young ones go naked in procession as well as the men, and dance at certain solemn feasts whilst the men stand around watching them."

"A splendid idea, Alcibiades! Since you've inherited your uncle Pericles' gift for taking command you may become the Archon yourself one of these days and bring it all to pass!"

"People have been telling him that ever since he was a pretty little boy!" Myrto puckered her prow shaped lips and blew Alcibiades a kiss. "Everyone eats out of his hand no matter what naughty things he says or does." She turned to Socrates. "What do you think about him?"

"I think Alcibiades is capable of doing whatever he wishes. Tell me, Agathon, as a dramatist you explore human hungers and ambitions. Could he be a ruler in one of your plays?"

"I am a writer of tragedies in which even the darkest of human events always contain a seed of hope," the young man replied. "First I might have the chorus sing a petition to the Oracle asking if Alcibiades should or should not be an Archon. Then I'd weave my plot around her reply. However politicians aren't good subjects for serious drama because their vision is limited to a craving for money and power. You Socrates, seem to want neither. How do you petition the gods?"

"Somewhat in this fashion," Socrates reflected. "Oh beloved Pan, and all ye gods of this place, grant that I may be made beautiful in my soul and that all external possessions be in harmony with my inner self. May I consider the wise man rich and may I have only such wealth as a self restrained man can bear and endure. What else do I need? For me that is enough."

"Splendid, dear Socrates!" Alcibiades cheered. Making a dramatic gesture he swept his arm in such a way as to bump Kallia. At this her already imperiled wine goblet fell from her hands and a stream of red wine poured across the white table cloth, directly into Xanthippe's lap.

"Forgive me!" he cried. "By Zeus how could I be so clumsy? But surely you understand my embarrassment, dear Xanthippe, for no one knows better than you how it feels to spill wine on a guest!"

Kallia, totally unlike the overbearing young woman of former days, was mute, her hands more than ever a-tremble.

"Don't worry, Kallia," Xanthippe told her, feeling the wetness trickling through the fabric of her new dress, "Alcibiades is quite right. I've done the same thing myself," she added, and caught a glance of gratitude from Critobolus. The others were looking on like spectators at a street scene.

"Here's a slave to fix the table," Myrto said, and if you will come with me, Xanthippe, I'll take care of your gown."

""My wife and I both thank you for what has been a splendid evening,"Socrates said. "But the hour grows late and we must be on our way. Xanthippe will easily erase the wine spots when we get home. Is that not so, my dear?"

* * * *

"Alcibiades upset that wine on purpose and ruined the first and only silk peplos I ever owned," Xanthippe fumed as they threaded their way through dark streets to Cerameicus Road.

"There is a good side to him but he's a troubled man. Don't make a face. Were he at peace with himself he'd feel no need to treat others shabbily."

"You wouldn't recognize evil if it came up and hit you in the face!" Xanthippe retorted. "You look handsome tonight," she added, observing how nice her husband's new toga looked swinging around his short legs as he kept easy pace with her brisk strides

"I'm seldom told that," he laughed.

Xanthippe's thoughts went back to his prayer.

Judging from that petition Socrates' attitude about money was even more eccentric than she had surmised and might well prove a major obstacle to their future financial success!

Chapter Thirty-five

Terror in the guise of shrieks awakened Xanthippe. Drowsily emerging from an unfinished dream she thought of ravens flying in the house. But the cries were Phaenerete's and, after the shock of learning that Sophroniscus had died in his sleep the thought occurred that so quiet a leave-taking rather suited the soft spoken old gentleman.

Cleina refused to go near him so the distasteful task of preparing the aged artisan for his journey into the under-world fell to Festus and Xanthippe.

After bathing and wrapping his body they placed a coin in his mouth to pay Charon, the ghostly ferryman who, following a proper burial, rowed dead people across the River of Woe to Hade's kingdom, Then Festus and Socrates settled him in the courtyard where he looked remarkably peaceful, lying in state, surrounded by tombstones of his own making.

With shorn head Socrates, and his family, all of them garbed in black, received visitors. Phaenerete, beating her breast greeted them with loud lamentations. Women drew shawls over their faces, a classic sign of sorrow, and men said nice things about Sophroniscus and recalled his good deeds.

When the funeral procession had wound its way up the road to the cemetery, chisels, wine, food, and items Sophroniscus would need in the hereafter were placed beside his body.

Sophroniscus' last rites were the first Xanthippe had ever seen. The hideous memory of bodies piled and burning on Athenian streets still seemed disconnected from reality. She had been too ill with the plague to attend the burials for either Yiayia Phyllys or Great Aunt Elpinice, and had, in fact, not even known that they were dead. It had all been so inconclusive.

"Zeus!" she muttered, "Is this how it ends, being dropped into a hole, like a cheese in a cooling cellar, with an oboloi between your teeth, and clods of dirt pressing down on your chest? In a way it was comparable to a Panathenaea where people pass by in endless procession until they vanish in a cemetery at the end of Cerameicus Road.

"I strongly believe that death is but a separation of the soul from the body," Socrates said at the funeral feast after having made his filial incantations. "While on earth, the desires of a man's physical body distract and hinder him from getting possession of Truth. That is why those who love wisdom practice dying, because death, to them is the least terrible thing in the world. Look at it this way. Why not go willingly to a place where there is hope of finding the wisdom they are in love with all through life?

"When the unhallowed get to the house of Hades they lie in mud with no use for the jars and tools with which they have been interred. But the purified go to dwell with the gods. Ancient legend tells us that such souls are continually arriving in paradise and, after an interim with the gods, coming back here to be born again from the dead. My father was a good man and, although his body is now an empty shell, I am persuaded that his soul lives on."

Following the funeral repast cook-pots were broken in accordance with tradition but, unconsoled by her son's words Phaenerete's complaints continued unabated into the night.

The lugubrious obligato of a neighboring hound awakened Lamprocles and he too began to weep.

"If only Sophroniscus had been the one to survive," Xanthippe thought and made a sign to absolve her guilt for allowing such a thought to cross her mind.

"Mother surprises me," Socrates remarked while his wife was comforting their disconsolate son. "I know she cared for my father, and that she is not what one might call a 'placid person', none the less I always saw her as a woman of fortitude. She seemed so self reliant, and capable of dealing with any crises, even the death of a loved one."

The next morning when Socrates left the house, Phaenerete was still in bed and, while Lamprocles busied himself with his terra-cotta horses Xanthippe wandered out into the court yard and appraised the row of tombstones that leaned against Sophroniscus' shop in mute testimony to their late maker.

"Kalimeera!" the potter's wife called across the fence. "May your little one come here to play with my children?"

Her offer was gratefully accepted. This dreary house was no place for a child. Lamprocles needed a brother. Like Elefterous and Marc, the two of them would have special games, secret hiding places, and a private language that no one else could understand. But where to put another?

"It's bad enough having to share a bed-chamber with one, let alone two," Xanthippe sighed, and went to take a bowl of cheese and olives to Phaenerete.

The idea of having a baby was still on her mind when, spade in hand, she went to stake out a bit of earth in which vegetables might conceivably be encouraged take root.

That night, worn but still awake, she contemplated the eerie certainty of death. So many people had come to her father-in law's funeral one might have thought it was a statesman being laid to rest. Crito, Critobolus and Kallia were there of course. She looked ill and shivered as if she had the ague. So who am I to talk about shivering when, at the sight of my former lover I quiver like a leaf in the wind, Xanthippe thought to herself.

Tired as she was when, past midnight, Socrates came home, she chose not to postpone the subject of their finances any further. "I have an idea," she said, trying to sound more cheerful than she felt. "Socrates?" she repeated. His mind was clearly elsewhere. "I despise having to ask someone to dole out money every time we need a measure of meal. Your mother is too unhappy to tackle our household accounts and I can do them. I'm good at numbers, I can also tell your disciples what to pay you for your lectures and that money will help a lot to ease our financial anxieties."

"What financial anxieties?"

"Oh for the godsakes, Socrates!"

"We get along. The uncluttered life is the sweetest. We're happier when our needs are few. People who seek felicity in wealth and possessions never find it. Desire is an insatiable taskmaster so, instead of fewer cares they burden themselves with more. I don't mean to say it's wrong to have wealth, but money can easily divert one's attention from the most beautiful things life has to offer."

"You speak of beauty yet I see none here. A little money would brighten up this place and make it more comfortable.

"My dear, there is no way that you can persuade me take money for what can only be given freely. Silver and gold are more devious persuaders than poetry. Were I to be paid for my observations I might be tempted to adulterate them to please my benefactors."

"You self-centered master of fly-brained frugality! You could give me every comfort and yet you refuse!" Xanthippe stormed. "Your harangues about virtue and truth may capture the fancy of an elite group of rich young men with nothing better to do than follow you around, but just show me one who's willing to live on nothing but 'food for thought!'"

That long-ago dream about being miscast among aliens in a drama that made no sense had come true. What was she doing here, yoked to a man who talked rubbish, and a crabby old woman who chewed like a horse, belched like a pig with every swallow, and smelled like a goat?

"Fill my wash basin! Empty the slops! Bring me some wine and cakes," Demands issuing endlessly from the bedchamber in which Phaenerete had confined herself ever since her husband's death. At times Xanthippe felt that one more outcry and she would burst like the jug of her father's kokinelli that blew up in the wine cellar. And she had less hope of escaping than the cat who fell in a well.

Once upon a time she had envisioned herself as an actor, earning her own money. But even were she to impersonate Zeus himself, neither she, nor any woman on earth, would ever be permitted to set foot on man's domain, the stage.

Training horses? Forget that too. The very day Papa came of age, his mother had been compelled to turn the farm she had managed successfully for fourteen years over to him. Nor could she, Xanthippe, even aspire to the gainful career of a hetaira because, as the daughter of an Athenian citizen, she was not even eligible to join their recondite sorority.

Chapter Thirty-six

When Socrates did not go to his disciples in the Agora they sought him at home. It was a motley congregation of wealthy nobles, ragged intellectuals, politicians, fellow townsmen and itinerant sophists who came together on Cerameicus Street to participate in Athens' most talked about cult.

Some were handsome young men with ideals and inexpressible longings to be godlike, Others so old they had to be assisted in their ambulations by slaves.

Xanthippe had come to know many of them, Simon the Cobbler, Aeschines, Zeno, Glaucon, Cebes, Antisthenes . . . Connus. There were also foreigners with strange unpronounceable names.

By now much of what Socrates said was as familiar to her as it was to those who crowded the courtyard.

"The unexamined life is not worth living. Listen to the Divinity within. There is but one Truth, and finding it is the work of eternity. If you must forsake family and friends to pursue it then do so!"

Connus, a broken down old maestro, came twice a week, not only in the role of philosophic disciple but to teach Socrates how to play the cithara. Once a celebrated composer he was now considered somewhat of an idiot. His shoulders were concave, perhaps from years of bending over his instrument and his teeth, visible through a broomstraw beard, were large and yellow, like those of an old horse. Even at a distance Xanthippe could tell who it was coming up the road. He had a gingerly way of walking, knobby knees lifted high with each step, and toes turned out as if he were traversing a sheep pen in bare feet.

When Connus tuned his cithara strings at one end of the courtyard, Chaerephon, the lanky singer, was usually at his side. While they played

253

and sang Socrates would whirl and stamp like a frenzied ram. "Dancing," he often said, "is a form of cure all, a healer of body, mind and soul."

They were at it again. Lamprocles, convulsed with giggles watched until the music and dancing ceased, then wandered into the kitchen court where his mother stood dejectedly plucking the remaining strands of meat from a well worked over chicken carcass.

"Mama! Mama!" His high thin plaint grated on ears still raw from the sound of Connus' twanging strings. "Mama! Listen to me!" He gave the hem of her tunic a jerk.

"What is it?"

There was no answer. Still whining he wandered around the kitchen poking small grubby hands into whatever lay in reach.

"You bad boy!" Xanthippe cried, seizing him by the ear when he upset a bowl of freshly ground grain on the floor.

"Now Mama, calm yourself," said Socrates, appearing in search of refreshments for his friends.

"Don't you 'Mama' me!" Xanthippe yelled. "I'm not your mother! Your mother is in her room calling for cakes and barley water! Mama indeed! I'm supposed to be your wife! Get out of here!"

Grabbing a pail of water she flung its contents with such vigor that both he and Lamprocles were soused.

"My wife's thunder turned to rain," Socrates jested when his friends came running to see what the commotion was all about.

"I must take my leave," Connus said, retreating hastily from the savage look on Xanthippe's face.

"And I. Thank you for a pleasant afternoon," said Chaerephon

"Is there no end to the horde of weird ones who think that this house is a taverna?" Xanthippe stormed when they had gone. "The food is free, and so is the entertainment! Those two fools couldn't wait to get away and tell their friends a new story about Socrates' wild wife. Godsname! Am I to be served up as a tasty bit of gossip for the rest of my life?"

That night she went to their bedchamber and sat by Lamprocles' cot. The little fellow was asleep, traces of tears still smearing his cheek. He looked very small and defenseless. How can anyone who loves a child as much as she loved him, allow her anger to go out of control. Temper! It could blow like the sails on a ship in a squall, knocking overboard anyone luckless enough to be on deck.

"It's as if I'd turned into Papa," she thought sadly. "Thank the gods I only threw water. It might have been hot broth!"

"Are you still angry with me, Mama?" Lamprocles was awake and watching her with the somber eyes of an owl.

"Of course not! I only acted as if I were because I was tired and my head hurt from all that squawking and scratching." What she did not say, at least not aloud was, "And because I am starving for love."

"What shall I play for you, little man?" she asked in a nasal voice. Picking up his hockey stick and holding it like a cithara she walked around the room, raising her knees and pointing her toes outward.

"Mama! Do that again. Be Connus some more," Lamprocles cried joyfully jumping up and down on his pallet.

"Would you not rather hear a song?" Now it was Chaerephon being mimicked.

"When God made you a woman the Theater of Dionysius lost its greatest actor. You are superior to any performer I ever saw!" said Socrates, standing in the doorway and sharing his son's mirth.

*   *   *   *

Xanthippe awoke early the following day to bake bread. By noon heat was pouring, like a red tongued invective, from the oven. A drop of perspiration trickled down her brow, and hung suspended from the tip of her nose. Impatiently she brushed it aside and, jutting her chin, blew upward at the strand of hair that was plastered against her face.

Long ago she had seen a fox in a trap, red eyes glinting crazily in its fear-damp furry face. Caught here in this hot hovel on a street that ended in the graveyard she had a good idea how that fox must have felt.

It was fruitless to talk about money. Remote as the Pindus Mountains, Socrates lived in a world of his own. Instead of paying attention to her needs he would try to assuage her with sophisms. The more he refused to take pay for the lectures he gave so freely to his horde of followers, the more her resentment grew. Nevertheless she would try again today.

"Socrates, your father left you five hundred drachmas that don't belong in a box under the bed," she said when he came in to he kitchen. "Crito is your friend. Talk to him. He'll be glad to help you invest your inheritance wisely so it can make a little extra for our needs."

"Stop worrying! The gods will look after us. They always do."

"What you mean is I always do. And I'm sick of pinching every oboloi, and buying cheap food."

"You have a way of turning simple fare into food for a king."

"Khesti!" "If you wish to put it that way," he said affably.

"By Hades' dog I do wish to put it that way, or any way at all if it gets you to hear what I'm trying to tell you!"

There were times when his perennial good humor was almost as aggravating as their lack of funds.

Before more could be said on the subject Phaenerete clumped into the kitchen where, day after day she sat, a somber figure swathed in black, morbidly indifferent to what was going on around her. It was as if she were disintegrating. Once the busiest midwife in Athens she now seemed incapable of moving away from the shadow of her loss.

"Forty seven years I lived with your father, Socrates," she sighed, grabbing her son's arm. "He was a part of me."

"Stop grieving, Mama," Socrates said, placing his hand over hers. "To die is a debt we must all discharge. It is the soul's journey to another land. We come together, we leave, we meet again. While we're on earth it is good to enjoy the gift of life until Hermes comes to tell us our time has come for the trip."

Phaenerete's tormented old face relaxed a little and, after giving her a light kiss on the forehead, Socrates hurried off. Today he was going to the Palaistra where others were probably already awaiting him.

"Sophroniscus and I never tired of talking to each other," his mother sighed, wiping her rheumy eyes and scratching her head beneath its widow's bonnet. "We were always pleasant. No harsh words. We enjoyed many happy conversations."

But Xanthippe herself did not recall hearing Sophroniscus ever utter a complete sentence in the company of his wife.

* * * *

Heading for the Palaistra, that monumental structure made for athletic contests and adaptable for debate, Socrates was unable to shake the image of Xanthippe's face. With her chin puckered, and her lower lip tucked under her teeth, she looked like Lamprocles, trying not to cry. Was anyone ever actually free from the child he or she had been? Her fierce angers could just as well be screens to hide a frightened little girl.

She was also an intelligent and indomitable woman and he loved

256

her. The day would come when she'd discover the meaning of inner peace, and the joy of a life free of ambition and dependence on things.

"What's wrong?" she asked in surprise when he reappeared.

"I decided to come home."

"Why? Was no one at the Palaistra?"

"I don't know. I got as far as Simon the Cobbler's and turned around."

"Are you sick?"

"Not at all. I was thinking that, regardless of what you do, what mood you're in, or what words come out of your mouth you are a remarkable woman. You express yourself in many ways. I enjoy all of them. I also returned to say, 'I love you.' "

"Godsname what's come over you? What is it you want?"

"Can't a man compliment his wife without having her suspect that something is amiss?"

"No. Not you anyway! Not a man who races away each morning with his last mouthful of breakfast still unchewed!"

"Stop flagellating yourself with housework. Sit down with me and let all this wait awhile," Socrates indicated the cluttered kitchen. "I see you have Cleina hoeing a patch of ground. I'll get Lamprocles to help her. When a lad is five he is old enough to do a few tasks.

"Now," he said, coming back. "Let's try to find the woman I married, the lovable sensitive you."

"Socrates, good husband, while I sit here and discover all manner of nice things about myself perhaps you will clean up this mess, prepare supper, empty your mother's chamber pot, and, in your leisure time, wash her soiled bed-covers. Then, when Cleina has finished hoeing, try badgering her into helping me with my vegetable garden so we won't all starve. That is if so much as a cabbage can be coaxed out of that clay!"

"Listen to me!" Socrates grasped her hands and held them fast. "I know life here is not easy for you. I realize that Mother is a difficult woman. You are remarkably patient with her. And you take loving care of Lamprocles, all three of us for that matter. But treat yourself to a peaceful pause now and then. Take time to listen to the gods, to the great God, and see how your tasks grow lighter and your troubles vanish!

"If I talk to the gods perhaps one of them will come and bake the bread! Go ahead. Take a look!" Stiff-armed, Xanthippe pointed her finger at crumbs that were being attacked by a battalion of red ants, bowls in which sticky farina had dried to a paste, and a tunic Lamprocles had left on the floor to sop up a puddle of spilled milk.

"I get so tired," she sighed. "Sometimes I wish I could sit all by myself on top of Mount Parnassus. Perhaps that way I'd get a few moments in which to 'discover who I am' as you say." Her chin quivered.

"You are an attractive woman with eyes like two green stars."

"I am an angry woman!"

"There is an angry person in everyone. At one time my own temper gave me great trouble. What a pity that Eryximachos can not remove rage as if it were a tumorous growth. On the other hand there are circumstances when indignation is justified, and the courage to express it can be viewed as a show of strength".

"My anger gives me strength."

"You have even greater strengths," Socrates persevered, ignoring her look of disdain, "a fine mind, a strong life force, and your own particular essence. I recall telling that to you the day we walked to the sea. Remember, I said that the brightness of you made me think of Clytie!"

"I think she died"

"Clytie?"

"No, the Xanthippe of whom you speak. She died and left an unhappy old nag in her place. What good is a mind when one is too tired to use it? A smart woman is a miserable one. You have to be dumb to put up with non-stop housework. I know I'm smart. Yet what good does it do me? Were I a man I'd have accomplished anything I wished. And, as you suggest, I would know who I am! My entire life has been circumscribed by my sex! What good has the education I got from Archos been? Whatever I learned, my sorry attempts to be myself, the things I questioned, all just served to get me into trouble. No thank you, Socrates. I'm not interested in discovering who I am because by the gods I do not like who I am!"

Instead of answering, Socrates sat quietly studying his wife's thin, mobile face.

"Why do you stare?" she asked. "Am I so beautiful you can't take your eyes away?"

"Yes", he said simply. "A unique kind of beauty, unmatched by any woman in Athens."

With a crow of laughter Xanthippe seized a knife and, raising her arm aloft, pointed it like a spear toward the sky.

"I think I've seen you before, Athena", Socrates laughed. "On the Acropolis!"

It was then that he noticed her old scar, looking more than ordinarily inflamed. Which was not to be wondered at. This kitchen court really was infernally hot.

"Tomorrow we shall go to the bankers' tables", he said.

"I can put your money out to loan. The returns will be modest but if we re-invest them you will gradually accrue enough to buy a small piece of land. There's no better purchase on earth than earth," Crito said the following day when Xanthippe and Socrates sought his advice. "In recent years Athens' population has soared to over 150,000 citizens, 35,000 resident foreigners and 80,000 slaves! What's more, I'm convinced it will continue to enlarge."

Xanthippe's spirits lifted. Despite everything, she respected this man. His direct approach, and crisp clean look instilled confidence when financial matters were at stake. No 'head in the clouds' folly for Crito!

How astonished he'd be to realize that she was the girl his son had preferred to Kallia. Or to know that she, Socrates' wife, had been in love with his son for fifteen years? He'd be all the more startled to discover what had taken place under the old hollow tree!

"Thank you for your time and care, Crito. We'll leave it to you to decide what we should do. As you know I am wool-headed when it comes to these matters. Now, if you will both excuse me, I am committed to joining Eucleides and Terpsion in the Agora."

"One would never know to look at my husband that he is so occupied with the thoughts in his mind he forgets to put food in his stomach. That would explain why he's hungrier when he's away from an audience." Xanthippe mused, following him with her eyes as he hurried off, looking awkwardly graceful. Like a goat.

"Stay awhile and keep a lonely old man company," Crito said, as if forgetting that he and her husband were the same age."Give me the pleasure of sharing a little wine and water with you."

"You have known my son and daughter-in-law for a long time," he said after they had chatted briefly about this and that.

She nodded.

"Have you seen either of them lately?"

"Not since Myrto's party."

"Kallia is unwell. Some people think she drinks too much but that just isn't so. Eryximachos was not able to diagnose her malady so he consulted other physicians. One claimed to have seen similar cases. It starts with noticeable tremors, especially in the fingers and hands. Then, gradually, muscles turn rigid and the speech blurs. The entire body slows down, all but that awful trembling. Even Kallia's face has become . . ." Crito groped for the word, "expressionless. Without laughter, like a mask. My dear, I can tell by your eyes, I have startled you. Perhaps you cared more for my son's wife than I guessed."

"I cared more for your son than you guessed," Xanthippe was thinking. Aloud she said, "It moves me to hear of anyone being so afflicted".

"Sadly enough, when these things happen many so called friends are no longer around. Hipparete visits once in awhile but, like other young matrons, she is occupied with children and the household matters. Socrates pays you a tribute, Xanthippe, when he says that you make him see himself more objectively, because you bring out the best and worst in him. "I'd be grateful if you would visit Kallia. At this point I wouldn't even mind if you managed to bring out some of her . . . not always cordial, disposition," he said with a rueful smile. "I'd see it as a progressive step toward her restored health."

"Your compliments are undeserved but I will visit Kallia before the week is out," she promised. "I know she loves sweets so I'll bake some almond kourabeides. Perhaps they'll please her even though mine aren't as good as Mama's."

Sometimes an expressionless face can be a boon. Get a grip on yourself. Say goodbye and leave. With these thoughts in mind Xanthippe thanked Crito for her drink and arose.

"So, how would you like to trade places with Kallia now?" she asked herself as she moved away from the bankers' tables.

Socrates could be right. Can a woman become so caught up in life's dull exigencies she forgets to live in the present, and savor the pleasure of just being alive and enjoying good health. Was she, Xanthippe, stuck in time, hanging onto something that happened a forgotten dream ago, as if it were a raft in the sea?

Walking home through a labyrinth of narrow streets and torturous alleys lined with the malodorous stables of Athens, Xanthippe looked up into a sail of clouds floating through a very blue sky. She could almost feel some of her pent up rage ebbing away in the dazzling sunshine, rebounding on her from white-washed walls. A black hoopoe bird probed his red bill between cobblestones for bugs and a grinning dog ran out of no-where to be patted. "I'll visit Kallia and try to think of Critobolus as an old friend," she decided. "Nothing more."

* * * *

Putting her misgivings aside, Xanthippe set out. She had given Crito her word and, by Zeus, she'd keep it.

When she reached her destination she lingered awhile at the gate.

Seven years ago she had spent a war-time summer in this beautiful place. After the war, instead of moving into her husband's family home, Kallia had insisted on residing here in the house owned by her father.

Which meant that now the man Xanthippe loved lived here with the woman upon whom she was about to pay a call,

"She will wonder what prompted me to come. We've known each other from childhood but we were foes, not friends. She will probably think I'm here out of spite, or curiosity, or to gloat over her misfortune," Xanthippe thought, giving the bell a pull.

A slave came to the gate and led her into the courtyard where Kallia was sitting in a curve-backed arm chair with not only her hands, but her entire body atremble.

"I remembered you always liked Mama's kourabeides so I made some for you." Xanthippe said.

To her surprise Kallia smiled. "It was nice of you to come" she replied, and, after tasting one of the almond cakes, "This is are every bit as good as the ones your mother used to make!"

Crito had tried to describe Kallia's condition but the reality of it was appalling. Her tongue, her hands, in fact her entire body seemed to be totally out of control. "At first I was so bitter about what was happening to me. I cursed the gods," she said, after a bit more 'small talk' had been exchanged. Seeing what a struggle it was for her to express herself, Xanthippe leaned forward, straining to hear and understand.

"After awhile I stopped being angry, at least to some extent," Kallia continued. "Critobolus was partly responsible because he kept quoting things your husband says, such as, 'If we are to know the sweet secret of contentment, even in times of trial, we must learn how to accommodate to any given situation.'

"He made me furious. I asked Socrates to come here and tell me what he meant by thinking that such silly advice could help anyone in my condition. I wanted to tell him, to his face, that he was crazy." Although there was emotion in Kallia's nearly inaudible voice, her face remained blank. "He came and talked to me about dying and being reborn. He believes in an all-powerful 'something-or-other' who sets things in motion and causes them to serve a good purpose, even when it's an illness as hateful as mine. According to your husband the 'Being' has no name but . . . Oh to Hades' pits!" Kallia cried weakly. "When

Socrates is here and says things like that they make sense and I feel better until he leaves. I guess you have heard all of this before."

It was not solely her garbled speech that kept Xanthippe from understanding everything she said. It was the comment she had made about being empowered by the physical presence of Socrates that was incomprehensible. Why could Kallia derive so much comfort from him when his own wife could not? Struck by a new idea she frowned. Was it conceivable that she still envied this pitiful woman named Kallia?

Wishing to change the subject, Xanthippe reminisced. "Mama often mentions the summer when Pericles ordered everyone who lived beyond the Great Walls to move to Athens," she said. "You probably remember that first summer when we had to leave the farm and your father insisted that we make use of this beautiful house. You should have seen Mama! She thought she was in paradise, and kept running about, all over the place. Every time she found something new to marvel at she would call the rest of us to come look. She wasn't the only one. I loved being here too. I kept trying to figure out how we could live in Athens for half a year, and spend the other six months at home."

"That's funny," Kallia's little laugh sounded pathetically like a hiccup. "The town girls wanted to live in the country. But that was mostly because we all envied you, Myrto too although she'd never admit it. We thought you were daring. You rode horses, even had one of your own! You drove a chariot, and had a big hollow tree that you pretended was the Theater of Dionysius. Hipparete told us about it."

Kallia was trembling more noticeably. "Visit me again," she said when Xanthippe said it was time for her to leave, "I get lonely. I . . . I'm different. I've changed. It's not just this sickness . . . Do you understand what I mean?"

"Yes. I do. And I'll try to return. May I bring you anything else? Some baklava perhaps?"

"No. Just come again."

"At the very time I was being jealous of those girls in town they were envying me! How little we know about what goes on in other people's heads," Xanthippe marvelled, homeward bound.

One thing was certain. From now on she would definitely not allow herself the luxury of daydreaming about Critobolus.

Never again! May the gods strike me dead if I do. And, considering the plight his wife was in, they might!

"I don't know what I'd do without Critobolus," Kallia had said. "By now most men would have turned their wives over to the slaves. He's very good to me . . . even though I never gave him a son."

Chapter Thirty-seven

Eyeing Xanthippe the black goat emitted one of his irritating giggles as, hoisting her skirts, she picked her way across the yard.

"Be still you silly fool" she snapped and shoved her spade into the ground.

To grow anything at all in this clay was a major feat but under her aegis it was beginning to produce, fortunately too, because the interminable war had food prices rising.

Dreams of immediate wealth had evaporated with Crito's reminder that Socrates' funds had not multiplied enough to allow an investment in property. Even if they had, dividends from land were slow to accrue. The same might be said of getting food from this plot she thought grabbing up a handful of malformed beets.

"What's going on?" she asked when back in the house she found her husband and son stamping and whirling in the courtyard

"We shall stop for now, my boy," his father said. "You have done very well. Run along and join your friends."

Gladly Lamprocles disappeared through the gate and they could hear him halooing to the potters' children to come and play.

"As you know, our son is five. It's time for him to be prepared for school. Since we are a family of modest means I myself shall tutor him, rather than engage a paidogogus. "Socrates said

Xanthippe's eyes widened. "You will WHAT?"

"Yes, my dear. We'll begin with lessons in dance, running and throwing, then gradually add memory work, history, and numbers. To be a whole person Lamprocles must develop his body as precursor to the expansion of his soul. Young men who spend all their time at sports become hard and savage. On the other hand those who study music and art to the exclusion of physical exercise get soft and lack courage."

"Man has two natures. When they are in concord his soul is both temperate and brave. There is little use in dancings, huntings, houndings, and gymnastic contests if communion with the Muse is excluded. A taste for learning and reasoning must also be developed to keep a person from becoming spiritually weak, deaf, and blind. His senses must be purified. I shall teach Lamprocles to expatiate both body and soul."

"A large order for a five year old. Even I could not understand half of what you just said."

Socrates chuckled and, still smiling, patted Xanthippe and bade her adio. As he loitered down the street with his absurd gait of a water fowl she watched him go. What was his secret, she wondered, what could it be about this maddening man, that had her caring for him one moment and hating him the next.

She had cleaned up after Phaenerete and was about to settle down to patching coverlets when the gate bell sounded.

It was Hipparete standing there. She looked quite thin and her violet eyes were shadowed.

"Come in!" Xanthippe exclaimed. "Sit here in the courtyard. Forgive the mess. I'll get to it one of these days."

"It's been so long since I've seen you," Hipparete sighed and sank down on a bench. "Why did you never answer my messages?"

"I never received any. I didn't expect to. I thought you were too busy with parties and friends to have any time left for me. Or this." Xanthippe indicated the shabby courtyard.

"Did you get the silk peplos I sent to replace the one my husband stained with wine at Myrto's party?" Hipparete asked.

"You sent me a dress?"

"Yes. I might have known I couldn't depend on Alcibiades to send either the peplos or my messages. Instead of trusting him I should have done it myself. I have been unwell, Xanthippe. Life with him is intolerable. It's worse since he became a General. Even his most devoted sycophants grow weary."

"Alcibiades may be rude to others but he has always adored you, or so I thought . . ."

"Xanthippe. you think everyone who has wealth and travels with the aristoi is happy. You're wrong. I've envied you because your husband is kind, and gentle, and full of laughter. You yourself loathe Alcibiades, so how can you think I find any contentment with him? Those who have seen him grow violent over some insignificant matter find it hard to believe he's the same man who can charm anyone he meets. His moods change at whim. He's neither truthful or dependable. His most recent escapade involves a plot with the city of Argos. They plan to break Nicias' Peace Treaty, one that he originally supported. It's as if he has forgotten everything Socrates ever taught him. He's a madman. Some of the things he does are horrible!

"Horrible?

What do you mean?"

"He participates in all sorts of ugliness, even to fouling the altar of the gods. And I found him . . ." Tears streamed down Hipparete's face and she had difficulty going on. "He forces me to engage in activities that sicken me and last week I found him asking our little son to -" She shook her head, unable to go on.

"Zeus!" "I can't talk about it," Hipparete said when she composed herself. "Remember how, when we were girls we talked about 'making love'? 'Making love' is not in his vocabulary."

Unable to think of anything to say in the face of such disclosures Xanthippe sat silent. She was acquainted with the darkness that lurked behind Alcibiades handsome face. He had killed Cerberus. She had also seen his orgiastic delight in torturing a tortoise.

"I'm so afraid of his temper I can no longer tolerate being under the same roof with him. Yesterday he used me in a cruel fashion, not as if he were pleasuring himself but more as if he were driven. He kept repeating obscene words over and over. The ridiculous thing is . . .,"

For a moment Hipparete's old gamin grin reappeared, "It's always some small matter that pushes a person over the brink. In my case it was the sound of his lisp when he said those damnable things that finalized my decision to leave."

"Where will you go?"

"To my brother Callias. After Grandfather Callias died the house went to him. He always knew my marriage was wrong and he has agreed to intercede for me in court. The reason our mother could get a divorce was that Pericles took care of it for her. Men get divorced when they please but did you ever hear of a woman who did so?"

Xanthippe shook her head. No one had ever heard of that!

"I tried to be a discreet wife, even in face of the scandalous affairs he carries on openly. But if I don't get away from him I shall die. Although I have no idea how it can be managed I must take my children with me when I go."

"I want to help you," Xanthippe said urgently. "You're the only real friend I ever had. I meant it when we pricked our thumbs and pressed them together to mingle our blood as a pledge of eternal friendship. Nor will I ever forget that you told Alcibiades you wouldn't marry him until I could be your bride's attendant. What a fight you must have put up to get him, as well as your father to agree to that when you so many other friends you could have asked."

"You, Xanthippe, were the only one of them with whom I truly had a happy time. You were fun to be with and fascinating, even when you were furious! You still are. I've wondered if growing up with horses, and being able to control them, was what made you seem superior to others. Did it give you a feeling of power, as if you were a god or a Centaur?"

"In a way perhaps. Why?"

"I always had an idea it contributed to your remarkable vitality. Alcibiades has a passion for horses but he's not a bit like you. He's strong but mean, and makes no bones about running down this man and that on the race track. He has maimed and killed people. I've heard him brag about how he edges a chariot until the driver fell beneath his horse. He says he does it to teach commoners not to tangle with their superiors."

For awhile they sat quietly then Hipparete spoke again. "Love is like phyllo pastry. If you stretch it too far it tears. If my husband really tried to practice what Socrates preaches he wouldn't abuse love the way he does. Yet I can't seem to learn how one can go on giving love without getting any in return."

"I've wondered about that myself. I'm not even sure I want to try doing that any more, not when love hurts too much to take the risk of loving! But tell me, what do you plan to do next?"

"Go to the Court of Justice. You asked if you could help me and I came hoping to persuade you to go before the tribunal with me so I wont be the only woman there. Besides, having you by my side would give me courage."

"I'll be proud to go with you."

"You're a remarkable woman," Hipparete said gravely. "As I've told you, Yiayia Elpinice thought so too. She said that any girl who had you for a friend could consider herself fortunate."

At this the old familiar lump invaded Xanthippe's throat. It was all she could do to choke, "That is a tribute I shall have to earn," she said gravely.

* * * *

Having decided not to speak to anyone about her mission, Xanthippe walked toward the Hill of Ares on a foot-path lined with great gnarled trees. The road itself had been made of marble slabs, mostly white but accented here and there by blocks of red, gray, orange and yellow. Lost in her own reflections, she saw none of it.

Hipparete was already standing in front of the 'Areopagus', an immense open ended quadrangle dug out of rock. Benches, within the three sided courtroom, allowed spectators to view proceedings, while the accused and their accusers, as well as those with private matters to be settled, stood before them on a platform of stone.

"I told Callias we'd meet him over there." Hipparete pointed to a small sanctuary, placed there for the Erinyes, those three venerable deities who punished crime, were feared by gods and men alike, and could be called upon to intervene in legal problems.

Timidly the young women seated themselves and examined their surroundings. "Yesterday I heard about two women who obtained divorces here a hundred years ago. But, like my mother, they had no need to appear because their cases were negotiated by men. I shall probably make history because, although my brother will be here to support me, I must state my own case. I hired a rhetorician to write it for me." Hipparete said, with a nervous glance at the roll of papyrus in her hand."

Both she and Xanthippe had fallen silent when, with a thunderous clatter a chariot, drawn by two black horses, came racing up the marble driveway. Sparks flew from the animals' hooves as they stopped dead in front of the Areopagus.

"Oh God, it's Alcibiades!" Hipparete, already pale, was now ashen.

The horses flanks were bloody as was the whip Alcibiades clutched in his hand. Flinging the reins to a slave he jumped from the cart and strode to the bench where his wife and Xanthippe were sitting, rigid with fear. His face contorted with fury he twirled the whip aloft and snapped it across Hipparete's legs.

"What do you think you're doing here?" he rasped, ignoring her cry of pain. "Are you crazy enough to think I wouldn't find out what you were up to?" Grabbing her by the shoulder, he jerked her to a standing position and accosted Xanthippe.

"You meddlesome bitch! Don't you ever dare to come near my wife again or I'll give both of you cause for regret!"

Savagely Alcibiades thrust Hipparete into the chariot. "Hang on or get your neck broken!" he yelled and, giving the lathered horses a lash, wheeled the chariot about and plummeted back down the drive.

Xanthippe caught the look of terror on her friend's face and winced. Helplessly she watched Hipparete being born away, knowing that there was nothing she could do to help.

Bitterly she turned away from the 'Hall of Justice' and walked back to Cerameicus Road.

When she got home Lamprocles was waiting for her at the gate.

"Mama, Grandpapa Palen's slave is here," he said.

"Where?"

"There". He pointed to a bench in the courtyard.

"I bring bad news," Andokides said gravely. "Your brother Elefterous is dead."

Staring in disbelief Xanthippe felt the blood drain from her face. It was too much. Hipparete, Now this. How could Elefterous be dead when he'd just returned from the war.

"What happened?" she cried.

From the slave's mumbled response she gleaned that there had been an accident, something to do with a horse.

"My brother is dead. I must go at once," she panted to Phaenerete and Cleina. "Look after Lamprocles and tell my husband." Hurriedly she threw into a sack and joined Andokides.

Before the donkey cart could come to a complete stop in front of the farmhouse she was already out of it and running.

"Mama!" she cried. "What happened?"

Shaking her head from side to side Nikandra pointed.

Bracing herself Xanthippe looked side-ways across the courtyard and saw, from the corner of her eye, a still figure on a long wooden plank. She clenched the chords in her neck to stifle a scream. This dare not be real. Not today. Not right after that horrible experience on the Ares Hill.

It was Marc who explained. After serving his term in the army Elefterous had hoped to surprise Palen by competing in the next chariot race. Enlisting the aid of Andokides and Marc, he would harness a team and practice whenever his father was away. But Palen seldom absented himself during the day, which limited Elefterous' time on the track.

Nonetheless he had been gaining confidence. Yesterday he had been maneuvering a sharp turn when Palen returned sooner than expected. Elefterous, caught sight of him, lost control, and was flung from the chariot. The fall broke his neck and, without regaining consciousness, he had died.

"Where is Papa?"

"Somewhere down by the paddock. He just sits there all by himself, and wont speak to anyone.

"He'll talk to me. Tell Mama, I'll be back as soon as I tell him I'm here."

* * * *

Xanthippe found her father in the tack room. He was polishing a stirrup that already shone with ceaseless rubbing.

"Papa, I came because of . . . what happened."

"A terrible thing." He scowled. "I thank the gods I still have Marc."

If only, just this once, he could have said, "Thank the gods I still have you and Marc." But no, that would not be Papa.

"I don't think any of us ever really got to know Elefterous, not really."

Xanthippe sighed, thinking about her brother's taut little grin, and his feckless pursuit of Palen's approval.

"I'm going back to the house. I'll see you there." she said when her father did not answer. He seemed not to have heard.

For a long time Xanthippe stood beside the slab on which her brother's body lay. Except for a few bruises on his face, one might think he was asleep. The longer she looked at him the more he appeared to be actually breathing. Her scalp prickled. Name of god where was Elefterous now?

Nikandra, looking dazed, was apparently finding solace in familiar tasks. She had broken a hunk of goat cheese into pieces and placed it in a bowl with olives, goat cheese, and green horta leaves. Now she was slicing bread. Wiping her hands she poured wine and water into cups and motioned Xanthippe to join her at the table. "We go from bad to worse," she sighed. "I was so thankful when Elefterous came home safe after serving his two years. And then . . ." She glanced toward the far end of the courtyard and her lips trembled.

In an effort to hold her own emotions in check, Xanthippe concentrated on watching her mother's lips as they moved. Miniscule lines had formed a lattice-work around them. Time, that most merciless of artists, was slowly but surely etching Nikandra's anxieties on her once pretty face. Her habit of nibbling the inside of her cheek was also more pronounced. There was a wispiness about her, a kind of fragility that brought to mind those little puffs of wool that float through the loom room with every gust of wind.

"Marc has to return for another year of duty in the army," Nikandra said "I always seem to be worrying about something. Worry. worry, worry. About so many things. I worried about Elefterous." She sighed heavily. "Lately I have received comfort from the Orpheans." The strained look on her face eased a bit.

"Orpheans?"

"Religious messengers from Thrace. I attend their meetings when I can get away. Don't tell your father."

"What do they do?"

"Chant and make prophecies. They're descendants of Orpheus the minstrel. You remember, the man who turned into a god. They believe that the soul is trapped inside the body as a punishment for wrong doings. I've often wondered what I did that was so bad. If one donates jewelry, and doesn't drink wine, she is pardoned. I gave my necklace . . . but I still drink wine."

"Mama! You didn't give them your gold beads?"

Nikandra's hands squirmed in her lap. She nodded. "The priests of Orpheus say if we live in purity and practice the rites we'll enjoy great happiness in the afterlife. We can even keep the souls of those we love from going to Tartarus." Again her teary eyes strayed toward the courtyard.

Briefly Xanthippe considered asking her mother if she actually believed all the things she'd been told by the Orpheans. The whole business sounded strange. On the other hand, why question anything that might help Mama get through her ordeal? "Early this morning I went to a little Orphean shrine in Cholargus and asked the priest to cast a spell for Elefterous. It made me feel better. Would you like to hear one of their chants?"

Xanthippe nodded.

Shyly Nikandra began, her thin voice cracking as she sang.

"Parched with thirst am I and dying,
Nay! Drink of Me the ever flowing spring,
Who art Thou? Who art Thou?
I am the Son of Earth and Heaven
But Heaven alone is my house."

Xanthippe was about to say something nice about the song when Socrates appeared. Not only was she pleased by his punctual arrival, but because he had thought to bring Lamprocles along.

Most of all she was touched by his solicitude for Nikandra.

As he talked with her one could see her face brighten. At one point, she even laughed at something he whispered in her ear.

* * * *

People had been notified by word of mouth that Elefterous would be buried in the ash grove and Lysicles was among the many who came to observe the Rites of Passage. But Nikandra was too blinded by grief to notice who was standing there beside him.

Xanthippe saw her right away. Lysicles' second wife had a heart shaped, high cheek-boned face, and the sturdy chin of a peasant. Her large eyes were the color of wood-smoke, and her lips so voluptuous they seemed to be dripping with honey and wine. Her ebony silver-streaked hair was modestly bound with a band. But especially notable was the look of calm serenity on Aspasia's face.

'Arrogant,' 'Plain' 'An unprincipled companion of men,' was how gossips described her. All of which made Xanthippe wonder if any one of them had ever seen her.

"I've looked forward to meeting you," she told Xanthippe when the rites were over and the time had come for mourners to gather in the courtyard and eat the funeral feast. Gifts of food had continued to arrive almost until the burial rites began. Aspasia herself had prepared a cassoleta of lamb.

It's so fitting, at times like these, to break bread together, and drink, and remember," she said. "I want you to know how sad I am for all of you who have suffered this tragic loss. When your mother is ready to talk, and share some of what she must be feeling, I shall come back for a visit with her.

"I am pleased to see Socrates," she said. "I found him to be a man of extraordinary perception when, many years ago, he and I undertook the study of rhetoric."

There was something about Aspasia that set Xanthippe to wondering who she resembled.

Who was it? . . . Someone with that same warm smile and earthy beauty.

Femma! Name of god where was she? Where had she gone? What could have induced her to leave her charming little house? Had she . . . the gods forbid, . . . was she, like Elefterous, and so many other dear ones, dead?

Chapter Thirty-eight

Abstractedly Xanthippe watched Socrates eat his breakfast and wondered if she would be able to eliminate the dilled olive oil he had splashed down the front of his cloak.

"What are you thinking about so seriously?" He gave her a quizzical look. "Is something bothering you?"

"What could possibly bother me?" Her voice was acidulous. "I have a roof over my head, one that leaks in only a few places, food enough to keep us from starving, provided I raise most of it myself, plenty of work to keep me occupied every waking hour, and I'm married to a cheerful eunuch who slops food on his garments and only comes home when he has no place to go. If I stabbed you with a knife in your fat stomach you would probably go right on urging me to find out who I really am while you bled to death on the floor." As if to illustrate, Xanthippe speared a loaf of bread and flung it to the ground.

"I shall never be in danger of becoming vain, not as long as I have you," Socrates chuckled.

"Will you listen to me? While you are trotting all over town telling rich people about virtue and truth, I am in the Agora trying to buy food with no money. I expected to marry a provident man. Instead I got a teacher who won't take pay even when it's offered. And, although you may be Athen's most popular Master, your own son isn't learning a fig. If we don't soon get enough money to hire a paidogogus the child may never get into school at all!"

Circling the table Xanthippe sat down beside her husband and put her hand on his knee. "We bicker. I tell you my troubles, you answer with a discourse on inner peace. That's all we ever do. Back and forth, back and forth, getting nowhere. "I beg you, stop debating with people.

273

Give it up," she urged. "What good does it do? Hundreds of words, all of them useless. You might as well spit in the sea. Half the people who tag after you do so only because they think it connotes cleverness to be seen in your company. Go back to being a sculptor like your father. As long as people continue to die there will be a market for memorial steles."

"I must continue to fight ignorance even if no more than one in ten thousand gains lasting benefit," Socrates replied. "For example, in going from poet to artist to craftsmen, I reached the conclusion that poets write by a sort of celestial inspiration. Like divinators, they say fine things without understanding the meaning of them . . . "It is as if, in a state of semi-consciousness, they are guided by a Muse. If their poetry meets with public acclaim, they immediately consider themselves to be authorities on all sorts of high matters about which they know little or nothing. Poets should be encouraged to think before they speak. That also applies to artisans. They at least seem to have a better knowledge of their craft.

"What does all this have to do with you?"

"By questioning people, the poets for example, some of them come to realize that, although they are blessed with skill, they don't know everything. I believe the Oracle called me 'wise' because I know and admit I am not. Only God is wise. He may be using me to search the minds of others just to illustrate that the wisdom of man is worth little or nothing."

"You pick, pick, pick at people, badgering them to search their souls until you have them so confused they can't even remember their names! You wouldn't try to change an octopus into an eel would you?"

"No. An eel knows he's an eel, and is content with his eelhood. But the average human pretends, even to himself, to be what he is not."

"To Hades pits with eels. You evade the issue which is my need for money to keep us from going hungry and threadbare. I keep putting patches on top of patches and I can barely get together enough thread to do that." Xanthippe's voice had risen to such a pitch that people in the street paused to listen.

"A poppy never worries about what to wear yet have you ever seen anything more gloriously garbed?" Socrates asked.

"Are you suggesting that I, your wife, and the mother of your son, emulate the poppy, and appear in the streets of Athens covered only by the scarlet thatch on my private part?"

With a roar of laughter Socrates seized his wife in his arms, intruding on her anger.

"Are you mad?" she shouted, pulling away. "What's come over you? It's six weeks since you approached me in bed, and now you tear at my clothes out here in the courtyard! We've scarcely finished breakfast!"

Later, still in his arms, she savored the languor of a nap before noon and woke only when he gently released her and arose.

"I'm on my way to the Palaistra to meet a wiley politician named Kritias," Socrates said. "He wants to introduce me to his nephew. The boy's name is Aristocles but they call him Plato because of his broad shoulders. He's only twelve yet Kritias claims he's so smart he can stand his ground with any Sophist."

"Have you forgotten your promise to accompany me to Agathon's 'Antheus' this afternoon?"

"Indeed not. I shall meet you at the appointed time."

"Take your good cloak with you when you go to the baths and be sure to use it instead of that thing you have on."

That afternoon, as she approached the theater, Xanthippe saw him, still wearing the signatures of everything he'd had for breakfast, and looking like a barefoot mendicant. Once again he had managed to make both of them the butt of jokes. No doubt his clean new himation was hanging from a peg in the Palaistra.

"For once I arrived, not only in time, but ahead of you," he greeted her cheerfully. "You're shivering, Agape Mou. You should have worn a cloak. Here. Take mine."

Snatching the odious garment, she flung it on the footpath, and stamped on it. "I'd freeze to death before I wore the filthy thing!" she raged.

"I thought you were here to see, not to be seen." he remonstrated lightly,

"Very nice, Socrates!" she retorted. "By tomorrow that sprightly comment will be on every lip in Athens. Even your husbandly quips have a way of turning into great wisdoms."

"That's a hard act for Agathon to follow!" someone yelled a others looked on in delight.

Socrates, unperturbed and underdressed in his tunic, took his wife's arm. "Shall we go in and find our seats?" he asked.

When the drama ended Agathon came to the stage and bowed to wild applause. As for Xanthippe, the afternoon had been a prolonged agony. She had disgraced herself again, this time before the whole world!

"I'm sorry I upset you," Socrates apologized on the way home. "The extraordinary conversation I had with young Plato erased everything else from my mind. At least," he chuckled, "I didn't walk into the theater wearing nothing at all. Like one of God's poppies, if you will."

"You would have looked better if you had."

"Don't grieve, Agape Mou. It wasn't all that bad. Look at it this way. Today you became the first woman ever to perform before a large audience at the Theater of Dionysius, or should I say, in front of it. We learn from each other, you and I," he continued, seemingly blind to her dark look. "I provoke you. You challenge me. No two people can co-exist in everlasting harmony. It is from friction and difficult days that character is built."

"If that is true I've amassed enough character to last me the rest of my life! I'd like to have a few days that didn't build it one whit!"

*   *   *   *

"What transpires? I have never seen you so stylishly clad!" a disciple, Appolodorus by name, exclaimed when Socrates ambled into the Palaistra wearing sandals and a clean unspotted cloak. Even his hair and beard had undergone a combing!

"It pleases my wife. I'm trying to be more thoughtful of her feelings." Socrates replied. "although, frankly, I take more interest in trying to cleanse the thoughts of my mind than clothing myself in a new unblemished garment."

"I gathered her feelings can become pretty intense when I witnessed her sensational exhibition in front of the theater. It is she, not Agathon, who should have been given a prize for drama. Shouldn't you have applied a bit of manual discipline?"

"So bystanders could form a ring while we were at fisticuffs and shout 'Well done', Socrates', or 'Hit him again, Xanthippe!' I think not. However, in view of what you say, this may be the time to consider the role of women in our 'ideal republic'."

Raising his hands above his head, he said, "I pray to you Nemesis, goddess of righteous anger. Since it is not as bad to kill a man as it is to deceive him in any way, help me to speak clearly, honestly, and well."

"Socrates, if we get into any trouble as a result of this debate we hereby acquit you of manslaughter," Phaedo, another follower declared.

"You're so pure you couldn't deceive anyone if you tried. Speak on!"

"Very well. I shall begin by asking if you think females in a pack of guardian dogs should share in the guard males keep? Ought they join in the hunt or be kept in the kennel taking care of puppies while the males do all outdoor work taking care of flocks?"

"They should work together," young Xenophon affirmed.

"Is it possible to use both male and female dogs for the same purposes if they don't have equivalent training?"

"Impossible."

"So if women do the same things as men must they be taught the same?"

"Yes"

"Music, gymnastic, matters of war?"

There were laughs and a few shouts of 'Yes'.

"You think this sounds funny? Agreed. The biggest joke of all would be naked women in the wrestling school, not only young ones but the old too, competing with men. And like the elders in the gymnasium not pleasant to look at but still fancying the game," Socrates said, rolling his great blue eyes sidewise.

"Very well," he continued, after waiting for the hilarity he'd evoked to subside. "Let refined people talk as much as they wish about such an upheaval and let us not forget the wearing of armor and riding horseback is also to be included."

"Socrates, good Master, I'm sure that as far as you are concerned the idea of women on horseback is not shocking," Xenophon said earnestly. "My father claims your wife was an excellent rider. But I myself don't hold with it. Women belong in the home."

"She *was* a rider of horses," Socrates corrected him. "Only because she is a female was she forbidden to continue. Suppose we ask ourselves, 'Do the natures of bald men differ from those of hairy men? If so, should we then forbid long-haired men to make sandals if short-haired men do?" He gave his listeners a roguish grin.

"Then, whether it be to prescribe medicine, or wear a suit of armor do we agree it is a woman's nature, not her sex that suits her for being a healer or, on the other hand warlike?"

"By my beard Socrates has proof that women can be warlike! Take a look at his wife," one of his listeners laughed.

"If we have everything in common, must the nurturing of children be shared too?" Socrates asked, ignoring him.

"That would be hotly disputed," a man named Adeimantos avowed.

"Should permissible sexuality replace monogamy, and the children of such unions be considered the children of all? Should women past the age of child-bearing be left free to consort at will? In conclusion," Socrates said, dousing the flames of argument he had ignited, before they could become a major conflagration, "Let me remind you again never to cease searching for wisdom and truth in all matters and to keep your gaze forever focused on the light that lies within."

"Where are you going now, Master?" Phaedo asked, keeping pace as best he could as they passed through the crowd that pressed in on them from all sides.

"To the baths. I'm going to dinner at the home of a pretty man so I must make myself pretty." Smiling enormously Socrates hurried away leaving chaps younger than he shaking their heads in amazement at his inexhaustible energy.

"Does he get it from that inner source he's always spouting about?"

"Time goes so fast when he talks that he's done and gone before you know it. It can be hours later but I still always feel as if we had barely begun."

"Yes. Time is a mystery. It seems that one minute you are involved in a heated debate and the next thing you know the whole thing is ancient history."

Chapter Thirty-nine

Sometimes Xanthippe wondered if she, like her mother-in- law, had become barren following the birth of one child. Now it was beginning to look as if another baby might be on the way.

By swallowing a dose of hydromel women could always tell if they were pregnant. When severe colic and nausea resulted from the elixir the answer was definitely 'Yes'. And that was Xanthippe's answer . . . 'Yes.'

"You look sick," Socrates said.

"We're going to have another child. I pray we can afford one. We should go to the Agora and ask Crito if we've made any money yet."

Socrates was obviously pleased. "I am very happy to hear that!" he said beaming at her. I'm glad to know that you and I are going to increase our family and that, at the same time, Athens will be getting another citizen!"

Because she had given him a son to carry on his line, Xanthippe now felt free to hope that the next one would be a girl. But, boy or girl, Lamprocles must not be made to feel supplanted the way she had when Marc and Elefterous were born.

Elefterous! It was still hard to realize that he was dead, and had been for close to a year. She had seen little of her parents in all that time. They rarely came to visit her, and she had not done much better.

"I think I shall walk to Cholargus tomorrow to see how Mama and Papa are getting along, and tell them the news," she said. "I'll take Lamprocles with me in his pull-cart. He loves going to the farm. Will you see if you can find where he went and tell him to come here and eat his breakfast? Cleina! Take the widow-Phaenerete her morning meal."

When everyone had eaten, Socrates went to the Agora, and Xanthippe went out into the courtyard. A few quiet moments to herself were the reward for seeing to it that trays of food were taken to the bedchamber of her cantankerous mother-in-law. In fact, the old woman's seclusion allowed more time to supplant the chronic chaos in the kitchen court with order. By now it was almost as tidy as Nikandra's.

Two crocks of olives had been cured and were ready to eat. A bag of cheese hung on the roof, dried to just the right consistency. The vegetable patch had yielded some cucumbers, a tomato or two and a few little cabbages. If she had some money to purchase a jug of wine life wouldn't be half bad!

"It's time to do something about this," Xanthippe thought, surveying the shabby courtyard. If it were, at least, clean, she might feel more comfortable about inviting someone to come in and sit down. How nice if that 'someone' could be Hipparete.

Two weeks following the day Alcibiades had flung Hipparete into the chariot and raced down the hill, a messenger had come to the gate. "The wife of Alcibiades asks me to say that you have no further cause for concern. Everything goes well with her," he recited. The worrisome thing was what came next. "She asks that you not try to get in touch with her." he had reported.

Beyond hoping Hipparete was no longer being mistreated, there was nothing Xanthippe could do.

"Call Festus and bring him with you into the courtyard," Xanthippe told Cleina when the dishes and food had been cleared away. "I want to hide these tombstones behind the house."

Festus had been saving every bit of money he could to buy freedom for Cleina and himself. He'd have to pay Socrates a good price which would come in handy but, in turn, there would be no more money coming in regularly from his labors in the shop. And Zeus alone knew how they'd get along without that, especially with a baby on the way.

"I won't miss Cleina," Xanthippe said to herself. "She does so little she seems to think she's already free and I'm the slave."

"Put a low price on these old grave markers and stack them behind the house where they can't be seen. Then take the ones that were were ordered but never claimed, the ones with peoples' names on them, and use them to make a fence that will keep the goats out of my vegetable patch." Leaving Festus to carry out her orders Xanthippe urged Cleina to help her go after the dust and grime.

They had been working for over two hours when Xanthippe, encouraged by the success of their efforts, brought her wedding gifts out of hiding. It was time for them to be seen and enjoyed (except for Alcibiades' gold goblets which she had decided to sell)

Late that afternoon she thanked the pair and dismissed them. "Before you go to your room, Cleina, will you boil the macaronia I made, and see to it that Mother-Phaenerete is comfortable? Lamprocles can play next door until I finish what I'm doing here."

Sunshine was turning the courtyard's mortared walls to golden pink. Stalks of leafy artemesia sprayed from a tall red floor vase, and some clumps of wild ivy, planted by the wall over a year ago, were big enough by now to partly conceal the blistered stucco and cracked paint.

Still not quite ready to quit, Xanthippe was standing on a bench trying to hang a colorful wall hanging that had been a gift from Hipparete's brother Hermogenes, when, hearing the gate creak open, she turned abruptly, and lost her balance. It was Critobolus who ran to catch her and kept her from falling.

For a moment she clung to him before forcing herself to pull away. It was not the voice of an inner daemon that had stayed her from remaining in his embrace, but a recollection of something she had heard Socrates say. "When following the dangerous path of desire one can quickly be pulled into disaster."

Shaken, less by her near fall than the emotions invoked by her rescue, Xanthippe drew away and, suddenly conscious of her appearance, pushed back her hair.

"You look lovely even when you do housework," Critobolus assured her. His voice, and the look in his eyes indicated that he too was disquieted.

"Well!" he said, on an exhalation of breath. "You have transformed this place."

"I'm getting all the work out of Cleina and Festus that I can before they leave for good. Festus has managed to buy their freedom, you know."

Critobolus nodded. "And then I appear in the middle of the afternoon and interrupt your task."

"I was ready to quit anyway. In fact I had already sent the slaves back to their room. Besides, I am glad to see you." To herself she whispered, "Be calm. Be calm."

"You must be wondering why I came. It's because I have something interesting to discuss with you. Is Socrates here?"

"No. He's in the Agora, lecturing at the Stoa of Zeus. If you wish you can tell me and I shall give him the message when he returns," Xanthippe said, grateful that her voice had not betrayed how she felt. It was a long time since they had been together with no one else present. Impossible as it seemed the last time had been that fateful afternoon in the ash grove. Small wonder she was finding it difficult to remain calm.

"Yes, by all means. It pertains to a matter that concerns both of you. But before we go into that, I want to thank you for the times you have visited Kallia. And for bringing her those treasures from your kitchen."

"How is she?"

"A bit weaker, perhaps but essentially the same. There's little change from day to day."

An interval passed during which neither spoke. Knowing danger lurked in the meeting of eyes, like moths circling a flame, they stared at one another.

"This must stop!" Xanthippe exhorted herself. "What am I thinking of? He has a sick wife, I have a husband and a son and I'm pregnant."

"What had you planned to tell me?" she asked hurriedly.

"Father came across an available piece of land, just beyond the Great Walls. It is so modestly priced we suggest that you buy it with some of the capital from Socrates' inheritance. It's beyond the city limits, but our feeling is that, someday, it will be worth more."

"You mean we have enough money to invest in land?"

Critobolus nodded. "We won't be using all of your capital. We plan to set a sum aside that can be used to loan out at interest so you and Socrates are assured of a small but steady source of income."

"How good you were to leave your banking table to bring such good news!" Xanthippe exclaimed. And, after a slight hesitation, "Stay awhile, Critobolus. Allow me give you a cup of cool barley water before you go! I have been longing to get this place clean enough to be able to invite a friend to come in and sit down!"

For a moment it looked as if Critobolus might decline. Then, "That sounds very pleasant," he said.

After bringing the beverage from her cooling cellar Xanthippe placed almond cakes on a platter and stood still long enough to regain her composure returned to the courtyard.

"I agree with Kallia. You bake the best kourabeides in Athens," her visitor said.

How handsome he looked, sun tanned and glowing with vitality. A bit older, but distinguished. Like his father.

For awhile they sat quietly enjoying the balm of a beautiful day.

When they spoke again it was as if time had rolled back on itself and they were still two young people, savoring their first conversation at the Apaturia. With one exception. Except that they were careful to avoid what was better left unsaid.

They laughed over the comical episodes that occur at banker's tables. They laughed again when Xanthippe imitated the way Festus made a sign every time he moved a tombstone. They spoke of politics, the theater, and how the on-going war with Sparta might affect the next Olympiad until it dawned on Xanthippe that they sounded like the potter and his wife.

"When will Socrates return?" Critobolus asked.

"He is usually home by sunset, but sometimes his debates last until dusk."

"I know. I often make it my business to leave the banking business behind in order to hear him speak. He's not only a brilliant teacher, he has the power to change peoples' lives! He gets them to think for themselves, and use their talents wisely. He is also the most honest man I ever met. "But let me say this, Xanthippe. He needs you. Don't ever underestimate the importance of what you do to provide him with food and comfort," Critobolus said earnestly. "There were times, before you and he got married, when he'd be so involved in his pursuit of wisdom, he'd forget to go home! Antiphon once said that if a slave were made to live so he'd run away!"

"The wisest man in Greece couldn't remember to go home?"

Suddenly they were laughing again.

"Socrates cares for you very much, Xanthippe." Critobolus returned to his subject as if willing himself to be serious. In a way, he seemed to be telling these things to himself.

"Time spent in your company passes much too quickly. I must be on my way," he said, glancing at the sky. When he stood up Xanthippe rose too. Their eyes interlocked, this time for no more than a moment. But long enough for Xanthippe to form a mental image.

It was that of two tall, slim people, Critobolus and Xanthippe. With minds and bodies seemingly matched they were analogous to a story told about the original man and woman who, until Zeus separated them, were one flesh. It was also Zeus who had given them their privy parts for purposes of procreation and pleasure.

"I must be going," Critobolus said again, giving his head a quick shake. "Talk to Socrates about that piece of property and, if he wants to go along with our suggestion, have him visit.

He had hardly left before a tearful Lamprocles appeared. The potter's boy had a hoop he would not share. Absently Xanthippe patted his head and he ran back out to play.

This was a busy, happy, unsettling day. The prediction of money to come from land outside the 'Walls' had thrilled her, But not nearly as much as the man who made it.

"I was playing in the street and look who followed me through our gate!" Lamprocles announced joyously. In his wake pattered a starved looking little mongrel whose mouth appeared to be grinning. A mouth that also consumed food.

But no child should be without a dog to love as she had loved Cerberus. Even yet it sometimes seemed as if her hound might appear at any moment. With a reminiscent smile she sat on the floor and stroked the head of Lamprocles' new friend.

Guiltily she jumped to her feet when Phaenerete waddled in. Xanthippe had almost forgotten she even had a mother-in-law!

She was stirring a bowl of eggs, cheese, and a shred of oregano when Socrates came home, earlier than usual.

"Is anything troubling you?" she asked, noticing a frown on his customarily serene face.

"Not really. I was thinking about what happened today," he said. "Young Menon and I were enjoying a splendid debate in regard to the definition and qualifications of virtue, when up came Anytus and pointed a finger at me,

'Pay no attention to this man!" he shouted. "Socrates is a doer of evil'. He is convinced that I influenced his son to defy him. He may be all the more vindicative because you were once betrothed to Astron and married me instead."

"Wrong! Anytus wouldn't sign the contract. Thank the gods!"

"In any case, the scene was a bit disruptive, but nothing with which to concern myself. Now, what was it that you were about to say?"

Chapter Forty

The air was intoxicating as new pressed wine and Xanthippe's mood matched the day. "Athenians walk with delicate feet through the most luminous ether." The words of Euripides came to mind as she traversed a webwork of autumn bright streets to the Agora. Upon gaining the vast market she stopped to watch a kid nuzzling its nanny while a flock of sheep stared at her in return.

Eight months had passed since she and Critobolus had enjoyed each other's company in her newly adorned courtyard. They'd had a lovely visit. Nonetheless he was no longer always on her mind. The intensity of her feelings for him had diminished. Soon she would have another child. Just the thought of it made her happy.

Something told her this one would be a girl. 'Phyllys' they would name her. How pleased Mama would be to have another little grandchild to call her 'Yiayia'!

"Have you heard that Alcibiades is our newly elected Archon?" asked the wheat merchant when she stopped at his booth to make a purchase.

"I don't believe it!" But she did. Alcibiades had never lost his power to bewitch people. The more flamboyantly he behaved the more he was adored. Lately, according to her informant, he'd taken to carrying a shield emblazoned with the figure of Eros. And this was the bastard who had just been anointed Ruler of the Athenian Empire!

Xanthippe still fantasized about bringing him to heel, but it had become more a habit than a firm ambition.

At least he was smart enough to realize that citizens everywhere loved and admired his wife. Nor could he help but know the political hazards inherent in the Athenian predilection for gossip. If anyone, even a slave, were to catch him treating Hipparete shabbily, he story would be spread and exaggerated all over Athens.

His new preeminence also might also keep him too busy to harass his wife. She might find a little peace now, some time to be with friends, possibly even the opportunity to take pleasure in the nice things that were due the wife of an Archon.

War and plague had removed too many people. Which made it all the more tragic to have a friend like Hipparete who was still alive but so inaccessible that there was no way to either see or speak to her. Or to Femma who had vanished like a phantom in the night.

Autumn drifted into early winter when Xanthippe's labor began. This time Socrates was at her side.

A younger midwife, one of those who had taken over some of his mother's obstetrical practice was there but Phaenerete, responding like an old general to the sound of a drum call revived sufficiently to quit her room and issue commands during the entire proceeding.

Xanthippe set her chin, embraced the pain, and following one last thrust produced a new life.

"A girl! You got what you wanted," Phaenerete said, examining her new grandchild.

Lamprocles surveyed his sister with suspicion, anxiously watching his mother smile and hug the baby to her breast.

"It makes me happy to see you so happy," Socrates said.

"You must rest now," the new midwife directed.

But Xanthippe was too excited. All through the night she rose at intervals to gaze enraptured at her daughter. Then she too fell into a deep sleep.

In deference to professional courtesy the younger midwife refused payment nor was it necessary to find money for a wet nurse because Xanthippe's breasts were swollen with nourishment.

"The gods always provide," Socrates moralized happily.

'Phyllys' the baby was named, without so much as a glance at the 'Pythagorean Book of Names'. "Look at her, full of milk and dozing like a kitten. See those wee hands and feet, how perfect they are! And her perfectly shaped little head. Beautiful!" Xanthippe gave Socrates a radiant smile. "She's three days old, and time goes so quickly that, in no time, we'll be telling her stories and teaching her games. Lamprocles, you will help her learn all sorts of things! She is going to love having you for a brother! My problem is wanting to play with her now when I should be in the kitchen court. If I don't soon get back to work we're apt to starve!"

That night she peeked at her baby one more time before going to bed, and it was barely dawn before she was up again looking into the crib to make sure that the advent of little 'Phyllys' had not been just a lovely dream. "You sleepy little thing," "Here I am awake and you haven't even begun to cry for your breakfast!" she said with a happy laugh.

Little Phyllys looked strange. There was something odd about the way she lay there, so still. Xanthippe's throat constricted with fear. She seized the tiny body. It was cold as marble and without life.

Then she screamed. "No! No! NO!"

Eryximachos, looking tired and careworn, came and tried to explain. But how could he when he himself had no notion what caused these things to happen? One could only lay it at the feet of the gods.

"It is not an uncommon tragedy, my dear woman," he said somberly. "You'd be amazed to know how many babies die in their crib baskets on the second, third, and even fourth day of life. There's no known cause. The only reason I can give is that from time to time the gods change their minds and decide they want a precious soul to return to them."

Failing to comprehend his words, Xanthippe stared at the physician while Socrates stood by in a passion of pity. "Cry," he begged. "There's no shame in tears. They bring relief."

But though her aching breasts were wet with useless milk. her eyes remained dry.

Hipparete came. Her wraithlike appearance jolted Xanthippe, at least for awhile, from her grief. "I heard about your baby, and I have no way to tell you how desperately sorry I am," she said, her eyes brimming. "What strange ways the gods have with mortals. I'm watched like a prisoner, but I came to you as quickly as I could. Luckily, now that Alcibiades is the Archon, he's away most of the time, so my own pressures are less. Oh, Xanthippe, I think of those happy days when you and I were children. Where have they gone? What has happened to us?"

"Your messenger told me all was well."

"Sometimes it is . . . but not always".

* * * *

Because of the generally held notion that newborns remain in a fetal state until they had survived ten days, one born prior to that time did not warrant a formal funeral.

However Xanthippe had her way and the body was taken to the cemetery in the ash grove at the farm. A doll was placed inside the little beehive shaped coffin so the baby would have one to play with in the Underworld but oh, name of God, Xanthippe moaned, she's such a little thing to be down there all alone with nothing but a toy to comfort her.

At least there was solace in knowing Yiayia Phyllys was there too. But would anyone think to tell her that she had a little namesake nearby to fondle and love?

Xanthippe could remember making a sacrifice of two turtle doves to the gods when Lamprocles was born. But this time, having disavowed the lot of them, she had not done so and they had taken their revenge.

One heart rending groan escaped her tightly drawn lips at the service. Only one, but the sound of it made others wince.

"My time to die is over due," Phaenerete wailed, "It should have been I."

* * * *

"By the dog I'd be grateful just to hear Xanthippe yell at me or throw a dish," Socrates sighed. Unable to swallow past the lump in her throat, she sat silently in the courtyard amidst its bravura of redecoration, while Socrates cooperated with Cleina and Festus in the doing of household tasks and marketing.

Whimpers like those of a forlorn puppy intruded upon her melancholy and she arose. As if in a daze she followed the sound and came upon her son, behind the house, leaning against one of Sophroniscus' tomb-slabs.

"Everyone wanted that baby but no one wants me", he wept, digging at his eyes. "Sometimes boys feel sad too, Mama."

Her heart lurched. Why must life and history go on repeating, repeating, repeating?

Fiercely protective, she swept him into her arms. "You are my dearest one, little man," she crooned. "I have recovered. You and I can smile again. I wont be sad any longer about the baby sister. She went with

'Zephyr' the west wind, and she is happy."

How could she have forgotten all her fine resolves to be thoughtful of Lamprocles when the new baby came? Immersed in her grief she had failed to remember that he had feelings much like hers. "I'm older than he, why can't I be wiser? Never let me do anything like this to him again," she prayed, not to any god but to herself.

Chapter Forty-one

A messenger came. "The wife of the Archon Alcibiades wishes to see you," he said. "She hopes you will visit her today, and asked me to tell you her husband is not at home."

"I must leave at once," Xanthippe told Cleina. "Give Lamprocles something to eat when he comes home from the Academaia, and look in on Mother Phaenerete. Right now she's asleep."

A year had passed since she and Hipparete had been together, the day after baby Phyllys' death.

In that time Alcibiades, as if goaded by the Furies, had refueled the cooling war between Athens and Sparta, until it nearly boiled over into renewed combat. His scheme had aborted. Once again, the Archonship went to Nicias.

When Xanthippe arrived at the house on the hill, and was ushered into the courtyard, she could not conceal her dismay.

"Yes, I guess it's obvious. I am ill. Come, sit here, across from me, and let me look at you." Hipparete pointed to a bench. Even her hand looked emaciated.

"I've been plagued with blood-wasting ever since my little girl was born. Eryximachos invited other physicians in for consultations. Each had a different medicine, but none cured me. I have no strength left to fight for my life, and I wanted to see you at least one more time before I . . ."

"Don't say it! If I had only known you were ill I'd have braved a pack of guard dogs to come. But I thought perhaps . . ."

"I know, I know! In spite of everything you still pictured me whirling around Athens covered with jewels!" Hipparete laughed weakly. "I was never the center of social activity you thought me to be. But then who wants to believe that a woman, to whom the gods have given position and wealth, can have problems like everyone else? In a way I'm like Cratinus the comedian. He knows he's an 'Oedipus' but no one believes him. They can only see him cast in his old role of 'satyr'.

"Truthfully, Xanthippe, the happiest times I ever had were at your house when we played games and peeked at the boys through that hole in the wall. What fun it was. And I haven't gone to a party since the one Myrto had when, oh dear, I still hate to think of the look on your face when Alcibiades shoved Kallia and the poor thing spilled wine all over your beautiful new silk peplos."

"And you tried to replace it twice. The second dress did come and was even lovelier than the one that got stained. I haven't had much opportunity to wear it but its nice to know it's there, waiting!"

"Thank you, Eudoia," Hipparete said when a slave brought wine. "Yiasus! To friendship." Deeply moved the two women smiled at one another and touched goblets.

"I'm glad you could come today. I needed to tell you how much you've always meant to me. And what strength it gave me just to know I could always come to you for support as I did the time I tried to get a divorce. You never hesitated a moment. That day turned out badly but your loyalty made the whole hideous business more tolerable. Although I'm afraid I left the scene too abruptly to thank you just then," she added with a sorry little smile. "Xanthippe, did I ever tell you that, even though Callias and Hermogenes were two of his best friends, Alcibiades gave orders they were never to be admitted to this house again because, like you, they stood ready to help me? Anyway here we are together again and I love you very much, dear one."

"And I you. Our friendship is the best thing that ever happened to me! You must get well, Hipparete. You can't, you just can't . . ." Xanthippe put her hands to her eyes. "You can't not get well," she said. "I'll bring you some of Phaenerete's herbal tonic. It tastes bad but she swears it will cure anything that ails a woman! Funny how an entire year can go by when we don't see each other but I always know you're somewhere here in Athens, and," she swallowed hard. "I can't imagine a world without you in it! There has to be a cure for what ails you! You're so young. You have two beautiful children who need you. And I need you."

Hipparete shook her head. "I didn't invite you here to fret over me. You have troubles of your own. I just wanted to be with you. I even hoped you'd do one of your funny imitations and make me laugh! Who knows? I may get well. Remember that tale about Athena appearing to Pericles and telling him how to heal the man who fell off the Parthenon Roof? Well, maybe she'll show up here!" She laughed, the ghost of her old infectious giggle.

"Surely Alcibiades treats you more considerately now?"

"When I became unwell he lost all interest in me, as a woman. Until the recent election he was occupied with the Archonship. He has other . . . personal interests too so, all in all he is seldom home. The slaves look after me. They're very kind . . .

"I don't mind being alone. I enjoy solitude. It gives me time to think. About marriage for example and the way betrothals are arranged for young couples who have no more idea what they're getting into than children who grab blindly into a games basket. One fetches up a knuckle bone and the other a toy shield but since both items are unrelated there can be no game."

"I agree!" Xanthippe nodded vigorously. "What you say reminds me of two merchants I overheard in the Agora, one from Egypt, one from Ionia. Neither understood a word the other said. Socrates and I are like that. When I married him I thought I was getting a companion, not the saviour of mankind. You and everyone else, even Alcibiades, see him as near perfect. People say he has godlike qualities. But, from a wife's point of view, deity is not a particularly desirable trait in a spouse. I remember Mama saying something or other about the trouble Mother Hera had getting along with Lord Zeus! Oh! I have tired you!"

Hipparete looking pale, was slumped against the back of her chair. "No!" she remonstrated, sitting upright. "Having you here is better than your mother-in-law's tonic. Besides I have more to say about Socrates. I've begun to view many matters in a new light because of something he said ages ago at Myrto's party. His divan was next to mine."

"What did he say?"

"We were having a conversation, similar to some you and I had about love and marriage. Critobolus said his father once told him that the gods punish anyone who disobeys his father by nullifying his betrothal contract to marry someone else. Crito claims that such couples invariably suffer dire consequences."

"Then what?" Xanthippe asked, her heart pounding crazily over her companion's inadvertent revelation.

"There was a lively discussion and Socrates said we should see life itself as a marriage, a union of good and evil. That we're all in it together because everyone is simply an extension of one vast Mind, a mind that is, in itself, eternally perfect and beautiful. So although it's up to each person to think for himself, the ultimate result is always right and good.

"Mama used to get nervous because she thought I was out-spoken," Xanthippe said. "Now I'm that way about Socrates. He talks too much about peoples rights, telling them to 'think for themselves,' that sort of thing, right out in public. It could get him into trouble. Papa used to say, 'Hold your tongue.' Well, I wish Socrates would hold his! You and I will never finish wanting to share all the things we think about and do, not even if we moved into the same house and lived to be a hundred! It was like that with . . ." She bit her lip.

She'd been about to say, 'Critobolus.

"With whom?".

"With Yiayia Phyllys," Xanthippe substituted. "You know after all these years I still think of her as being nearby. I'm going to leave now and let you get some rest. I shall return in a week with some delicious broth she taught me to prepare. It's very strengthening. And I'll bring a supply of the tonic I told you about."

Still Xanthippe lingered, not wanting to go. "You are a wonderful friend." she said, bending over to touch Hipparete's pale forehead with her lips.

"Wait," Hipparete whispered. "There's something else. I have watched little Elpinice come to love and admire you. It isn't only because you have a way of making her laugh but children have an instinct about people. Please, Xanthippe, in whatever way you can, when Alcibiades is away will you try to spend some time with her? You could give her what our grandmothers gave us, love and inspiration."

It was a year since Xanthippe had been unable to speak because of the lump in her throat, but there it was, getting in the way again. "I just can't let you die," she said huskily. "Nonetheless, rest assured, I will watch over little Elpinice as long as there's breath in my body."

* * * *

Instead of taking chicken soup to her friend, before the week was up, Xanthippe attended Hipparete's funeral rites.

It was an eerie day with a film of silvery fog hanging so low that the snow peaked ramparts of Mount Parnassus were barely visible when mourners watched the box which held what remained of Hipparete given the final shove that implanted it in a rock walled tomb inhabited by Hipponicus, Pericles, his two sons, and a host of former Alcmaeonids.

Scornfully she watched Alcibiades sob and beat his breast in a dramatic show of grief. "Look at her face, hard as stone," said one of the mourners, nudging her companion. "And to think that she and Hipparete were supposed to be such friends!"

"By now I should be accustomed to the omnipresence of Death but it only gets worse," Xanthippe told Socrates when the rites were over. "I want to be alone for awhile so you go on to the funeral feast without me. Please. I never want to enter the house of Alcibiades again . . . unless I'm there to kill him." It interested her to note that sometimes even her impassive spouse could still be startled by something she said. But, upon seeing young Elpinice, alone and looking breathtakingly like mother, she changed her mind.

"I knew you'd come and I was looking for you," the child said, her eyes crystalline with tears. "Mama loved you so much. Before she . . . went away she told me that no matter what happened you would always be my friend."

When old Eudora came to accompany the little girl to the nursery Xanthippe, still needing to be alone, took the well travelled road west from Athens and walked to the harbor at Piraeus.

Choosing a large flat rock on the deserted beach she sat, a solitary figure in the pale sunlight, watching the mist merge sea and sky together in delicate swirls, and thinking that perhaps spectres of the dead moved through a similar haze in their sad kingdom.

Does she know where she is? "Do you, Hipparete? Are you here beside me, silent and invisible? Have you seen my baby girl? Or any of the others?" Xanthippe breathed her question into the soft salt breeze as she rocked from side to side in a paroxysm of grief.

Now she knew who it had been, that dark terrifying Presence she'd so often envisioned coming up behind her on the old outer stairway to her bedchamber, ready to grab her by the heel. It was Hades, King of the Dead! Waiting. Always waiting.

When Socrates came home that night Xanthippe was in bed, but very much awake and longing for the warmth of a caress. It was not marital union that she craved but simply the comfort of human arms enfolding her, easing the pain.

However he looked so abstracted she knew this was not apt to occur.

* * * *

For the next three months Alcibiades elicited such public sympathy over his wife's demise that it played directly into his political hand. Laying aside his golden shield of Eros he went about in starkly black silk that eddied gracefully about his feet and his head bore a crown of hyssop interwoven with black ribands. In the face of such theatrical mourning fickle Athenians, up for more excitement, saw him as their man. Again the mild peace maker Nicias was deposed whereupon Alcibiades, glorying in his return to pre-eminence, shed his somber dress in favor of brighter raiment.

When the little island of Melos refused to knuckle under and pay dues he persuaded Athens, the most humane state in the world, that 'might makes right!' The Melians were ordered to yield. Because they continued to refuse he directed a massacre of all their men of military age. He had the women and children sold as slaves.

Upon hearing the gruesome details Athenians sobbed and beat their breasts. Shock waves of revulsion had them shuddering with remorse for this foulest of deeds, this blight on the entire Empire.

Socrates wept in the privacy of his courtyard. Xanthippe, thinking of the enslaved widows and orphans of those murdered men of Melos once again cursed the day that Alcibiades was born.

Chapter Forty-two

"Lamprocles, here's something for you to think about." said Socrates, handing the conch shell he had given to Xanthippe as a wedding gift to his son. "Put this to your ear. Listen! That little hum you hear is the sound of the universe.

Cautiously Lamprocles accepted the object and did as he was told.

"Now, take your tablet and stylus into the courtyard and do your sums, the ones we went over yesterday. And no nonsense! Remember, with bulging eyes like mine I can see sideways, like a horse."

"You make Lamprocles smile but when it comes to giving him an education . . . Alright, I must admit, you did manage to get him into the Academaeia." Xanthippe reversed herself to say, "

"His attention span is that of a dancing flea. Without constant supervision he jumps off his study bench at every whim! He thinks all he needs is . . ." Socrates, interrupted by a summons from the gate-bell, went to see who was there.

"Crito!" Xanthippe heard him say, "What kindly Fate takes you from the bankers table so early in the morning? Come in!"

"Have you forgotten? This is the first day of the Celebration of the Greater Mysteries? Bankers never work on Holy Days so I went to the Stoa Poikile and heard the Priest-Archon name those eligible for the eight day retreat at Eleusis. Then I came here.

"We observed religious days on the farm better than we do here in a town full of temples," Xanthippe said. "It's lucky for us that attendance at 'The Eleusionion' is not compulsory."

"I have news," Crito said, handing Socrates a jug. "This wine is not in celebration of the Holy Day but to toast the first notable earnings from your father's estate. Awhile back a client came to us so eager to get a loan in a hurry that he offered an exceptionally high rate of interest. Something told me he was essentially substantial and I took the risk. In consequence a sum has accrued that will ease your financial situation for awhile although of course it doesn't allow for luxuries. Xanthippe, will you fetch three goblets?"

"No, Socrates," he was saying when she returned, "It is I who am indebted to you, a debt not easily discharged. You have taught my son to think. Over the years, you have also opened my mind to a new way of looking at things. I'm no longer as short-sighted as I once was. Ah, Xanthippe! Permit me to pour the first cup for you.

By the way, has your husband told you about the compliment Archelaus paid him?" he asked when they had toasted the success of their financial adventure and were enjoying the unaccustomed pleasure of wine with breakfast.

Puzzled, Xanthippe shook her head.

"Well, since he's so modest I shall tell you. Archelaus is eager for the prestige that Socrates would lend to his literary club so he has offered to pay him a handsome sum if he will agree to join. Mind you, his is a very select group. Many people would be only too glad to put up an exorbitant fee merely for the privilege of having their names on the roster."

"No, he did not mention it," Xanthippe replied, prickling with annoyance. How many lucrative offers did he receive and reject without a word to her?

"My daemon negated the idea," Socrates explained. "Why, pray, should I bind myself to what is, in truth, a covey of artificial seekers after wisdom?

"I can tell you why!" The words burst from Xanthippe's mouth the moment Crito had gone. "Because it would put a little money in my purse, that's why!

You and your precious daemon. It must be convenient to blame everything you do on a spook! I think I shall dream up one of my own. It would have been so easy for you to go along with him. You snob!"

"And you, my dear, are an angry woman. As you have heard me say, I believe it is fear that engenders anger. Tell me my dear, of what are you afraid?"

"Keep an eye on Lamprocles. I'm going to walk to the sea for a little fresh air," she rasped. Ignoring his question, she strode through the gate and walked all the way to Piraeus

Gusts of wind from the sea tumbled her hair and snatched at her tunic. A gull, tugging at a plump translucent jellyfish, sensed her presence and flew away, triumphantly clutching a morsel in its black beak.

It was good of Crito to bring such welcome news, she reflected, as she strolled along the shore. One thing for which to be thankful was that Socrates' lifelong friend also happened to be a banker, doing all he could to save her from total poverty. At the same time, she did have to concede that her husband was right in that, so far at least, neither he nor his family had gone hungry. No one who lived in Athens did. Meals might be slim and inelegant but there was always enough to eat.

On the other hand, hunger took different forms. What about heart hunger, that unfulfilled longing, more troublesome than an empty gut? Or a woman who, like rich ripe fruit, was ready to be taken and savored? Or perhaps, after a long succession of hurts, heart-aches, and tragedies, she had turned sour..

Her father had once owned an overly active bitch hound. Gorgon, her name, was a 'skirter', so called because of her untamable wildness. great curiosity, and her refusal to stay with the pack. Ordinarily Papa would have simply put her down. But 'skirters' are sometimes correctable if they are turned over to a new trainer. That had been the case with old Gorgon.

Suppose that, years ago, the Fates had intervened in a her life, and she, Xanthippe, like old 'Gorgon' would have been given to another 'trainer'. What if today she, not Kallia, were the wife of Critobolus? If so, would she be spoken of as a noisome scold? Or would she instead be composed and serene like Yiayia Phyllys and Great Aunt Elpinice?

"Why do I go on cluttering my head with silly illusions? What's to be gained?"

Savagely Xanthippe pulled up a clump of seaweed and threw it at the surf. Despite what had occurred years ago, today she was, fundamentally, a virtuous woman.

"Fear not thy wife, Socrates, for exceedingly prudent she is, and knows what is right." It would be interesting to know what had prompted Alcibiades to recite that particular stanza from 'Odysseus' as a wedding toast. The likelihood was that he had done so to show off by proving he had read at least one of Homer's works. Or, perhaps, in one of his rare lucid moments, he knew that, to the best of her ability she would fulfill her marriage vows by being a trustworthy wife.

Chapter Forty-three

It was nice to be back.

"Why did you not bring the boy?" Nikandra wanted to know.

"He's in school, Mama."

"Such a little one in school?"

"Mama! You know perfectly well Lamprocles has been going to the Academaia for over a year!"

"I forgot."

Prior to Elefterous' death Nikandra had already started to age. Today the process was even more visible.

"Gryllus was here the other day. Said he'd soon be on his way to Sicily," Palen remarked. "I hadn't seen him since Xenophon's wedding and already the old war horse has a grandson!"

"Did I ever tell you that Xenophon studies with Socrates? He's very opinionated, especially about women, and not nearly as amiable as his father. I pity his wife. Poor Philesia!".

"Has your husband come to his senses or does he still refuse to take money for teaching?"

"He still doesn't believe in taking money for teaching."

"If he's so smart he should know people don't value what they get for nothing," Palen said with a crooked grin.

Xanthippe pursed her lips. Dear old Papa. One could always depend on him to bring up at least one sore subject. Yet there was something different about him. It wasn't that he looked older. Actually the gray streaks in his hair and beard were becoming. It was his expression that had changed. For one thing he looked less harried, and he smiled more often.

"What are they saying in town about in Sicily?" Marc asked. "I hear we've sent troops there so I'll probably be going myself one of these days. I wouldn't mind. It might be fun to see another part of the world."

"Oh may it please the gods, no!" Nikandra despaired.

"Someone should get Alcibiades in a dark alley and wring his neck" Palen caviled. "To think I once liked and admired that scoundrel! How can voters continue to supplant a proven leader like Nicias with such an 'oephole'? It looks like they'll never learn."

Alcibiades' latest gambit as re-elected Ruler had been to persuade Athenians that by getting control of Sicily, particularly its coastal city Syracuse, they would cut off the Spartan's supply of grain from that area. It could then be redistributed to Athens whose greatest weakness lay in a growing inability to feed herself.

Troops were being readied to cross the Sea of Adria. However Alcibiades was no longer entirely trusted. Therefore Nicias, who was still a dedicated peacemaker and had opposed the entire venture all along, was, by general demand, also joining the expedition to keep him from running wild.

Shadows on the slopes of Mount Parnassus told Xanthippe that if she wanted to be in Athens by suppertime she must be on her way.

She was almost home when the woman who lived two doors down from the potter's house came to her fence waving a hand. "Have you heard the latest?" she shouted.

Xanthippe groaned. This one could talk for hours about who emptied whose slops into the yard next door, owned a chicken killing hound or diddled his slaves.

"Alcibiades and his crowd had a party in the home of that crooked politician Charmides," she said, enthusiastically moistening her mouth with a long salacious tongue, "And they got drunk and parodied the Sacred Mysteries of Demeter! People say it's common sport for them to make fun of the gods! Only this time they became so crazed that their filthy acts were reported to the authorities." She licked her lower lip again, as if enjoying a buttery piece of lobster.

"From what I hear Alcibiades dresses up as Lord of the Underworld and performs obscene acts on young slave girls who are bought to impersonate Persephone. Then the others follow his lead. I was shocked to hear that Kritias and Charmides participated." She paused, took a long breath, and gave her listener a shrewd glance.

"Their nephew Plato is one of your husband's disciples isn't he?" Something about the way she said it sounded as if she pictured Socrates himself participating in the orgy.

"My family is looking for me, I must go," Xanthippe said hastily, anxious to stem the unholy tale. Impiety toward the gods! Athen's unpardonable crime! Philosophers were free to argue fine points of religion but even they dared not contravene temple traditions or the Priest Archon's dictates.

Socrates could be implicated just for having been seen in the company of Kritias and Charminides!

"Father walked home with me from school," Lamprocles reported when she hurried into the house. "He said to tell you he's gone to a symposium at Xenophon's. I learned a riddle today, Mama. See if you can guess the answer. "A man, not a man, saw and did not see a bird, not a bird, sitting on a stick, not a stick, and hit it with a stone, not a stone."

"That's too difficult for me to guess!" Xanthippe exclaimed smiling at her son. "I give up. What is the answer?"

"A eunuch caught a glimpse of a bat sitting on a reed and he hit it with a piece of pumice," Lamprocles said, watching her eagerly.

She rewarded him with a look of astonishment. "I'd never have been able to guess that in ten years!"

"The big boys told it to me. They said I must ask the great Socrates to guess the answer because he thinks he's so smart. Poor Mama, you could not guess it in ten years, you said so yourself!"

Although Lamprocles resembled her, the boy's impish grin reminded Xanthippe of Elefterous. Giving his tunic a tug to straighten it she looked at her carrot- haired son, with love, fierce, protective and proud.

Using her tongue to moisten a corner of her tunic she wiped a yellow trace of egg from his chin then reached to hold him close.

"Oh, Mama," he protested, as, with lofty disdain, he squirmed himself free from her maternal grasp and ran.

With the new dog snuffling happily at her feet Xanthippe kneaded barley cakes. It was nice to have him there. 'Argo' they had named him, for Odysseus' famed white canine.

"What made Xenophon's symposium so remarkable that it went on all night?" she asked Socrates when he came through the gate."

"For one thing he had the most skilled troupe of dancers I ever saw," he replied. "No part of their bodies was idle, but neck, legs, hands, and arms were all active together. Ah to be so supple! How I should like to learn from their dancing master! By the dog, I could be a professional myself." He gave his rotund body a few twirls.

"Some of the younger men aren't in as good physical condition as I. I warn them to cultivate bodily health by exercise and lack of excess.

They don't mind the exercise. but, as for excess, that's another matter and harder to sell . . .

"Xenophon is thinking of going to join his father in Sicily. If so his party may be the last of such occasions for awhile. Did I tell you that he and Philesia have eschewed Gryllus' town house for a place in the country?"

"Yes. It will keep Kalia and Critobolus from having to move which is fortunate."

"How is she?"

"Dreadful. Yet, somehow, she manages to cope."

"Critobolus was there last night. I had a beauty contest with him and he won."

"Name of god what were you doing in a beauty contest, and with him of all people?"

"He asked whose nose was the more beautiful, his or mine. I insisted mine was because noses are to smell with and while his points to the earth mine spreads out so widely I receive odors from every quarter. I also maintained that my thick lips could give a softer kiss than his and the young upstart said to hear me anyone would think his mouth was uglier than an ass's."

"Was Alcibiades there?"

"No."

"Did you hear that he and his crowd parodied the Sacred Mysteries of Demeter?"

"Yes. A grave matter," Socrates said somberly. "For a man in his position, such a scandalous show of irreverence could undermine the government. It shocks me more than I can say. I always have found it hard to understand how Alcibiades can be so discerning one day and turn into a maniac the next. He knows as well as anyone that what he did could mean his death. I find it equally difficult to fathom how and why Charmides and Kritias got mixed up in such a foul business.

To change the subject, how is your family?"

"So you did notice I was not at home yesterday! They are well, thank you, although Mama is becoming forgetful. "However" Xanthippe lowered her voice, "Your mother looks sick. Her skin is the color of hawk meat, and it's all broken out with little red sores. She can't get enough sweets and she's always thirsty. Then, as soon as she drinks, she has to empty herself. It's as if a conduit ran from her mouth to her private part. She also complains that her vision is blurred."

"Perhaps we should send a message to Eryximachos. I'll go have a chat with her." Socrates said.

* * * *

"Po po po, we must get you back on your feet", Eryximachos told Phaenerete, in a loud hearty voice. "What will all those expectant mothers do without you?"

"I may be sick but I'm not deaf," she retorted. "And you know as well as I that they have been getting along without me ever since my husband died, you old rascal"

After prescribing bloodletting and a daily pharmacopsis of fenugreek the physician suggested that, before evening meals she take oil of castor bean to which a small quantity of hiera, a sacrificial offering, had been added.

"Sit in an infusion of aromatics and warm water," he concluded.

"Go sit in one yourself", the midwife snapped peevishly. I have been prescribing those same herbs and infusions for years and know as well as you do that unless the gods are favorable none of them do an oboloi's worth of good. As my son says, It's all 'in the mind".

Taking no offense Eryximachos bade her 'adio' and went to speak in an aside to Socrates and Xanthippe.

"I fear your mother has a debilitating illness sometimes associated with heaviness and a taste for honey," he said.

Xanthippe showed surprise. Phaenerete's complaints had come so unremittingly that, like the lad's cry of 'Wolf' in Aesop's story they had for some time now fallen on deaf ears.

In spite of strict adherence to Eryximachos' orders, and the nourishing broths Xanthippe concocted from carefully hoarded bits of lamb and chicken, Phaenerete's condition worsened.

"Talk to me about the gods," she commanded her son.

"I shall speak of Hermes," Socrates said, taking her withered old hand in his. "Hermes, the Divine Herald and messenger of Zeus, who comes with winged sandals on his feet, to lead souls to another, lovelier realm. I can picture Father, standing in radiant light, waiting there to welcome you.

"You have been a midwife for many years, Mother, the best in Athens. But the day comes for each of us to be delivered into a new life. However I doubt if that transition is as alarming as the one in which we are forced, as mortals, to emerge into the world."

With exquisite tenderness he stroked Phaenerete's forehead and when Xanthippe saw a look of peace replacing the fear in her rheumy eyes she found it easier to understand what made people follow Socrates in droves wherever he went.

"The immortals will send you to Elysian Fields where there is 'No snow, nor heavy winter storm, nor rain, and Ocean is ever sending gusts of the clear-blowing west wind to bring coolness to men'."

In the autumn when leaves floated from trees to drift in the streets, Phaenerete began to chill. Then she became feverish and, despite the application of cool packs, her body felt as if it were on fire. Finally her breathing became so labored that she was probably grateful, at the last, when Hermes came to take her.

Once again Xanthippe and Socrates sheared their hair and donned black garments in accordance with the rites of mourning. It was not so much the death of her mother-in-law but memories of Hipparete, Baby Phyllys, Yiayia, and the rest, that caused Xanthippe's throat to tighten at graveside. She coughed to clear it, then found it difficult to stop coughing.

Three drink offerings, one of mead, one of wine, and one of water were emptied into the pit and white meal strewn over all.

"Why are they putting Yiayia Phaenerete into that hole?" Lamprocles cried with compassion born of understanding. Xanthippe clasped his hand in hers.

"We must be on our way," Palen said. He, Nikandra, and Marc had come and Xanthippe was sorry to see them leave. Her restored courtyard had helped to make the funeral feast a surprisingly pleasant affair.

"You have become celebrated for posing questions that provoke strong debate," Plato said to Socrates when he, along with others, stayed on. "What started you on this search for knowledge? What drives you?"

"I seem compelled to ask questions. You might say that, like my dear mother, I am a midwife. But my task may be even more important than Mother's in that mine is a 'maieutic method', that is to say, a 'bringing forth' of new understanding. After people undergo labor in my care they give birth to themselves! However I cannot, nor can anyone else adequately describe the birth of his own soul."

"What about death? We have had many opportunities to observe that you, yourself, have no fear of it," said Xenophon. "You've proven it time and again in battle. How can you face it with such equanimity, not only the prospect of your demise but the passing of loved ones as well? What makes most of us so afraid to die?"

Fear of death! Now Xanthippe was fully alert. Death, her ultimate enemy! Even more to be loathed than was Alcibiades. When Hades, the

King of Death, becomes your foe, you can no longer dream of revenge.

"Death spells change and most people are deeply fearful of change even when it leads to truth and liberation," Socrates replied. "Yet, in a way, we die a little every day. Moment to moment, we are constantly dying and being reborn. Think about it. Who is the 'I' who is sad one minute and happy the next? Who and what lies behind the appearance of the child, then the youth, the adult, and ultimately the old man who is still one and the same?. Are the changes all illusory?

"If you wish to find the answers, you must distance yourself from blandishments and demands, and stay aloof from any desires that divert you from searching for them within yourself.

"You've heard me say so many times. May I add that it takes the highest form of heroism to examine one's own secret thoughts and motives. Or do our thoughts think themselves?

"I view death as being akin to the trip I took with Sophocles. We sailed to Chios, and when we got there I found myself in hitherto unknown territory. None the less I was, in essence, still the same man who left Athens..

Quietly Xanthippe watched and listened. These men were fanatically devoted to her husband. Critobolus too, standing there with a rapt expression on his face. Socrates, tranquil, imperturbable, and evidently free of ordinary emotions, seemed able to motivate them, and, by his very presence, empower them with some of his vitality.

"The hour grows late," he said.

"Please, Socrates don't stop now. Tell us, are any of the thoughts that you bring forth from others as beautiful and wise as your own?"

"The ideas I deliver are sometimes noble, sometimes not. I can only ask the questions that help a man discover whether his concept is true or false. At times, when I expose someone's 'darling notion' to be a mere shadow, that person is ready to bite me as if I had actually grabbed a child from its mother!

*　*　*　*

It would be false to pretend she missed Phaenerete, Xanthippe reflected, a month or so after the funeral.

Yet oddly enough her memories were also laced with compassion, more of it, by far, than she had ever been able to feel when her mother-in-law was still alive.

In some ways the mid-wife had been a courageous woman. But she was gone now and, for while. there ensued, in the house of Socrates, a time of peace.

Chapter Forty-four

Xanthippe had just finished feeding Argo the few scraps remaining from breakfast, when a fearful commotion arose from the street.

"What could have happened?" she cried, as the shouts and outcries increased in volume. Followed by Socrates, and Lamprocles, she ran outside.

"Our Herm! Some fiend has mutilated our god!" the potter's wife screamed, pointing wildly at her gate.

Her home, like every other house and temple in Athens, was guarded by a symbol of Hermes. Made in the form of a tall rectangular slab of marble, or stone, the figures were posted at every entrance. Each was surmounted by a sculptured head of the god, and below, on the same flat surface, a carved representation of his genitals.

Hermes, the guardian, gatekeeper, conductor of dreams, and ultimately of persons, was a god so revered that, at eventide, Athenians everywhere offered him the last libation of the day. His image had been defiled, not only in front of the potter's place but all up and down the street!

Clusters of neighbors, artisans, and herm-makers were all talking at once. "Probably the same ones who parodied the Mysteries!" they said.

"This has to be the work of Alcibiades and his crowd of crazies!"

"Only a bunch of rich ne'er-do-wells could conceive of such madness!"

All the Herms had been divested of their privy parts, all that is save one. The god in front of Socrates' home still stood intact.

"Some people are fortunate to have friends in high places," the woman two doors down sneered. Others stared at the inviolate Herm knowingly.

Stung by their sideways glances Xanthippe grabbed Lamprocles' hand and marched stiffly back into her courtyard."

Soon it was learned that similar mayhem had been wreaked throughout the city, and rewards were being offered for information that would lead to the apprehension of those responsible. Some people claimed that the mockery of Demeter's holy rites and the laceration of the Hermae were all part of a plot to overthrow the Democracy. Everyone did agree that it could not be considered just a prank, but a conflict of religious thought, and, as such, highly treasonable.

Tensions heightened when a reliable witness was found. A man on his way to collect wages from a slave who worked in the Laurium mines thought he had seen the conspirators by moonlight, attacking the Herm standing guard in front of the Theater of Dionysius!

"If Alcibiades actually is at the bottom of this, it proves he's forgotten everything I ever taught him," Socrates said sorrowfully. "He's been so over-ruled by conflicting desires that they have darkened his mind and obscured his soul."

He sat down heavily, his forehead furrowed by an uncharacteristic frown. "It never fails. When lusts storm a man's soul, and find it devoid of noble practices, they purge him of all goodness. Then, having swept away honor, they bring in their friends, Violence, Anarchy, and Licentiousness. All my warnings that he beware of wrong desires went unheeded. I mourn him as if he had died. In a way he did, when he perpetrated that massacre on the people of Melos."

"You use many words to describe what I can say in four, namely, 'Alcibiades is a monster.' You and Hipparete were his only link to goodness but neither one of you stood a chance."

"I believed that because I loved him I could help him become a better person." Socrates appeared to be talking to himself.

"Are you at home, dear Master?"

It was uncanny to see the source of their conversation come charging through the gate. Behind him walked a slave, weighed down with baskets. Determined to avoid Alcibiades at any cost, Xanthippe dodged back into the house.

"Kalimeera," Socrates greeted the caller. "You appear to be out of breath."

"I'm hurrying to get everything in order before I leave for Italy. But I can't leave without your blessing."

"That I must deny you, Alcibiades. Blessings on this venture are something I can not give. You have been a son, a brother, and a compatriot to me. You saved my life in battle. I love you, and I shall never cease to pray for your welfare. But your actions I cannot condone."

"I need your approval!"

"What I said must stand."

"Well then, blessing or no, before I leave I beg you, do me the honor of accepting these." Alcibiades motioned to the laden baskets that his slave had placed at Socrates' feet. "Permit me to repay just a small measure of the debt I owe. Whatever I do that is commendable, I learned from you, Socrates. You taught me, inspired me, and poured your energy into me. Nor can I ever forget your incredible bravery in saving my life at Potidaea!"

"Your words are kind, but, I can only repeat that, by accepting your gifts, I would break my time honored custom." Socrates raised a hand as if to push away even the thought of assent.

Through the half open door Xanthippe saw the two men grip each other's shoulders, and kiss one another on each cheek. Then Alcibiades, and the slave lugging the laden baskets walked back out into the street.

"Socrates, how could you? After all you've done for him what would have been so wrong with accepting those gifts? He's so rich he can't even count his money! How could they act as a bribe when he's about to leave the country? I hate Alcibiades. But that doesn't mean I wouldn't welcome the food and wine he had stowed in those baskets! As it is you don't have a damned thing to show for the years of free time you've given him."

Stalking back into the kitchen court she thought of other times when Alcibiades had arrived bearing lavish offerings. Once he'd minced in at mealtime with fine cheeses and a flagon of wine from Italy, all of which Socrates had refused, even though there was nothing but bread and a few wretched turnips to put on the table that day. And today she had to watch the Ruler of Athens send those treasures back to his chariot!

Following his implication in the Hermes scandal, Alcibiades knew better than to begin a hazardous journey with suspicion hanging over his head. He was also aware that even those who were convinced of his guilt would hesitate to convict him for, should he be judged guilty and removed from command, several of Athens' allies were likely to withdraw.

What's more, despite all he'd done to discredit himself he still had most Athenians believing that, in his saner moments at least, he was a brilliant general. So he demanded a trial and was informed that he must nevertheless set sail and stand trial upon his return.

As the fleet's departure drew near a sort of giddy gaiety overtook Athens. Revelers roamed the city, laughing and shouting drunken toasts to victory, convinced that the conquest of Sicily would make them all rich.

"Uncle Marc will be there! He's going to Sicily on the biggest trireme in the world! Please come with Mama and me!" Lamprocles implored. Socrates wanted no part of the celebration. Nevertheless his son's pleas brought consent, and he accompanied his family to see the most splendid armada ever assembled set sail.

Regrettably the time of departure fell on the Day of Adonis, an unfavorable sign, because the ships might fade in glory as had the youthful beauty of Adonis. Soothsayers and priests had an even more ominous report. The first fleet had already left during the unlucky days of the Plynteria!

Equally sinister, the statue of Athena Pallas was not yet entirely regilt, a matter always completed of before a launching. The Polemarch in charge of sacrifices to the war god Enyalios had constant ringing in his ears, one of the worst possible portents!

Nor did Athenians ever set out on the seventh day of the month but even this happened and as one ship left the harbor there was a strange flight of crows into the wind.

"Many wrongs are done by the nightmare of superstition," said Socrates, inveighing against the prophets of doom. "It's a mighty evil. Men who are enslaved to it, try to force others to think as they do, and they despise those who don't. Anyone who does believe them lives in constant terror."

How well Xanthippe knew what he meant. What he said brought dark recollections of a raven beating its wings against the loom room walls. That and others. She shivered.

Even before the entire fleet left the harbor its generals had begun to disagree.

* * * *

Within two weeks of the embarkation Palen appeared.

"Your mother is taking it hard about Marc going to Sicily," he said glumly. "If you visit her she'll straighten up. How soon can you come?"

"As soon as I can get away," Xanthippe promised. How like him to expect her to drop everything, obedient to his call, "Come girl! Fetch girl! SIT!"

Of course she went, as soon as she could, and found her mother sitting alone in the loom room staring vacantly into space.

"We've come to see you, Mama," she said. There's no school because of a Holy Day so I brought Lamprocles."

"Xanthippe? Lamprocles!" A smile teetered across Nikandra's face and was just as quickly gone.

"The gods didn't give me time enough to stop grieving for Elefterous before Marc was sent to Sicily," Nikandra lamented. "Just when he was able and old enough to take over the farm. We were planning to find him a wife. Then came his orders to sail."

"Don't worry, Mama. He'll be home soon. Syracuse will never be able to stand against our fleet," Xanthippe said, hoping that no one would come along to contradict her by revealing what the soothsayers were saying.

For awhile Nikandra relaxed. "Back when I was a bride I wanted more than anything in the world to meet Aspasia. Now here I am, her friend!" she said with a show of animation. "She is ever so kind. Lysicles adores her."

"I don't wonder! I thought she was lovely when I met her here. . . " It had been the day Elefterous was laid to rest, "Tell me, Mama, do you still feel drawn to the Orpheans?"

"I'm not sure. They were glad enough to get my gold beads but all the things they promised would happen . . . didn't." Nikandra replied haltingly. "Yet I must say that my prayers at the shrine and the nice thoughts helped. I still sing the chants when I'm by myself. They make me feel less alone."

* * * *

Following her marriage a girl's childhood ties are supposedly severed, but separating oneself from one's family is more glibly said than done. In less than a month Palen was at the gate again. "Your mother is getting on my nerves," he complained. "She cries a lot. Come back and cheer her."

Thinking she could use a bit of cheer herself Xanthippe collared Cleina and again admonished the reluctant old woman to watch over

Lamprocles when he returned from school. "I'll stay overnight this time", she said. "There are melons and cucumbers in the vegetable patch and I'll leave a pot of rice on the brazier. Be sure my husband and son eat before they leave in the morning."

At noon, when Xanthippe walked into her parents' courtyard she was appalled by its derelict appearance. One of the hounds must have run amok because the big amphora was broken and its bouquet of decorative field grasses strewn everywhere. Then she saw her mother.

Nikandra was slumped in a chair, her mouth crooked and drooling. One of her eyelids was partially closed in a macabre wink and, fixing her daughter with the other, she mumbled, "Shumshing jusht happened to me. I can't move". Her head lolled to one side and, with a moan she toppled to the floor.

"Papa! Andokides! Someone please come!" Xanthippe cried.

When they had carried her into the boy's old bed-chamber Palen rode into Athens to summon help.

Eryximachos (who no longer made calls in the country) sent his apprentice, an eager young man who explained that a seizure of this nature was not uncommon in people Nikandra's age. Possibly she had already suffered similar but less severe attacks. A gentle manipulation of the jaws, he felt sure, would restore her ability to speak, and daily manipulations with tincture of Egyptian bacchar would benefit her weakened limbs.

"It is well known by now that healing is often brought about by the laying on of hands. Permit me to demonstrate," he said. As, with thumbs and forefingers, he pressed her jaws, Nikandra's one focusing eye rolled wildly .

"There's another new way to hasten recovery," he informed them." the new doctor informed them. "The vapor of urine, boiled in a lamp pot, greatly rouses the senses of persons in this condition by warming congealed nerves."

It was not Nikandra's nerves so much as her face that appeared to have congealed into one of the little social grimaces she made at weddings and clan meetings.

"Rest, Mama, and I shall prepare some of the 'kota yahni' Yiayia used to make when one of us was sick," Xanthippe said, and, turning to the doctor, "Please, sir, when you return to Athens, will you be so kind as to have a message taken to my husband. He's to be told that I must remain here with my mother and that I depend on him to supervise what goes on at home."

For several days she helped Pausimache and Leah carry out the physician's orders, and did what she could to ease her mother.

Meanwhile it was conceivable that, on any given afternoon, Socrates would come home from a debate, leaving his son waiting for him at the Academaia gate. If he wished, he could do anything to perfection, as when he'd taken charge after baby Phyllys died. But one never knew when he would be so inclined.

The cabbage, cauliflower, and eggplant would rot if they weren't picked and preserved. Cleina, euphoric over her impending freedom could, conceivably, leave the chickens to perish of thirst or the goat to go un-milked until its udder split. How sad it was to have to worry about such matters when Mama was too ill to move.

With no way of knowing whether Socrates attention was on these matters or 'in the clouds' she dared stay here no longer. With growing apprehension she went in search of her father and found him hurling objects against the stable wall

* * * *

She had not been home a fortnight when Andokides shuffled through the gate. She was to return at once he said. Mama was dead.

This time Socrates and Lamprocles were crowded into the donkey cart with her when Andokides drove it back to Cholargus.

Palen was waiting. "It happened last night", he said dully, "and I can't even tell Marc that his mother is gone."

According to Socrates, Mama was already awake and able to talk, walk again, even to dance in another realm. But whatever he might say concerning life in the next world Mama had irrevocably departed this one. One of her legs was twisted and bent upwards, and her left hand curled like a bird's claw. She looked fragile, and smaller, as if somehow in dying she had shrunk.

Grimly Xanthippe watched Lysicles and the others lower what was left of her into a grave next to that of Elefterous.

Again Aspasia was there. "I enjoyed being with your mother." she said. "She was kindly and sweet. I told her so."

"Did I ever tell Mama that?" Xanthippe searched her mind and was glad to recall that, on a few occasions, she had.

Those who knew Aspasia well said she had been so adored by

Pericles that he kissed her warmly every time he left the palace, and again upon his return. She was so brilliant and well-educated that men in high places had brought their wives to hear her speak. Yet she had come to this modest farmhouse to brighten Mama's life by telling her she was kindly and sweet.

Lysicles joined them. When he and Aspasia were together they drew others to them he way a warm blaze draws those who are chilled. When they left the gathering it was as though a light had been withdrawn from the room.

Love, Agape . . . words much discussed in Socrates' circle of friends. Some people know without trying to define them what those words really mean.

* * * *

At home again on Cerameicus Street Xanthippe stretched a rope between two trees, hung her black mourning garments on it and watched them flap like pinioned bats in the breeze. They had suffered far too much use. In fact she wondered if either she, or they, could endure one more time of mourning.

Too many funerals, one following upon another, faster and faster, or so it seemed. It was too dreadful, this knowing that the God of Death was always there, leering and lurking, just around the corner, waiting to grab some hapless victim. Sometimes it was almost as if he were breathing in her ear.

Turning her back on the clothesline Xanthippe raced, shivering, back into the house.

Chapter Forty-five

No city had a law more fair to slaves than Athens, a law that gave Festus the right to gain liberty for himself and his wife, by using their savings to buy it from Socrates.

"Proof again that the gods always provide enough for household needs and some to lay aside," he moralized.

"By now the gods should know we need it,"

Poking at a few expiring embers in the stove Xanthippe bent to their warmth. Without Festus, fires had a tendency to die unnoticed. She missed him. But not grumpy Cleina who, although never openly defiant would, when asked to wash the churn, be apt to seize a broom and go out to sweep the street.

"The cost of food has risen so high that even people with plenty to spend are horrified," she chafed. "All because of this accursed war with Sparta. I feel as if it had been going on all my life."

"In a way it has, Xanthippe, at least for one third of it."

Sometimes a single day could seem endless, which made it hard to believe that Marc had been gone for two years, News filtered daily into the Agora but never a word from him.

It was reported that Alcibiades, in disfavor again because of dismal war reports, had been recalled to stand trial for mutilating the Herms. Instead he escaped to Sparta. There, in return for being granted immunity he offered that country his aid against Athens and bragged, "I'll show those fickle fools that I am still very much alive!"

The Spartans were enchanted to see this luxury loving Athenian cheerfully accommodate himself to their rigid ways, even to sharing a plain diet of black pudding with the soldiers.

With no apparent limits to his treachery he encouraged them to disregard Nicias' peace treaty and send help to Sicily against Athens. Most shocking of all he persuaded them to fortify Decalea, the very same area he'd persuaded Athenians to fight for and take.

"He's deranged," horrified former supporters gasped. "He got us into a war with Sicily, now he helps her to fight us!"

Members of the Assembly tried him 'in absentia', reached a verdict of guilty, confiscated his property, and condemned him to death. They also ordered priestesses to curse his name!

Xanthippe was not the only one to say "It serves him right!" Yet in a way she hoped he would not be executed until she herself found a way to even her own bitter score.

In the evening neighbors gathered to share the reports that continued to pour into town. The latest concerned Nicias. Like any prudent general he had offered a sacrifice before embarking. Every one of his ships bore the emblem of its god and carried a sacred fire. He had been careful to take the customary troop of diviners, sacrificers, auspicers, and heralds. But in spite of all precautions he was suffering cruel losses and defeats. The evil omens under which Athens' fleet had set sail for the west continued to multiply!

News filtered back that a flight of crows had injured Athena's statue, and a man had mutilated himself on an altar. Nicias, suffering from severe kidney disease, was now convinced that Alcibiades' ill conceived war in Sicily would be fatal to him as well as to Athens.

What happened next was not to be believed!

Nicias had been preparing his fleet for a return to Athens while the sea was still free. But his chief diviner saw an eclipse of the moon and claimed it was an unfavorable presage. So he had commanded a wait of nine days during which further sacrifices could be made to please the gods.

Alas, that very delay played directly into enemy hands, giving them just the time needed to destroy the entire Athenian fleet! Everyone aboard the ships that ended at the bottom of the ocean had been lost!

Six thousand men surrendered, and after a horrific massacre of his own troops Nicias had capitulated. Even then, Athenians, knowing him to be a man of unflinching courage, did not blame him, save for one thing. He had taken the advice of an ignorant diviner, when even the man on the street could have told him if a moon conceals its light that is a very good omen for an army in retreat!

When Socrates came home from the Agora, and told Xanthippe what had happened, she clasped her hands to her cheeks and groaned. Marc was somewhere in that disaster.

* * * *

"I have made a discovery!" Socrates said, appraising his wife. "Your hair is turning pink, Agape Mou." He smoothed a lock away from her forehead. Where has all that fire gone?"

She shrugged.

"You look tired. I can tell you are worried,"

"Yes. I can't sleep for wondering about Marc, not knowing if he is dead, or a slave, or which would be worse. And Lamprocles has been making life all the more difficult.

"In what way?"

"He scolded me today because he was hungry and dinner wasn't ready. He said I had neglected my duty. I told him he was a spoiled brat, and then he called me 'old adder tongue' and said that's how everyone refers to me." Reeling from that blow she had run to her garden and flung herself face down on the ground.

To Xanthippe's surprise Socrates embraced her. "We can have no more of that," he said, gently stroking her back. "I'll speak to him and dispel any ideas he might entertain about you being his slave. As for your brother, we can only pray he still lives and has the gods watching over him. Your muscles feel tense. Let me massage them as they do athletes in the Palaistra."

"Tonight is the first time we have been close in quite some time," she said later, when, after succumbing to the strong persuasion of his hands they made love.

"Something tells me that there is something else you wish to say."

Xanthippe nodded. "Why does a man with your virility and passion so rarely approach his wife?" she asked.

"Did you ever hear the story of Apollo Pythias?"

"Which one?"

"About the dread serpent Python who lived in the caves of Parnassus and devoured people. After a severe contest Apollo killed him with an arrow. Like all myths, this one has a hidden meaning."

"Which is . . .?"

"That there is a serpent in all of us, and to tame him we must be vigilant in our practice of bodily, mental, and spiritual discipline.

When once we master the 'Python' we can savor perishable delights without necessarily being bound to them. Better yet, we have freed ourselves to taste the imperishable sweetness that transcends all physical satisfactions. That, my beloved, is a rapture no one can describe."

Involuntarily Xanthippe looked at the snake on her arm. A symbol of her own Python, there to mock and remind?

"Too often I forget how much younger you are than I," Socrates said, cupping her face in his hands. When I do remember I am grieved that, in my pursuit of self discipline I deprive you of pleasures that are rightfully yours."

"It is said that the men in your circle of friends love each other more than they love women . . ."

"You mentioned something to that effect on our wedding night. The answer is in what I just said. But let me tell you another story. This one is about love. "On the day Aphrodite was born the gods held a feast. 'Plenty', the son of Neverataloss was there and when all had dined 'Poverty' came in to beg. Noticing that, by this time, 'Plenty' was drunk she decided to have a child by him so she lay at his side and conceived 'Love'.

"The opposite natures of his parents are evident in his duality. Neither mortal nor immortal, he is, at times, tender and beautiful, then again hard, rough, homeless, and dwelling in want. From 'Plenty', his father, comes Love's desire for good things, his bravery, and his high strung temperament. He is a wizard, always weaving devices, but he is also a philosopher, sorcerer and sophist. Sometimes he is dying, but again, through his father's nature he gets renewed life. Yet, sooner or later, whatever he gains trickles away.

Because Aphrodite is beautiful and 'Love' was begotten at her birthday party he is always a lover of beauty. In a general sense, love is a desire for good things and happiness, whether it be found by way of moneymaking, writing poetry, or in a taste for sports, horses or philosophy.

"Love of having good things for oneself always, it is the breeding and begetting of the beautiful in both body and soul. To love a thing one must be fond of it altogether.

"Another thought in regard to your question about the affections of men is that youths in their bloom, see little of women other than their mothers. So they sting and stir, admiring one another's bodies and finding them worthy of attention and a kiss. And because a lover must always see the beloved as beautiful he will praise one with a tilted nose and call him 'Gracie', another's hook is seen as a royal nose. Like those who are fond of wine they make any and every excuse for a drink.

"Some grow beyond the physical to a closer communion and a firmer friendship. Others turn to women and beget children, a few perhaps only because they want to secure immortality for themselves.

"A man with divinity in him, one who, from youth, is pregnant in soul more than body, seeks and goes about to find the beautiful thing that he himself can beget. If he finds a similar soul he gladly welcomes that person and embraces the two, body and soul, together. To those few who taste the Divine, physical desire diminishes, or ceases to exist. Have I made myself clear?"

"Not really. You remind me of the man who, when asked to tell about his journey at sea, began by describing in great detail, step by step, how a boat is built. You gave me a complicated answer for what I thought was a simple question. In truth, what you said makes me feel no more truly married to you than I did before.

* * * *

"Tell me my boy, do you know any men who are termed ungrateful?", Socrates asked, putting his hand on Lamprocles arm.

His son gave a nod.

"Do you know how they come by this bad name?"

"Yes. It describes people who don't express thanks for the good things they receive."

"Do you take it then that to be 'ungrateful' might also mean to be 'unjust'?"

"Yes. What are you getting at, Father?"

"Be patient and you'll find out. Together we will solve a riddle. I have another question. Would you say ingratitude is unfair to friends but justifiable with enemies?"

"I think it's the same one way or the other."

"Then you're saying that ingratitude is injustice, pure and simple?"

"Yes."

"And the greater the benefits received the greater the injustice of not showing gratitude?"

Another nod.

"What deeper obligation can we find than that of children to their parents?

Parents to whom they owe their being, their portion of all fair sights, and all blessings. Do you think it's only lust that provokes men to beget children when the streets are full of means to satisfy that? I think it's fairly obvious that we males select wives who will bear us the best children and marry them to raise a family.

"The woman conceives and bears her burden in travail, risking her life and giving of her own food, and with much labor. Having endured bringing forth her child she rears and cares for it although she receives no reward, and the babe neither recognizes its benefactress nor can make its wants known to her."

"Still she guesses what is good for it and what it likes and seeks to supply these things. And she goes on rearing it for a long season, enduring toil day and night, not knowing what, if any, return she'll get."

Socrates paused, poured two cups of water, handed one to Lamprocles and took one for himself. After downing his in a gulp he exhaled and continued.

"Nor are parents content just to supply food. When their children seem capable of learning they teach them what they can and if they think another is more competent they engage him and strive their utmost to see that the children turn out as well as possible."

"But, Father," Lamprocles protested, by now recognizing the direction in which he was being led, "even if Mama has done all this how can I or anyone put up with her when she acts like a beast?"

"Which do you think is harder to bear, a wild beast's brutality or a mother's?"

A semi-smile lurked on Lamprocles' lips. "I'm not so sure!"

"Many people get bitten or kicked by a beast. Has your mother ever done you an injury of that sort?"

"You know she hasn't but she says things that are almost as bad."

"And how much trouble do you think you've given her with your peevish behavior? And how much pain when you were ill? You know full well there's no malice in what your mother says to you! On the contrary she wants you to be blessed above all other beings. If you can't endure a mother like that you can't endure a good thing.

"You cultivate neighbors, companions, school mates, don't you think courtesy is due your mother who loves you more than all? My boy, if you're prudent you will pray the gods to pardon your ingratitude toward her lest they in turn refuse to be kind to you, thinking you an ingrate."

Lamprocles, looked thoughtful, did not reply.

"Well?"

"I think I understand what you mean, Father."

"Then go apologize to your mother. It helps to realize that you prove your strength by being able to admit that you have been wrong.

* * * *

Barber shops in the Agora were rookeries of rumors but the disintegration of the Empire was so slow a process that, like nightfall, no one was precisely aware of the darkening.

People reminisced about the way things "used to be." Something precious was being lost. Athens looked less well kept, education was deteriorating, and there had been an increase in crime.

"Perhaps we have forgotten how to pray and the gods are displeased," people said.

"Nothing has gone well for us since the Herms were destroyed."

It was handy for some to lay the blame at the feet of Alcibiades who by now had lost favor with the Spartans and was negotiating with Tissaphernes, the satrap of Persia, in an effort to gain Persian support for Athens!

"The bastard bounces from side to side like a tipsy scale," Menon, a disciple of Socrates, remarked. "He'd lie and cheat on the grave of his father if he thought to gain by it. Can there be anyone left who still believes a word that scoundrel says?"

"You'd be surprised," Socrates replied. "At this very moment there are people in Athens who would like to see him re-elected Archon!"

Menon frowned and looked as if he had more to say. Instead he glanced at Xanthippe who was sitting not far from him making a baby garment. The entire discussion had been taking place in her own courtyard where she could hear every word. Everyone knew she was a very temperamental woman so this was no time to mention a story being circulated about Socrates' association with Alcibiades. Nor, since she was expecting another child, was it appropriate to bring up the fact that citizens were being urged to enlarge families decimated by war. Even strict legitimacy laws had been stretched and bigamy, long abolished, was, at least temporarily, once again looked upon with favor.

Chapter Forty-six

It hadn't mattered to Xanthippe whether she had a daughter or a son. All she wanted was to have this one survive. Her wish had been granted and little Sophroniscus was a healthy, sturdy child. However, in his first year of life there had been death and defeat in Sicily, and revolution everywhere.

Athenians had been hopeful when a council of wealthy citizens replaced an oligarchy of terrorists. But the 'Four Hundred', as the new leaders were known, proved to be so unpatriotic, inept and unprincipled that war flared anew, this time spreading beyond the eastern Aegean to Byzantium.

Meanwhile Alcibiades switched allegiance yet again, and was joined by ousted Democrats in Samos where he claimed that he personally would effect a durable peace with the enemy.

"I had a feeling that our interminable wrangle with Sparta might finally end but, evidently, it was kept under control just long enough to make us think that Thracybulus and Anytus would be able to redefine Nicias peace treaty," Socrates remarked to a group of young men who, glad to have survived so far, still collected daily in his courtyard. Some, notably members of the 'aristoi', had begun to affect the 'Master's' haphazard attire, possibly in the belief that, by dressing as he did they gained a look of wisdom.

Overhearing his words, Xanthippe's nostrils flared with scorn "Only a fool would trust Anytus," she mumbled.

"As individuals how can we achieve a healthy unity of body, mind, and spirit?" Socrates asked.

"Perhaps our knowledge of the musical octave helps us keep things in harmony and balance," said Plato. "That, and as you said, sir, the surrender of attachments."

But one needs to know that he is loved, and love is an attachment," Apollodorus protested. Like all rhetoricians whose job it was to sway opinions, he always sounded a bit contentious. "How can a man be happy if he denies physical desires? When I die my body goes into the ground and that's the end of it, so why not enjoy it while I'm still here?"

"I don't say you shouldn't. The body is the vehicle through which everything on earth comes into being. Our bodies are sacred. So is marriage. In true love there is nothing that is not. Sex is a sublime gift for which we can thank God. And God is the pure creative energy from which all things come. So in love or not, look into the motive and intentions behind your actions.

"Never forget," Socrates continued earnestly, "that when one is solely in love with and beguiled by the body and its desires, he may come to believe that truth exists only in physical form, to be seen, touched, and tasted to gratify his lusts. But such thinking breeds hates and fears and prevents him from seeing the intellectual principle because, to the bodily eye, spiritual things are dark and invisible. My belief is that after death he, and all such persons are compelled to wander tombs and sepulchres, imprisoned in corporeal form, until finally they into asses and animals of that sort.

Plato was writing every word the Master uttered. at twenty one he had already distinguished himself as an athlete and a military man. Xenophon, also back in Athens, was equally conscientious in transcribing the master's sayings. Otherwise the two young men were notably dissimilar.

When I married Philesia she was so young she still lived in leading strings," Xenophon said pompously when attention was turned to the fictitious republic that still dominated most discussions. "She saw, and said little. But I made sure she learned how to turn a fine cloak if only to teach her slaves. She's quite docile yet sufficiently well educated to carry on a conversation. And since the gods made women less able to endure toil than men she's content to maintain our home and nurture the tasks ordained for a man's mate."

"You're not exactly in accord with your father are you? He advocates outdoor exercise for women," Socrates rejoined.

"I find nothing more absurd than the practice which prevails in our country of men and women not following the same pursuits with one mind. It reduces the power of the State by half. Everyone, without exception, should enjoy a spontaneous unanimity, knowing it has the backing of the gods."

"It's evident that you two have given these matters much thought" Socrates applauded. "And you, Plato, imbue your convictions with a virtuous light. To return to earth and our immediate situation, I am appalled by the thoughtlessness with which our fellow men are blithely and casually vote either for or against matters that will affect Athens forever. In our effort to devise a saner world, I implore you to stop, think, and take stock", Socrates said, gazing affectionately at the group of young men who, whenever he spoke, listened so intently one could hear a leaf drop.

"The day is waning so I shall try to sum up what has been said. We grope for wisdom and courage, all the while struggling with our humanity trying to moderate our irrational impulses.

"In striving for virtue we find ourselves yearning after One, the Beautiful, and the Good. In sharing the goal of creating an ideal republic we hope to contribute our part to each generation, each age, and the thousands of lives that stretch before us. One might say we are part of a 'Great Panathenaea', moving from star to star until we vanish into the Infinite from whence we came."

Overhearing this, Xanthippe, gritted her teeth. Always the same, day after day, Socrates trying to cram wisdom into men's heads while she had to come by enough food to put into his and her sons' stomachs. It would be a lot easier to stand around gabbing from dawn to dusk than to find grain enough to coax eggs out of a few hens!" She aimed a bowl at the wall. The sound of its crash was pleasing her ears but less so to the men in her courtyard.

"Why don't you train your wife?" Antisthenes asked when she passed them and slammed the gate behind her.

"My life with Xanthippe is like that of a horseman with a steed. When he masters one such he can cope with all. So I, in the company of my many faceted wife, learn to adapt myself to all temperaments. In so saying I compliment her because, to me, she is like tincture of catharitis, the irritant that brings blood to the surface for regeneration. She teaches me to affirm without anger. My father was a sculptor who polished marble with abrasives. In like manner she, with her tumultuous nature, polishes me." Socrates explained with a grin.

* * * *

Hunched against the chill, Xanthippe seated herself beside big water pots, hugged her shawl to her shoulders and folded her hands over the other across her midriff. "By Pluto's beard," she thought, "I shiver like Mama. Or am I shaking with anger at Socrates, this stranger with whom I am in a marriage gone as sour as a pail of goat milk in the sun?

'And beneath it all lies my anger, anger stronger than all reason, anger, the greatest of all evils, which brings the worst of woes upon men'. A passage written by Euripides, spoken by Medea, and learned under the tutelage of dear dead Archos.

"I hate being an angry woman. But that is what I am. I need to get away from here awhile. By now Papa must realize how much he depended on Mama for the comforts she provided. He still has Andokides and Pausimache, but slaves are not family. I will bake him some cakes and take the boys to Cholargus."

She had seen little of her father since last past year he had come to celebrate little Sophroniscus' Day of Recognition. They had exclaimed over the baby's resemblance to his maternal grandparent but he had behaved rather strangely and stayed only a short time.

"How are you getting along without her?" she had asked him when he told her that Leah, Andokides second wife, had died.

"Well enough," had been his bland reply. "Don't worry about me. Things seem to get done."

Beyond that, he had been notably uncommunicative.

Her eldest son was embarrassed when she, at age thirty six, had given birth. If his peers had any babies around they were nephews, not brothers. A little trip to the farm would do him good. The boys should get to know their grandfather. It was time for him to get acquainted with them.

Lamprocles, in a rare good humor, took turns with her pulling Sophroniscus in the baby cart. All three of them had a splendid time, making jokes, laughing, and pausing along the way to eat the treats she had packed for the long walk to Cholargus.

Xanthippe smiled to herself every time she thought about how surprised Papa would be. Instead it was she who got the surprise. As they neared the farm house she saw a lad who looked exactly as Marc had when he was about ten years old.

At that point the courtyard gate opened and there, as if in some dimly remembered scene from a long ago drama stood Femma. She had changed little since the day they cast love spells with wheels. But what was she doing here? And who was that boy?

"Xanthippe!" Femma exclaimed. "I knew you'd come one of these days! I kept begging your father to visit you and try to explain every thing. However, as you know, he's stubborn. He kept putting it off, probably because he was uneasy about how you'd receive what he had to say. Anyway, thank the gods, you're here. And with your sons!"

"You must be Lamprocles," she said. "And little Sophroniscus! Oh po po po, look at him walking already! Philip, go to the paddock and get your father. Take Lamprocles along. Xanthippe, you and the baby and I will go into the house. I must have divined you were coming because I cooked a big pot of Kapama just this morning. Can the baby digest chicken and vegetables?"

* * * *

Xanthippe looked around the kitchen court. It appeared much as it had when her Mama was alive and well. She rubbed her forehead. All this, Femma, the boy, everything, was comparable to the disconnected events of a dream.

"Dear one, how could you be anything but bewildered to find me here? I am going to pour us some wine. Then we'll sit down and I shall try to explain." Femma said, sounding flustered, as if she had mislaid her characteristic calm.

"Long ago, even before you ran away and ended up eating bean soup with me in my house, I knew who you were." she said, collecting herself. "You were such a bright enchanting child and . . ." Her story was interrupted by the appearance of Palen and the boys.

Until now Xanthippe could not recall ever having seen her father ill at ease. In an attempt to regain his composure he made clucking noises at Sophroniscus.

"What brings you to the farm?" he asked still wearing that 'caught-in-the-cakes-crock' look on his face.

Only when they had eaten a meal that smelled and tasted as good as that still remembered bean soup, did he relax.

"You tell her, Femma," he said. "Philip, take Lamprocles to the stable and give him 'Artes' to ride. She's easy gaited, Xanthippe.

While Pausimache, the sole reality in an otherwise unreal scene, cleared the kitchen, Xanthippe put Sophroniscus down for his nap. Then the story unfolded, bit by bit.

"Your father and I are married. It was about three years ago. . ." Femma hesitated, " not long after your mother was taken." There was another pause. "However I had been with him before."

"Obviously," Xanthippe thought as she listened, dumbly bereft of speech.

"I knew you wouldn't understand," Palen said testily.

Her face flamed. 'Wouldn't understand,' he said, this parent of hers who, except for when Yiayia Phyllys died, had made little or no effort to understand the longings, passions or heartaches of anyone other than himself.

"About Philip," Femma said. "He'll soon be eleven. Back then the law made it impossible to give him a 'Day of Recognition' but one look and anyone who knew Palen would realize . . ." Her eyes sought Xanthippe's. "Dear one, I know this is hard for you. I wish I could spare you. At least now you know why you have seen so little of your father," she finished lamely.

"When did you and Papa meet?"

"Shortly after you were born. I was fourteen. My mother had died, leaving me an orphan with nothing of value beyond our little house. I didn't even have relatives. Had it not been for. . . friends I would have lost that. But I knew how to bake so . . ." again Femma hesitated, "That is, in part, how I was making my living when I met your father. Later on, not too long after the last time I saw you, I became pregnant, sold my house, and moved into Athens."

Xanthippe's first impulse was to grab her sons and return to Athens as fast as she could. But that would be impossible.

"You must stay the night," Femma insisted. "It would be far too hard on all of you to travel all that way, back and forth, in one day. Besides, look at the way those boys are enjoying being together."

Lamprocles, puzzled at first by the sudden advent of an 'uncle' two years younger than he, was having a glorious time. Xanthippe, on the other hand, felt as if she were being ripped apart, not only by anger, but jealousy. Although her son, as a novice equestrian, was doing remarkably well, Philip, having had the advantage of daily tutelage and practice was, naturally, far more adept.

In spite of Femma's efforts to initiate conversation, the rest of the day passed so slowly that, except for the boys, everyone was obviously relieved when the time came to retire.

"Do please stay longer," Femma urged the next morning.

"No. It's impossible. I must be on my way."

"Then promise me you will come back soon."

Wracked by conflict, Xanthippe did not reply. Bidding Femma, Palen and Philip a cool 'adio' she departed.

Sophroniscus laughed and babbled cheerfully as he rode along. Lamprocles too was in high spirits. As for Xanthippe, the walk back to Athens seemed endless. She was angry at Femma who had betrayed her. And at Papa. True, other than for his comment about her 'not understanding', he had been as genial as Lysicles. Yet it was his very good humor that added to her ire.

The sheepherder and the horseman, both so quick to find new wives, one a former hetaira, and the other a whore! It was as if Mama and Lysicles' wife had never existed.

And her father's newly legitimized bastard would take Marc's place if Marc did not return. By fair means or foul Palen would have a son to repeat the Mysteries at his grave. By Zeus she would not be caught dead going back to Cholargus. Not ever!

Goaded by indignation she took such long strides that Lamprocles asked her to slow down before Sophroniscus was bounced out of his cart.

Chapter Forty-seven

There were shadowy rings beneath Alcibiades' eyes and his once handsome face was cross-hatched with lines. But his lips were still cruel as a crocodile's.

"Stop staring and allow me to enter," he demanded. "I'm here to visit your husband and was hoping you would not be at home. Ah! There he is! The man I returned from Samos to see," he cried, pushing Xanthippe aside when she opened the gate.

Flinging a gold crested cloak aside he embraced Socrates. "Dear Master, had you given me your blessing before I left Athens, it would have spared me much grief. But here I am, in spite of my many trials, the conquering hero, home again!"

Gleefully he described how, after taking Byzantium, he had sailed to Samos and, from there, back to Athens in a fleet decked with trophies of his victory. Two days later the Assembly had acclaimed his conquest, restored his property, placed a gold crown on his silvering head and invited him to address their august group.

"Naturally I denied all charges and, again, avowed my fealty to Athens. Then they re-elected me general, this time with sole powers by land and sea!" he finished exultantly.

"So this is how our Senate rewards a traitor," Xanthippe seethed. "Were it not for Alcibiades there would never have been any war in Sicily, and Marc, as well as legions of other young men would be right here in Athens and not be drowned or enslaved somewhere in a foreign land, but alive and home where he belongs."

"I want to regain the peace I find only in your presence, Socrates." Now Alcibiades' sounded less frenzied. "Please say that, despite all my shortcomings, you still love me."

"Nothing you do can destroy true love. You are my son, my brother, my friend, and I pray for you daily."

"For which I am grateful," Alcibiades said gravely. "Do you recall Agathon's symposium? The topic was 'love' and when it came my turn came to speak I confided how, in my passion for you, I invited you to dine? And how, after we ate you wanted to leave but I begged you to stay because I was bitten by a viper in the most painful spot, the soul, an esoteric issue upon which you, in your philosopher's madness, often expound"

Xanthippe felt she heard a hint of madness in his giggle.

"Remember how everyone shouted and laughed when I put my arms around you and tried to seduce you but you were wholly unmoved by my tender advances? I compared you to those little replicas of Silenus that sit in statuaries shops and, when they are opened down the middle, you can see the gods inside, just as when you, Socrates, are very earnest and opened out I see divine, golden, radiant images within you!

"I kept trying to imitate you. At times I almost succeeded. The reason I finally gave up was because I feared it was too late for me to change. Yet, dear Master, after all these years I am still awed by your impregnable chastity. To this day it has a way of making me feel ashamed."

"Ultimately it will be the curse of his overwhelming ambition that will destroy him, poor fellow," Socrates said heavily when their visitor departed.

Neighbors had collected in the street to ogle Alcibiades' jet black stallion. Their attention was quickly diverted by the appearance of the mercurial aristocrat himself.

His ivory and gold shield was engraved with a figure of Zeus, hurling a lightning bolt, and on his thumb (a phallic symbol) he wore a signet ring, engraved with a charm, sacred to Aphrodite, and said to augment the wearer's virility.

People were still gaping when he rowelled his horse and charged down the road.

"He justifies his extravagance by saying it exalts Athens," said the woman with hair on her upper lip.

"I hear Alcibiades paid you a visit," the grain merchant remarked the next day while he was weighing out a packet of wheat for Xanthippe in the Agora.

"Did you know he put Antilochus, one of his jackass friends, in command of what's left of our fleet and sent him to attack Sparta's General

Lysander?" he asked. "Well, that Lysander is nobody's fool. A report came this morning saying that we have already suffered heavy losses. At this very moment the Assembly is having an emergency meeting to get Alcibiades removed. My guess is he'll run to that stronghold he has in Thrace and sulk 'til a new majority votes him back into power. How long can such a rogue go on gulling people?"

* * * *

Socrates had left the house and Lamprocles was in school when Xanthippe returned from the Agora next morning, hauling Sophroniscus behind her in his cart, When the baby had been fed and put to bed, she went into Phaenerete's old room, the one she and Socrates now occupied, and was giving the coverlets a shake when her little curio box from home flipped onto the floor and discharged the long dormant eye of Artemis.

Instead of replacing it she thrust it into her work-tunic pocket, went to the kitchen court, poured herself a cup of broth, and carried it outdoors. The mess in the kitchen could be dealt with later.

Aimlessly she circled the cup rim with her finger. The sky was overcast, but pierced here and there with fitful rays of sunshine. Somber clouds streamed by, swift as chariots in a race. The day, like her mood, was dark and unsettled.

"I'm sorry you're downcast," had been Socrates' response at breakfast when she mentioned feeling sad. "We'll discuss it later. Right now I must hurry on to meet Plato. He wants to show me some of what he has been writing."

Socrates spoke glibly about equality for women, but his words appeared not to apply to wives. Clearly he saw them as minions, whose duty it was to bear and care for his children, have food ready whenever he chose to come home.

Insistent as a fish-monger, he kept reiterating that the unexamined life was not worth living.

He also loved to tell a story about people who lived in a cave and thought that they themselves were the shadows on the wall, cast by the light of flickering flames. Sadder still was their failure to see an opening in the end of the cave, that could lead them into a brighter, more beautiful, world.

335

It was not fables she, Xanthippe, needed, it was love. The kind Yiayia-Phyllys meant when she said that no vocation or sport afforded a greater challenge than that of taking a chance on relating to another human being.

"A man can risk having his hound bite him, or his horse throw him, but he can only find his manhood when he dares to give his love, unreservedly, to a woman." she said.

Some of Yiayia's ideas had been similar to those of Socrates, except that he gave little, if any thought to meeting the needs of a wife. He was not interested in being a caring companion, or sharing some of her interests. He was not one who savored living in his body. His preference was, as Aristophanes put it, to 'dwell in the clouds.'

"What about my preferences? Xanthippe asked herself. "I want things I don't have and I have things I do not want, all because I was involuntarily committed to spending the rest of my life with a man whose only desire is to probe people about the meaning of Virtue and Truth and to tell everyone he meets to search his soul and discover who he (or she) is.

A curiously disturbing demand.

Hipparete had owned a shiny metal mirror. Xanthippe still recalled holding it up to her face and staring directly into her own eyes, The experience had been unnerving. Like coming unexpectedly face to face with a stranger. Could it be that she, like Socrates' cave-dwellers, was less afraid of her own shadow than of that unknown 'Some one' who returned her gaze?

How to go about discovering who, or what, one is?

"Get on with it," she said aloud, and was startled by the sound of her own voice ere in the courtyard.

'Kokeeno'? Papa's carrot haired daughter who should have been a boy.

To her brothers she was Tippy, and to Mama 'Penroula', Bad child. A name that hurt. Yiayia's 'Kale Pai' had been kinder.

'Agape-Mou', my beloved, sounded nice, except that, in Socrates' eyes, everyone was his 'beloved', even Alcibiades.

Other memories surfaced, some of them seeping like drops of blood from an unhealed wound.

Cautiously she scrutinized them, one by one.

She had owned, at least she thought she had, a mare named Iris. Until then Papa had seemed god-like, After the Iris episode she'd come to realize that he was as mortal as anyone else. Yet to this day she'd catch herself doing everything in her power to emulate him. Poor Elefterous had died trying.

Did anyone ever succeeded in pleasing Papa? Perhaps Femma, At least so far. But she had only pretended to care for his daughter when, all along he was the one she loved. Enraging!

Encounters with Hipponicus? Horrible.

Alcibiades had been the real thorn in her flesh. It was when he called her a 'Nobody's Nothing' that their never cordial relationship had turned into implacable hatred.

The memory of her first fight with Kallia brought a smile. She, and the other girls who lived in town, had made it obvious that they did not want Palen's daughter for a friend. Not only did they scorn him because he was a breeder of horses, they disliked her just for being whoever she was. So who was she? According to Socrates, she didn't know!

Friends, relatives, enemies, moving in and out of her life like dancers in a drunken dithyramb. And she?

The mimic of them all.

Characters in dramas seemed more real. Medea, for example, saying, "Ladies of Corinth, of all creatures that live and reflect, women are certainly the most luckless. First a great price must be paid to buy them a husband. After that everything depends upon whether the choice was good or bad.

"She is plunged into a way of life entirely new to her and must learn what she never learned at home, how best to manage him who masters her body and shares her bed. If she works all this out well and carefully, and if her husband is agreeable, life can be happy indeed. If not she may as well be dead because a man who does not enjoy what he finds at home, leaves the house and puts an end to his boredom by turning to another diversions."

A happy memory was the swing Papa had hung for her. How lovely it was to sit on it, arch her back, point her toes toward the sky, and pretend to be Artemis, flying across the moon. Had that Xanthippe taken happiness as her due? Riding, racing the chariot, and playing games with Hipparete seemed more like a dream than an experience.

As did those magic moments with Critobolus. Her feelings for him still went unresolved. Was it true love? Or had that also been no more than a game of pretend?

Does the remembrance of things past delude one into seeing them through more benevolent eyes?

Xanthippe stirred uneasily. The atmosphere was becoming more oppressive. Startled by a sudden streak of lightning she upset her broth. It was lukewarm but the episode recalled a pot of scalding stock and beads of sweat formed on her brow.

With a sinister rumble, black clouds turned to sluices of rain but, making no move to go indoors, she continued to sit, tense and still, watching the storm accelerate. It was early afternoon but the world was enveloped in darkness, and the crashing of thunder so fierce one might think Mount Parnassus was being shattered.

She braced herself, expecting to be struck. The God of Thunder had killed others. Was she to be his next victim?

A jagged flare pierced the gloom and hit the trunk of a sycamore tree beyond the wall, searing its bark. Flashes of hot white light jumped toward her over the hard earth floor, and the air reeked of smoke and the odd pungency of that bolt

"Zeus!" she cried. Her answer was a jagged dagger of light splitting the darkened sky.

"Go ahead! Get on with your game. Show your power." Xanthippe's shout vied with the elements. "Knock me to my knees!

You've done it before, why not again?"

Tears were beginning to flow, unchecked, down her cheeks, mingling with the torrent as if she and the tempest were one.

"You win, Zeus. If you don't like me as I am what can I do about it?" she sobbed. "I surrender! I give up."

She did not know how long she wept but the source of her tears seemed fathomless. Tears over long dormant hurts, tears of regret for errors that could not be rectified, tears still trickling, the salty taste of them good in her mouth.

Gradually the rain began to abate, clouds dissolved into light and with one last celestial rumble, the turbulence ceased, and the sun emerged like a dazzling surprise.

Heedless of sodden garments and streaming hair, Xanthippe reseated herself and felt her burden of anger and remorse falling away like wet leaves dropping from the wounded but still staunch sycamore tree.

Puddles of water were opalescent prisms, dotting the courtyard floor. Streams of gold glistening on a lattice-work of leaves, brought back the day Hipparete had exclaimed, "Look! All the trees are wearing clean green tunics!"

Socrates believed in a singular god who made matters right even when they appeared to be wrong. Possibly that same god had the power to wash away hurts and heartaches somewhat the way she gave her baby a bath and hugged him before his nap.

Time had moved on but, evidently, she had not. Perhaps, like a temple girls who must be purged with brine before they are ready to dance, she herself needed a storm of rain and tears to help her let go of the past, live in the present, and walk boldly into the future.

Thoughtfully Xanthippe withdrew the eye of Artemis from her pocket and studied it. Artemis and Aphrodite . . .

Virginity and Desire, Sunshine and Storm, Rich and Poor, Love and Hate, Time and Eternity, opposites all, yet one and the same.

Penroula and Kale-Pai? A mean-mouthed vixen, plagued with desire, yet, simultaneously a woman who knows what it is to laugh and to love, one who finds joy when she sees a battalion of sea-gulls standing at attention beside the sea.

"That is who I am. It is ME, Xanthippe!" She marvelled. A growing sense of stillness within her was part of the quiet that now reigned in the courtyard.

How lovely if one could always be this content. Socrates claimed that few people, other than fools, could abide in a state of perennial good cheer. "In the rest of us there always lurks a meanness, even a savagery of disposition."

"I heard noises in the sky. They scared me," said little Sophroniscus, coming out and toddling into her arms.

Still holding him, Xanthippe got to her feet. Socrates and Lamprocles would soon be home. It was time to prepare the evening meal. And the breakfast things weren't even washed!

"From now on I shall be the nice, pleasant Xanthippe if it kills me!" she muttered, heading for the kitchen court.

Chapter Forty-eight

The wintry month of Gamelion brought a brief lull in the war and a visit from General Gryllus. He looked older and a bit grizzled but otherwise the same.

"Xanthippe, I'm here to thank you for the care you gave my daughter," he said, accepting a cup of her carefully hoarded wine. "What's this I hear about Anytus telling people you separated him from Astron?" he asked Socrates.

"I'm sorry that Anytus bears me a grudge. But it's his vendetta, not mine." Socrates replied evenly. "Astron no longer holds with everything his father believes. But I told him nothing I wouldn't freely say to anyone who cares to listen, namely, not to take anyone's word, including mine, unless he personally accepts it as valid. Then, truth, once realized, be adhered to, even if it alienates loved ones. But I admire Anytus for trying to restore political accord."

"The only thing Anytus wants is to further himself, and may the gods help any man who contradicts him. He's dangerous."

"Far be it from me to stand in his way!"

"Why pay him a compliment in return for the malicious tales he spreads about you?"

"Because he's a good politician."

"You said there is no such thing as a 'good politician'."

"I said 'there's no such thing as an honest one! But, by the dog, there soon will be! I am about to become one myself," Socrates declared, giving them a droll wink.

"You what?" Xanthippe and Gryllus eyed him with disbelief.

"I own this house and, as a property owner, have often been approached about serving a term in the Prytaneum. I declined because, to hold public office would conflict with a mission I consider more meaningful. Had I chosen to engage all my time in politics I'd have perished long ago, and done no good to either Athens or myself.

"No man who strives against the lawless, unrighteous deeds that are done for the so called 'good of the state' survives. To stay alive he who fights for the right must have a private station. But I believe my time has come to enter the arena."

Xanthippe's face was a mix of incredulity and delight. As a senator Socrates had to accept a salary! Which meant she'd be able to restock an impoverished larder, renew family and buy wool with which to weave new covers!

"Well!" Gryllus exhaled. "We urgently need men of courage in office. And the power of your oratory might persuade others to want to get rid of the frauds who seem determined to destroy the very foundation on which Athens was built."

Soon afterwards Socrates was taking his meals within the august walls of the Prytaneum. However, because senators were served bounteously at state expense, he ate sparingly.

Xanthippe and her sons fared better at home. "I'm getting fat!" she said after an unprecedented dinner of roast lamb. They were laughing at her joke when Crito arrived.

"First let me tell you that, albeit ever so slowly, money continues to accrue from your initial investment," he said, lowering himself heavily onto a bench.

"For me that is very good news, as you know," Xanthippe replied. "But I can tell by your face that something's amiss."

Yes, Xanthippe. I live in a house of sorrow."

"Kallia?"

"She fell down a flight of stairs and broke her neck. You saw how difficult it was for her to keep her balance. At least, death, at the end, no longer held any fear for her. You were so very kind to visit her often, and always with a treat you'd made just for her. She was truly grateful. We all were."

So, once again, out came the garments of mourning. It was the grain vendor who said, "What with war and the plague, there are so many people in the Underworld it's a wonder there are any of us still up here!"

She shed a few tears at the funeral, not just for Kallia but all the rest. Papa had forbidden her to cry but nevermore would she gag on a lump in her throat. She would weep if she wished and to Hades' pit with all those dry-eyed Spartans.

* * * *

Toward the end of the year dying embers burst into renewed conflagration near the Arginusae. Then a triumphant bulletin. The Athenian fleet had overwhelmingly defeated the Spartans who lost seventy ships, along with their General Callicrates!

After the good news came a report that Athens had lost five ships in the fray. Worse yet, hundreds of Athenian had drowned, all because the eight generals it had taken to replace Alcibiades were busy arguing strategy when they should have been paying attention to what was happening at the moment.

By the time they got around to deciding how to effect a rescue, the seas were so rough that, of all the sailors who had been clinging helplessly to driftwood only a few survived.

Two of the generals fled. The six who returned to Athens were arrested. All could agree they had been victorious leaders, and that 'War is war'. Nonetheless they had committed a crime.

What made their action all the more reprehensible was that dead men who are not given funeral rites are doomed to wander through eternity unseen, never at rest, neither part of this world nor the next.

Bereaved families, clothed in black, their heads shaved, stormed the Prytaneum, demanding vengeance.

"Death to the generals," They chanted.

It happened to be Socrates' turn to preside in the Prytaneum on the same day that Callixenus, the chief magistrate, delivered a fiery speech against the generals, demanding that all eight, including the two absentees, be put to death.

"Gentlemen of Athens, hear me!" Socrates shouted. "I refuse to entertain Callixenus' motion, or let it be put to a vote."

His suggestion met with such vociferous opposition he had wait until the arena became quiet enough for him to proceed.

"It is contrary to Athenian law to try more than one man at a time for any crime, no matter how heinous or seemingly collective the wrongdoing might be. As long as I am president of this Council I must demand that we adhere to the law!"

Impeach Socrates," someone yelled. Others took up the cry.

The clamor provided Callixenus with an opportunity to leap to his feet insisting that all the generals must die.

"What Callixenus asks is illegal," Socrates said, standing his ground at the rostrum. "Each general deserves to be tried separately. It may be proved that one, or perhaps two, did things possible to save the drowning or recover their bodies."

"For opposing my motion Socrates is a traitor to Athens!" Callixenus, bawled so loudly that everyone began to shout.

The mob won. Ignoring its temporary chairman they voted with Callixenus, unanimous save Socrates. His was the lone 'Nay.'

"Impeach Socrates!" Arrest the traitor!" Their howls followed him when, after the verdict was read, he arose and without haste, departed. It was no surprise for him to see citizens suddenly contradict themselves by showing disfavor for one who had, only yesterday, received their acclaim. Just as, for little more reason than the fact that he looked like a god they would re-embrace a perfidious man like Alcibiades.

At home he found Xanthippe looking so pleased with her new situation that he did not mention anything about today's events,

The generals who came home were executed immediately. In their ranks had been Pericles the Younger,last surviving son of 'The Olympian', the one who had been born of Aspasia.

When Xanthippe learned that he had died she sat, her mouth turned down thoughtfully. Can anyone truly mourn with, or move into the grief of another human? Impossible.

Nonetheless she set out for Cholargus, to offer sympathy to Aspasia, and visit Palen and Femma. It was time to let them know she bore no grudge. It was as if she, like the bark on that old tree, had been stripped clean.

Naturally the idea of having a half-brother inherit the farm still rankled, as did a suspicion that Papa behaved like a moonstruck calf because Femma had either cast a spell on him, or dribbled a love potion into his soup. He was not the man whose tantrums had kept Mama in a constant state of agitation.

"I have a way to go before I get to the state of bliss and contentment my husband extols," she sighed. His admonition that 'Only a torturous path leads to enlightenment.' might be true, but for a surety it was more pleasant to permit one's thoughts to wander freely than to face unlovely truths about oneself.

Chapter Forty-nine

At seventeen Lamprocles' name had been duly inscribed on the roll of the clan of Antioch. Today he stood on the podium of the Temple of Aglauros, prepared to repeat a solemn pledge, one committed to memory by all newly inducted 'ephebes. Like his mother, he was tall, slender, and had the same copper bright hair.

"I will not disgrace my sacred weapons nor desert the comrade who is placed by my side," he vowed, in the richly resonant voice of his father. "I will fight for things holy and things profane whether alone or with others. I will hand on my fatherland greater and better than I found it. I will harken to the magistrates and obey the existing laws and those here-after established by the people."

"I will not consent unto any who disobeys the constitution but will prevent him, whether I am alone or with others. I will honor the temples and the religion my forefathers established. So help me Aglauros, Ares, Zeus, Thallo, and Athena."

"He didn't miss a word!" said Socrates, smiling broadly.

Xanthippe's eyes glowed. Her boy! How handsome and solemn he looked, up there in an army tunic, with his hair shorn to signify adulthood. He and she were on their way to becoming friends again. "Mama, you yell a lot, but you're a very nice person," he had said yesterday.

In return for the (dubious) compliment she had offered him a freshly baked piece of flat bread and, in view of his forthcoming induction into the army, a cup of wine.

"One can only pray the time will come when people learn to settle their disputes peaceably," Socrates said two weeks later seizing his son in a farewell embrace on the day Lamprocles was to leave with his contingent of 'epheboi'. "I too have served Athens in battle, my boy. The experience taught me that if you want to be thought of as good at this business of soldiering you must make every effort to be so. That's the quickest, the surest, the best way. May the gods be with you!"

Xanthippe thought about Marc who had gone and not returned. She shuddered. Lamprocles would be away for at least a year, patrolling Attica's borders and forts.

However her face was a carefully composed mask as she waved 'adio' until he was out of sight.

That evening she and Socrates, accompanied by seven year old Sophroniscus, sacrificed two doves to Athena and prayed for Lamprocles' safe return.

Later, alone in the courtyard, she kicked a copper pot across the courtyard. Its clatter, tumbling over the hard earthen floor, provided a brief and somehow satisfying diversion. But it did nothing to ease the pain in her heart.

* * * *

"In the name of Athena I pray you don't carry out this scheme," Desperately Alcibiades warned Athenian generals who were activating plans to vanquish Sparta's General Lysander and his troops in the eastern Aegean. "You can't win. Lysander can't be beaten! He's too formidable, too powerful! Take my word for it! "

"Take my word for it" the generals mocked. "Who wants the worthless word of a double traitor? What proof have we that you're not working in behalf of Sparta this very moment? And lest you forget, you're the man who assured us we could conquer Syracuse!"

Wild, unruly, and double dealing though he might be Alcibiades was undeniably one of the most gifted commanders in Athenian history. His intuition as to when and where to move troops was so uncanny that many were convinced that had Nicias not been at his side he might have, on his own, achieved victory in Sicily.

Unfortunately intuition was a quality sadly lacking in the generals with whom he pleaded. This time instead of embracing him they sent him away, proceeded with their plans, and sailed to the attack.

Lysander trapped Athens' fleet at Aegospotamia. Nine of her one hundred and eighty ships escaped, one was sunk with all aboard, and the Spartans added the remaining hundred and seventy to their own navy.

The 'Mistress Of The Seas' had been raped and three thousand Athenian prisoners of war put to death.

An eerie sound of wailing awakened Xanthippe and Socrates. Hurriedly they slipped into their clothes and ran outdoors.

'Paralus' the State Trireme, had sailed into the harbor at Piraeus with tidings of the disaster. Agonized laments moved from person to person, through the long walls of the city, one man passing word on to the next.

"It is over! . . . FINISHED!!!!!"

After thirty years of fighting, heartbreak, and destruction the Peloponnesian Wars were over in a single battle.

No one slept that night, all of them mourning not only for the dead but for the suffering they themselves might have to endure, suffering such as they had inflicted on the tiny island of Melos years ago.

Although he was no longer a senator, Socrates attended an emergency session of the Assembly where it was unanimously voted to blockade the harbor and prepare for siege.

Xanthippe found it difficult to focus on the catastrophe that had befallen Athens. The only thing that really mattered to her was knowing that Lamprocles, on patrol far north of the Aegean's watery scene of defeat, was safe! Glad to be, once again believing in the gods she thanked them.

"Total surrender!" shouted the Spartans closing in on Athens like a vise. "The Walls must come down!"

In despair the Assembly sent an ambassador to Sparta's King Agis offering to become his country's ally, asking only that the 'Walls' be saved.

"No!" His straightforward answer was fast in coming.

There was no more food, no ships to bring it, no allies left to come to the rescue. Some one stole two of Xanthippe's hens so she brought the rest into the courtyard and barred the gate.

It was not just a shortage of food but famine gnawing at the bellies of rich and poor alike and Athenians dying of hunger and thirst. The city capitulated. What else was there to do?

Peace terms were decided upon. The Great Walls would be demolished and, of the ships that still remained in Athenian waters, only twelve could be kept. The rest went to Sparta.

Xanthippe was scraping remnants of cabbage and rice into a pot of herb water when Socrates came into the kitchen court.

"These are terrible times but at least our son was not in that battle," she said, noting the sadness on his face, "You look as if you'd lost your last friend."

"Not my last friend but a dear misguided one whom I loved."

"Who?" Xanthippe's voice was hesitant.

"Alcibiades. He's dead," Socrates replied tonelessly and cleared his throat several times before continuing. "He ultimately so enraged the Spartans they sent mercenaries to kill him and his death was as uncommon as his life. He had been living with a woman named Timandra, and he told her of a dream in which he had seen himself lying in her arms while she robed him in women's' garments and painted his face.

"You may find this hard to believe but three days later hired minions set fire to his house and when Alcibiades rushed out they killed him with javelins and arrows. And it was Timandra who took his dead body in her arms, dressed him in her own sumptuous robes and vows to give him the finest funeral money can buy."

Socrates covered his face with his hands. "What a tragic waste," he said, looking up again. "I speak, not so much of Alcibiades' death but his life, a life destined for greatness and destroyed by wrong thinking. In a way he represents our country, beautiful, brilliant, highly civilized, but undermined by greed, superstition and decadence."

Xanthippe had been five years old when she encountered Alcibiades for the first time. From that day on he had done everything in his power to make her life miserable. Now he no longer existed. Yet she could still see his mocking face, just as if he were standing here before her.

In imaginary confrontations she had challenged him with brilliant rhetoric, humbled him before the world, and demolished him for every cruel blow he'd ever dealt.

Along with these flights of fancy she had also, in actuality, mocked him on various occasions, most notably by triumphing over him in a chariot race. But nothing she'd ever done could excuse the murder of her hound, the loss of her mare, or the torture inflicted on Hipparete.

Although he was not totally responsible for Marc's disappearance he was, in some measure, even to blame for that.

Now, here she was, diminished by his death because, in going permanently out of reach, he had forever ended her cherished plots of ultimately destroying him. How strange, that even the death of an enemy can be a form of bereavement.

In a sense one might say that his had been the final triumph.

Chapter Fifty

In the year following Sparta's triumph, her leader, Lysander, had come with a corps of workmen, and torn down the Great Walls. Heartsick over the devastation of their city, disciples continued to assemble in Socrates' courtyard. Here, more than anywhere else, they could, for awhile, forget the chaos prevailing elsewhere. And thanks to Xanthippe's perseverance it was a pleasant place in which to be.

Socrates' clean well patched toga proved that she was also gaining the upper hand in regard to his apparel. Beyond that he never seemed to change. At sixty six his bulging blue eyes still sparkled, and his voice was as vibrant as ever.

"Homer says a small rock can hold back a great wave. Perhaps you and I might be described as pebbles trying to stem the downfall of civilization," he was saying. "In my lifetime I have been privileged to experience the golden days of Greece. Our beautiful Athens was the center of the world. Every important writer, thinker, and artist aspired to visit and be accorded honor here. But now, as we yield to tyranny, I am forced to see her humiliated. The complexity of such a tragedy would defy the quill of Sophocles!"

A hand was agitated to gain his attention. "We are only in this plight because of wars that began before I was born," Phaedo, its owner stated. "We had rulers who made Athens great but, unfortunately, not wise. That's why now we are paying the price."

When the ensuing volley of comments and questions subsided it was agreed that Athenians had begun yielding to a dictatorship long ago but it had progressed so slowly that only a very few saw what was happening.

Well," Socrates concluded, "I think we've cogitated enough for one afternoon. May I offer you some refreshment? I shall see if my good wife has something for us."

Xanthippe put down the broom she was fashioning from a bunch of bristles "Smile! Be content!" she reminded herself, and shook her head in wonderment. Here was a man who, in spite of his reputation for having great wisdom, couldn't get it through his head that there was barely enough food in the house to feed a family of four. But oh no! He just had to go right on making the same mistake over and over again.

"Excuse me, Master," she heard Plato say, "but I managed to dig up some cheese and a jug of wine. And don't give me that look! This gift is not for you! I brought it out of sympathy for your long suffering wife. And I am going to go find her and request that she join us."

There was a shout of laughter and, when he returned with Xanthippe, a burst of applause.

Everyone had a splendid time and not until dusk did anyone think of going home.

* * * *

Having successfully demolished Athens' Great Walls, Lysander chose thirty Athenian aristocrats on whom he could depend to serve Sparta's interests. Among them were Plato's uncles, Kritias and Charmides, whom he elected to be leaders of 'The 'Thirty', as the group was dubbed.

Under their direction fifteen men, including Socrates' long time friend Polemarchus, were executed in a series of murders more despicable even than the massacre at Melos.

"No one is safe, especially people who, like Polemarchus, own covetable property," Socrates mourned.

"I'm worried about what happens next," Xanthippe said.

She had good reason. The very next day Kritias and Charmides came to the house hoping to implicate Socrates in their nefarious schemes. Claiming to have heard him inveigh against the democracy, they asked him to help them arrest Leon, a wealthy merchant from Salamis. What they forgot was his detachment from any political party or system that ran counter to his theories about an 'ideal republic' which their nephew 'Plato' was transcribing in voluminous detail.

"I want nothing to do with your growing list of murders!" he said flatly.

Xanthippe swallowed. Only the miracle of a counter-revolt could save him from the consequences of his defiance. That was exactly what happened!

Following a valiant battle, Democrats deposed 'The Thirty' and put all of their leaders to death.

"Kritias and Charmides were Plato's uncles. It was their treachery that got them killed," Socrates said. "How sad and bewildered he must be."

"How long can this nightmare go on? I am fearful for you, Socrates! Xanthippe wailed. "You were right when you said that people wore masks. It's getting so you can't tell a friend from an enemy! Any one of the men who meet here in our courtyard and appear to be so devoted to you, could turn on you in a moment!" I think it's time you quit teaching."

Contrary to his wife's suggestion that he discontinue his lectures, Socrates welcomed the eleven men who showed up that very afternoon. Among them was Plato who made no effort to hide the fact that he felt no need to mourn his uncles.

"Why should I?" he asked. "They sought to betray my Master, and, in so doing, they betrayed me. From this time forth I am their nephew only by an accident of birth. I'd as lieve be the nephew of pigs."

Alone in her kitchen court, Xanthippe heaved a shaky sigh. It was damnably difficult to be cheerful in times like these, when, day and night, you feared for the safety of both your husband and your first-born son.

Chapter Fifty-one

The new year was hardly into its first lunation when the courtyard gate burst open and Socrates came in like a whirlwind.

"Good tidings for a change!" he shouted. "The list has been posted in the Agora! Our boy is coming home!"

"When? How soon?"

"Any day, praise the gods!"

And praise the post-war demand for loans that sent interest rates up, which meant a small gain from their modest investment and would allow enough money to spend on winter wheat for Lamprocles' favorite honey cakes, Xanthippe thought.

"I like parties," Sophroniscus said, licking the bowl as she pushed a tray of confections into the oven.

"Are you expecting him to arrive with his entire troop?" Socrates inquired. Where did you find all this food?"

"I've been getting enough vegetables from my garden to take care of us and still have enough to preserve. The hens are laying better too. Just be glad I grew up on a farm."

"You're to be congratulated. I have heard you complain that the only thing anyone could get out of our backyard was a clay pot and now look what you've done! Your happiness over the homecoming of our son becomes you! You've never looked more fit. Even before the good news about Lamprocles I have noticed a change in you, you seem . . . happier somehow."

Contentedly Xanthippe sniffed the three crisp brown loaves. The baking of bread was a satisfying challenge. There was life in bread, and it nourished the lives of others. It also rewarded one with a savoury smell

"Now, fetch some water to wash the floors, Sophroniscus," she said when her plans for a home-coming feast were in order.

"Mama!" he demurred, "Lamprocles will be so glad to get home he won't see the dirt if there is any left!"

"Go!"

On hands and knees she scoured. Then, taking her best coverlet from a chest she went into the room that had been turned over to the boys after Phaenerete's death and placed it on Lamprocles' pallet.

One by one she fingered the souvenirs of childhood that still lay there, a terra cotta elf astride a goose with a broken beak, a leather bag containing five smooth stones, a hoop, a hockey stick, the dusty skin of a snake . . . Ah, if only for awhile he were a child again and she could hold him close. "I'd be different, not so strict, nor easily upset over spilled milk and broken bowls. I'd be gentler." She sighed, stretched, and rubbed an aching back with the flat of her hands. "But that's in the past," she reminded herself. "What counts is to be alive and enjoy today.

"Now," she decided, after a final survey of her domain, "I can do something about my own appearance. All this house cleaning must have me looking like the one who's come home from a war."

That same afternoon, toward sunset, a loud haloo sent the whole family running.

"Mama! Father! Sophroniscus! It's me! I'm home!" shouted Lamprocles, loping through the gate

Joyfully Xanthippe gazed at the lean young stranger who was her son! His face looked more mature, his body was trim and muscular in the tunic that signified his combat unit, and he bore the treasured shield and spear given to ephebes upon the successful conclusion of their formal training.

Having discovered that tears served in times of happiness as well as those of stress, Xanthippe permitted her eyes to brim.

At supper, Socrates, Lamprocles, and young Sophroniscus wore garlands on their heads and their thanksgiving oblations and prayers seemed more significant than ever before. Even the tragedy of Athens' defeat could not dampen their celebration.

"Mama, you amaze me! How did you manage such a feast?" Lamprocles marvelled. "I heard all the food stalls were bare, And the swill we got at camp wasn't fit for rats!" He made a wry face. "I kept dreaming about these!" He waved one of the cakes that had been baked expressly for him.

"I have done the same thing myself," Socrates laughed and rubbed his belly. "Yes, Agape Mou, tonight you have truly outdone yourself!"

Nine months after Lamprocles' homecoming Socrates was accepting good natured teasing about his virility, and congratulations on the birth of a third son. For a woman to have a baby when she is forty-four is remarkable in itself but when the father is sixty-seven the tale becomes even better.

"Menexenus has a congenial sound," he said when they discussed. "Meno, Menon, Menexenus! You've met Menon, the young Thessalian nobleman, He would be a conscientious godfather."

"I like him too, and his name," Xanthippe agreed.

Sophroniscus was happy to have a younger brother. Not so Lamprocles who was mortified, even more than when Sophroniscus was born. "I'm old enough to be his father!" he grumbled.

Sick of war, he, like his peers, refused to re-enlist.

"Decide where your talents lie and in what field you wish to excel," Socrates advised, having decided that the time had come to address the matter of his son's future. "Then, having made up your mind, follow that path courageously. Is there anything in particular you would like to do?"

"I want to have a good time and meet some girls."

"Perhaps you and I should discuss this further, son, Sit down." said Socrates, pulling up a bench. "As I've previously mentioned, there are girls who can be encountered on the city streets. As they are of dubious virtue, you'd do well to avoid them. You will see many women but I urge you to temper your passion with wisdom. Glands often speak more loudly than brains, but you must ignore their siren call. First of all, choose and pursue your career. In the meantime your mother and I will help you to find a suitable wife."

"I don't want a wife. Wives yammer and scold."

"Yes, and geese hiss but they lay eggs! One of these days you're going to want a son of your own. That's why the wise choice of a mate is so vital. A man should breed for strength, health, and stamina, and definitely for wisdom." Earnestly Socrates sought his son's eyes. "As a soldier you have served Athens well, but you still owe a debt, to your family, your country, and your species and that is to leave sons who will inspire and create. I pray this is what you will do."

"Is that why you married Mama?"

"Yes. But by the time I married your mother I was mature enough to choose my own wife. There's more to it than that. She's part of my destiny, I always loved her. I still do."

"Somehow I would not have guessed that," Lamprocles said, casting his parent a dubious look.

"I don't want you and Father picking a wife for me," he told Xanthippe later in the day.

How long ago it, she wondered, since she had said the same thing to her mother while they were in the kitchen court, making macaronia?

Chapter Fifty-two

"I wonder if Xanthippe is sick," the neighbor on the other side said to the woman next door to her. "I haven't heard her yell at Socrates or the children in the gods know how long!"

"Perhaps he put a curse on her loud mouth."

However, it was no curse that accounted for the quiet, but the fact that Xanthippe and Socrates were at peace. On occasion it occurred to her that she loved him. Stranger yet, she had taken to asking the 'questioner' questions and was doing so today as they sat together in the courtyard.

"If, as you say, I'm part of the 'Nous' and 'It' is part of me, why can't I say, 'Nous', I need money, jewels, and a house full of slaves to do my bidding?" she asked. "Godsname I've been around you and your disciples for so long I've begun to sound like one of them!"

"You have indeed! And my answer is that the danger in asking for something specific is you're apt to get it. And if your wants are limited to the items you just mentioned you'll never be satisfied. As I've said a thousand times, you just go on wanting more and more things. But if your goal is, purely and simply, to align yourself with the 'One', the Good and the Beautiful, sooner or later, those troublesome cravings go away and leave you transformed. Do I make myself clear?"

"As clear as this bread dough I'm kneading!" Xanthippe retorted. "Would that my supply of grain were as plentiful as your words. If, as you suggest, we are all members of one vast 'body' then you must be the teeth, biting, crunching, and spitting out ideas that are difficult to swallow."

"And you, my dear, are the tongue! And a clever one."

"You find me clever? Then pay attention to what I say. I've heard that you contradict the priests, and even fly in the face of elected officials. Any one of them could accuse you of impiety if he wished and I implore you to be more discreet about voicing your opinions in public. "

"Why should I be considered impious because I promulgate the need to decry existing evils? I am entitled to my own opinion even if it happens to differ from that of a priest, or a politician. Our 'inner voice' tells us right from wrong, and blesses us with the knowledge of goodness and virtue, so why damn me for saying that 'only in virtue can one find truth?"

"I'm not sure," Xanthippe replied. In a way he was right. Wealth, for instance, no longer seemed quite so important. Nor did the fact that, according to law, she could be neither an actor nor a breeder of horses. As for membership in the 'Young Arrephorai', she had never wanted it. That had been Mama's desire, not hers.

For a time she and Socrates sat quietly, and said no more. Then she stood up, stretched and went back into the kitchen court to do her chores.

Oblivious to a mass of clouds heaped high against the sky, gray on white on blue, Socrates' mind was on 'The Clouds' as written and produced by Aristophanes.

Xanthippe was closer to the truth than she guessed. The wave of public distrust, instigated by that ignoble performance twenty two years ago, along with disquieting rumors about him and his precepts, was still rampant and growing louder. What people were saying was no secret to him.

Anytus, for instance, with his statement, "Socrates' gift of oratory bends the minds of men! Look at me, a broken-hearted father because my only son, Astron, has been so seduced and deranged by what Socrates teaches that he wont enter my profession and he is drinking himself to death!"

In another diatribe he called Socrates "a meddling busy-body who scorned his father's trade to gad about pretending he was a Master . . . and he didn't even own a pair of sandals."

"Leave it to a leather merchant and seller of footwear to think of that," onlookers laughed.

Still, they were listening . . . and agreeing.

"Socrates discounts stories of the gods and calls them no more than 'vulgar mythology' that is full of cleverness fit only for children and the childlike."

"He associates with drunks and n'er-do-wells!"

"Well, as Homer says, 'Zeus pairs like with like'."

"Which explains why he married Xanthippe. Her tongue clacks like his, only louder!"

People on Cerameicus Road fueled the gossip. "Strange things go on in the house of Socrates," said the woman three doors down. "Many's the time I've seen Alcibiades, Charmides, Kritias, traitors all, entering his gate!"

"For shame!" the potter's wife chided, "You seem to forget who went around the neighborhood during the plague, comforting the dying, even helping some to recover! Day or night he was out. We wondered if he ever slept! I should know! It was he who saved the life of our eldest son!"

Her husband and a handful of others, nodded vigorously.

"What are you brooding about?" Xanthippe asked him upon returning to the courtyard. It was awhile since he'd heard that sharp edge to her voice. "I have a feeling that you're keeping something from me. Why was Antisthenes here today? I don't trust that sneaky dog."

"He came to tell me Chaerephon died, probably from all he was forced to endure as an exile in Samos. I shall go to his funeral. Ah, Xanthippe, will you ever forget how beautifully he sang on our wedding night?"

"As I recall it was a song about death. But what else did Antisthenes say? Surely it didn't take him all morning to tell you about Chaerephon."

"No, we also discussed Anytus and some of the harsh remarks he's been making lately in the Agora."

"Nice people die, others, like that damned leather-dresser, seem to go on forever," Xanthippe spat, "His name is Trouble. Speak up, Socrates! What nastiness is he up to now?"

"I shall try to explain. Recently Menon and I were having a fine battle of wits over the meaning of virtue, when up walked Anytus with a dour look on his face.

"My dear Socrates', said he, 'You Sophists are a canker and a destruction to all those unfortunate enough to find themselves within hearing distance of the garbage that comes out of your mouth. May no more of my relatives here or abroad ever again have the ill fortune to fall into the madness of listening to, and becoming tainted by, your foolishness!"

"He's evil! Also powerful enough to hurt you."

"Relax. He just can't face his own culpability in the matter of his son's drunken state, so he has to hang the blame on someone else, me. But he's too ambitious to risk criticism by doing anything villainous. Ah! See who's here!," Socrates chuckled as little Menexenus, weary of wrestling with the dog, came to be petted. "He'll be tall, like you, Xanthippe. Think of it, two years old and already five hands high! Thanks to your loving care, he's the image of health! I never asked, but I have wondered, were you sorry we had another boy?"

"I wouldn't trade my Menexenus for any girl on earth," Xanthippe replied, giving her youngest son a hug.

Chapter Fifty-three

One way for malefactors to expiate their guilt was to make a goat the surrogate for their wrong doings. Once it has been placed on the altar and sacrificed, culpability ceases.

But something more extraordinary than a scape-goat was needed to release Athenians from bouts of post-war remorse. Casting about for someone upon whom to dump their bitter load they came up with a name . . . Socrates!

Crito came early in the morning.

"A pleasant surprise!" Socrates greeted him, and leaped to pull another bench alongside the kitchen court table. "May we give you some bread and dipping oil? Olives? My wife cures the best olives in Athens.

"You make me wish I had not already broken my night fast," Crito said. "Forgive me, Xanthippe, for coming here at this hour, but I must speak to your husband."

How unlike him to exclude her, Xanthippe thought to herself when the two men arose and left her still sitting at the table.

"I have agreeable news for you," he said when, after what seemed an interminable time, they returned.

"Your property is no longer considered to be 'outside the city'. When the Great Walls came down its value increased. In fact I'll wager that when order is once again restored Athens will continue to expand. So, rather than sell now, my suggestion is to bide your time. Prices will go on rising and, though you won't get rich you'll have less need for concern about the future."

"May I have a horse?" Lamprocles asked eagerly.

"You missed some of what I said, young man," Crito laughed, "The part about not becoming rich! You'll have food but I can't guarantee the cost of fodder! I must go. Forgive me for interrupting your morning meal."

"You look gloomier than a hired mourner," Xanthippe said when he left. "I'm sure Crito wasn't here so early in the morning to discuss property! What else did he say out there?"

"He said Xenophon wanted to be the one to tell me he was joining Cyrus' Persian expedition but, because he had to leave sooner than expected, he asked Crito came to relay the news."

"Poor Philesia. She's expecting a child."

"He should have stayed in Athens."

"I've lived with you long enough to know that isn't what's troubling you." Xanthippe compressed her lips, put her hands on her hips and faced her husband squarely.

"Very well. It's this matter of Anytus. He's trying to persuade a certain young chap, not yet dry behind the ears, to lodge a trumped up charge against me."

"How dare he!" Xanthippe cried, clapping her cheek in dismay. "I warned you to watch what you said but you never could hold your tongue!"

"As long as there is breath in my body I will speak out and try to eradicate what is false by speaking the Truth!"

"But you infuriate people, telling them things they don't want to hear, and in an imperious way that makes them angrier yet. Of what crime does Anytus accuse you?"

"He pretends to charge me in behalf of craftsmen whom he claims I unfairly malign. He quotes me as saying that artists, beyond their singular gift for painting, poetry, or sculpture, can rarely boast any real wisdom. Which, by the way is true. But don't worry, All of it will blow over like a summer rain."

"What if it doesn't?"

"Use your mind, Xanthippe, Of what am I guilty? Stirring up a few doubts? Inducing people to think? These are hardly criminal offenses! In any case, something new will come along to entertain the populace, and all will soon be forgotten."

However, her anxiety unallayed, Xanthippe went to the Temple of Zeus and resorted to a custom that, for her, had gone long unobserved. At the portal she bought two doves and took them to be sacrificed by an altar priest. This done she stood before a tall bronze statue and stared up into its face.

"I'm no longer afraid of you, Zeus," she said in a low voice. "I told you to do as you wished with me, even if it meant killing me with one of your bolts, but, not my husband. He's a good man and I've only begun to get along with him."

When she got home there was a crowd outside her gate. Separating himself from the rest, Critobolus took her by the elbow, led her into the house, and told her that Anytus had prodded Meletus, a second-rate poet, into bringing an indictment of impiety against Socrates.

"Don't be afraid," he entreated. "Many of us would deem it an honor to contribute whatever is necessary to get the whole thing called off. Or, should he prefer, Socrates can use the money to take you and your boys to Thessaly or Thebes until it blows over."

"Crito says he and others have money ready to get us away from Athens and out of this mess," Xanthippe was quick to inform Socrates when the crowd outside their gate dispersed.

"No." He shook his head. "To leave now would be a denial of everything I believe and have tried to teach. I counsel others to either abide by the laws of the land or do what they can to amend them in a legitimate manner. Admittedly Athens is not perfect, but she protects me, supplies me with care and gives me gifts. She is my parent and I owe her my allegiance."

"I fail to see why we can't go away for awhile and come back when this affair has been forgotten."

"Were I to run away it would not only disgrace me but you as well, you and our sons. I've done no harm. In fact I have done much good. Having been duly implicated under the laws of Athens by which I always lived, I intend to abide by them."

"Then you must hire a good rhetorician to write your defense, and don't choose Antisthenes."

"With the help of God and my daemon, I shall defend myself."

"Stay home, Xanthippe. I'll see you the moment this trial ends," Socrates vowed the morning of his trial.

Accompanied by a crowd of well wishers and curiosity seekers he marched to the Hill of the Areopagus where hundreds were already crowding into the Court of Justice to secure advantageous seating. This, people said, was probably the most celebrated trial ever to be held in Athens. A few went so far as to suggest that it would go down in history!

Although bets were being wagered on the outcome, most everyone was surprised that the farce had been permitted to come this far. The consensus was that Anytus, having made his point, would be satisfied to see Socrates remove himself by voluntary exile, thereby getting the case dropped by default.

Three accusers, sitting in a row, faced the spectators. Meletus, a hook-nosed mean young man with dirty hair and a scant beard, was on the left, next to him sat Anytus, grimly upright, then Lycon, the third man of the nefarious trio.

There was a stir and the chief magistrate had to rap for order when Socrates announced that he would speak in his own defense. When order was restored, the charges were brought.

"Socrates denies the gods recognized by the State and introduces new divinities in their place."

"He corrupts youth and encourages them to disobey their parents."

"He teaches his hearers to despise the institutions of the State."

"He numbers among his friends, living and dead, the most dangerous representatives of both oligarchial and democratic parties and is therefore guilty by association."

"He habitually quotes mischievous passages from Homer and Hesiod to the prejudices of morality and decency."

"How you have been affected by my accusers, oh Athenians, I cannot tell. But I know they almost made me forget who I am, so persuasively did they speak," he said with a waggish tilt of his head. The following ripple of laughter brought further blows of the gavel.

When the trial ended for that day Critobolus hastened to Cerameicus Road to tell Xanthippe what had transpired.

"Socrates was brilliant. He confused and confounded the idiots who were trying, in every conceivable way, to convince the jury that he's a money cadging teacher of false doctrine.

I wanted to applaud when he spoke out against Aristophanes and called 'The Clouds' a slanderous piece. He said it ignited rumors that have smouldered for twenty-two years until now when they've become a deadly conflagration."

"What else?"

"He pretended ignorance by saying there were some matters that puzzled him greatly, and he invited Meletus to set him straight. His questions made that arrogant young ass sound an even greater fool than he already is, and got him so flustered he ended up not knowing what he was saying. If I didn't loathe Meletus I'd have almost felt sorry for him. I think a few spectators actually did!"

"I can't believe this is happening."

"Don't worry, dear lady. Socrates is bound to get out of this. His rhetoric is flawless, and he himself so persuasive, no one in his right mind will find him guilty of wrong doing.

"But if worse comes to worst we'll bribe the jailer with such an imposing sum he'll be glad to look the other way when we run off with his star prisoner."

"The jailer may be easily persuaded but you know how stubborn my husband is when it comes to matters of integrity."

"Yes," Critobolus agreed. "Few men dare to speak out as boldly as he. But we'll see what tomorrow brings. This is for you." He thrust a basket into Xanthippe's hands. "You were good to Kallia. Now, do me the honor of accepting a few treats for yourself and the boys. There's some wine too. It will help you sleep. You must get some rest, Either Father or I will be here tomorrow to give you another report."

It was his kindness that brought tears.

"I never saw you cry" he said haltingly, "not even when you had good cause. Let the tears come, Xanthippe. One of the most deplorable things about this whole nasty business is what it forces a gallant woman like you to endure."

He reached out as if to draw her to him then pulled back abruptly and ran out into the twilight.

Chapter Fifty-four

Perhaps a man can be too forthright, too clever.

"Arrogant," Assemblymen muttered, not liking Socrates' confident air of authority. They resented his crisp speech, detecting in it a note of condescension, such as that reserved by school masters for dull-witted disciples,

When he told jury members he was guided by a daemon they looked askance. He said he had asked his family not to come to the trial because he scorned those defendants who brought wives and children into court to elicit sympathy which, of course, antagonized spectators who had done exactly that

"As for me, I will be tried on truth and merit alone. You must know however that there are some sentences I deem unfeasible," he added doughtily. "For example, I prefer death to exile or imprisonment."

Then he announced that what he really deserved was to be given maintenance for life as a public benefactor because he had done far more good for Athens than Olympic winners who are rewarded with fortunes. That outraged everyone.

He handily demolished each accusation, one by one, and made his accusers appear to be simpletons. Thrown into confusion and unable to dodge the perspicacity of his questions they came up with senseless replies.

"I must tell you again not to interrupt me," he insisted when another uproar broke out. "Kindly remember that you initially agreed to allow me to speak in my accustomed manner."

"In deference to Crito, Critobolus, Plato, Simmias, Cebes and others here present who have volunteered to stand surety for me I propose a maximum fine of three thousand drachmas. I myself do not possess three thousand drachmas because, contrary to what has been said here today I've never asked for, or permitted anyone to give me money for telling the truth".

Perversely the tide turned against Socrates. In a foment of rage jurymen, suspicious that he was making fun of them were insulted past reason. By a majority of sixty they found him guilty and gave him the penalty of death!

It was agreed that major religious rites being observed on the Isle of Delos augured a delay, hence not until next month when the sacred ship returned with her Athenian emissaries, and docked at Piraeus, would Socrates have to die.

Onlookers, reluctant to leave, clustered in cacophonous groups, recalling the day's events.

"He said he preferred death!"

"With a wife like his who wouldn't!"

"You've met her?"

"No but a good friend of mine knows someone down the street from her who says for a fact she's a fire-tongued woman!"

Together Crito and Critobolus hurried to Cerameicus Street before anyone else could get there with the shocking verdict.

As gently as possible they told Xanthippe the truth. "How could they?" she gasped, white faced and stunned. "We wont submit to this insanity", Crito promised. "Early tomorrow I shall go to the jail and persuade Socrates to let us get him out of town. There are visiting hours for women. Would you care to have one of us go with you?"

"No, . . . no," Dazed she shook her head.

"A slave will be here shortly with food prepared and ready to eat. He can stay on to help with household tasks. It will give you a chance to get some rest," Critobolus said.

"I can manage. The older boys will help."

"Don't protest, Xanthippe. I consider it an opportunity to repay a debt.

"The gods have granted us extra time," Crito comforted her. "All executions must be stayed. The Delos Mysteries will keep anything from being done until the sacred ship returns. By then we will have spirited all five of you away. Now, my dear, we will leave and return again tomorrow."

When they were out of sight Xanthippe could no longer contain her sobs.

"Please, Mama, don't cry," Lamprocles begged. His face, like hers, was the color of limestone.

Sophroniscus, bewildered by her tears, began to wail, then Menexenus set up a dismal howl, and had to be soothed.

"You heard what Crito and Critobolus said. Everything will work out. Don't worry, my loves, we'll get along," Xanthippe assured them, wiping her eyes. But," she added hastily, "There are times when crying helps so don't ever be ashamed of tears."

Alone in bed that night she abandoned herself to grief, like people everywhere who must submit to unjust laws. She wept for her three sons who stood in the shadow of their father's imminent demise, and for herself, faced with the curse of widowhood. But she had lost her terror of Death.

Critobolus' gift of wine was on a table by her bed and she poured some into a cup. Instead of sleep it produced a semi- somnolent state in which reflections continued to come and go in hazy succession.

People said Athens, the golden city of the world, was being punished for craving too much prestige, power, and wealth. The same words might be said of me," Xanthippe thought. However, Athens had known the rich fullness of life whereas she had not. By the gods, this was not the end of Athens or Xanthippe! Two aging women, down alright, but far from dead!

She drummed her brow with a forefinger, the digit used for divination. Possibly she would receive a message in her sleep that all would soon be well.

* * * *

"Father bribed the prison guard to let him slip into jail before sunrise," Critobolus said on his next visit. "He told me that the room to which he was shown is so spacious it seems more like a stoa than a cell. Socrates was still asleep when he got there so, not wanting to awaken him, he just sat there and marvelled at his serenity.

When Socrates finally did awake Father asked him how he managed to remain so calm under the circumstances. His answer was that he had no reason to be otherwise because he expects death to open gates into a splendid new world where there is neither misunderstanding, illness, or darkness of night, and friends can converse honestly and freely."

"Then what? Will he let you get him out of jail and away?"

"Father did everything in his power to persuade him. It could be done so easily, however . . . " Critobolus hesitated.

"However what?"

"His reply was always the same. A man must obey the law of his land. As a citizen, I gladly entered into an implied contract to do so because I would not be able to stand living in a lawless state. You know how it is. When he makes his points he's invariably right. How can one refute him? He agrees there are certain procedures and policies that should be changed. But he won't run away because foolish men misinterpret the law, and choose to put him to death. He's right in saying that people rarely stop to think. Instead they vacillate from here to there, as eager to bring a man back to life again as they are to kill him in the first place. Look what happened to Pericles!" Critobolus took Xanthippe's hands. "Even father, his oldest friend, couldn't dissuade him," Critobolus said somberly.

"Tomorrow I shall go to the jail myself and insist that he find an alternative to this madness," she declared. "I won't let him do such a terrible thing to me and our three sons!"

* * * *

Shall I wear the black peplos and cape?" she asked herself the next morning.

No! She was not a widow nor would she dress like one!

Head high, she walked down the road that led to the prison and encountered Antisthenes who was just leaving.

"Kalimeera," he made a slight bow. "I had a pleasant visit with your husband. He tells me he is content to die because it is better to perish for a cause than to become slowly old and infirm and lose one's mental powers."

"You've already lost yours," Xanthippe bristled, sweeping past him into the jail.

She was grateful to see that Socrates was alone.

"I know this is difficult for you," he said, "but you will be cared for. My friends have promised to look after you and our sons. Menon assures me that he will take charge of Menexenus' education, and Crito says that although Critobolus never complained about Kallia's inability to bear a child he always wanted one. He told his father that he loves our boys,

370

especially Lamprocles, as if they were his own. As you know, both Crito and I belong to the clan of Antioch, which means that Lamprocles, having been initiated into the same Mysteries, is qualified to repeat the prayers at their graves. Never fear, my dear, everyone will be well cared for."

Xanthippe's green eyes blazed. "Name of God!" she exploded, "Years ago I tried to tell you it was you I married and not your parents. Well, neither did I marry your friends! It was you, Socrates, and not any of them, who begat my three sons! I am not ready to let you go! Don't do this to us. Godammit, I don't have the strength to bear it. Besides, I thought that you and I were finally leaning how to enjoy being together!"

"We will always be together, now and in eternity.

As to your being weak, that is not so, my love. I have watched you break free from a load of needless burdens to become the strong self-reliant woman that you are and always have been."

"I'm sick of being a strong, reliable woman! Just for once in my life I'd like to be a weak, cosseted one. I beg you, Socrates, go into exile."

"The court's decision was made according to the law of Athens. I can do nothing other than accept it. If I did bring myself to disobey, and run away like a coward, it wouldn't work. No matter where I went I would antagonize people, as I do here, by speaking out for what I hold to be right. Nor would I wrong our sons by depriving them of that which I hold so dear, Athenian Citizenship."

"You think nothing of depriving me of what I hold dear, namely an unbroken family and marriage, because you think that making a martyr of yourself is more important."

"I am a martyr. A martyr and witness to Truth. The final witness is the one who goes all the way, even to the sacrifice of his life, for Truth. That, I believe is the most eloquent and powerful way available to make my final statement, to disclose the infinite in the finite. Others greater than I, will come after me, also advocating Truth, and again there will be those who will try to silence them by death.

"Truth cannot be silenced. Those Athenians who do this deed will find out how badly they erred in taking my life. But some good will come of it. Someday you will come to know why this was the only path I could have taken. "Look!" he said suddenly and pointed to her arm, "Your scar is barely discernable."

He was right. Xanthippe had not actually looked at it for some time but, sure enough, the snake was almost gone!

"I asked Asclepius to erase it and, with it, your sorrows. Perhaps we have a sign that my prayer was heard and is being answered. This must be our farewell, 'Chriso Mou', until we meet again in another realm. And, instead of fretting over yesterday or tomorrow, keep remembering to live in the 'Now' . . . "Listen to your heart and do what it tells you, knowing it will be with my blessing," he said gently, when the jailer came to tell Xanthippe that the time had come for her to leave.

"I ask that you do not come here again. At least not before the ship returns from Delos." Socrates said, in parting. Yet, until the sacred vessel docked, a stream of visitors continued to stream into his cell as if it were a stoa. Or his own courtyard!

* * * *

The day for Socrates to die had arrived. With Menexenus in her arms, Xanthippe came in, wearing her old green peplos, and feeling as if she were walking in her sleep. Sophroniscus was at her side, and Lamprocles, lagged behind, frowning and furious because his father had elected to desert them.

Seated upon a couch, Socrates, acknowledged them with a brief salutation, but said nothing further. Xanthippe, biting her lip, moved, with the children, to where Critobolus and his father were standing, side by side. Next to them, General Gryllus, whose son Xenophon had already sailed to Persia, told her that Plato had grieved until he was too ill to come.

Others were also regarding her with sympathy. "This grievous thing should not be, Xanthippe. You have my true sympathy. I will pay you a call soon. Then we will talk." Myrto said.

Hipparete's children had become young adults. "You have been like a mother to me since Mama died. Now I shall try to help you," young Elpinice said, embracing Xanthippe,"

Aspasia was there, with Lysicles and an older woman whom others addressed as 'Theodote'. But what almost undid Xanthippe was the sight of Palen and Femma, emerging from the crowd. Silently they came to her side and pressed her hand, their faces laden with compassion.

Some people wept openly, others showed traces of tears.

No one but the condemned man seemed truly at ease. One might have thought he was attending a clan gathering.

Apollodorus, losing a struggle to gain mastery over his emotions burst out in a loud passionate cry.

"Come now, what kind of disturbance is this?" Socrates asked gently, "Be still, Apollodorus. A man should be permitted to die in peace."

He should not be dying at all, Xanthippe thought, gazing at this stranger to whom she had been wed for twenty- six years. She had no fondness for Apollodorus, but his grief was that of all the eager idealists who found meaning to their lives in Socrates' company.

Sensing his mother's distress Menexenus made noisy little hiccups of despair. Sophroniscus too was obviously miserable, and Lamprocles, her soldier son, the picture of gloom.

It was too much. Overwhelmed, Xanthippe sobbed aloud and beat her breast. "Socrates!" she cried, "This is the last time your family and friends will be able to speak to you and you to them!"

Never before had Socrates seen his wife cry. Those tears could be his undoing. "Not now," he told himself. "Not now do I dare react to her sorrow!"

This assembly, especially his sons, must see him accept the inevitable with tranquility. In dying he could teach them that the God of Death was not to be feared. Death, man's great initiation into the afterlife, was to be his final statement here on earth, and it must be done with dignity and grace.

There was no doubt in his mind. No other path could be taken. Nor had his Daemon attempted to dissuade him from choosing to die rather than to negate those truths for which he had lived.

As Euripides said, 'This is courage in a man, to bear unflinchingly what heaven sends'.

"Take her away," Socrates told Critobolus. The brusqueness with which he spoke was unintentional, but were he to betray the tenderness of his feeling for her it might be misconstrued as fear or lack of conviction.

"I must go," she said in a husky whisper to Palen and Femma. "You will never know what it meant to have you here with me today. Return to Cholargus before it gets dark. And visit me soon I pray you."

Come, my friend," Critobolus said, throwing his arm across Lamprocles' shoulder. "It's up to us men to look after your Mama and the boys."

Giving him a grateful look, Lamprocles squared his shoulders, took his mother's elbow, and assisted her into the cart. After putting his brothers in the back he wedged himself in beside them.

With Xanthippe at his side, Critobolus took the rein. "Father will be with him until the end." he assured her as they went along. "We will come tomorrow to make arrangements, and to assist in any way we can. You gave me support when I needed it, now I want to help you. We have been many things to each other, Xanthippe, but, above all, we are friends"

She nodded and they continued on in quiet compatibility.

"Socrates asked Father to buy a fine cock for Asclepius and sacrifice it for him. He said he owed him one." Critobolus said after awhile. "Possibly because the rooster is a sacred creature, and its sacrifice befits a candidate's introduction into the final Mysteries. But why to Asclepius? The last thing Socrates said to me was "Do what your heart tells you to do, Critobolus, and know that it is with my blessing. What do you make of that?"

Xanthippe stroked her smooth right arm, but did not mention that there may have been two reasons for making a sacrifice to the God Of Healing. Nor did she say that Socrates had also advised her to do what her heart told her to do.

There was frost in the air. Alone in her courtyard, she could not stop shivering. It was like having an ague.

Critobolus volunteered to stay awhile, as did the potter and his wife. Pleading exhaustion, she had sent all three away. Her sons, worn by this day of horror, were already asleep.

'Chriso Mou'. The first time Socrates had ever called her by that name had been his farewell. Strange to be addressed as his 'precious one' Much of the time she had felt unidentified as his housewife, companion, or sexual partner. Yet now she was about to become, undeniably, his widow.

It was getting colder and she moved indoors to huddle by the cook stove. Still no warmer she went to her room, lit the lamp that had been a gift from Mama, and rummaged until she found Socrates shabby cloak, the one she had torn off him in front of the theater. The garment was soft and carried the agreeable scent of his body. She pulled it over her shoulders, feeling that by wearing his cloak she was still with him. It was reminiscent of Palen's work tunic, hanging on a peg in the stable, yet still bearing the identity of its owner.

Gripping her arms tightly across her breast Xanthippe rocked in a paroxysm of grief.

Her husband had evoked a gamut of moods, love, hate, anger, rapture, resentment, but never passivity. When a man and a woman live together for many years they are bound in more ways than one. Even now, at this very moment, she felt as joined to him as if she were still in that jail room, an integral part of everything that was taking place.

Contrary to custom, it would be the condemned man, cheering the rest, while he himself serenely faced the God of Death. When asked how he wished to be buried the cheerful answer was sure to be, "Suit yourself, do with my body what you will, I shall be long gone." As if he were planning a voyage at sea!

In her mind she saw him, bathed and ready for what was to come. And the jailer, bearing his sinister goblet with its one lethal dose of a white mousy-smelling potion that derived from hemlock. Hemlock, the plant sacred to Hecate, the goddess who nested in a yew tree!

Socrates would drain the cup without pause.

Xanthippe's teeth were chattering. Thank the gods, no, thank Critobolus, for his gift of wine. She poured some into a goblet, took a few sips, and felt warmer.

The lamp wick exude pungent smell of olive oil. She looked at its brightly painted flowers, fingered its embossed figure of Artemis, and cupped it in her hands. The terra cotta surface felt warm and smooth to the touch. Its spear of light piercing the gloom was comforting.

She did not know how long she had been staring into the flame when she began to feel uneasy. It was as if she herself were experiencing Socrates' mysterious transition into the kingdom of Hades.

The hemlock, all of it, swallowed in one mighty draught. Now the poison, moving irreversibly. The feet, turning frigid and gray, a heaviness in the calves. Death's cold, sullen stream, finding its way into the thighs, groin, hips, An icy weight in the belly, stealing into the chest, robbing it of breath, Eyes closed and unseeing. Constriction of the lips. Trying to talk without words. A live body turning to stone.

The mind! Oh God! Does that go too? Whirling down, down, down into a vortex where everything is dark and blurry. How long does it take to die? A million years? A moment?

"Xanthippe! Chriso Mou!" Socrates, calling her name! The lamp flickered, then flared, unaccountably brilliant, brighter than anyone could imagine. So very beautiful. Everything, the whole world, shimmering with infinitesimal rainbow-like particles of light.

The sound of a child's wail brought her back. It was Menexenus crying in his sleep. No child should have such a day. No woman should have such a day!

Somehow she knew that the man who, for twenty-six years, had been a part of her life was gone. But it wasn't yet real.

Socrates believed that he and she, even in conflict, were completing themselves. He had called her 'strong.' Maybe so. Perhaps she was an unknowing beneficiary of the force with which she had seen him imbue others. She was less afraid . . . of everything from ravens to poverty. But, considering what she had so far survived, what was left for her to fear?

She and Hipparete had discussed marriage as comparable to a design on a loom, where strands of every hue and shade, darks and lights, are successfully worked together, although, at the outset, they look like an uninspired combination.

Curled up in a coverlet Xanthippe rested her back against a chair, and looked intently into the lamp's flame. It recalled a day when Plato was reading from one of his endless rolls of papyrus. She hadn't really paid much attention to what he said, yet some of those lines came back to her now.

"This kind of knowledge is a thing that comes in a moment, like a light kindled from a leaping spark which, once it has reached the soul, finds its own fuel."

Still gazing into the brightness, she pondered the mystery of them. Then she lay down on the floor and slept.

Chapter Fifty-five

For a long time after Socrates' death Xanthippe felt numb. It had been Crito, Critobolus, and other sorrowing friends who made the burial arrangements. Even the memory of Lamprocles reciting the Mysteries for his father at the grave-site was still as insubstantial as a dream.

It was a fortnight before the full realization of her situation struck like a blow. Her teeth chattered, her body quaked, and, alone in her room, she had wept.

'Spinsters lead a sorry life but it's the poor widow whom I pity. Being widowed is the worst thing that can happen to a woman." Nikandra's words, returning to haunt her daughter.

"Widow". A word seldom used without its prefix 'poor'. Even wealthy women were called 'poor widows'. and, were it not for Crito, she would be one of the financially impoverished ones as well.

Surprisingly Myrto came to the rescue, arriving with a savory concoction of barley and lamb. "It's my cook-slave's secret recipe. You'll like it," she said. "Since I too have been widowed I can guess what you are going through. You are probably too scared and miserable to eat, which just makes matters worse. But warm this and, after one mouthful, you'll find yourself eating all of it. Then you'll feel better. I won't stay now but later on we will talk."

Whether it was Myrto's lamb stew or her surprising show of friendship, Xanthippe actually felt better after she ate,

Unfortunately, her chills and fits of trembling were replaced by the same wrath and frustration that had assailed her when Socrates first chose to throw his life away to prove what?

. . . Nothing.

Grief followed anger. Now that he was gone beyond recall his eccentricities seemed less reprehensible. Instead she remembered his quick wit, genial disposition, easy laughter, and the way he enlivened people just by his presence.

Ordinarily when someone dies it's hard to recall his face, let alone the sound of his voice. But Socrates was one whom death had not erased. The likelihood was that he would remain forever vibrant in the minds of all who knew him. He had been gone for a year, yet she still sensed his presence. Sometimes she'd think she saw him coming up the street, with that odd walk of his, half dance step, half waddle.

Should the day come when her sons were no longer at home, much of what she had learned as his wife would stand her in good stead. She had often been an unwilling listener, still, over the years, she had come to view herself in a new light. And, by Socrates' almighty God she was going to cope with widowhood, or whatever else might come her way, Socrates had chosen to die. She chose to embrace life. And she would. To the fullest!

Xanthippe was still coming to grips with her emotions when, true to his word, Palen came calling, with Femma and Philip. Their visit had been cordial, and ever so pleasant.

Palen had begun to age visibly. His hair was white, and his gait that of an old man. Femma looked the same. It was likely that she had been altogether sincere in her early show of affection. To love was apparently part of her nature.

After the funeral Critobolus and his father had come to review Xanthippe's financial situation. As usual they brought gifts of food, wine, and fruit, "probably just because I'm the widow of their beloved friend and Master," she told herself. Since then she had seen Critobolus only when in the company of others.

Her feelings for him were ambivalent. Whatever his reason for staying away might be, nothing, absolutely nothing could, or ever would, be the same.

Kallia had been gone for some time. Critobolus was a widower who quite likely wanted to leave it at that though, as. the most sought after unattached man in Athens, he could marry anyone, even including a rich, beautiful fourteen year old, if he wished.

No longer caring to escape into foolish fancies Xanthippe asked herself a straightforward question.

"If he did, how would I feel?"

In all the years, from that never again mentioned act of love to this day, their relationship had, as far as she was concerned, remained undecipherable. When they did encounter one another he had little to say that was not related to financial matters. Yet, the last time she'd seen him, the expression on his face was the one she had seen years ago, a guarded look that told her he had something on his mind with little to do with her budget, or his banking table.

Certainly she had no need to worry about being alone! Not with three sons to look after! But when they are grown and married, everything I learned, as the wife of Socrates, will have me better prepared to live with myself," she mused. For one, his frequent absences had accustomed her to getting along with limited companionship.

Furthermore, although she may have been an unreceptive audience, what she had heard when he taught in the courtyard, had changed her outlook in many ways. Little by little, she had come to view herself in a new light.

Strange thoughts to be going through the mind of a woman so recently bereft. In any case she was far from ready to make any commitments. She must learn how to handle her modest financial interests, not with the idea of becoming rich, but simply to give her sons a feeling of security she, herself, had been unable to enjoy.

She intended to pursue a few interests of her own, such as reading books, memorizing a few more of Sappho's poems, and spending more time in the company of intelligent women, Myrto for example, and others like her who were interested in more than recipes, gossip and crude jokes. Women, Xanthippe had found in chatting with the potter's wife were more articulate than men when it came to sharing innermost feelings and thought.

Nor would she forget Hipparete's daughter! That lovely girl must be given the same love and strength that she, Xanthippe, had received from Yiayia Phyllys and Great Aunt Elpinice.

Another matter to be contemplated was the thought of living, once again, in a land no longer shattered and torn by war. How glad Socrates must be that, even though thirty years of fighting had left Athens scarred and beleaguered with monetary problems, political strife, and sorrow, she was, once again, at peace.

"How glad Socrates must be." Xanthippe repeated the words she had said to herself just as though he were still alive! Like a few nights ago, when she awakened thinking she heard him softly snoring beside her in the bed.

Frequently, when people die, one can scarcely recall the sound of their voices, or how they looked. But once in a very long while there is someone whose living presence is so extraordinary that even death itself cannot quench it. Possibly for the rest of her life, she would sense the presence of Socrates, here, or in the next room, or the courtyard. . . . Or she would see him coming down the street with that strange walk of his, graceful as a bear.

It was conceivable that Chaerophon had been telling the truth when he claimed he had asked the Oracle to name the wisest man in all of Greece, and she had said, 'Socrates'. In all likelihood she had been correct.

"I can't give you happiness," he had said. "No one can give that to another. It's up to the individual to find it within himself."

By the Almighty God of whom he often spoke, she would show the world she could cope with the burden of widowhood, whatever it might entail.

It was a pretty day. She would prepare an omelette and eat it with the boys in the courtyard. Surely one way to make a fresh start was to let them know that, even with one parent missing, they were still a united family.

"I'm coming!", she called to her sons.

Chapter Fifty-six

Last night she'd had a dream. Even now, with the sun in her eyes, it was as real as something that actually happened

She had been in a cave. At first it was so dark she couldn't see a thing. Then, gradually, a glimmer of light filtered through and she found herself entering a tunnel. Fearful, and uncertain of her footing, she ventured further, but was only able to progress by pushing aside innumerable curtains that seemed to be made of filmy, gray mist.

"Never fear, Xanthippe," someone said. His voice was low pitched and comforting, He had taken her by the hand and guided her still further into the tunnel. It was quite dark but she could see that his eyes were extraordinarily bright and beautiful.

"Who are you?" she had asked.

"My name is Hermes," he replied and disappeared.

She was trying to find him when, in the distance, she discerned people silhouetted against a near blinding light. Now that she thought of it, they seemed to glow,

They were coming toward her and, seized by inexplicable excitement, she hastened her steps. Then, she saw who they were and, her heart pounding wildly, she started to run.

Mama, looking healthy and young, was laughing and hurrying ahead of the rest! Behind her came Yiayia Phyllys, accompanied by a young girl whom Xanthippe knew at once must be baby Phyllys, looking as she would today, were she alive. Great-Aunt Elpinice was there too, and Hipparete, and Archos, all of them smiling and approaching her with arms outstretched.

Then she saw Socrates. He too was luminescent. But, instead of hastening to meet her, he remained where he was. "Not yet, Chriso Mou!"

he said quite clearly. "Go back. You still have much to do and many experiences to enjoy."

With that the brilliant light, and the people faded from view.

She awoke in the dark, knowing she would never have any need to dread death again.

Wide awake now, she sat upright in bed. How good it was just to be alive on so beautiful a day. She must get up quickly to bathe and dress!

Yesterday one of Critobolus' slaves had come with a message. "My master wishes to pay you a call tomorrow morning, I am to tell him if that is agreeable with you."

"Tell him 'Yes," she said. It would be agreeable.

Menexenus would be occupied with the paidogogus Menon had insisted on providing for his god-child, even though the lad was not yet five years old. Sophroniscus would have left for school, and Lamprocles was in Cholargus to spend a few days on the farm with his grandfather and Philip. To Xanthippe's delight, the trip had been Papa's idea.

All of which meant that by the time Critobolus arrived, the house would be quiet.

Why was he coming?" she wondered, selecting a peplos instead of her work tunic. Perhaps he simply wanted to clear the air by letting her know he had no wish to resume a relationship that ended right after it began.

He would phrase what he had to say cautiously, so as not to offend. Being a banker, he might begin by saying the time had come for her to enjoy a bit of relaxation. Possibly he would suggest, as he had on prior occasions, that she allow him to lend her one of his slaves to lighten her chores. It was pride, so far, that had kept her from accepting those tempting offers yet, if the subject came up again, why not? He had more slaves than he could use. What's more, if he, or any of the others, had been permitted to pay for her husband's lectures, she could have bought slaves of her own!

By the time he arrived she had come to a decision. Whatever he might say, marriage was too flawed an institution to hold any further appeal as far as she was concerned. Her parents had seen fit to free her from the stigma of spinsterhood. She, in turn, had given Socrates three sons.

Today, one year after his death, she was ready to put an end to her mourning, and to enjoy life as she saw fit. With this in mind she sailed into the courtyard and opened the gate.

"It's good to see you, Xanthippe" Critobolus said.

"It was nice of you to come," she replied. "May I offer you some of the excellent wine with which you and your father have so generously supplied me?"

"Yiasus, Xanthippe," Critobolus said, raising the brimming cup she handed him.

"Yiasus, Critobolus." She lifted hers in return.

"How are you getting along?"

"Better. As you know, these things take time. It may sound strange, but at first I was furious! I was like that when Yiayia Phyllys died. The difference this time was that Socrates elected to die."

"I had trouble with that too, Xanthippe. It was when my father and I discussed the matter that I began to realize it was the only choice Socrates could have made. Had he gone into exile he would have negated everything he taught. Again and again we all heard him say that, once we find Truth, we must be willing to leave family, friends, even, if necessary, to die for what we know is right . . .

"His death could be the most powerful statement he ever made. You will also be interested to know that, in talking about Socrates, Father and I became better friends."

"In a way I can relate to that," Xanthippe reflected. "After years of not seeing eye to eye with my husband I began to listen to him and find much of value in what he said. He was so scrupulously honest about practicing what he preached. Take duty to one's country. He compared Athens to a nurturing mother. 'You may not agree with her but you always love her', he'd say."

"True. Whenever the command came, he went to war. As he saw it, no citizen of Athens should even dream of running away when duty calls. His idea was that the time to fight for peace is when we are not at war," Xanthippe said, finding it comfortable to be able to share her feelings about Socrates with Critobolus.

"In recent years I began to question him. I wanted to talk about weightier matters than what we were going to eat for supper. I admit that having some money in my purse helped take my mind off finding food to put in my cook-pot. Marriage has a way of making a woman dull! What disturbs me the most is that, just as I was finally beginning to get acquainted with my husband, along came that horrible trial."

"I take exception to what you say about marriage making a woman dull." Critobolus said, smiling, "You couldn't be dull if you tried! I have relished every conversation we ever had. I also anticipate many more.

First, however, you and I have some unfinished business to which we must attend."

"I thought everything was in good order."

"It is, in regard to your budget. But, for too long a time I have been burdened with a need to keep silence where the two of us are concerned when I wanted to tell you, to explain to you . . ."

"No!" Vigorously Xanthippe shook her head. "If you are referring to something that happened years ago, allow me to relieve your mind. We behave impulsively when we're young. When I listen to Lamprocles I can hear myself at his age so there is no need to . . ."

"Hold on, Xanthippe! This has to do with more than the impetuosity of youth. I betrayed you! Stop shaking your head and hear what I say. At sixteen, my friends and I saw ourselves as warriors, ready for the fray. Marriage was the last thing on our tablet of interests." A rueful grin came and went on his face. "I thought only old men past the age of nineteen or twenty got married! Then I fell in love with you."

Xanthippe's eyes went wide.

"You heard me. I fell in love with you. In a way it happened when you were still a wild little girl, crashing about on a big horse. Then came that Apaturia when you sat down beside me and I looked into your incredible eyes. From then on I had trouble concentrating on anything my Masters said. The only thing I had on my mind was you."

"I'm dreaming," Xanthippe thought and did not answer.

"I loved hearing you talk, and I wanted you for a friend. I still do. But I wanted you in other ways. Yet, I swear by the gods, I had no intent to force myself on you."

"You never did. Had I wished I could have fought you off," Xanthippe murmured. "If I had so much as tried I know that what happened . . . would not have happened."

Surprised by her candor, Critobolus was, briefly, silent.

"I went home and told my father I had met the woman I wanted to marry." he continued. "He demanded to know who she was, but, if you can believe me, I at least had enough honor not to tell.

"That was when he informed me that I was betrothed to Kallia. And I, the brave warrior, did not have the guts to challenge a betrothal contract in which I'd played no part."

"You need not go on, Critobolus," Xanthippe said softly, "this is difficult for both of us. Yes, I was upset. Yet the longer I live, the more I realize how helpless boys, as well as girls, can be when it comes to making their own decisions. How many people do you know who had any choice in choosing a mate? When two persons with nothing in common marry, they can't help but have problems . . . It was like that with Socrates and me although he always said that our marriage was ordained by the Fates. Who knows? Maybe it was. But had I said I didn't want to marry him, I think he would not have insisted.

"His honesty and goodness added to my guilt, because, in spite of all he taught, I could not stop loving his wife." was Critobolus' reply.

"I would be less than honest if I let you reprove yourself, and didn't admit that I never know for sure whether my motives in visiting Kallia were as pure as they should have been," she said quickly. "Each time I went to your house I hoped against hope that I would see you. And I was always very happy when I did!"

She had not meant to reveal that much. Unfortunately, despite all of Papa's admonitions she had still not learned to hold her tongue!

"Xanthippe, will you marry me?"

The suddenness of it left her speechless.

"What would people say?" she gasped, when she caught her breath. "Oh for the godsakes, I'm beginning to sound like my mother!"

With that Critobolus laughed and the last vestige of tension evaporated.

"Let them say what they wish! All I care about is that, the gods willing, you and I will have years ahead to be together like this, sharing our thoughts, and loving one another. I have made mistakes . . . you seem to think you have too. But if you're willing to give it a try, I think that, together, we can make a good marriage. I promise you, it will be one that will allow you freedom to do what-ever you enjoy doing."

Could she believe him? True, after all these years he was still single but . . .

"Take a good look, Critobolus, she said, lifting her face to his. As you can see I'm no longer that young girl who raced around on a horse. I'm getting old. You may well end up wishing you had married a pretty sixteen-year- old! You could, you know!"

"As far as I am concerned you are the same person you were back then. If anything, you're more desirable. If love is real it lasts, Xanthippe. I don't want some young girl. What would we talk about? You and I not only have the future, we've shared the past. Our conversation today, about Socrates, Kallia, and all the rest, leaves the door open for us to speak unreservedly in the future . . .

"I won't press you for an answer. I waited this long and, if necessary, I'll continue to do so. But the next time you lift your lips to mine I shall take you in my arms and it will be 'for keeps'. "I shall leave now, and give you a little time to decide. Will tomorrow be too soon for me to return for your answer?"

* * * *

When Critobolus had gone Xanthippe sat very still, hugging his words to her heart. "I love you . . . I love you . . ."

He was willing to take a chance. Now it was up to her. Did she have the courage?

If what he said were true she would still be free to make new friends, read books, memorize verses, and all the rest. She had seen other old couples who obviously loved one another and enjoyed being married. As Critobolus had pointed out, it wasn't as though they had just met! Can individual freedom be found within the confines of marriage? He seemed to think so!

Her three sons were already fond of him. They would be delighted if he were to become their surrogate father.

"It's up to you," she said to herself. "What do you want? What have you always wanted more than anything in the world?"

Love . . . to give and receive love. Even at this late date the prospect of gaining such a relationship was tempting! And the risk of marrying again would be tempered by knowing that, this time, the choice was hers to make.

Critobolus claimed he'd be willing to wait. Should she ask him to? Neither of them was getting any younger . . . What if something were to happen to him? She shivered. Socrates' belief that one lived on after death, was of little comfort. His 'Live in the Now' made more sense.

She was six years old when, seated beneath the hollow tree she had vowed that when she 'grew up' she would marry the handsome Critobolus. What if the Fates shared Socrates' unique perspective of time, and had ordained that she be given a longer stretch of it in which to mature!

Suddenly a beatific smile lit Xanthippe's face. She had arrived at a decision!

"Do what your heart tells you." One of the last things he had said, to Critobolus, and to her. Which was exactly what she intended to do!

Cast of Characters

Only the names accompanied by an * are fictitious. The rest have been taken from history.

XANTHIPPE — b.445 B.C.? (zan-TIP-ee) was the wife of Socrates. Some historians say she belonged to the family of Pericles. She had a poor disposition and a bitter tongue. Later generations believed that Socrates married her to discipline himself but there is no proof of this. (World Book Encyclopedia, 1960 Edition)

ALCIBIADES — (Al-suh-biades) 450-404 B.C. Orphaned at four when he and his sister Ariphon became wards of their uncle Pericles, Archon (ruler) of the Athenian Empire.

AGATHON — Handsome, popular playwright.

ANDOKIDES* — Palen's slave.

ANYTUS — Politician, owner of leatherworks.

ANTISTHENES — A friend of Socrates.

ARCHOS* — A paidogogus (tutor).

ARISTOPHANES — 448-335 Comic statist, authored 'The Clouds'.

ASPASIA — A hetaira (woman educated in the art of giving pleasure to men.)

ASTRON — (Name fictitious) Known in history as the son of Anytus.

CALLIAS — 508 B.C. The richest man in Greece. Negotiated 'Peace of Callias' to end war with Persia in 446 B.C., and later, a peace treaty with Sparta.

CHAEROPHON — Socrates' friend who asked the Oracle at Delphi to name the wisest man in Greece and was told, "No man is wiser, more liberal, just or possessed greater self control and prudence than Socrates."

CLEINA and FESTUS* — Slaves in Socrates' parental home.

CRITIAS and CHARMIDES — Aristocrats, Plato's pro-Spartan uncles.

CRITO — Prominent banker, father of critobolus.

CRITOBOLUS — 448 B.C. The man Xanthippe adored.

DIOTIMA — An Arcadian prophetess, one of Socrates teachers.

ELEFTEROUS* — Xanthippe's younger brother.

ELPINICE — A celebrated beauty and the wife of Callias.

ERYXIMACHOS — 470 B.C. A well know Athenian physician.

FEMMA* — Xanthippe's friend who lived in the hamlet of Cholargus.

GALA* — The potters wife and Xanthippe's neighbor.

GENERAL GRYLLUS — prominent army man. Palen's friend, father of Kallia* and Xenophon.

HERMOGENES and CALLIAS the 2nd — Sons of Hipponicus.

HIPPARETE — 448 B.C. Xanthippe's dearest friend.

HIPPONICUS — 475-450 B.C. brutish father of Hipparete.

IODICE — Elpinice' great-niece.

KALLIA* — 446 B.C. Daughter of General Gryllus, sister of Xenophon.

LAMPROCLES — 422 B.C. Xanthippe's firstborn son.

LYSICLES — Tall, jocular sheepherder who lives with his beady eyed wife on the farm next to Palen's.

MARC* — 438 B.C. Xanthippe's amiable youngest brother.

MELISSA* — A slave in Palen's household, married to Andokides.

MENEXENUS , 404 B.C. Socrates' and Xanthippe's third son.

MYRTO — circa 446 B.C. Daughter of Lysimachus, Granddaughter of Aristides 'the Just'.

NIKANDRA* — 465-414 B.C. Xanthippe's mother

PALEN* — 470 B.C. Husband of Nikandra, and father of Xanthippe. A breeder of horses and member of the Alcmaonid clan.

PERICLES (Pehr-uh-KLEEZ) — 490-430 B.C Elected the Archon and sole master of Athens in 441 B.C. According to the Plutarch he then changed and became more stern with the people, controlling them through the double-edged sword of hop and fear. At the same time he took care of the public good and despite his great power and opportunity, he never added a single drachma to his estate. His foreign policy was less than successful, nonetheless he was elected year after year and known as "The Olympian" and the general of generals'.

PERICLES THE YOUNGER — 445-406 B.C. Bastard son of Pericles and Aspasia. Given citizenship by special franchise in 429.

PHAENERETE — 487-417 B.C. A midwife and the mother of Socrates.

PHYLLYS* — 494-429 B.C. Palen's mother and Xanthippe's 'Yiayia' (grand-ma).

PLATO — 427-347 Disciple of Socrates, surnamed Plato because of his broad shoulders. "As I see it," he said, "the human race will have no rest from its evils until philosophers become kings, or kings become philosophers."

THE POTTER* and THE POTTER'S WIFE* — Xanthippe's neighbors.

SAPPHO — 612 BC Writer, dancer and teacher who lived on the Isle of Lesbos.

SOCRATES — (SAHK-ruh-TEEZ) b.469 B.C. (4th year of 77th Olympiad) d.399 B.C. Preached the doctrine of man's essential goodness.

SOCRATES' SONS — Lamprocles, Sophroniscus and Menexenus.

SOPHRONISCUS — father of Socrates and husband of Phaenerete.

SOPHRONISCUS the second — Socrates' and Xanthippe's middle son.

XENOPHON — 434-355 Son of General Gryllus, and Clymene* A disciple of Socrates.

Bibliography

Arrowsmith, William, Translator, 'The Clouds' by Aristophanes' New American Library

Andrew, S.O., 'Homer's Odyssey' J. M. Dant & Sons Ltd., London, England

Bartlett, John, 'Familiar Quotations' Little, Brown and Co. Boston, Toronto

Beye, Charles Rowan, 'Ancient Greek Literature and Society' Anchor Books, N.Y.

Botsford & Robinson, "Hellenic History' MacMillan & Co. Publishing

Bowder, Diana, 'Who Was Who In The Greek World, Washington Press Square & Pocket Books N.Y.

Boxer and Black 'The Herb Book' Octopus Books Ltd. London, W.I.

Burn, A. R.,'The Pelican History of Greece', Penguin Books

Cooper, John Gilbert, 'The Life of Socrates', R. Dodsley at Tulleys Head, London 1750

Cavendish, Richard, 'Man, Myth, and Magic, Marshall Cavendish Corp. N.Y.

Church, F. J. & Cumming, Robert D. Translators, 'Euthryphro, Apology, Crio', Bobb-Merrill Ed. Publishing, Chicago

Copplestone, Trewin, 'World Architecture', Hamlyn Publishing Group Ltd., Feltham, England

Cornford, Francis M. Translator, and Notes, 'The Republic Plato', Oxford University Press

Cornford, Francis M. Plato's 'Timaeus'

deCoulanges, Fustel, 'The Ancient City', Doubleday & Co. N.Y.

Delhian Text, Part 16, Delphian Society

Dover, K. J., Greek Homosexuality, Vintage Books, Random House, N.Y.

Downing, Christine, 'The Goddess' Mythical Images of The Feminie Crossroads, N.Y.

Finiey, M. I., 'The Greek Historians', Fellow of Jesus College, Cambridge

Fitts, Dudley 'Greek Plays, In Modern Translation', Dial Press, New York

Freeman, Kenneth J., 'Schools of Hellas' 1907, Macmillan & Co. Ltd. London

Fuller, Edmund, 'Plutarch's Lives of Noble Greeks'

Gildersleeve, D. L., 'Brief Mention'(from a magazine published in the 1800's. Can be found in the O.S.U. Library.

Glover, Terrot Reavely, 'Springs of Hellas and Other Essays', Cambridge University Press

Godley, A. D., 'Socrates and Athenian Sciety In His Day', Suley and Co. Ltd. London, 1896

Grant, Michale & Hazel, John, 'Who's Who In Mythology', Hodder and Stoughton, London

Graves, Robert, 'The White Goddess' Noonday Press N.Y.

Grene, David and Lattimore, Richard, translators, "Euripides 1' Washington Square Press, N.Y.

Guthrie, W. K. C. 'The Greeks and Their Gods', "History of Greek Philosophers' Vol. 3 'Socrates',
    Cambridge University Press, N.Y.

Hamilton, Edith, Mythology' New England Library Ltd., Little, Brown & Co. Boston

Heiderstadt, Dorothy, 'A Book Of Heroes', Bobbs-Merrill Inc. N.Y.

Herzberg, Max, 'Classical Myths', Allyn & Bacon, Boston 1952

Ions, Veronica, 'The World's Mythology in Color', Hamlyn Publishing Group Ltd., Middlesex, England

Jowett B., 'The Trial of Socrates' 'Two Dialogues of Plato', Crown publishers, N.Y.

Jowett Benjamin, 'Plato's Symposium'

Jowett, Benjamin, 'Plato's Protagoras', Translation revised by Martin Ostwald, The Liberal Arts Press, New York

Marchant, E.C., 'Xenophon In Seven Volumes', Harvard University Press, London

Oates, Whitney J. 'Seven Famous Greek Plays' edited, 1938, The Modern Library, N.Y. Random House N.Y.

Roget, 'Thesaurus' 3rd edition

Roloff & Stassinopoulos, 'Gods Of Greece', Harry N. Abrams Inc. Publishers

Rostovtzeff M. 'Greece', Oxford University Press Oxford, London, New York

Rouse W. H. D., 'Great Dialogues of Plato', New American Library New York and Scarborough, Ontario

Runes, Dagobert D., 'Pictorial History of Philosophy', Philosophical Library, New York

Sanford, John A. 'The Life Within', Lippincott, New York

Scott, Kilvert, 'Plutarch's Rise and Fall of Athens', Penguin Classics

Silverberg, Robert, 'Socrates', G.P.Putnam

Tatlock, Jessie M., 'Greek and Roman Mythology' 1917, D. Appleton-Century Co New York

Tmomson, George, The Prehistoric Aegean', Penguin Books Ltd. Middlesex, England

Toynbee, Arnold, 'A Study of History', Oxford University Press, Distributed in the United States by American Heritage Press (McGraw-Hill Co.)

Walker, Benjamin, 'Sex and the Supernatural', Castle Books, Ottenheimer Publishers Inc.

Webster, T. B. L., 'Life In Classical Athens', T. B. Batsford Ltd. London

Winspear, A. D., 'Who Was Socrates?'

Zane, Eva, 'Greek Cooking For the Gods', 101 Productions Publishers, San Francisco